Where Heroes Run

The American K9 Elegy

The "Big Boys" Collection Special Edition

Smokey Joe

Big Boys In The Sand

Big Boys In Blue

Big Boys Don't Cry

Big Boy Games

Big Boys In The Wild

With never before published chapters

Celebrating the courage, sacrifice, and silent heroes who
never stopped running toward danger...

By

H. Jack Dunn

Where Heroes Run

The American K9 Elegy

The 'Big Boys' Series & Collection Special Edition

Celebrating the courage, sacrifice, and silent heroes who never stopped running toward danger...

Special Collector's Edition

With gratitude to my family, friends, and colleagues whose support, insight, and encouragement made this work possible. Thank you for believing in the story - and in me.

A special thanks to Lowell Dunn and my wife, Lori Dunn, for their guidance, patience, and dedication — your help has been instrumental in bringing this edition to life.

Copyright filed with the U.S. Copyright Office January 2026

ISBN: 979-8-9990921-6-8

Table of Contents

Introduction

The Heart of the Line

Sometimes writing something like this isn't just about storytelling… it's about reckoning, and sorting through what still lingers, and what is carried too long.

Every story has a beginning, though we don't always recognize it when we're standing in it. For some, it starts with a first ride on a horse, or having a dog bounding toward you with unwavering loyalty, or the first call on duty that changes everything. For others, it begins in silence - the pause between danger and decision, the breath held before life shifts forever.

I've spent a lifetime walking that line. I've learned what it means to carry responsibility, to bear loss, to witness courage, and to discover the quiet strength that comes from standing beside those who refuse to let you fall. From dusty barns and the open ranges of my youth with Smokey Joe, to the streets patrolled, or with a K9 at my side, to the wilds… of life and death in the line of service. I've seen firsthand that the measure of a person isn't in what they win, but in what they protect, and who they protect it with.

Smokey Joe taught me that respect, patience, and humility aren't learned in victory, but in listening - to the land, the animals, and the lessons they quietly offer. **Big Boys in the Sand** showed that courage isn't always loud, and that the bonds we forge in youth shape the men and women we become. **Big Boys Don't Cry** reminded me that grief is not weakness, and that sometimes the hardest battles are fought in the heart. **Big Boy Games** proves that life doesn't always make sense - chaos and danger often arrive without warning - but the people who stand beside you, who watch your back, become the true measure of survival.

These stories are about loyalty: to a partner, a family, a friend, a cause, or a dog who refuses to leave your side. They are about resilience: how we carry the weight of loss, the scars we bear, and the choices we make when every instinct tells us to stop. And they are about humanity: the quiet moments of reflection, the courage to be vulnerable, and the understanding that the wild - whether mountains, streets, or life itself - will strip us to what is real.

As you journey through these pages, you'll meet people and animals who teach, challenge, and sometimes save one another. You'll witness the grit it takes to survive, the compassion it takes to lead, and the humility it takes to love without reservation. These stories are real in their heart, inspired by real people and events - even if the names and events are dressed in fiction. Because these lessons are carried, and come from lives lived on the edge, in service many forget, and in the company of those who refuse to abandon one another.

This is a story of survival, yes - but more than that, it is a story of why we keep standing. Why we keep showing up. Why we love, why we fight, why we endure. And most importantly, why we honor those who walk beside us, whether they have fur, four legs, or a heartbeat like our own. Because…

There is safety in the darkest storms…
Behind me.

Chapter 1

Learning Lessons

I was fifteen years old before I realized my first name wasn't "boy." That's what all the old-timers called us kids. They weren't being disrespectful - that's just how it was back then.

When we were young, we learned to work. And when a kid like me - with a hard life, no money, and no dad - found someone to look up to, it was more than finding work or learning a lesson. It was friendship.

And for old man Hawkins, I think he found something in me that he needed too. His son never came home from Vietnam.

Charlie was the kind of man who would never give you the shirt off your back, but he'd never let you go without one either. He was old, but he worked harder than most men half his age, though the weight of years showed in the curve of his shoulders and the slow lift of a hay bale.

He would say the wrinkles on his face were the stains his smile left behind, and the gray in his hair was a gift. He taught by example that a man wears a hat, works hard, and does the right thing when no one is watching. That's what he taught his son. I never knew his son – Charlie simply called him 'Junior' because he said he named his only son after himself.

Charlie would say the lessons he was teaching me were the same lessons he taught his son, and it's what I needed back then. He would say that's what made all boys become real men.

I spent countless afternoons, and so many weekends working at his ranch, doing chores, tending horses, and learning the rhythm of the land. I learned that tools, patience, and a steady hand could solve nearly any problem. I learned that a dog, or a horse, like a man, responds to respect, consistency, and sometimes a gentle correction. I didn't mind earning a little extra money either.

Charlie had a way of making every lesson stick. "Boy," he'd say, "if the tool ain't right, the man ain't bright." Or, "Don't turn a pile of cow slop into a problem - make it fertilizer." Simple words, simple truths. And as I grew, I began to understand them.

I also began to see the quiet shadows behind his smile - the gap left by a son lost too soon, the loneliness that even a full ranch and a hard day of work couldn't fill. In those moments, I realized that growing up wasn't just about learning skills. It was about learning empathy, responsibility, and courage.

It wasn't long before Charlie asked me to join him on a longer journey - a trip to a distant ranch in Wyoming to see breeding stock, test horses, and share the work of men who lived their lives in sweat, sun, and soil. It was my first real adventure outside the familiar fields of home, and it taught me more about trust, observation, and responsibility than I could have imagined.

We traveled through miles of open country, over dirt roads, past small towns and grazing cattle. Each stop, each careful check of a hitch, each shared joke or quiet moment of observation, was a lesson. And every hour on the road reminded me that patience, preparation, and focus were as important as strength and skill.

At the ranch, I met men and boys whose lives were measured in sweat, grit, and the bond between a man and his animals. I saw horses that could outrun the wind and learned that true mastery comes from respect, practice, and understanding. And as I sat on the porch that first evening, feeling the cool Wyoming breeze, I realized that the boy I had been was already learning the ways of a man - ways that would one day shape courage, loyalty, and service.

That night, I thought of a horse I'd heard so much about, the promise of a ride, and the lessons yet to come. And I understood, for the first time, that life's real heroes are those who run toward responsibility, toward courage, and toward danger - not because it's easy, but because it must be done.

I don't know if my night was restless from the anticipation of seeing these ranchers work their Arabians, or simply from being in a strange place. But I was excited to see the prize champion that everyone admired.

The restless night came to an end with the breakfast that didn't feel heavy even though eggs, bacon, sausage, toast, and strong ranch-house coffee could weigh down anyone. Perhaps it was excitement, or maybe I was getting used to this place.

The morning was calm, a stillness that seemed to carry confidence and a quiet comfort that embraced you. Through it all, I couldn't help but notice the "big" barn behind the house. Inside, the rows of stalls seemed endless. Tack rooms held equipment of remarkable quality - like some saddles made in 1875, still in daily use.

Our host, Calvin, led Charlie and me to his best breeding stallion, Smokey Joe. I expected a velvet-lined stall and pristine buckets, but there was only the usual care - Joe didn't need frills. I thought the name was silly for such a magnificent animal, but as our eyes met, I could swear he knew what I was thinking – like he was assessing me… Smokey Joe gave me a look – and a smirk, like he was silently saying "What kind of punk-kid are you?"

I stood in awe. Joe's breathing carried the weight of the barn, each movement precise, and calculated. No move wasted. His chestnut coat hinted at bluish smoke beneath the crimson, impossible to describe fully. I realized Joe didn't exist to impress anyone - he simply was, and he was a lesson in dignity, focus, and presence.

Calvin asked Joe if he wanted to go for a walk. Joe nodded. I didn't realize it at the moment, but I was about to ride a million-dollar horse for the first time. Charlie's smirk told me I was about to learn more than horsemanship.

I mounted, and Joe walked with the patience of a general inspecting his troops, reading my balance, my confidence, my hesitation. Down the corridor, out the barn doors, past the other horses… the surprise of him springing to action – was more like launching a rocket – forced me to cling to the rigging tighter than I'd known before.

We went - with power, agility, and enough speed to make my eyes water. Smokey Joe ran with a rhythm like a motorcycle hum under me, every hoof-fall deliberate.

The irrigation ditch loomed ahead. I held tighter, expecting a jump. Joe simply glided over it, smooth as air, the music of motion perfect and precise. I learned quickly: he was in charge, and my job was to trust him.

We reached a pond five miles from the ranch and stopped. I slid off, patting his neck, marveling at the intelligence and presence in his eyes. Here was more than speed or endurance – Joe showed me he had reason, compassion, and awareness. A creature capable of understanding and teaching. A silent mentor.

I realized the ride wasn't about mastering a horse. It was about learning the value of trust, respect, and connection. A moment of understanding passed between us, wordless but profound. I wasn't showing off; I was learning.

Over the next days, the bond grew. Joe seemed to read my intent, my hesitation, and my growing confidence. He taught me patience, observation, and empathy - lessons that, I realized, could apply to any partner in life, human or animal.

On my final morning, I slipped into the barn alone. Joe knew me instantly. We stood in silence, comfortable, a mutual understanding in the shadows of the stalls. I patted him one last time, whispered "thank you," and felt the dust and wind from the trails blur my eyes once more.

I slid my boots against the planks of the barn floor to turn – to walk away, and before I left – Joe turned one more time. As our eyes locked – I swear I could see him smile at me… one more time.

Charlie, Calvin, and their mother said their goodbyes, and I joined them outside. Calvin hugged me like a father I never had. Charlie handed me the keys: "You drive for a bit, son."

I climbed into the truck, but my mind lingered on Joe. That ride, that connection, that lesson - I carried it with me. A quiet understanding that courage, respect, and trust weren't just for horses. They were for every living thing willing to run with you, follow your lead, or watch your back.

And when I got home, I knew exactly what that meant when it came to my four-legged partner of a different sort. Buddy.

It was now January. The kind of cold that bites your lungs and makes your bones remember. I packed light - too light. No firewood, no plan. Just a sleeping bag, a can of pork and beans, a bag of potato chips, my little dog… and a whole lot of pride.

We called it Mine-Pass, tucked up in Rock Canyon. An old cave from a long-abandoned mine. I'd been there before. I knew the way and what to do, or so I thought. I figured I'd have one of those "rites of passage" nights - man versus wild. What I got was something much more important.

By the time I reached the mine, I'd already trudged a mile and a half through deep snow, drifts sometimes three feet high. Wet, tired, hungry, but I never stopped.

There was no dry firewood anywhere. I hacked away with my pocket knife, trying to spark a flame from damp shavings. Nothing worked. Cold pork and beans became my dinner - eaten straight from the can - shared with my shivering companion, nestled inside my sleeping bag.

The night was long, nearly sleepless. Every shadow, every whisper of wind seemed to have intent. At one point, a strange noise echoed through the canyon - a bray, maybe a mule, maybe not. I stayed still, listening, heart hammering.

Morning brought no comfort. Stale doughnuts, cold hands, frozen pants. The hike back down was worse than the climb up. The Wild had reminded me of its truth: you weren't ready. Effort alone didn't count. Survival demanded awareness, respect, and preparation.

That was lesson one. But there were others.

Another time – summertime – I camped alone with my dog on the last highest hump of a nearby Mountain, just a secret hideaway that overlooked the valley. My little mix-breed cattle dog followed my every step, alert to what I couldn't see or hear. Even armed with a pistol and a double-barrel shotgun, the lessons I learned from Charlie – even ol' Smokey Joe – were to trust my dog Buddy's instincts over my own eyes.

Dinner cooked over the fire, smoke spiraling into the rising stars. Silence fell, broken only by the shuffle of paws. It was silent until my dog stiffened, then shuffled - ears up. Something approached - a shadow, slow and deliberate.

I leveled the shotgun, fired twice into the dirt just ahead of it. I knew an injured animal was more dangerous, and I didn't need that... The shadow stopped, hesitated, then slowly retreated, leaving no trace behind.

I didn't sleep that night. But we watched, listened, learned. The Wild had spoken. Not in words, but in truth. It reminded me of my place – I was small, fragile, and reliant on my partner, my dog, for senses I did not have.

By sunrise, everything seemed unchanged, yet something had shifted. My dog and I had a silent understanding: I could not see all, hear all, or predict all, but he could. Trust, observation, and respect were everything.

That was lesson two: the value of a partner who reads the world in ways you cannot. The connection that would later shape every relationship I had with animals - from horses like Smokey Joe to the dogs who ran at my side.

And maybe, just maybe, that was the first step toward understanding how a dog could become a hero... loyal, perceptive, and brave enough to run toward danger when I could not.

My childhood friend Wade – I'd known him since kindergarten... he and I would also take many of these little adventures together – even he learned to trust Buddy as more than a companion, but as a partner.

Chapter 2

Testing Ground

The snow told the story before we ever saw it. Hoof prints torn wide, blood frozen in dark splashes, a trail leading up into the timber. Something big had come down from the hills in the night. We were sent to find out what it was.

The snow had hit hard – deep, and whatever that something was… it wasn't hungry for deer anymore.

Wade crouched low, gloved hand brushing the print. "Cougar," he said. His breath steamed in the cold.

I knew it before he said it. "At least we know now – that answers that question."

Calves had been turning up dead, half-buried in the snow – the snow deeper this year than most. We'd find some with ribs cracked open like kindling – others dragged off to the hills.

We weren't out here for sport - this was a race for survival. The 'wild' wanted to eat, and we had a job to protect the livestock. This was the kind of work old man Hawkins trusted us with.

Wade and I busted a trail through the snow while Buddy padded behind us, ears sharp, nose working. He didn't understand the rules this time. To him it was all scent and shadow, a game of chase.

We continued up the mountain.

I held up my hand – made a fist… I turned my head slightly with a motion to keep silent and then crouched down slow so I could lie down on the snow. I didn't have to say anything to know Wade was doing the same.

I heard a growl – low and intense… "Wade – can you shut him up?"

Wade hushed my dog as I focused on something few ever get to watch.

A shape seldom seen but often felt by ranchers. It was a vision that burned through the timber, its shoulders rolling slow, tail nearly dancing back and forth. It wasn't running. It was pawing at the calf that only hours before was safe within the herd. For a heartbeat, I thought maybe it would turn and go. I watched in near awe – its golden fur shuddering for a moment as it began to eat.

I couldn't help but watch while the light skiff of snow – with flakes so small they were hardly recognizable – speckled its golden fur and spotted the blue steel of my rifle. For a moment, nature and man seemed tied together, sharing the same silence. But beneath it lingered the old truth: unity was only borrowed, and conflict was inevitable.

I whispered "You think we can scare it off? So maybe it won't come back?"

Wade tried to answer as quiet as he could "I don't know, but…"

Before he could finish his words the golden cat froze – turned toward us, its eyes locked onto us.

But Buddy bolted first, barking, trying to rush toward it. The large cat lunging toward my dog – fangs ready, and the scream that can haunt dreams.

I didn't think. I moved. And when the shot cracked the air, I already hated myself for pulling the trigger.

The snow crunched under our boots as we turned back toward home. Buddy kept close now, tail low, ears pinned back. He didn't understand what happened - just that the game had ended with thunder and smoke.

Wade slapped me on the shoulder, his grin hidden behind his scarf. "Hell of a shot, Jack. Dropped it clean. Old man Hawkins'll be proud."

I nodded, but the praise didn't settle right. The rifle felt heavy, heavier than it should've. My gut twisted at the thought of golden fur melting into the snow. The cougar wasn't evil… it was hungry. And hunger wasn't a crime.

By the time the fences of Charlie Hawkins's ranch came into view, the weight of shooting the cougar hadn't lifted. Even though – it was to save Buddy.

Charlie was waiting at the gate with his coat buttoned tight, and his gray hat rimmed with frost. He looked past us to the ridge, then down at the rifle in my hand. And he could tell by the look on my face…

"You boys did what had to be done," he said, voice low but steady. Then his eyes landed on me. "You didn't do that for sport." And then looked at Wade "Killing for a trophy don't make a man. Feeling the hurt of it… that's different. That means you understand life matters. More than most do."

I swallowed hard and just nodded. Wade smiled and leaned his rifle against the fence. Buddy brushed against my leg, pressing close. Wade shivered, and before reaching back down for his rifle shuddered his words in the cold "we got down before the weather turned bad."

Charlie tipped his hat "no such things as bad weather boys – just bad clothing choices." And then he gestured toward his house "Come on in – the Fire's still warm. Let the dog rest. The world'll still be wild tomorrow."

He'd been around for so long; I thought he'd last forever. Ol' man Hawkins was wiry, stubborn, and always full of stories. Charlie was the rancher who taught a couple of rag-tag boys how to be men.

His ranch was small by some accounts, but big enough for adventure. That's where I "really" learned the value of working with my hands. Sure – chores at home – what some *could* call a family farm – was different. Working for someone else made me feel like the expectations were higher, and the lessons learned – were cemented into my mind.

And through it all was Wade and a mix-breed cattle dog… Buddy.

I met Wade at recess when we were in kindergarten. We were playing in the sand-box, became friends, and have been ever since.

We'd taken most of the same classes together – the usual required classes, and then there were the ones we liked… shop, auto mechanics, and the FFA (Future Farmers of America). I didn't struggle with the mechanical stuff, but Wade seemed to be a natural. School was one thing, but where we really learned was on the farm.

We learned everything and anything - from wiring irrigation pumps to building fences and patching barns, from carpentry to wrangling his animals. Life on the farm was learning, and the first lesson was always the same: work hard.

I lived on a small family farm. It was mostly for us at home, but Wade talked me into helping him work for some of the other local farmers and ranchers... we'd done it for years because Wade was always talking me into doing something. I didn't mind. Helping others helped me learn. Helping others made me feel good.

It was the first cut of hay – now late spring, and winter's heavy snow-pack gave us an abundance of moisture. It looked like it was going to be a good year for the ranchers. We were out in Charlie's fields... the air sharp with dust and alfalfa. I swung another fifty-pound bale onto the bed of the truck, sweat rolling down my back. Our rhythm was steady - methodical - like we could do this all day without complaint.

Wade, by contrast, grinned through the work. He moved quicker, tossing bales with a little extra snap like he was proving something. Every once in a while he'd crack a joke, just to see if he could get me to break my calm focus.

"Think this counts as Army training?" Wade puffed, grabbing the twine of another bale. "Hauling hay's gotta be tougher than push-ups."

I may have smirked a little, my eyes narrowing against the sun. "Maybe. But the Army doesn't pay you by the bale."

We both laughed, then kept at it - boots scuffing the dry earth, hands raw from twine burns. The truck creaked under the growing stack, the sweet-grass smell thick in our lungs.

Wade swung a bale like it weighed nothing, grinning. "Bet I can stick this one faster than you!" I tightened my grip, lifting with care. "Maybe, but I'll make sure it doesn't fall on us."

When the bale slipped and nearly toppled Wade backward, my hand shot out, steadying him without hesitation. Wade caught his breath, gave a sheepish grin. "You've got reflexes like a cat."

I shrugged a bit, calm as ever. "You've got nerves. That'll count for something."

We went back to work, side by side. Different styles, same grit. By the time the last bale hit the stack – high and the truck loaded, the sun was low and the valley glowed gold. We sat on the top row, legs dangling, catching our breath as we looked out over the patchwork of farms and the far-off mountains.

Wade broke the silence. "Jack… you ever think about what's next? Like… after this?"

I didn't answer right away. I shaded my eyes then squinted at the horizon, the mountains shadowed in evening haze. The future felt big, bigger than the fields, bigger than this valley.

And for the first time, I wondered if maybe Wade was right - maybe the Army was the next field to work, the next mountain to climb. Wade's talked about it for some time now – I wasn't sure. But he kept at me.

Old man Hawkins – Charlie – watched us unload the hay – the lights of the barn only hinting at the day we'd just conquered. Right about the time we were brushing all the dust, dirt, and hay from our clothes – Charlie told us there was a problem with the hay baling machine.

"I think the 'knotter' is jammed" Charlie said with some frustration – pointing to the part of the baler that ties the string holding the bales of hay together. Wade smirked, and I knew that he knew – exactly what to do.

Without any thought – he ran over to the tractor – still hooked up to the hay baler – and began to tear into it – cutting away the baling twine that was caught up in it – and gave the parts some grease – then put it all back together.

"There Ol' man" Wade said with a chuckle "this should get it going for ya…"

Charlie said that he'd tried, but couldn't get it to work, but Wade turned, and with that huge grin said "the secret is – like this one old guy taught me – ya have to be strong enough to break it free – to fix it – without using so much force ya break it."

Charlie nodded his head remembering what he taught us a long time ago, and then smiled saying "that's advice you boys can use anywhere" – then invited us in for some dinner…

**

I hated to see the weekends come to an end. Especially when I could be earning money working for the farmers. But school wouldn't last much longer, and graduation was just around the corner. The thoughts of my future nowhere in my mind.

I choked down my breakfast, and waited for the sound of that old '73 Chev pickup. And I could hear it coming all the way from the street. He pulled up to the house – I ran out to meet him through the dust from him coming to a quick stop.

We headed into town – even though our town stretched across a lot of the farms and ranches where we lived, and worked. We stopped for a doughnut and coffee before heading to class. Small rituals we liked to start the day – just right.

We sat impatiently through math – English… couldn't wait for the good classes, but then the Principal made the daily announcements… the pledge, the daily events, and then…

"And students – before third period we will meet in the auditorium for an annual test. We will be assisting in administrating the ASVAB with the Army recruiters…"

Wade turned around to look at me from his desk – just smiled. One girl asked the teacher "what is an ASVAB test?"

The teachers' brow furrowed and she said "this test is an 'Armed Services Vocational Aptitude Battery'" with a puzzled look on her face… "it's something we do every year…"

Another girl piped back interrupting her "what if we don't want to go into the military?"

The teacher smiled… "You can either skip going to the auditorium or go directly to your next class, or… you can do badly on the test!"

The bell rang – and instead of heading toward the door to leave class, Wade jumped from his desk, and waited for me. "Come on Jack – let's get a good seat up front – it'll be fun!"

"I'd have thought you'd planned this – if I didn't know any better…" I chuckled.

We shuffled through the crowded hallway toward the auditorium, and made our way to the front. The seats were mostly filled with all the high school guys simply wanting to find a way to skip their next few classes.

The auditorium smelled faintly of dust and chalk, the old fluorescent lights buzzing overhead. On each one of the seats was a scratch pad, a No. 2 pencil, and the thick booklet of the ASVAB. Fifty years of high school kids had sat here, but for us, it felt like stepping into a different world - one where every question counted. I didn't know what I wanted to do after high school, so maybe this could be an option?

I flipped open the booklet and swallowed hard. The first section was math - arithmetic reasoning, algebra, fractions, and percentages. My hand itched to work it all out, slow and steady, while Wade leaned back in his chair, grinning like it was no big deal. Wade always seemed pretty cool when it came to stressful situations.

"Hey, Jack," he whispered, nudging me, "what's 17 divided by… uh, never mind. Just scribble something."

I glared, but a snort escaped when he winked.

Hours crawled by. Word knowledge, paragraph comprehension, mechanical concepts, and shop problems - I'd never thought vocabulary could feel like a marathon. Wade cracked a small smile every time a tricky problem tripped me up. I'd shoot him a glare, but he just shrugged, completely at ease.

One kid next to us had his pencil break. It looked like he tried to bend it, and then it snapped. He was scribbling so fast it looked like he was trying to start a pencil fire. Another kid looked puzzled – kept sticking his pencil erasure in his ear… Another girl whispered, "If anyone says 'vocational' one more time, I'm dropping out."

Wade, of course, whispered back, "You mean like a professional complainer?"

By the time we hit the mechanical section, I was sweating over a diagram of a gear train. Wade leaned over, peered at it, and then shrugged. "Looks like my grandma's washing machine. Turn the thing clockwise. Done."

I rolled my eyes, but couldn't help laughing quietly. Somehow, Wade made this torturous test feel… lighter.

By the time they called the final section, our hands were sore from pencils, our shoulders stiff from sitting, and the room smelled faintly of pencil eraser and nervous energy. A few kids looked like they were dozing in their seats, heads bobbing; others scribbled furiously, eyes wide with panic.

"Think we're gonna make it?" I whispered to Wade.

"Piece of cake," he said, flipping a page with the confidence of someone born to do this. I wasn't so sure, but I admired the ease he carried.

When the last pencil scratched its final answer, the proctor collected the booklets. Relief washed over me, and Wade leaned back with that familiar smirk. "See? Told you it'd be fine."

I just shook my head, exhausted but oddly exhilarated. Four hours, or maybe five - of testing, of thinking, of trying not to let the fear of failure creep in. Somehow, the ASVAB felt like another mountain to climb, one that we'd survived together. I almost wished we'd gone to class instead.

By the time the testing was over – school had already let out for the day. We walked out the doors of the school into the daylight – both of us squinting – to see a Sheriff's department truck next to Wade's '73 Chev.

We got closer to Wade's truck – the tall Deputy – a Lieutenant in a deep voice asked Wade why he missed classes – his tone was serious with an accusation as if Wade wasn't in school today…

"Funny – Dad…" Wade grinned "you knew right where we were today… all day!" as Wade's dad started to laugh too.

"Just checking to see how it all went" he smiled.

I shook my head – maybe out of exhaustion, as Wade came back with a "it went great – no problems – easy-peasy if you ask me."

Wade's dad smiled: "The real tests don't show you how weak you are - but how strong you are."

I started walking around to the other side of the truck to get in – Wade's dad still smiling – telling his son not to be late for dinner… Wade hollered to his dad "maybe - tell mom we'll grab a bite at the diner… we're on our way to Charlie's place to help him with some chores…"

Wade was still laughing under his breath – the whole way to Charlie's little ranch. The mood changed when we pulled up to Charlie's barn…

Several of his neighbors' – the 'new to the area' kind of people – looked distressed. They wanted advice on how to keep their chickens from getting eaten by predators. They even asked us if we could hunt down the predators that had been killing their chickens. Before Charlie could respond – I couldn't help myself…

"We've had chickens for years… and we've never lost any to – well – any kind of predators… if you're going to have 'em – then you need to understand how to 'predator-proof' your chicken coops – like we've done."

They looked puzzled. Charlie looked proud. But their chatter didn't calm any – in fact they may have even become more insistent on us hunting for them… that it could even be a 'sport' for us. But Charlie in his old – wise way simply put his hand on my shoulder and stopped me: "the boy is right – if you're going to raise any kind of livestock – you need to take into consideration what lives in these hills – these mountains near us."

As he tilted his old cowboy hat back a little, he said, "Raisin' livestock means you're gonna take some losses. Sometimes it's weather, sometimes it's predators. That's the cost of runnin' stock. Where you put 'em, and how you tend 'em – well that's where you make the difference."

He shrugged, grin tugging at the corners of his mouth. "That's why I keep hogs closer to the ridges. Ain't much comes down outta the hills looking for a meal when a field full of hogs is waiting. They're meaner than coyotes, and smart enough to keep their own."

He scuffed the dirt with his boot and added, voice turning more serious. "But when a predator turns on you… then they don't leave us much choice."

Wade and I understood what he meant, though I wasn't sure the out-of-towners did. Charlie just smiled, letting the weight of his words settle. "Coyotes, wolves - even cougars and foxes - the difference between them and us is, they don't hunt for sport."

It may not have calmed their nerves – or their anger about losing their animals, but Charlie was right – and they knew it. When we live where the wild lives… we live by their rules.

Wade and I went about the chores Ol' Man Hawkins set out for us, but the thoughts of those neighbors kept at me… and bothered me. I looked at Wade – and said "how do these people think? How can they – not understand what living around here is like?"

Wade looked back at me with the same questioning look on his face… "I don't know man – too many of these kinds move here not knowing what it's like – they buy up our old properties – come from the big cities and then… try to change everything."

"I know" as I paused a little… "I guess I know at least…" as I saw Charlie walking out to where we were putting some tools away, and then I paused again before I continued saying "I may not have had a dad like you Wade, but I've had your dad…" as I turned and smiled at Charlie – "and I've had a 'Charlie' to fill that for me also."

Charlie just smiled a bit – looked at us proud "you know boys – no matter what you two do – you'll be just fine. I'm proud of both of you, and even though you're a bit scrappy at times – well I know you boys are going to be just fine."

"What ya mean?" I asked.

"I know you boys took that Army test today – and, well – I know you guys can't stay around here forever…" as he sat down onto a broken bale of hay… "Not every path was meant to be followed - some are meant to be made."

There was something hollow in his words – worry maybe? The fear of losing "his boys?" I knew he'd never stop us, but I could tell something was hiding behind his smile.

The ride in an old Chevy truck got quiet when we left the dirt road behind and pulled onto the pavement. It stayed quiet as I could tell Wade's thoughts mirrored mine.

Graduation was only days away. The future stared at me through the lights from Wade's dashboard. I've known this guy – my friend from even before the first grade… words weren't always important. Words were never that important when you can almost read each other's thoughts – and I could tell what he was thinking – because I was thinking what Charlie said…

"Not every path was meant to be followed – some are meant to be made."

Chapter 3

Changes

There has always been a comfort in living where you can almost guess how each day will be. Each day brings the same thing. Each season brings just enough change to make the predictable years come and go as they should. Nothing to guess - everything a reassurance that life simply is what it is.

Even the surprises? These were normal too - the unexpected things like weather, wild animals, or the price of grain… They really weren't that unexpected… Well – It's all just part of an endless cycle of life we'd all come to know. So how was a teenage boy supposed to describe the feeling of uncertainty he'd never known?

Sure – things changed from time to time – Like when my dad had run off when the youngest was still in diapers. I guess Mom in a way… never forgave me for looking so much like him. She wasn't unkind, just… distant. Being the oldest of five meant I was the one patching fences, milking cows, and keeping the younger ones out of trouble while Mom did her best to hold a job and keep the house together.

But the little differences in my years didn't unfold the security – the reassurance of life's 'warm blanket' this town had wrapped me in. I've lived with the comfort of always knowing my world would never change.

And maybe that's the difference. For me the certainty was - knowing that tomorrow will look the same. I carried that kind of trust my whole life.

It was cemented into my mind and to this valley one afternoon when I was eight years old. I walked out of a grocery store and saw a couple of kids giving away puppies. I picked one up and fell in love. "Mom - can I keep him?" It is the cliché that lives in the heart of every child, and is feared by every single mother.

"Yes… you can keep him."

He was never supposed to come in the house, but found his way through the doors and into the hearts of our family. "Buddy"

A 'Mutt' by any standard, but is it *really* a Mutt when you can tell what it is? The kids at the grocery said he was part Border Collie, but I could see some of the 'speckling' a 'Red Healer' has through the fur on one of his legs, and he had many of the similar markings of an Australian Shepherd. But none of that mattered when a natural born cattle-dog does what it does, and does it well.

He was stocky and strong - never tired from work, and never tired from chasing a ball. And he never wanted to leave my side. Whenever Wade would talk about going away and joining the Army, Buddy would look at him like he knew what Wade was saying.

When Wade and I were driving home from Charlie's house we would silently look at each other. When I closed the door to Wade's ol' Chevy there was a familiar nose at my side, and eyes that looked long and hard wondering why today - he didn't go to work on the farms with me.

Wade pulled away waving to us and I turned to see my mom with a look that said 'time for my chores here at home.'

So Buddy and I got started. Even in the dark the work on a farm was never done. No matter how small it is…

It was late by the time Buddy and I walked into the house - to a snack and a scolding. Even though my mom wasn't the real social kind of lady, she told me she still wanted to attend the high school graduation. But I didn't. I didn't think all that ceremonial 'stuff' was necessary. And then she changed the subject when she asked me:

"You ever find out where those raccoons have been nesting?" she asked with a bit of a snap.

"Not yet" I said respectfully, "but - they aren't bothering anyone - they haven't gotten into the chickens, and I've made sure they can't get into the garbage cans."

I didn't know why the little bandits bothered her so much. Buddy liked chasing them, and it was almost a game for all of them.

I got dressed for bed, and climbed into the comfort I've always known, but it seemed to stir something I couldn't explain. It was a comfort that seemed to be at the cusp of going away even though I didn't want it to.

I looked into the eyes of this pal resting beside me - thinking he too would be something I could count on… forever.

Only a few days of school left, and then what? I tried to make these last few days of routine seem normal, but they weren't. Kids were excited about the changes that were coming, but I wasn't.

The next day I told Wade to go to Charlie's place without me - I had to catch up on some things at my place. He tried to convince me, but ended up going without me. I walked home, and before I got to the little dirt road that led to my house - Buddy was waiting by the side of the road.

We didn't even go into the house - I started my chores, and watched Buddy play with a ball, and chase the raccoons. Whenever I had to clean the chicken coop, Buddy would sit by the door and watch. The chickens never wanted to leave while my 'chicken-hound' kept watch by the door…

And then he bolted away.

I was shoveling and scraping while listening to a joyful bark. I just pictured in my mind him chasing and playing - trying to catch the little bandits. Then his bark turned ferocious. I dropped my shovel and ran to see what was alarming him.

I ran around to the back of our tool shed, and found him nearly half-way under the shed - digging and pawing while growling and barking. I pulled him away quick holding onto his hindquarters, and while he was still in a near frenzy - I told him to calm down…

His face was scratched and bleeding. It wasn't bad, but still bad enough for me to take him into the house and get him cleaned up. My mom helped - even though she tried to put on a brave face I could tell she was concerned. While she was tending to his scratches I went back out to the tool shed and found where the raccoons were nesting. They'd burrowed underneath the shed, and hollowed out an area underneath. I had to flood it with a hose to chase them out - then grabbed some bags of post-mix concrete and filled in the hole.

By the time I was finished - I felt the presence of my shadow now inspecting my work as if he approved. His face clean and all smiles now, he followed me so I could finish the chores I'd started.

Even though my mind told me school was coming to an end, and I would have to adapt to the world around me – I looked at Buddy and somehow thought – this… this would never change

**

The next day at school Wade and I left the High School campus and were having lunch at a little diner. We didn't like eating in the cafeteria. He asked me if I was going to the graduation dance, and said we could double-date if I want…

"Naw - I just don't want to" I said taking a sip from my coffee mug. But Wade - always trying to talk me into something - wanted me to go with him and his childhood sweetheart Charlotte. I never did.

Wade chuckled "you know it's a tradition to 'smuggle' in something like a pizza - or something like that during the graduation ceremony?"

"What are you thinking about 'smuggling' in Wade?" I asked with a chuckle.

"How about a watermelon" he snickered nearly spraying me with his soda.

He never snuck a watermelon in, but did manage to show me a large hoagie sandwich he hid under his graduation gown… and yes - he shared it with me. Callahan and Duncan - we sat close enough to each other it wasn't hard for us to share some laughs… and a huge sandwich.

We never had a manual for growing up - just a lot of sunshine, some trouble… and stories like this we'll laugh about forever.

During the ceremony I was listening to the traditional speech about us being at the crossroads of our life. I thought about that gnawing feeling that seemed to creep up - the one I can't explain… where the comfort I've grown to love met the unknown I was about to face.

The music played the pomp and circumstance while we all marched the way we'd rehearsed – up to the stand so we could get our diploma… and right before Wade's name was called for him to walk across the stage - he reached into his pocket underneath his robe, and smiled that huge grin of his, and I knew something was 'up.'

He started walking. And as he climbed the stairs to the stage - he placed the funny glasses with a huge nose and fake mustache onto his face and met the principal to receive his certificate. The principal just smiled, reached up and snatched the gag off of his face, and put them on himself. The audience laughed.

Like I said - I didn't go to the dance with Wade and his girlfriend. I stayed home. It just felt right. I just wanted to be home. I just wanted everything to stay… normal.

For a week or so it almost felt like I was skipping school - you know, that 'playing hookie' sense you get when you know you 'got away' with something. I spent more time at home now - teaching my younger brothers and sisters how to do the things I was doing around our place - in case I got a job - maybe working more full-time hours for the other farmers and ranchers. And as always… Buddy went with me everywhere I went.

It was about - maybe I'd say it was a little more than a week, or could have been ten days after Buddy 'got into it' with the raccoons under our shed when I noticed it. We 'd spent the day at Charlie's place, and when we got home Buddy was hopping out of our '65 Ford pick-up, and he stumbled.

Something he'd never done before. Yeah - he was 10 years old, but still acted like a pup. He was always full of energy, and full of life. Never a day he wasn't sharp and on his game. But he stumbled. His back legs gave out for a moment. I picked him up - dusted him off, and rubbed his side…

"You Ok boy?" I said with some concern. He just gave me a look like he wanted to smile, but didn't.

Later that evening I noticed he was starting to drag his back legs. I felt him all over again - checking for any injuries - for anything broken. He sat patient letting me, but I couldn't find anything wrong. The next morning it was worse. He couldn't move his back legs at all.

I picked him up, and carried him to the truck, and we drove to the Vet's office. My mom was concerned how much it would cost, but I told her I had enough money - that she shouldn't worry about it.

I was confused - and getting a little worried. I wasn't sure why my big Bud wasn't walking. I carried him into the waiting room, and the staff could tell I was uneasy - maybe a bit anxious. They didn't waste any time escorting us to an exam room. I knew this wasn't normal either.

Our old-time Vet - Dr. Mortensen - came in and introduced himself, then asked me to put him on the exam table. He began to look him over carefully - he couldn't see anything wrong. He asked me if he'd been hit by a car? Was he in a fight with another dog? I told him that Buddy had been with me nearly the whole time - I couldn't think of anything… other than him 'getting into it' with the raccoons.

"Raccoons?" his brow lifting… then he asked me if he could take some blood and tissue samples. I agreed. I didn't know what else to do.

He told me he'd put a rush on the tests so we could see what's wrong with our boy. But I didn't want to wait… I hate waiting.

I carried Buddy back out to the truck, took him home, and made him a bed in the front room - where he was never supposed to be. I didn't care.

I gave him water - some of the food he liked, but nothing would get him to move on his own. For two days he sat there. Nearly helpless. And then our phone rang. It was the Vet's office with the test results.

"Coonhound paralysis."

The Vet told me that in most cases the sickness would run its course in a little more than a week. That the paralysis would gradually take over his body - then start to go away slowly. He did say that maybe one percent or so of the cases would cause respiratory failure and that it could become fatal, but that would be rare.

But so was Buddy.

Wade and his dad came by - even Charlie came to the house when I told them Buddy was having a hard time breathing… we were all gathered there when…

His breathing slowed, and became shallow. I held him tight against my chest. Then he let go, and just like that he closed his eyes for the last time.

I felt like my whole world stopped. Everything I knew was changing.

Some people will never understand how much someone can love a dog, but that's ok… Buddy knew. Buddy taught me about unconditional love, and losing him was my first lesson about profound grief…

It was a lesson – sure, but even more… it was the door I was walking through leading to a path that would change my life forever.

Chapter 4

A New World

The farm work kept me busy, but busy didn't mean the same thing anymore. Without Buddy shadowing me from dawn until long past chores, it felt like something had been ripped out of my days. Wade knew it. He didn't talk much about it, but when we drove together in his old Chevy, I'd catch him glancing over like he was checking on me without wanting me to know.

The same way he did ten years ago when my dad left.

It was Wade who kept the idea alive. The Army. He'd talk about it while hauling hay, fixing fence, or even while we were sitting on the tailgate drinking from a shared thermos of coffee.

"You ever think about how far we could go?" he asked one night, looking past the headlights into a dark road that seemed endless. "Past this valley? Past all of this?"

I didn't answer right away. I'd never been much for dreaming out loud. But maybe that's what Buddy's leaving had done. It made me realize nothing stays the same. Even the warm blanket gets pulled away sooner or later.

A week later, Wade's dad, Lt. Callahan, sat us down at the kitchen table with a cup of black coffee steaming between his hands. He wasn't the kind to give speeches, but when he talked, you listened.

"Basic training isn't like fixing a water pump or stringing barbed wire. It's long. It's slow. And it'll test your patience before it tests your muscles. But the Army's a good experience if you tough it out."

We nodded like we knew what he meant. Truth was, we didn't. Not yet.

When the recruiter called and told me my ASVAB scores came back higher than most - high enough to get me considered for any of the jobs I'd like - like the K9 program - my heart jumped. Wade's score opened the door to technical jobs – like EOD - Explosive Ordinance Disposal – which seemed right for him.

I was always the calm one, but Wade had the steady hand when things got tricky. And then it was official. In a few weeks, the two of us would be boarding a bus. But I was headed for Fort Benning for my basic training… Wade wasn't.

It would be the first time – for a lifetime… the life I knew wouldn't be right by my side.

I lay in bed that night staring at the ceiling, thinking of the farm, my mom, my brothers and sisters, and the valley that had been my whole world. I thought of Buddy too, and how he'd been with me in every season of my life so far.

I whispered into the quiet room, like maybe he could still hear me somehow: "Wish me luck, Bud. I'm gonna need it."

**

The morning air at the bus station carried a heaviness I couldn't shake. Mom hadn't come. Maybe she couldn't – but I knew she didn't want me to join. Her words still echoed in the back of my mind: *"I just don't know how we'll keep the farm going without you."* I tried, in the weeks before leaving, to teach my younger brothers and sisters everything I could - how to fix a busted fence, how to tell when the calves needed doctoring, how to handle the tractor without grinding the gears. I hoped it would be enough, but a part of me knew it wouldn't.

It was Wade's dad, Lt. Callahan, who drove us down and stood with us at the depot, a hand on each of our shoulders like we were already his soldiers. He didn't say much, just the kind of quiet strength that made us straighten up without even thinking. And in that moment I was glad I couldn't see the man that fathered me in the crowd. I already had a dad.

As the bus engine rumbled to life, I caught sight of a familiar figure across the lot. It was old Charlie, standing near the feed store with his hat in hand, waving with that same easy grin that seemed a little hollow this time. It hit me like a stone to the chest. Something about that wave felt final, though no one said it out loud. Wade grinned and waved back, but I just raised a hand slowly, swallowing hard.

When the time came, the two of us climbed aboard. Wade pressed his forehead briefly against the window, giving his dad a nod. I sat back, staring out at the horizon, telling myself that this was just another kind of fieldwork - another kind of fence to mend. Only now, the stakes weren't cattle or crops.

And as the bus lurched forward, my last glimpse of home was Charlie's arm still raised, fading in the distance.

The bus finally pulled into that tiny nowhere town in Missouri like it had all the time in the world. Fort Leonard Wood. Wade gathered his duffel and grinned that lopsided grin I knew too well.

"Guess this is where we split, brother," he said.

Split. The word sounded wrong. Too permanent. I shook my head, but didn't argue. We hugged quick, firm, like men who didn't want anyone on the bus to see.

"Don't forget me when you're some big-shot bomb tech," I said.

"And don't let 'em drop you on your head at Airborne," he shot back, and then he was gone. Just like that.

The bus moved forward again, and I was alone. For the first time in my life… I was really alone.

Basic training was a machine built to chew men up and spit them back out in uniform. My world shrank to boots, bunks, rifles, and sweat. Every second counted, every mistake punished, every word measured. I learned to move before thinking, to stand taller when I wanted to curl up, and to keep my mouth shut unless I was sure I wouldn't regret opening it.

Letters from home were gold. Short, rushed, and read over and over until the paper softened. So when I'd get a letter with mom's words saying she was proud of me, I kept it like a rare thing. Because it was. And then, every now and then, Wade's handwriting showed up. Scribbled, messy, but somehow full of life. He was buried in explosives manuals and schematics I couldn't quite picture yet, but I imagined him grinning through it all.

Fort Benning was another kind of beast. Airborne men walked differently, like they had already beaten gravity. I wasn't there yet, but I wanted to be.

They drilled us until running in full gear felt like breathing, until the world seemed to shrink down to the sound of boots and wind whipping past.

And then, the jump.

The C-130 waited – patient in the humid Georgia morning like a beast with its mouth – open waiting to swallow us. Above the door, stenciled in bold letters, it read:

"Remember: your parachute and this plane were both made by the lowest bidder."

Comforting.

They shoved us to the edge, one by one. My turn came too fast. The sky looked too big, the ground too far. My legs shook. I jumped anyway - or maybe I was pushed. Arms pin-wheeled like a windmill gone mad, every bit of training evaporating in the freefall that lasted for only a second.

Then, a jerk. The chute snapped open. My body slammed upward, my stomach went somewhere I didn't know existed, and my pride… well, it landed long before I did – beaten and bruised on the ground below.

I hit the earth in a heap. Legs sore, ego worse. The sergeant grinned like he'd seen it a thousand times.

"Welcome to Airborne, son. Only four more to go."

I swallowed hard, dusted off, and grinned back. Somehow, I'd survived. Somehow, I'd made it back to the ground with both feet – while I looked around in the red Georgia dirt for a little bit of my dignity.

Each task – each jump, and every adventure led to that final day. Graduation. All the guys welcomed family and friends, but the letters I'd received from home told me what I expected.

Money is tight – no one to watch over the small farm, and every available help… was now taking care of Charlie's place… helping his extended family sell off the estate.

Every part of my world seemed to be a memory fading.

But I stood proud – alone. I was pinned with the wings of an Airborne. And no one was there to see.

All the guys had weekend passes, but I stayed on base – I had nowhere to go – no one to see. I just waited for my new orders, and when they finally arrived I already knew what they would say, but it's always a surprise when an **Army** guy gets sent to… the 341st Joint training center at… Lackland **Air Force** Base… where all the Military Working Dogs – for all branches and even Federal Law Enforcement are trained.

If it weren't for the rising and setting of the sun – I wouldn't have been able to know which way was what… I'd lived and learned how to tell where I was by the towering mountains, and now… nothing but wide open skies, and a sprawling flat earth…

Texas.

The first time I saw him, he was no bigger than a loaf of bread. Black and tan, ears too big for his head, eyes like he already knew the world was full of rules he didn't care about.

I took his leash for the first time and the trainer – or Kennel Master as we called him - introduced me to him. "Gunner" he said, and his name stuck before I even thought to ask why.

We didn't exactly start as a team. He nipped at my boots more than once, and I nearly tripped over him trying to get him to follow the commands. Every time he barked, I felt like barking back in frustration, and every time I tried to be gentle, he leaned harder into mischief.

But slowly - like learning a new rhythm - we figured each other out. I wasn't just learning how to be a K9 handler, but a master trainer, and Gunner? He was learning – no – growing into the role of both protector, and companion.

I learned when to push, when to back off, and when a soft hand meant more than a harsh word. Gunner learned that I wasn't just another drill sergeant, that I could be trusted, and that following me didn't mean losing his spark.

Because I remembered what Charlie taught… "Strong enough to fix it, but not so forceful it breaks."

We ran courses together, crawled through mud, jumped over walls, and he learned how to sniff out things no one wanted found. With every trip, tumble, or mistake – we learned, and it only made us stronger. By the time we got to the final evaluation, we were a team. A little scrappy, a little stubborn, but solid.

Graduation came in the gray dawn. A small ceremony, a row of officers clapping, and me standing there with Gunner by my side. No family, no friends, no one to throw the hat or clap the loudest. Just me and this little dog. This wasn't the kind of graduation I'd expected in a way – like having Wade there to make it fun… this was different… just me and Gunner. I watched him grow, and he watched me change. Together we forged a bond, and he had become my world in a way I hadn't expected.

And yet - I didn't feel alone. Not anymore. Gunner looked up at me with that same spark in his eyes, tail wagging, ready to face whatever came next. For the first time, I realized that navigating a new world didn't feel so hard when you had a buddy who had your back, no matter what.

Whatever did come next – we'd face it together.

By now, Gunner and I had become more than a team; we were a unit. He followed my every step, and sniffed out problems before I even saw them. Somehow he made the chaos of all these temporary assignments feel like a rhythm we could manage. We'd learned to trust each other without question. Every success – even the small ones – felt like a victory we shared. During these 'temporary duty' assignments – we called TDY – we were sent all over the world.

From cargo inspections to training drills - from simulated hazards to finding the real thing… Gunner never failed. We moved around so much it seemed like our letters from home were always a few steps behind. But we kept busy – and that's what we liked. When we found our way back to Texas – Lackland AFB where we were training other trainers – Gunner almost acted like a puppy again.

But that wouldn't last long…

Letters from Wade kept arriving in the barracks, folded and tucked carefully into my gear. He wrote about fixes and repairs, about long hours spent troubleshooting equipment, and the quiet satisfaction of a job done well.

I could see him growing into his own strength, steady and reliable, always calm, always thinking ahead. And I could almost hear his voice when I read his words, reminding me of the bond we'd formed long ago.

Recognition came quietly. A superior noticed how smoothly Gunner and I moved through the exercises, how I didn't panic when things went sideways, how this little German Shepherd grew into a force to be reckoned with, and he seemed to anticipate the worst before it happened. It was enough to earn me a promotion – Sergeant. Not that anyone back home would know; the farm, my family, the life I'd left behind – it all felt miles away. But Gunner didn't care about medals or ranks. He cared about the work and the moments we shared, and that was enough for me.

Rumors of growing tension in the Mid-East began to reach us. News reports, hushed conversations in the mess hall, subtle hints of movements in Kuwait and Saudi Arabia. Something big was coming. I'd learned the rules, the drills, and the ways to keep calm. But nothing could prepare me for the unknown of what lay ahead. New orders came in… Another long flight, and another new experience.

I'd never heard of it before – most people haven't. A small sliver of land just south of the Equator in the Indian Ocean… Diego Garcia. If it weren't for the work – it could have been a tropical paradise.

We spent long hours inspecting cargo and walking security checks. Gunner was a key player in making sure the preparations for a big operation – was a success. And yet, standing there on a little island in the middle of the Indian Ocean there on the tarmac one evening, we watched a transport plane disappear into the twilight, I felt a strange calm.

Gunner nudged my leg, tail wagging, like he already knew what was coming next. And then a dry palm leaf blew across the tarmac, bouncing along in the tropical wind. My first thought was home and the long stretches of dirt roads. I thought of the dusty fields, the quiet rhythm of life on the farm.

But Gunner… oh, he remembered too. With a sudden burst of energy, he leapt forward, chasing that palm leaf like a puppy again. His ears upright and sharp, teeth snapping, with all the seriousness of an attack. And yet he was playful as he remembered our play time in Texas.

For only a moment the seriousness of the day was forgotten. I couldn't help but laugh. For a moment, we were just a boy and his dog again, running in the sun, nothing but the open world ahead.

Gunner pranced back to me tail wagging, as if to say, "*look what I got*" with a few busted shreds from the broken leaf still in his mouth. I chuckled again – then knelt on the ground and hugged him. I could feel his confidence that said "*yes – we we're ready.*" Gunner looked confident, and I believed him. Whatever did come next – war, challenges, danger – we'd face it as one. And for the first time, I realized that no matter how far I went from home, I wasn't alone. Not really.

The desert was waiting, and soon, so were we. And in that instant, I knew: whatever did come next – the desert, the unknown, the war – it would be Gunner and me side by side. Ready for whatever the world would throw at us.

Chapter 5

Letters From Home

The orders came with a weight I couldn't fold up and tuck away like the papers in my pocket. Texas was behind us now, and the world ahead was nothing I'd ever seen before.

The staging hangar smelled of oil, sweat, and jet fuel. Rows of green duffels sat like sleeping men, and men sat like green duffels - waiting, shifting, and staring into nothing. Gunner's crate waited for him wedged between my rucksack and a stack of boxes. His ears twitched at every metallic clang of the C-5's ramp as if he already knew this wasn't just another drill.

Hours blurred. Briefings, more waiting. A ride back to the tarmac. A line of shadows climbing the ladder into the belly of the transport. The engines roared and it rattled my chest, as usual Gunner's eyes never left me. I held him close to me and kept scratching his ears until the loadmaster waved us aboard.

It was just another flight - a rhythm of noise and silence. Engines howled, men slept. I couldn't. The cargo bay was cold, my knees pulled tight to my chest, helmet digging into my side. Somewhere over the expanse of the tropical ocean and the desert, I drifted off with the thrum of turbines and the rattle of loose bolts above my head. My hand never leaving Gunner.

Nothing to do but think. And while I was lost in thought – I thought how Gunner and I had seen the world. From Germany to Japan we showed the world how special he is. From one cavernous hangar and fluorescent lights to another… we weren't tourists – we had a job to do.

By now it is so early in the morning the sun was barely waking up. Out here time zones are meaningless. For 10 hours it was nothing but coffee in paper cups, powdered eggs from a 'MRE' and us - looking at men stretched out on webbed seats like fallen dominoes. Gunner knew this drill, but I sat beside him, whispering low just to keep us both steady. His tail thumped, and for a moment the war felt far away. Another day lost to the sky.

The desert sun finally caught us as the ramp lowered in Kuwait. Even in January the desert air carried no mercy - dry, gritty, and sharp. The sun pressed down hard enough to make the sweat bead, though the thermometer only read seventy. It wasn't summer's furnace yet, but you could feel it lurking, waiting its turn. Sand blew against my boots, fine as powder, endless as the ocean.

I tightened my grip on Gunner's leash when we walked out onto the tarmac. His nose to the wind, ears up. I followed his gaze toward the horizon where brown met blue and thought: "here we go boy... it's the real thing."

Somewhere between the heat, the dust, and the endless noise, I realized how long it had been since I'd heard from home. From Wade. From anyone. Out here, comfort didn't come in warm meals or soft words - it came in letters, folded and worn, passed from one world into another.

Gunner stretched as we walked away from the air strip. His head held high nose to the dry air – dust and all. We'd spent so much time working temporary assignments – sniffing around cargo holds – aircraft ready for deployment and such – but this new world far from home... was a new world indeed.

And again – the world we were used to... was to wait. Hurry-up and wait... not that this military cliché was any comfort. But this wait wasn't long. It was only hours this time. A young Corporal – a 'Specialist' who was our company clerk for "W" company found us... I guess we weren't hard to spot. Not a lot of soldiers arriving in the desert – the sand and dust of Kuwait... came with a dog.

We didn't talk much. We just walked through the maze of planes, transport trucks – cargo and equipment... and he opened the door to the Hummer...

Gunner hopped in without command, and I settled into the front passenger side... and we drove... We watched the endless sea of nothing pass before we arrived at a post they called Ali Al Salem. There we finished our final checks and paperwork before boarding a convoy. And it wouldn't be our last. For now...

The convoy kicked up a wall of dust as we rolled north, the horizon painted in the dull gray of burning oil wells. We passed charred wrecks that lined the roadside - burned-out tanks, twisted trucks, from the initial air campaign. The sand itself seemed scorched, black scars scattered across the pale earth.

Gunner pressed closer to me, nose low, as if he, too, understood this wasn't just another assignment. This was war's calling card, littered across the desert for anyone brave or foolish enough to follow.

Gunner had his nose pressed against the small opening in the canvas, ears flicking at every distant sound. He didn't like the smell of this place, and neither did I.

Hours bled together, broken only by checkpoints, cleaning the filters for the engine, and soldiers stretched thin on too little sleep. Someone passed a canteen my way, and when I nodded my thanks he said, "Heard some of your team are already up ahead. One of 'em said he's from your neck of the woods."

I wanted to ask more, but the convoy jolted forward, and conversation scattered like sand in the wind. Still, I held onto that one line. Someone from home? Could it be Wade? I knew he'd be good at doing what he was trained for – and if anyone would have the nerves to diffuse the bombs and "IED's" out here – he could.

Gunner hopped up to the front with me, and shifted against my leg, restless, and I scratched behind his ear.

Letters from home had stopped coming a while ago. It wasn't totally out of the norm for the ARMY to start forwarding mail to your new duty assignment, but somewhere in the back of my mind I'd convinced myself not to expect them anymore. Out here, maybe a familiar face was the only letter I'd get.

The sun sank low, casting long shadows over the desert. Ahead, the road stretched into Iraq - unknown, unwelcome, unavoidable. I tightened my grip on Gunner's leash, feeling the weight of every mile between me and the boy I used to be. We hadn't gone far before the desert began to change. Whatever waited beyond that border was a world away from anything I'd ever known. By now – I had no idea where I was.

It was even worse when the sun went down.

The hum of the engine began to wind down a little – Gunner lifted his head up by my shoulder like he was trying to see what was in the lights ahead of us. I turned and looked at him – all I could think to say was…

"I think this is home – boy…"

The darkness was only broken by the scattered lights strewn on makeshift poles. The yellow from the lights blending into the sand cast shadows from the neighborhood of canvas and plywood. There was a familiar sound of tractors, and even generators… and everyone shouting just to be heard from the constant noise.

I hadn't even finished stretching when a booming voice rolled through the noise like thunder. A man strode toward us, broad-shouldered and barrel-chested, pointing left and right – directing the soldiers from the convoy where to unload supplies - his voice carrying above the chaos. He barked orders with the authority of someone who had been doing it since before I was born.

Then his eyes landed on me.

"You! Are you Sgt. Duncan?" He chuckled, deep and rumbling. "You gotta be - you're the only one with the dog."

That was the moment I met First-Sergeant Braxton.

He told me to follow him, and Gunner padded close at my side. A couple of Privates grabbed my gear and started off in the opposite direction. I opened my mouth to protest, but Braxton's voice cut me off without even turning his head.

"They're taking it to your billet, Sergeant. Relax."

We stopped at the 'Charge of Quarters' office. The CQ office was where 'W' Company was headquartered - though calling it an office was generous. It was just a wide canvas tent – above the flaps was a plywood sign "**W** Company." Inside there was a folding table, a stack of binders, and a couple of overworked soldiers pretending to look busy. I handed over my paperwork, and Braxton gave it a quick glance before looking back at me.

That's when he smiled. Big, unbothered, all white teeth shining against his dark complexion. It wasn't the kind of smile meant to put me at ease - it was the kind that said he'd already sized me up and decided where I fit in his world.

Braxton glanced at the paperwork, then at me, then down at Gunner, who was already sniffing the corners of the tent like he owned the place. The First Sergeant's grin widened. "Yeah, you'll do just fine here, Sergeant Duncan. Welcome to the **Wolf-Pack**."

He clapped me on the shoulder, turned, and barked at another soldier to get moving. That was the last I saw of him for the night.

By the time I reached my billet - a narrow canvas cot pushed against the wall of a two-man tent - they'd already dumped my duffel inside. Gunner circled twice and dropped at the foot of the bed like he'd been doing it his whole life. I sat, stretched my legs, and finally let out a breath "well Gunner" I chuckled – "home."

That's when I saw it. A small bundle of letters I'd probably get to later, and another small brown box set neatly on the cot. It was a package from home. Inside was a small Bible – maybe six inches by four – and its pages thin as tissue. Tucked between them was a folded note in my mom's handwriting:

"Jack - I know you've never been a religious boy. This is the only way I know to protect you. I'm not good with words but I wanted you to know that we are all proud of you – Mom."

I must've read it three times before sliding it back into the pages. The tent around me faded. The sand, the noise, the war. It all slipped away, and for a moment, it was just me, Gunner, and my mother's words pressed against my chest.

The morning sun spilled through the edges of the canvas tent, warm and low. I felt a wet nose nudge my face and I opened an eye. Gunner, tail wagging like a drum beating against the canvas wall, he was ready to start the day.

I swung my legs out of the cot, yawned, and followed him outside. My head bumped something rough. It was another plywood sign, hand-painted and tilted just enough to catch me on the forehead:

"Dog House."

I chuckled, rubbing the spot on my head as Gunner sniffed the sand like a pro on patrol. Then a familiar laugh cut through the morning air.

"Did you make this, or did Sergeant Braxton hire a carpenter for my wake-up call?" I called out, squinting toward the sound.

"I made it! Thought you'd need some orientation for your new quarters!" Wade stepped into view, grinning from ear to ear. Gunner barked, running in circles around him.

It was the kind of reunion that didn't need words. Laughter, shouts, and a wagging tail filled the space between us, as Gunner got introduced to Wade. It was a moment that washed away the distance of the past few years. And in that moment, the desert didn't feel so foreign, the deployment didn't feel so heavy, and everything that had been waiting for us - the new life, the danger, the unknown? It could all wait while we just caught up.

Gunner followed us as Wade showed me where the mess-tent was… we walked through a maze of canvas, chords, and the constant sound of generators. The tractors building the airfield were just getting started by the time we sat down for our breakfast of powdered eggs, toast, and mess-tent sludge.

I wasn't quite finished with my third cup of 90-weight coffee when the air shook dust and rattled the canvas walls of the mess-hall. A loud explosion, close enough to feel it in my chest, sent everyone scrambling.

Chaos hit before the smoke even cleared. Wade grabbed my arm. "Move! Get geared up! Choppers are probably inbound!"

Instinct took over. Gunner's leash was already in my hand, but he ran by my side before I even clicked it onto him. I started running back to our tent before I fully registered what was happening. My fingers fumbled through the harness, sliding straps, clicking buckles into place. The dog didn't hesitate - he knew the drill, and we'd run it a hundred times in training - but this was different. No practice rounds, no second chances.

The distant drum of rotor blades cut through the desert air, whipping sand across the canvas tents. Dust stung our eyes. The ground trembled as the choppers came closer, the air vibrating with the rush of spinning metal.

"Let's go! Move!" Wade's voice carried above the roar.

I tightened Gunner's harness again for good measure, and felt that surge of adrenaline that came before a mission. We weren't running exercises. We weren't running drills. This was real.

We sprinted across the gravel, bodies hunched against the wind and blowing grit. Gunner's paws pounding beside me. The smell of hot metal and fuel burned in my nose, but I barely noticed. Every step, every second, was about getting ready, getting on the choppers, and making it count.

The first shadow of the aircraft passed over us, and I could see the pilots' helmets glinting in the sun. A gust of air nearly knocked me off balance. Gunner pressed against my side, ready.

No time to think. No room for hesitation. Gunner hopped across my lap and I clipped the final strap securing Gunner to my web-gear. I checked the lines, and with a nod to Wade, we were moving - hearts pounding, eyes sharp, every muscle primed.

This wasn't training. This was the desert. This was now.

The bird groaned under the weight of five soldiers, their gear, and one very impatient K9. Gunner's straps clicked into mine. He was snug against my vest, every buckle a reminder that this wasn't a drill. The rotors chopped the air into a frenzy of dust and noise, and I almost didn't hear Wade calling instructions over the chaos.

The pilot leaned forward, scanning the desert below. "Two minutes out," he said, a grin tugging at his lips. Then, with a flick of his wrist, a CD spun up somewhere in the cockpit. The opening riff of AC/DC's "*Highway to Hell*" tore through the Black Hawk, bouncing off canvas, metal, and gear.

I couldn't help the smirk that cracked through the tension. The pilot grinned back at me as if he was saying 'we'd do just fine.' Gunner's ears perked up at the noise, tail wagging in anticipation. Two minutes. That was all the warning we'd get before stepping into the storm.

Welcome to my first day… playing in the Sand-Box.

Chapter 6

Sand Box

The Black Hawk groaned banking for its final turn with five soldiers and one very impatient K9. Gunner laying across my lap - strapped and clicked tight into my gear, snug against my vest, every buckle a reminder this wasn't training. The twin gunships flanking us kicked up dust in waves, tracers streaking the sky, and for a moment, the desert below was nothing more than a blur of sand and heat.

I could barely see the insurgent vehicle now - a battered Toyota pickup crawling across the dunes. From our height, it was just a dot. The gunships roared closer. At first I didn't see what they'd hit and I didn't need to. The explosion shook the bird, flames licking the horizon, and I felt the heat even through the cabin walls.

"Touchdown in ten – on my mark!" The pilot shouted over the rotors, eyes fixed on the target below. Gunner whined, tail high, nose twitching. He knew. And I could tell we were all counting down…

The bird slammed onto the sand, skidding slightly on the loose surface. Dust clawed at my face as I flipped the safety catch on the side of the restraint holding Gunner to me – then I hit the center release while we scrambled out, Gunner leading the charge. He was a blur of black and tan, ears pinned, nose down, tail stiff. Gunner - instinct kicking in like we'd done it a hundred times before. But this time, it wasn't a drill.

We hit the dirt running – dust, dirt, smoke… and the sand blowing from the gusts from the rotors stung my face and for a second – I couldn't see Gunner. I could barely see anything.

The chopper lifted off leaving us in the wake of wreckage from the gunships fire – as the only surviving insurgent sprinted toward an abandoned compound of brick and clay ahead of him, gun in hand – carrying whatever else he could.

Gunner running faster – barking, was gaining on the insurgent, fast and precise. We ran as fast as we could - together, a single, silent unit slicing across the desert chasing Gunner… who was chasing our bomber… Bullets kicked up sand around us as we got to the compound, the clay walls offering minimal cover. Gunner pressed forward, teeth bared, instincts sharp. I fired controlled bursts, covering the perimeter as he flanked left, cornering the insurgent against the crumbling walls. I hit the weak cover of the clay wall – dust and dirt breaking away as bullets were flying past us – at us… I called Gunner back – shouting.

For a second it was quiet. I could hear Wade panting beside me. Then the other three – Privates First-Class fell-in behind us. I didn't know their names – only minutes ago we were sitting at breakfast… and now?

Gunner's head turned – tilted the typical German Shepherd tilt when they hear something – I listened – I held my fist up to try and keep the others quiet – as best I could.

I heard the slight click of someone seating a fresh magazine into a Kalashnikov "AK-47" – Gunner tense and ready.

I turned my head – spoke slow and low – not a whisper… since whispers travel further than speaking low… "Wade – have one of your guys circle around that tower, and another double back and try to get behind that wall – see if we can pin him in…"

Wade nodded – jerked his head silent – his guys knew what to do…

They moved quick and silent – one circled around as instructed – the other weaved around the debris and headed around the other side of the compound… Gunner taking it all in. His eyes locked toward the opening of an old building – beaten and blasted – torn apart by war. I could only make quick peeks before more blasts from the Kalashnikov tore away more of the wall keeping us safe.

Another quick peek – and I could see a dull, olive-drab tube resting in the insurgent's hands, its rear flare catching the sunlight, ominous and still. The muzzle glimmered slightly, a hollow promise of fire and fury. He shifted his grip, tensed, and for a heartbeat, all I could see was that unassuming cylinder pointed in our direction - a small, simple thing that could ruin everything in a heartbeat.

I knew the weak crumbling walls of this abandoned compound would be no protection against a Rocket Propelled Grenade. I turned quick - back to Wade and choked out "RPG" and pat Gunner on the side saying "we gotta move now." For a heartbeat, I froze - time slowed. One second too long and the walls wouldn't have mattered. But instinct kicked in…

I knew we only had one chance – and since he put down the rifle we'd only have seconds to make this count. And Gunner moved faster.

He crossed the alley in mere seconds leaping onto the guy as he fired the weapon. The shell went high and wild. Gunner had him pinned but the rebel still fought reaching for the rifle. I leveled my M-16 slapping the side of the magazine in my rifle to let Gunner know to release. He backed away as the Kalashnikov pointed in my direction. I fired first.

The man fell, wounded but alive. Gunner pinned him with a quick shift of weight, nose to his shoulder, tail straight - rigid like a warning. I kept the insurgent covered with my weapon while Wade applied the restraints - zip-ties tight - and he went from combatant to prisoner under Wade's hands.

"Good boy," I whispered to Gunner, feeling that surge of pride that only comes from trust earned in the chaos. Wade clapped my shoulder, grinning. "Looks like you two just leveled up."

The desert stretched behind us, silent now but for the wind and our breathing. Wade had one of his PFCs call in that we needed a ride back to base… our team plus one…

I pulled out a Marlboro, and smoked while we waited. Wade just chuckled "reminds me of Charlie" as he shook his head.

The combatant sat while we listened for our ride. We all just stared for a moment at the smoldering wreckage, and what little remained of those who were with our prisoner only moments ago… a grim reminder of what can happen out here… where big boys… play in the sand.

For a few minutes the desert was peaceful, but I felt the weight of the real world settle around me. The desert hadn't changed. We had.

The ride back was quieter than the first. The rotors beat a steady rhythm, hot air pushing in through the open doors. We couldn't hear the pilot, but we could see him talking into his mic, lips moving quick, one hand tight on the stick. Whatever he was saying, it wasn't for us. All we could do was sit in the noise, the smell of smoke and sand still clinging to our uniforms, Gunner lying across my lap, eyes half-shut but ears still twitching.

The bird flared, and then set down near the edge of camp. The airstrip was coming together - a mile and a half of scraped earth and rolled dirt, big tractors lumbering back and forth with a sound that felt like industry trying to tame the desert. Off to the side, men wrestled with canvas and poles, raising a tent so big it looked like a circus.

"What's that one for?" I asked Wade, pointing with my chin.

"Hospital," he said, wiping grit from his face. "We'll need it."

The MP's and their Criminal Investigation team – or CID – was waiting when we touched down - the pair of MPs in crisp desert camo, and mirrored shades were hiding whatever they thought of the dust-covered mess we'd brought back. The insurgent sat slumped between them, wrists bound with zip-ties, face streaked with sweat and blood.

An interpreter stepped forward, a lean man in a clean uniform, his boots already coated in the same dust as ours. He said his name but it was hard to understand him through his accent. He said it was something like Asad – or Aman – or even a Shlabobble for that matter, but he said his last name was Salam. I caught that much.

He offered a quick nod before turning to the prisoner, rapid Arabic spilling out. I caught a few words that sounded 'American,' nothing more.

The MPs led their man away, Salam following, voice sharp and steady. Just like that, he was gone - from insurgent fighter to a case file in the space of minutes.

The First Sergeant was waiting when we stepped away from the choppers. His grin was wide enough to split his face in two. He clapped my shoulder hard enough to sting. "Not a bad first day on the job, Sarge. First day in and you already earned yourself a combat ribbon."

First day on the job? I almost laughed. It had barely sunk in that this wasn't the usual assignments, or training anymore, and now I was already collecting medals. Wade leaned in, still grinning. "Don't get too comfortable. It's only lunchtime."

Gunner padded beside me, no leash, matching my stride like we'd rehearsed it. We headed for the mess tent. The smell of powdered eggs and burnt coffee still hung in the air. As I stepped in with Gunner at my side, The 'mess-hall' sergeant – Master Sergeant Collins – a 'career' man hardened and crusty from a long Army life… but he blocked the way, with a frown sharp enough to cut. "Dog's gotta be restrained in here."

I kept walking, Gunner right on my heel. "He is restrained," I said. "He does whatever I tell him."

The Sergeant didn't argue, just shook his head as we found a table. Gunner sat at my side, posture perfect, like he knew he was being tested.

Lunch tasted like cardboard, but it was hot and it was quiet, and that was enough. Afterward, Wade told us we'd earned some downtime. Showers, maybe even a real bed for a change.

I snuck Gunner into the showers with me. The others didn't care - most of them thought it was funny. The smell of wet dog filled the canvas stall, and somebody yelled, "Guess we need more soap now!" The laughter carried through the steam, echoing against the tin drains. For the first time since touchdown, it almost felt normal.

But I'd come to learn – normal never lasts long out here.

I pushed open the flap of my tent, the first real quiet I'd had since hitting the ground. Gunner padded in behind me, tail flicking once as if to say this was his place now too. The cot creaked when I dropped my things on it, and for the first time all day I started unpacking for more than a temporary stay. Boots lined under the frame, gear stacked neat by habit, a corner cleared for Gunner's blanket. Home… or close enough.

Outside, the world kept moving. Heavy engines growled overhead – I could hear the long belly of a cargo plane banking low on approach. I thought "The runway must've been close to being finished." In the distance the sounds of another convoy rattling into the camp, axles squealing under the weight of crates and fuel tankers heading for the air strip.

Voices rose and fell in a constant churn, Privates sweating through their uniforms as they raised more canvas, stretched more lines, hammered plywood until the whole desert seemed to come to life with the rhythm of a city being built from scratch.

Gunner lifted his head when someone knocked on the post outside. The Company Clerk ducked in, still a little out of breath from the walk across camp, a folded paper in his hand.

"Orders from First Sergeant," he said, handing it over. His eyes flicked to Gunner before settling back on me. "Evening detail."

I scanned the message. Routine sweep - choppers, cargo planes, fuel, and ordnance stores. Gunner's ears perked, nose twitching as if he already knew.

"Looks like we're back on the clock, boy," I muttered, unfolding the paper then reading over the details – "report time 19:00 hours – full gear." Gunner's tail thumped once against the cot when I told him "we got some time to kill boy."

I finished unpacking. Even the little package from home – the Bible, and the letters. For a few minutes – I just sat and read.

I tried to lay down for a nap, but Gunner had other ideas. He kept nosing at my duffle bag – I asked him "What?" with a chuckle – "What ya want in there boy?" as if I didn't already know.

I reached into the side pocket slowly… Gunner smiling. I rattled my hand around pretending to look for something – Gunner 'sat' like he knew he'd found something.

I slowly pulled out from the pocket… a black rubber racquet ball and Gunner could hardly contain himself. It was his connection to comfort… his attachment to stability. He stayed – he shook with anticipation, but when I gave his release command and tossed the ball in the air – it was nothing but teeth and joy… and Gunner knew it was his turn… To play in the sand.

Chapter 7

Patrol

The tent was dim, canvas walls glowing with the last light of the sun as I sorted through my gear. Boots lined, pack squared away, rifle cleaned and set within reach. I pulled my Kevlar vest from the cot, checking the straps by habit, and then paused when my hand brushed something tucked in the corner of the duffle.

The small Bible. The one Mom had sent. I turned it over once, the cover soft. I thought about her hands as she must have placed it in the box – the look on her face, or maybe a tear in her eye… it was all in my imagination. But it was enough for now. Then I slid it into the upper-left pocket of my shirt. Close to the heart. Close enough.

The Kevlar vest settled heavy across my shoulders as I tightened it into place. Outside, the desert was falling quiet, the horizon painted in red and gold.

"Almost 1900 hours," I muttered, scratching behind Gunner's ears. "Time to report for duty, boy."

We stopped at the mess tent first. Dinner was quick - powdered potatoes, overcooked meat, and burnt coffee. Wade slid in across from me, his grin the same as always.

"Routine patrol tonight," he said, jabbing his fork at the tray.

"Routine until it Ain't," I answered. "If we trip over a bomb, I'll make sure to holler so you can come neutralize it."

Wade chuckled, shaking his head. "Generous of you, Sarge."

By the time we left the mess, the heat was bleeding out of the day. Desert nights come fast - one minute you're sweating, the next you're shivering. Gunner padded beside me, nose down, tail straight, already on the clock.

The perimeter stretched for miles - planes lined wingtip to wingtip, choppers huddled like beetles, stacks of fuel drums and crates of ordnance marked with stenciled warnings.

Our trail wound around it all, sand crunching under boots, Gunner's ears flicking at every sound. Boring work, maybe. But boring meant safe.

MP Humvees rolled past now and then, headlights cutting sharp across the sand. The gunners who were standing through the top of the vehicle gave us quick nods, sometimes slowing for a word or two - small talk, curses about the chow, or the usual "stay safe." Then they rolled on.

Hours wore on, and the desert fell into rhythm - rotors in the distance, the smell of jet fuel, Gunner's steady breathing. Nothing unusual, nothing alarming.

By midnight, we'd circled back to camp. Gunner shook sand from his coat and sat as if waiting for dismissal. I scratched behind his ears again, feeling the weight lift.

We finished our end of shift report at the office – spent a few minutes with the Lieutenant. I didn't feel like talking – I just wanted to get some rest… today was a long day. I was dismissed – then turned to Gunner:

"Good job, boy. We're through for the night."

The next week was beginning to look like our routine again – just another base – just the same old food. It was a week of watching our neighborhood grow into a city. More soldiers – more staff – even contractors hired to put out oil-well fires – a regular metropolis.

Gunner's and my days were filled with split shifts – between evening patrols and being 'on-call' for entry inspections – catching sleep when we can – meals whenever convenient.

One afternoon Wade was busy with inspecting some of the explosive ordinance arriving – assigning it to one of the storage bunkers… so I went to the mess hall to get some chow – with Gunner.

We sat – silent – choking down our dinner. It really wasn't that bad, but it's more fun to make fun of it – than not. So we ate.

Gunner raised his head a little – when a guy came to sit with us. He introduced himself – as "Father Patrick" – our Company Chaplain. We had some laughs – some casual conversation – and then… the inevitable question "why haven't we seen you at Sunday services?"

"I don't know 'Padre'" I huffed while trying to swallow "maybe Gunner here isn't as religious…" as I chuckled.

"You know Sarge" he continued – "your pal Gunner is always welcome with us anytime you think "**he**" wants to join us."

"I don't know – Sir" I hummed – "Gunner and me – well we walk a pretty hard road out here – not sure if your congregation is ready for us."

The Good Preacher – Father Patrick just smiled and said: "Maybe your path is harder – son – because your calling is higher."

He stood up – quiet and just smiled… "Just think about it… just think about it…"

Gunner followed obedient as I cleared my tray and then we walked back to our tent to gear-up for the evening. He watched – intent like he was waiting as I finished lacing my boots. I slipped on the rest of my gear – Kevlar vest – extra mags and ammo – and every night I'd put that little Bible in my pocket… just for my mom.

We headed out toward the airfield first – like we were counting the rivets on the planes, and the blades on the choppers. Then we'd make our way through the fuel supplies and ordinance deposits before we made our way to the perimeter for our walk around.

By now the sun cast its final shadows, and the loneliness of the night was only comforted by the partner at my side.

In the distance I could see the silhouettes of the Hummers and their crews – making their way around the camp. Their shapes painted shadows through the yellow lights of the camp. Gunner was sniffing every inch of the path we were walking. Nothing.

We kept walking. Until…

Gunner froze. Ears up, nose quivering, tail rigid. He sniffed the wind, scanned the shadows, alert. My gut tightened.

I crouched beside him. "Something's up, boy?"

He let out a low, warning growl. My hand went to the radio. "MP patrol - we might have a sniper. Perimeter Check – Quick – at the northeast quad bearing 1-5 degrees, over."

A beat later: shots rang out. Sharp, sudden, echoing across the desert. My M-16 went up instinctively, firing controlled bursts. I felt something hit me in the chest.

We hit the ground and Gunner crouched low, instincts razor-sharp, guiding me through the chaos. The Humvees responded, suppressing fire, sweeping the area until the sniper was neutralized - another small insurgent attack ended before it could escalate.

By the time the dust settled, we were quiet again. Gunner shook sand from his coat, eyes alert but calm. I patted him on the shoulder, feeling the adrenaline drain as I checked him over for any wounds. "Good work, boy."

More Humvees pulled up - soldiers arrived in patrol formations spreading out searching for more threats. I finished standing up and looked down at Gunner – still at my left side – but I noticed the fabric of my Kevlar was torn and frayed. I put my finger into the hole, and knew I'd been shot.

But I didn't feel anything.

I let the patrol Lieutenant know I'd been hit – but I was ok. He told me I'd have to get checked out at medical before being dismissed from duty.

Wade must have heard the calls from the radio traffic, and probably figured he could meet me at the new 'hospital' that was now in operation. I got out of my ride, and walked in proud with my partner at my side. By now – it was widely known – wherever I went… Gunner went too.

My nurse – a tall lanky First Lieutenant named 'Dave' – seasoned and no stranger to these kinds of deployment – he checked me out – told me I'd have a pretty good bruise for a while – but nothing to worry about. Dave shook his head a little "sounds like you were in a pretty tight situation – they said it was a pretty good firefight…"

"It wasn't as bad as the last one I was in" I smiled back.

"You think it makes you want to go home?" he smirked.

"No" I responded… "I've learned to look the enemy in the eyes – but I don't ask 'why-me?' – I stare 'em down and tell them 'try-me.'"

Nurse Dave called over to the CQ – Charge of Quarters office - told them that I was cleared for duty… but I'd need to have a couple of days rest.

Wade walked us back from the hospital – he and Gunner were the only family I had at the time – he might have felt it was his duty as my 'older' brother.

Back at our tent, I began to finish gearing down. Gloves off, helmet set aside, tossing my vest onto the cot. That's when I really felt it - a sting at my chest. I sat on my cot. My fingers traced the small wound through the Kevlar. Heart pounding, I looked at the vest fully… the rifle round penetrated all the way through it.

I felt through my shirt – opened the pocked and removed the little Bible. And there it was: a round, stopped cold by that little Bible.

I pulled it out gently, turning the worn cover in my hands. The pages of the Bible tangled and torn, but stuck together. I opened the remaining pages to John chapter 10, and the point of the bullet had stopped right on verse11. My eyes scanned the page: "I am the good shepherd. The good shepherd lays down his life for the sheep."

I looked down at Gunner. His tail flicked once. Eyes steady, unwavering. My lips curved into a smile.

"You're my Shepherd, boy," I whispered.

And in that quiet desert night, with a Bible between me and death, and Gunner at my side, the world felt momentarily right.

A couple of days-off… would be nice.

**

Wade caught up to us before we got to the mess tent – and we enjoyed some real eggs now – mixed in with the powdered ones of course. Wade laughed quietly "not quite like your farm eggs, but this isn't too bad."

I agreed quietly – and we walked back to our tent while Wade went back to work.

Waiting just outside our billet was the good Father – Patrick. Smiling he said "I heard about the message…"

"Message?" I questioned – a bit puzzled.

"Yes – the message… you really think this was all just a coincidence?"

"What ya referring to Father?" when I pretty much knew what he was talking about…

We talked for a little while in my tent – Gunner resting at my feet – his nose flickering toward the pocket of my duffle – knowing where his ball was. Father Patrick was trying to convince me that having the bullet stop right at that passage… was a message… meant for me.

I sat on my bunk while Father Pat left – and Gunner rose to 'attention' when I reached my hand… for his ball.

We spent the day playing – resting and showering. And while we could hear the war in the sands far away – for a moment – I felt like I was home.

Two days – made all the difference. I'd learned to drown-out the now normal sounds of the generators – the tractors – the building of a desert city… and the coming and goings of people I really didn't want to get close to.

Wade was like my brother. Gunner was like my child. For now – that was all I needed. And when morning came again… it was time to get back to work.

Wade was at my tent door before I could even make my way all the way out of it…

"Hey bro" he called out… "We got a new assignment. Gunner's gonna need his flight gear for this…"

I poked back into my tent and geared Gunner up for a ride in the chopper, while Wade explained what we would be doing, and then we all headed to the flight pad.

I climbed aboard – Gunner followed – and hopped onto my lap again – he seemed to know what to do. I clipped in – strapped us down, and the engines wound up – the rotors blew dust and sand… Wade just smiled.

About 20 minutes out – we landed soft, and the pilot shouted over the sounds of the rotors and smiled "have fun guys – I'll be waiting for your call…"

I would walk ahead of the EOD team – and Gunner would sniff-out any land mines – or IED's. We needed to clear a path for troops so they could move through.

Walking slow – Gunner was on his 20 foot lead ahead of me. Back and forth he swept the area, and went stiff… then sat - nose pointed at the dirt - we knew what that meant. I planted a little flag – nothing more than a piece of yellow fabric on a stiff wire. Wade and his crew would do the rest.

Hours passed – and a dozen flags planted. Lunch was merely a MRE meal packaged in cardboard… and the cardboard would have tasted better. I gave Gunner a generous drink of water – he gulped it down. It wasn't extremely hot, but hot enough. One of Wade's 'Privates' told me not to give Gunner so much water… I coughed back at him choking on some of the dust and sand from my throat:

"Give him a break… he's the only thing keeping you alive right now."

Wade piped back: "he's right guys – besides Gunner here is kind of our mascot now – he's the real 'Wolf' in our Wolf-pack."

The kid just shook his head, I stayed silent, but Wade continued "I've seen him in action – and he's earned the respect…"

Then Wade stood and said – "our group – we gotta stay strong – united, proud like wolves…"

Then I stood – took my place beside Wade – Gunner followed, and then Wade simply said:

"I'd rather run with a pack of wolves than a flock of sheep… because when danger surfaces - sheep run while wolves stay and fight."

Chapter 8

Leap of Faith

All I could do is look at Wade, and smile. Gunner just looked at the crew, he smiled too. I gave Gunner a little more water and smiled. Wade knew what I was doing. I looked back down at my 'little' partner, and then back at the crew – smiled and said "Gunner? When he's mad - even the demons run for cover."

The desert breeze picked up a little – Gunner drank – his fur blowing like movie star in a hero scene… when he was done drinking he looked up at me and I asked him "Ya ready to go back to work?"

The rest of the crew rose – maybe with a little more respect for our mascot. And even more before the day was over.

The desert breeze picked up a little more – wasn't too bad really, but irritating enough to wish it was calm. We kept on the trail – the team checking maps, and compass readings – making sure we'd be on the right trail for the troop movement.

An hour passed – a few more flags – and the team removing the threats. It would have been routine, but one wrong step or one missed clue meant disaster. Gunner and I were a little ways ahead of Wade's team – so we held up for a minute – another drink of water, and we waited for them to get closer. I crouched down and stroked him and I held him while we waited.

Wade was walking in front of his crew – toward Gunner and me. Wade was approaching one of the flags I'd planted in the dirt when Gunner broke from my arms. He charged toward Wade, lunging at full speed and hitting him hard. Gunner stood tall staring at the scared team that followed – eyes wide with panic. They didn't move – too afraid.

Gunner turned from Wade – stood stiff pointing at the ground where Wade was about to step, and then sat.

I rushed back toward Wade – now picking himself up from the ground somewhat stunned, and before he could get mad at Gunner – he realized if Gunner wouldn't have pushed him away – he'd have stepped on a land mine. A bomb meant for our troops – this time – for Wade.

The flag I planted... blew away in the desert breeze. Gunner saved Wade's life. He didn't move from the bomb until I planted another flag...

Wade coughed a little – trying to recapture the breath Gunner knocked out of him. Wade's team still stunned – amazed at their wolf – gained that respect Gunner had already earned.

Wade was finally able to make the call on his radio – then turned to us and said "I think we've done enough for today guys... how about some chow?"

Wade never looked at Gunner the same way – ever again.

**

As we approached the helipad I noticed another group of soldiers and support personnel disembarking from a transport plane. I didn't even notice the jets flying overhead any more. The air campaign was in full swing – and our city growing every day.

I told First-Sergeant Braxton – we needed more K9 teams. He laughed "you want more wolves for your little wolf-pack huh?" I just nodded and laughed back.

Wade told me to wait on dinner – he wanted a shower first... he told me it was his turn to 'buy' – that he wanted me and Gunner to eat with him. Both Gunner and I needed a shower too.

When we walked into the mess hall – word had already spread. Wade's team couldn't wait to recant the events how Gunner saved Wade's life. How Gunner 'flew' and pushed Sgt. Callahan out of harm's way. We walked in – and the room went silent.

Wade looked at me – I looked at Gunner – Wade shouted out with a laugh "*Yes Folks – I'm Alive*!" when cheers started breaking out and Wade continued – loud and proud – "*I'm alive because of our 'Corporal Gunner*!"

Amid the cheers, laughter, and clapping – the Master Sergeant - Collins even gave Gunner a special little treat he'd cooked for him. Yes – he served Gunner some roast that was reserved for Colonel Nettleton - the base Commander…

He smiled – put his finger to his lips and did the whole "Shhhhh" thing.

And every day – Gunner's fame continued to grow. Soldiers from surrounding Companies would recognize us – mainly Gunner.

And maybe it wasn't really protocol – but… in the growing heat as spring turned toward summer – our evening patrols turned into casual walks – a routine that in some ways shouldn't have become so routine. I would wear shorts and my boots – and many times I'd "forget" to wear my protective vest and gear.

I'd grown accustomed to the growing security around the base, and our 'walks' were now more of a formality, but then again… were they?

**

I met her in a foreign country… she was blonde and beautiful…

**

One morning when I was dressing for the morning patrol, and getting Gunner 'geared-up' – Wade knocked against my center post that held my tent up…

It was a routine now – in spite of the constant firefights and insurgents, but normal in a world that isn't normal? Well… that's where our world differs from the movies and TV – it's a place that most people who have lived through it – don't want to talk about.

It is a place of adrenaline – and horror… a place of peace and violence. The world I lived in with Gunner – with Wade – was so far from where I came from… I didn't know if I'd recognize what normal was… I was now living in a world where the line between safety and danger – was a blur – a figment of my imagination… I could only hope for – even pray for… something to ground me back to reality.

We walked in silence – a silence that said more than a thousand words. Before we got to the mess-tent – I asked Wade how he was doing…

The day before - Gunner 'hit' on an 'IED' and – I backed away quick… knowing these could be detonated remotely. Wade donned his "blow" gear as he called it – his bomb disposal gear. But in spite of Wade's careful – precise manner… it still went off… Wade was lucky… but shaken…

"I'm fine" he grunted… although I knew him better than he knew himself at the moment.

"You sure?"

"Yeah."

"It was a close one – you know… I didn't want to lose you." I said with the emotion I was doing my best to hide…

Wade was diffusing a bomb – but it went off… and he didn't want to talk about it… and I respect that. But…

I could tell it shook him.

"Every time I think I know what these bastards are doing – they change how they detonate them." He said with some resentment in his voice…

"I know bud" I said with as much strength as I could muster – "but as close as it was – you're still here…"

We ate breakfast in silence. Wade's usual humor and joking was missed throughout the mess-hall. Yes – I could tell it got to him. If it weren't for his protective gear… my childhood friend wouldn't be sitting here next to me.

I didn't know what else to say. I just put my hand on his shoulder and gave him the look… as if to say 'let's get back to work.'

We walked out to the sunrise breaking over the bleak horizon. If I didn't know where we were – I might have thought it was kind of nice. Maybe my sense of normal was more skewed than I'd have thought.

The routine. Gunner on my lap – the clips – the straps – the winding of the engines. Gunships to our flanks and the desert ahead of us. Just another day… playing in the sand.

The pilot calls out again – "two minutes out." While the 'rock' music played I start to reposition my partner nestled in my lap – ready to make the routine jump back into the sand… and clear a trail of safety for the soldiers who need to walk the path they trust…

I've learned to recognize – even at a distance – the shapes and silhouettes of ours – or even enemy vehicles. But Gunner?

I knew a patrol was working a trail we'd cleared the day before – when Wade – well… when Wade was nearly blown to bits by an IED Gunner located… and right before touchdown – Gunner caught a brief sight of the patrol, and as I clicked the release ready for our jump – he jumped first.

Dragging me along.

It wasn't a long fall – just a hard one. Gunner started off to find 'the bad guys' but…

As I called him back – I tried to catch myself from landing hard – my ankle twisting hard. I collapsed against the dust, dirt and sand. Gunner turned – quick – and came to my aid. He could tell I was hurt, and wouldn't let anyone help me. Not even Wade.

I tried to tell him "it's ok boy – Wade's trying to help me" – and he relented – as I tried to be brave and let Wade and his team help me back to the chopper.

The ride back was more embarrassing than painful… from everything we've been through – and now this?

I've been shot – shot at, and nearly hit by RPG's. But a broken ankle? Really?

I tried to put pressure on it – even tried to walk on it when the bird landed back at the base… but no. When the medical team from the hospital arrived with a stretcher – I was even more humiliated.

They did let me sit in the Hummer that took me to the 'hospital' – and Gunner never left my side.

A medical tech met us with a wheelchair, and before I refused – the First Sergeant – Braxton – told me to let them treat me… and of course… I reluctantly agreed. So did Gunner.

I was wheeled into a treatment room. I sat in pain for a minute – my hand at my side with a handful of fur and eyes concerned if I was 'ok.'

And there she was.

Yeah… she was blonde and beautiful…

Amid the chaos of a makeshift hospital, the smell of Army canvas protecting us from the dust we could never seem to escape… there she was. She looked at my sprained ankle, and as she moved it around I winced in pain…

"Don't be a baby about this Sergeant" she said with command – even though there was compassion in her voice – while sporting a kind of half-smile and a chuckle "it only hurts for a minute."

The Army doctor said I'd be fine – and I let her treat me as if I had a choice. But I looked into her eyes – and as she treated my hurt… she captured my heart.

She was wrapping my ankle – careful and gentle… she smiled at me. "You're little friend here is beautiful" as she looked at Gunner… "He looks like he can hold his own." As she continued to smile at me.

Gunner watched her close as she carefully wrapped my ankle. Nurse Isabel Carter – 1st Lieutenant U.S. Army… chuckled again… as she watched Gunner watching her…

"Are you trying to do my job for me too?"

I couldn't help but laugh through the pain, but couldn't help but say "You know – Gunner here – would like you to join us for a cup of coffee?" I said with a bit of question in my voice and a half smile…

"Yeah – I bet 'Gunner' would really love that." She smirked back with a wink in her eye…

This was a smile – a smirk, and a love I swore I'd protect for the rest of my life.

And I did…

We had that cup of coffee, and a lot more. We learned we could lean on each other in a place where loyalty, trust, and love weren't a luxury – it was survival. I knew from that day on… this would be a bond that would last forever.

We were walking to the mess tent... me limping still... but I coughed out a laugh and said "Well – Lieutenant – Um... does this mean I have to salute you when we go out on a date?"

"You bet – Sarge – you better know whose boss over here" she said with a giggle...

Yeah – that cup of Army sludge turned into a lifetime together – that one cup of coffee would eventually turn us – into a family.

Yes – the war went on... the bombings – the constant air campaign... the noise and the constant threats... but amid the chaos – the continuous life living with a gun at our sides... we found love.

I wrote home.

Mom wasn't pleased when I told her I was filling out the papers with the Army... she always thought she'd be there to see her oldest son get married, but yes...

I was going to ask Nurse Isabel to marry me.

Chapter 9

Wedding Bell

Father Patrick simply smiled. I could tell he wanted to say more, but didn't want to make me feel uncomfortable. It was the first time I walked into the canvas chapel for Sunday morning service… Nurse Isabel – Bell… walking me in – arm in arm… Gunner at… *her* side.

I tried to convince Wade to join us. I still didn't feel very religious.

Bell was happy that I – well that Gunner and I joined her that morning. She grew up in a neighboring state, and her mom raised her to be religious, but her dad was more like me and Charlie. It would be hard to convince us to… believe.

After the service we decided to get some breakfast… that's when Wade decided to make his appearance – for chow. And it was nice… Bell added a new dimension to our meals – that is… Wade seemed to be a little more 'mannered' when we ate. I thought it was funny.

"Is it me? Or is our food getting better?" Wade said – politely…

"Naw" Bell said sipping on her coffee "your taste buds are just getting numb." As she laughed.

I knew Bell would fit right in with us.

Our Sunday breakfasts became a pleasant routine Gunner seemed to love as well. One morning even Father Pat came to join us. And while we were having a pleasant discussion – Gunner stood sharp – alert, and started walking toward the kitchen… Wade and I rose and started to look around. We couldn't hear any alarms – there was no one else who appeared to be alarmed…

But – only Gunner.

He started to walk slow toward the food prep area… then sat. Wade hollered out – "Evacuate the Mess-Hall – NOW!"

Everyone scrambled – chairs dropping to the ground – tables turning over, and Gunner inching slow now – closer to the kitchen. Bell grabbed Father Pat's arm and jerked him out through the mess-hall opening. I drew my sidearm and inched my way following Gunner while motioning to Wade to get his gear on. He rushed out and for a moment - it was quiet.

Inch by inch sliding my boots against the rough dirt – smoothed only by the constant foot traffic in the tent… Gunner eased his head through the opening of the kitchen. I tried to peek through and at a slight glance I could see the 'mess-Sergeant' standing on a table – petrified – frozen…

"What is it?" as I tried to ask quietly, knowing some detonations could be triggered by sound. All Sgt. Collins could do is shake his head. I pat the side of my leg – Gunner 'fell-in' to the 'on-me' position simply backing up slightly. I pat my leg again that told him to heel. And we inched our way again slow around the corner of the table… and saw it.

It was carpet viper – or Saw-scaled viper (Echis carinatus) - One of the most dangerous snakes in the region. Although they're small, usually less than two feet, being sandy-colored, they blend perfectly into desert terrain. They're extremely aggressive and responsible for more bites in the Middle East than any other snake. Their venom causes internal bleeding and can be fatal without treatment.

I held up my palm motioning for the Sergeant to hold still. I stepped to my right once again to get a closer look at the snake – Gunner matched my every move. The snake was trying to raise itself toward the scared chef, and it was the only thing I could do, but…

I fired my pistol. The snake went limp. Color came back to the face of our mess-Sergeant.

I walked over and kicked the dead snake away from him so he could climb down from the table, but he was still leery and tried to step away as fast as he could but turned to me…

"How… um – how did you know?"

I could hear Wade busting through the outer 'doors' to the mess hall, and I nodded to Gunner – who let out a bark to let Wade know where we were right as I was telling the chef – "Gunner alerted us – maybe he could hear – or smell it – don't know, but it was Gunner here – who let us know."

The large mess-hall Sergeant looked down at Gunner and smiled – even pat him on the head and told him "good boy… you're welcome in **my** chow-hall anytime boy."

Wade entered the kitchen – all geared up for bomb disposal… with that intent look in his eye, and the determination to save us. I backed away – Gunner still on 'command' inched back with me. I pointed toward the dead snake with the muzzle of my pistol still in my hand. Wade made a quick glance at it and then looked back at me through his protective face shield, then pulled his helmet off.

"Really?" Wade's voice stern…

"Yep" I laughed although the chef wasn't laughing with me. But I continued "since you're all geared up for disposal – maybe you could dispose of this???"

Wade just shook his head "you killed it – you clean it – that's what Charlie always told us… so – this is on you!"

I asked the chef if he had some kind of trash bag I could put the snake in. He was still speechless, but fumbled around into some boxes and pulled out a huge black plastic bag… I looked at him and smiled "ya got anything smaller?"

Sgt. Collins could only shake his head, then choked out: "it's the only size we have."

I turned and looked at Wade – raised my brow as if to question – "uh – um… maybe help me find a stick or something – would ya Wade?"

Wade handed me the end of a broken table leg, and I used it to place the venomous carcass into the bag. We all walked out of the dining hall – me carrying the black bag – to the cheers and applause of the crowd that once occupied the large room.

Wade turned to me – asked "how'd ya know what kind of snake it was?"

Bell looked puzzled too, but I simply said: "first rule is – always know what you're walking into... I read-up on what the desert was like when Gunner and I were still stationed back at Diego Garcia."

Wade hollered when he saw the crowd gathering back around... "Anyone want to volunteer – to help get the chow-hall put back together?" and everyone was all too happy to pitch in so we could get back to business.

Bell simply walked up to me... wrapped her arms around me, and I handed the big black bag to Wade as Bell and I kissed... this time... in front of everybody.

And we got an ovation of cheers and another round of applause...

Father Patrick just smiled. Wade – still in his disposal gear, shook his head, chuckled and said: "I guess – well I'd better 'dispose' of this."

For months we'd worked in the scorching heat, the dry desert air, and the dust that we could never escape. We stood there in an embrace I wished would last forever – Gunner leaning on us, and then I felt something more than Bell's arms around me. I felt more than the love that was growing...

I felt rain.

The first drops fell without warning, tapping against canvas and dust in a rhythm that felt out of place here. The air carried that strange sharp smell - wet dirt and oil - like the desert was exhaling after months of holding its breath. Within minutes the ground turned slick, boots sinking, tracks filling with muddy water.

Gunner shook himself, ears twitching, not quite sure if he liked it. Wade walked back toward us then tilted his helmet back, grinning at the sky as if it had just told him a joke. And Bell - Bell just stood there in it, letting the rain run down her face, her smile softer than I'd ever seen.

For me it was different. The gunfire had faded weeks ago, but until that moment the war hadn't really ended. Standing there, soaked through, I felt the shift. A new season. A new tone. Maybe even a new kind of normal.

And there in the mud – amid the world of canvas and crowd of desert camo, I got down on my knee with Gunner by my side... and simply asked Bell...

"Would you like to marry me?"

She said yes.

That was all Father Patrick needed to hear. He processed the paperwork and we waited for the final approval… I may have even seen some of the rain from the sky… coming from Wade's face…

Mine too.

The desert hadn't given us much in the way of beauty, but that morning… it gave us just enough.

The seasons had changed, and so did the war. We were now more involved as peacekeepers and ordinance disposal – although minor skirmishes arose, and no matter how small… combat is still… combat.

But sometimes peace is what we create – even in chaos.

The sky was a pale blue, washed clean by another rare night's rain. The sand outside the camp was firm, almost holding its breath. A makeshift chapel had been pitched in our canvas mess-hall. No stained glass, no polished wood - just folding chairs, ammo crates, and strips of parachute silk tied up along the entry like a banner of defiance.

Bell didn't wear white. She didn't need to. Her desert camo was pressed, boots shined, and her hair tied back under her cap. Somehow, she looked more radiant that way - like herself. No pretending, no costumes.

Wade stood at my side, best man in name, brother in spirit. He'd tried to comb the dust out of his hair, but true to himself he gave up halfway. When he caught my glance, he smirked, like "don't you dare start crying before she gets here."

Then the tent grew quiet. Everyone rose.

And there she was.

Bell walked slow, steady. But it wasn't her alone. Gunner walked beside her, his chest out, tail high. Gunner didn't need a leash, but Bell held one lightly in her hand. More symbolic than anything. His ears twitched at every sound, but his eyes never left me. He was proud - proud of her, proud of this moment. For all the firefights, the chaos, the nights he kept us alive… it was here, in silence, that he became something more.

When they reached the front, Bell knelt, gave Gunner's fur a final scratch, and whispered something only he could hear. Then, with a soft smile, she handed me the leash. It was her way of saying, he's yours, but so am I.

Father Patrick cleared his throat, his voice carrying strong and steady over the gathered crowd:

"We are here, in the midst of war, in a place not known for peace… to witness something greater. Love has its own courage. It stands in the dust, in the danger, and still chooses to bind two lives together. Today, Jack and Bell give us a reminder of what we're fighting for - and what we hope for."

He paused, letting the words hang in the still air. A rare breeze fluttered the parachute silk above us.

For the first time in months, maybe years, the world felt whole.

The vows had been spoken, the rings would come later. Father Patrick's blessing echoed through the makeshift chapel. Cheers filled the tent, boots stamping, a few helmets banged together like makeshift bells. Bell laughed through tears, Wade clapped me on the shoulder so hard I nearly staggered, and Gunner barked once - loud, sharp, like he wanted everyone to know he approved.

It was the kind of moment that felt untouchable.

The mess-hall-turned-chapel started shifting back toward something else - men and women stacking chairs, dragging tables, our mess-hall chef whipping up a feast and the aroma sifting in through the smell of damp canvas. Makeshift toasts with cans of soda – the radio in the corner playing music. It was a room full of smiles – celebrating… joyful.

Then we heard it.

Low at first, like a growl rolling through the clouds. Engines? Jets?

The sound built fast, echoing over the canvas, rattling the poles. I felt my heart kick. A flyover? A salute for us? The timing was uncanny.

But then the tone changed. Any of us who'd lived under airpower knew the difference. These weren't friendly birds skimming the sky for show. The pitch was wrong, the formation too tight, the approach too direct.

The first whistle cut through the air.

"DOWN!" someone screamed, and the party dissolved into chaos.

The ground trembled. Out beyond the wire, fire bloomed - the ordnance dump had been hit. The desert that had just been our chapel's backdrop lit up like a second sun, the shockwave ripping through canvas walls and scattering the parachute silk like torn confetti.

I grabbed Bell, shoved her low, Gunner pressed between us. Wade already had his rifle up, scanning the perimeter with the reflex of a man who never stopped being at war.

And just like that, the honeymoon was over before it even began.

Chapter 10

The Storm Returns

Smoke and dust still hung in the air, curling through the torn canvas of the mess-hall chapel. The acrid tang of burning cordite and sand filled our lungs. Screams and shouts carried over the chaos, soldiers scrambling, pulling wounded comrades toward the field hospital.

Bell was already moving, hands steady, eyes sharp. She barked instructions, guiding stretcher-bearers, assessing injuries, applying pressure where it was needed. Freshly married or not, there was no time to pause - this was what she was made for.

I grabbed my rifle, checked my ammo, and signaled Wade. Gunner, ears pricked, he stayed close at my side, ready for any threat. The ground still trembled with aftershocks caused by the explosion from the munitions storage.

Wade geared up quick. I did too. We were scanning the perimeter, our eyes searching everything from our scattered makeshift buildings, our tents – to the supply depots – out to the horizon. The rest of the camp moved like clockwork - trained to respond, even when our hearts were still catching up from the shock.

Every second counted. Every breath could be the one before the next strike.

Wade shouted – kneeling by an injured soldier Bell was treating "he said they weren't jets – missiles…"

First Sergeant Braxton's voice crackled over the radio as he reported the strike to command, his tone tight, controlled. Gunner stayed at my side, eyes focused between me and the smoke-hazed horizon, waiting for my lead.

We had to know: where did it come from?

Gunner and I were nearly running, but I forced myself to slow down so my partner had time to detect any other threats. Between what Gunner and I were doing – and the others… the entire camp and the perimeter was quickly swept. More soldiers 'posted-up' around the camps border watching for threats.

The blast area – one of our munitions storage areas had been marked with something, but what? We kept checking.

Soldiers checked all angles – all areas. Dunes, sparse brush, and the other supply depots. Nothing moved. Nothing obvious.

I made my way back to the center of camp to check on Bell. We passed by the many who were still stunned – some soldiers – others were civilian contractors like the firefighters and the interpreters. We walked and Gunner growled softly, sensing the shift.

Bell glanced at me, her hands still steady as she pressed a dressing on a soldier. The wedding glow was gone, replaced by the sharp, cold clarity of war.

I passed by First Sergeant Braxton, shook my head "The missiles didn't just appear. These were too precise…"

And that's when the first seeds of suspicion - and the shadows of doubt began to creep into my mind.

**

Gunner stayed tight at my side, ears shifting like radar dishes, his tail stiff. He was my calm in a storm that refused to die down. I checked the perimeter again, moving between sand ridges and sparse desert brush, making sure no secondary strike was coming, radio squawking intermittently. Wade was working on the other munitions storage areas – making sure they were stable.

Once the injured were stabilized and moved to the field hospital, the camp slowly began to take shape again. Soldiers lifted tables back into place, reattached tarps, and swept debris into piles, all while scanning the horizon for movement. The missiles had hit precisely - too precisely. Someone had known exactly where to strike.

That thought weighed on me as I moved through the wreckage, looking for anything that might explain it. My boots scuffed against sand and shattered plywood when something caught Gunner's attention. He nosed at it – sniffing carefully like he was memorizing an invisible memory. It was a scrap of paper, half-buried under the dirt and debris. I bent down, and carefully brushed off the dust and sand. I looked at it – no – I read over it with disbelief…

Coordinates. Small notes. Marks on a rough sketch of the camp. Potential targets.

I froze. Gunner nudged my hand with his nose, sensing my tension. My pulse picked up. Whoever had left this wasn't just guessing - they knew the layout intimately.

I carefully folded the scrap and tucked it into my vest pocket. One thing was clear: this wasn't over.

Somewhere in the camp, someone had been watching, waiting. And now, they'd shown us they had the power to strike with deadly precision.

I went back to where Wade was disarming unexploded ordinance from the blast site – his job was far from over. I showed him the map – the scrap of paper… he couldn't believe it either "Jack – get this to the first Sergeant – and Captain Knight – quick."

I did.

As the Captain was looking at the map – over and over – he nodded back to Braxton – then our first Sergeant was on the phone – calling in the CID investigators. Captain Knight asked if we'd checked the air traffic station, or JTAC to see if they had a fix on where the missiles came from.

"We're checking Sir" they responded – the camp was in a frenzy of gathering Intel and getting put back together.

Braxton calling in the 'situation report' – or SITREP with one hand, and confirming missile trajectory from JTAC with the other.

For now, that's all we could do. It was 'get the camp back in order' and brace ourselves for the next move. We worked without drama. That was the thing about real danger - people fell into roles: Bell keeping the wounded stable, medics corralling stretchers.

It all moves quick. Almost like slow motion even… not like time standing still, but a surreal distortion where speed doesn't seem quite so fast. And we still had work to do – and it wasn't even lunch time yet.

Knight and Braxton want another sweep of the camp. They want us to find something – anything that can point to how this could happen.

Security patrols were already scouring and surrounding the aircraft, and the other ammunition and explosive ordinance areas. Maintenance crews were searching through the damaged areas while trying to get them put back together. Gunner and I started 'sniffing' through the areas on the edge of the blast zone. I kept thinking how this missile strike could be so precise? I kept thinking – wondering what we were looking for.

Was it sabotage? Where would someone hide something that would lead us to it?

I could hear the transport and cargo planes bringing in reinforcements and supplies. I followed Gunner as we began to work the edge of the wreckage. We walked through - and past a row of supply trucks. He threaded between crates and then stopped at some battered vehicles burned in the blast. His nose was working the unseen trail past the familiar scents – to focus on what was different. He paused – his attention now aimed at a gap in the driver's door of a Humvee – its tires still smoldering from the heat of the explosion.

I pried the door open – Gunner hopped in. Inside, under a folded tarp on the front passenger seat, something was tucked away: a thin composition notebook, its cover scuffed, pages penciled with cramped handwriting - more coordinates, circled areas, little margin notes.

"Don't touch it," Braxton barked at my shoulder. He'd come up behind me. He snapped on gloves and carefully bagged the notebook, sealing it like evidence. "I'll log it for chain of custody. We'll get it to Captain Knight."

I watched Gunner sit by the vehicle, eyes bright, and then look back at me as if to say, "*I found it. Now what?*"

Gunner followed me and Braxton. Captain Knight read the notebook in a tight silence. He didn't shout. He didn't need to. "This is deliberate," he said finally. "Someone inside the wire fed them a plan."

Braxton radioed a SITREP up the chain: status, casualties, probable origin unknown, evidence recovered. The camp tightened. Guards moved to stricter posts. CID and Intel started lists and names. For now, the notebook was a single thread. It was a solid lead that could lead to anybody.

Gunner rested his chin on my knee. I rubbed his ears, feeling that same knot in my gut. We'd found a clue. Now we had to follow it - quietly, or we'd alert whoever was watching.

The command center was a rush of calls, confusion, and communication. Gunner sat close as we watched, and waited. One of the intelligence officers was listening close to radio 'chatter' from the airwaves. He hunched slightly – raised his hand as if to quiet the room…

"I think I've got something…" he said in hushed tones – "but I can't make out what they're saying – do we have a 'Terp' that can translate for us?"

Braxton – overhearing this – motioned for one of the clerks – a Private – to run and get the interpreter… quick.

It didn't take long – and the Private escorted in one of the locals hired as a contractor.

"This is…" as he hum-hawed for his words "Aman Salam – or something like that" as he half-smiled looking at Aman like he was questioning whether he got it right or not. "Some of the guys call him Aman, but his papers say Asad?"

Salam nodded in approval, and in heavily broken English said "I can go by both name." Then he stepped over to the radio and listened close… made notes, and strained at times as if trying to get each burst of Arabic talking just right.

Gunner was resting quiet at my feet while I was finally able to get a cup of coffee and a cigarette – watching the command center commotion turn from confusion into an organized operation. Then Gunner raised his head, stood and looked around.

I stroked his fur – told him he was a good boy, and he began to walk around – sniffing around like he does. Not like he was on a patrol, but – you know – just how dogs sniff at everything… I could tell he was curious, but Gunner? He was always curious.

One by one – he made his way around the room sniffing at each of the team members. Each time he met someone – they'd give him a small pat on the head – or a stroke of his fur. Gunner got close to the communications table – and again – the intelligence officer reached down and gave Gunner a small pat on the head…

Gunner sniffed around the "Terp" as he was taking notes. When he looked and saw Gunner – he nearly jumped out of his seat. He tried to calm himself, and then he tried to push Gunner's head away. Gunner didn't budge. He kept sniffing and I could tell our interpreter was getting a little annoyed. So I called him right before I could tell he was about to sit – so he wouldn't interrupt what the "Terp" was writing.

Captain Knight – was in and out of the room while directing the efforts to get his camp back in shape. He watched, and was interested in the developing Intel. He walked over to Gunner, and me… "It's been quite a day" he said shaking his head. "We didn't see this coming… and we should have."

I could tell the Captain was not only puzzled how this could happen, but concerned that it did. He stood and watched – he was intent yet quiet. He turned back and looked at me again "You guys probably ought to get some chow – and take a break… we'll let you know if we find anything… and… I know a nurse who would like to spend some time with ya."

He was right. It was a long day. I walked Gunner back over toward the hospital tent. It seemed quieter now, but still busy. Bell was getting some of the staff brought in to help - get up to speed on the patients, and where things were stored. She made a quick glance toward me, and smiled. Gunner and I waited patient while she finished her conversation.

"You hungry?" I asked… she didn't answer – she didn't have to. She just grabbed my arm, gave Gunner a quick hug, and we walked. Before we even got to the 'doors' to the hospital I asked "where we going?"

"Not telling" she giggled.

And we headed toward the mess tent. We walked in – it was dark and quiet. Standing by a lone table was our mess-tent Chef. Master Sergeant Collins. He lit a candle, and motioned with his hands for us to sit. All three of us.

He clapped his hands the way a real Chef would, and several cooks walked out of the kitchen area with plates – real meat – steak… real mashed potatoes – the works. He just smiled - with his gruff voice: "Compliments of the Captain."

After a long day – we ate in peace. It was nice. Even Gunner ate like a gentleman. As far as that goes.

"The Captain wanted us to have some time together" she smiled.

By the time shadows grew long and we walked in silence toward my tent I knew I'd never look at this place the same way – ever again. But I couldn't find my tent. It wasn't where it was supposed to be.

Bell just smiled. "Wade's been busy… real busy."

Wade built us a new tent – from canvas and plywood… Wade built us our first home. He stepped out from behind with a huge smile… Polaroid camera in hand… "I thought you two might like this."

He told us where to stand – in front of the new tent, and before he snapped the picture…

"Hold on…" as he ran to the side of the tent… "One more thing…"

He reached down, picked up that little piece of plywood – ducked behind us… and hung that little sign he made for me when I first got here…

"Dog House"

Wade just laughed while he took our picture. The three of us standing in front of our home.   Home.

We thanked Wade for everything he'd done for us. We all hugged… like family. We really were a family. We always would be.

I was too tired to carry Bell 'across the threshold' – and she understood. Nothing about today was a normal 'wedding day.'

But as we settled in for our first night as husband, wife, and Gunner… all she could say as she turned out the light… was…

"We'll never be able to say… our wedding day – wasn't a blast."

Chapter 11

Changing Winds

The smell of smoke and acid still filled the air. The camp still lay quiet in the morning sunlight. It made the mist rising from the damage hint of lurking danger. While things appeared quiet on the surface, there's still danger present... there's always danger present in a war zone, but this was the deceptive calm after violence.

Every time we heard our jets fly over on their increased patrols it reminded me of that instant right before the missiles hit.

Bell held my hand – tight. Her smile was the only thing that made this morning feel just right. Gunner stretched as he walked out of our tent catching up to us. I couldn't help but laugh a little: "thought you'd sleep in a little – boy?"

He just looked at me straight-faced like he just woke up and wasn't ready for humor. We walked down "Wolf" street – nothing more than rows of tents, and they named it that because of "W" company, and the fact – that's where our "Wolf" lived.

We arrived at breakfast to a hefty applause, cheers, and jeers. Bell and I just looked at each other and smiled... Gunner – wasn't amused.

We were almost finished with chow when the company clerk slipped through into the mess hall and announced "Sergeants staff meeting in 30."

I walked Bell to the hospital, gave her a kiss and chuckled "I'll see you tonight after work – dear."

She just shook her head smiling "dear?"

Now – Gunner thought *that* was funny...

Staff meeting was informative – most of it above my pay grade. Security was increasing, and reinforcements were arriving as our mission was changing from combat to enforcing the no-fly zone. There would be updates to facilities – in part for contractors – mainly for us. We'd be getting a better kitchen – better food.

I turned to Wade and said in a low voice "maybe we can start getting bacon to go with our powdered eggs?" Wade chuckled.

Captain Knight and Colonel Nettleton brought us up to speed on the changing times – that 'nothing would be normal' now – as if getting shot at and being bombed… was normal. Gunner popped his head up for a second when they addressed our part – they were bringing in some help for us.

Knight chuckled as he turned the attention to me and Gunner: "It looks like Duncan and Gunner won't be the 'lone-wolf' in the unit anymore."

Nettleton continued – looking at me – "Jack – you'll be in charge of getting the new '*M*ilitary *W*orking *D*og's' in shape – get them used to the operation, and how it all works around here. And to make it official" as he motioned for me to stand by them… Gunner followed and the Colonel continued: "You're getting a promotion to E-6 Staff Sergeant… I know this isn't the 'ceremony' we usually get, but for now it's all we got."

Wade smiled big, but I wished Bell was here with me. At least someone from my family was here to see this. As Gunner and I were returning to our seat we were given our outline for the upcoming changes… Captain Knight began to tell us:

We were going to resume increased security patrols with the 'MWD's' and expand the camp to facilitate more helicopters and cargo planes. "If you guys thought our little town was big, well it's going to get a lot bigger for a little while." I'd seen it before in other places – even though the camp was changing – there wasn't a lot of difference in what Gunner and I – or the other K9's would be doing… as long as we did our job – they usually left us alone.

The Colonel also said they'd be changing ordinance disposal operations to be more efficient and safe. He clapped his hands and smiled "Let's go to work folks."

As Wade, Gunner, and I were turning to walk out of the CQ office – The Colonel and Captain turned to meet with some of the CID and Intelligence team. I couldn't tell what they were talking about – not really, but I had a good idea.

Wade and I walked Gunner back toward 'Wolf Street' and – we bumped into the 'Terp' who smiled big, and gave Gunner a nice pat, and he pet his fur while Gunner smiled. His greeting seemed genuine, his smile was pleasant. He didn't seem irritated with Gunner at all. He seemed different... somehow, but I couldn't put my finger on it. I shook it off.

Wade was all smiles – almost giddy... I had to ask. He told me instead of removing land mines and IED's by hand – they now get to 'blow them up' in place – that all I had to do was find 'em – and they would get to destroy them.

"Yeah... I get to walk out in front while you guys hang-back and have all the fun." We kept walking toward our tents so we could get geared-up and back to the field.

Gunner watched me... and waited for me to get him ready. We met Wade outside – it didn't take him as long. We were walking past the mess tent, and again – we saw Salam our interpreter. It looked like he was finishing a sandwich – or something he had – wrapped in a napkin.

Wade smiled at him and joked "ham sandwich?" but Salam just shook his head silently saying "no." But this time – he looked nervous when he saw Gunner, and quickly stepped back into the mess hall until we passed by. I thought it was odd, but then again – maybe Gunner's combat outfit made him nervous.

We stepped away toward the perimeter – I half whispered to Wade "they don't eat ham – or pork of any kind – it's part of their religion."

**

We were about 10 miles out of camp in a sea of dust and sand. I turned to Wade – thinking out loud "what'd we ever get from the radio transmissions that – that Salam guy was writing down?"

"They said it was just normal stuff – like workers talking back and forth" Wade muttered... "It was nothing much."

And for several weeks it became the norm. Gunner would 'sniff' 'em out, I'd flag 'em, and Wade would blow 'em up. Day after day – we'd come home from work – have dinner as a family – all four of us, and do it all over. It was becoming a routine. It was almost boring. But monotony can make you complacent, and that can get you killed.

Working with the new K9 teams was nice – Wolf Street was becoming quite the place for all the dogs. Gunner had friends to play with.

One evening after Bell, Gunner, and I finished up the day, we headed into the mess hall to meet Wade for dinner, and heard hammering – sawing, and all sorts of clanking… we walked in to see a heap – a mess of two-by-four's and tent poles, and things like ammo boxes being scraped together in the corner with the head cook – the Chef-Sergeant… working on something.

"Sergeant Collins?" Bell hummed with a question… "Um – what are you doing – what ya making?"

He turned his shoulder slightly from his kneeling – looked at us with a serious kind of smirk…

"A Christmas Tree."

Wade blurted out – "you know we can get things shipped in don't you?"

Master Sergeant Collins paused… looked at us for a moment and then: "so what ya got in mind?"

Bell bent down to help him hold a couple of sticks in place – smiled "maybe we can get some care packages with chocolate Santa's, or – something like – I know – maybe we can make paper snowflakes, and you guys can round up some spent shell casings – we can polish 'em up for ornaments, and – we can even get some 'chem lights' – oh – I know… we can have everyone get pictures from home we can use as ornaments too – this'll be great!"

Collins paused again, and then stood up slow and just looked at us. He tilted his head – smirked, but still had a hollow sense about him that showed in his eyes "follow me… you guys get a special dinner."

Then he turned and looked down at Gunner – tried to soften his gruff voice "you too boy – got something for you too."

Bell watched him as he turned slow to walk into the kitchen. Her look – compassionate and yet concerned. "I shouldn't have said anything about pictures from home…"

"Why's that?"

"Because – I think he's been in the Army so long – alone – that maybe he doesn't have anyone else to send him pictures."

"Got something in mind?" I grinned… "I bet you do."

"For now – just maybe? We could adopt him into ours." Bell's smile saying more than her words.

Collins returned with our 'special' dinner – and a big plate for Gunner. Bell smiled and before the Sergeant could turn away she giggled "where's yours – aren't you going to join us? – it can be like a family dinner."

For a moment – I could see through the years of crust and layers of isolation… I could see something he was trying to hide. He slowly slid his chair to the table as Gunner finished his meal – then rested his head on Sgt. Collins lap as we all ate… as a family.

We chatted – we laughed… Gunner sniffed… I would address Bell, and Wade by their first names and that's how they'd address me. And while I can't say I feel bad – I was a bit sorry for not asking earlier… Sgt Collins – our Chef – finally said… "My name is Ray."

**

The next morning we all – yes all of us – met for breakfast. Even Father Pat joined us. It was a good time. It was a pretty good breakfast too. The eggs were better – although Wade commented they weren't as good as our farm-fresh eggs… but we had bacon and sausage, hash browns, and coffee.

But then… something struck me funny. I hadn't really given a lot of thought – or even noticed when our 'Terp' Salam went through the tray-line to get his food. But it was when I noticed him out of the corner of my eye – a couple of tables down from us… he was eating… bacon.

I thought out loud – loud enough for the others to hear "I thought 'they' weren't supposed to eat bacon – or any kind of pork for that matter."

Father Pat swallowed but said "that's right – but some of the more unorthodox will adopt some of the 'Western' ways – even our diet, but that's right – most won't eat any kind of pork."

Ray shook his head – puzzled in a way, but added "I know – some days he's real picky about it, and other days – he'll eat ham or something like that…"

That really bothered me. Bell could see it in my eyes. "Something's going on in your head – what is it?"

I looked at our little group – then focused on Wade: "Remember what ol' Charlie used to say? If you can't be true to yourself – who can you be true to?"

"Yeah – I remember, but what ya getting at?"

I scratched my head a little – Gunner raised his head thinking I was going to give him a signal… but I looked at Wade and said "Charlie once told me 'Some people are just going to think you're hard to deal with - because you aren't that easy to fool.' And I don't like being fooled. Something's up… watch this…"

I got up from the table – Gunner sprung to his feet. I gently walked over to the tray-line as if I was clearing my tray. I made my way right past Salam and he turned slightly from eating as I passed. He smiled and gave Gunner a little pat on the back.

I got back to our table – said: "You guys see that?"

"See what?" Ray questioned.

"Sometimes I can walk Gunner past him – and he's fine – other times it's like he's about to jump out of his skin…"

Bell interrupted me "what are you thinking? He's got split personality or something?"

"Maybe not a split personality Babe – but the confusion over his name the other day in the command center – and this? Maybe Mr. Salam is more than…"

"You think he's two different people?" Wade blurted out.

I motioned with my finger to my lips and shushed him… "Not so loud… I think I've got an idea."

"Wade – remember what we used back on Charlie's ranch - the purple dye we'd smear on a treated cow to keep track of it?"

"Yeah – I remember…"

A wild idea hit me. "Ray – you got any red cabbage in the kitchen"

"I believe so…"

We followed Sgt. Collins into the kitchen, and he found me some red cabbage. I boiled a few leaves, thickened it with cornstarch, and added a dash of baking soda… The result wasn't pretty, but it would do.

"What's this going to do?" Bell asked.

"This – this'll let us tell 'em apart – not that Gunner can't – Gunner can tell… but Captain Worthen with CID needs proof that Salam is two different people… but then again… we have to ask… why?"

Chapter 12

SWITCH

We decided to put our plan in place at lunchtime. I crouched by the tray line, glancing at Aman - or was it Asad? We'd soon find out. Gunner sat at my feet, ears twitching, tail flopping. Bell leaned close, whispering, "So… you really think this will work?"

"I hope so," I muttered, swiping the tiny smudge of dye onto a folded corner of a napkin I'd tucked into my hand.

Sgt. Ray Collins stirred the gravy, humming under his breath.

I edged closer, pretending to bend down to grab a fork that 'had dropped' to the ground. Salam seemed nervous around Gunner. I remembered the name he was going by at the command center that day he was nervous around Gunner – this one had to be Aman.

As he brushed past me, the corner of the napkin brushed lightly against the back of his collar. A faint, almost invisible mark transferred to the back of his neck.

Gunner's hackles twitched. A low, subtle growl vibrated in his throat. I glanced down, catching the dog's signal. That was the one.

Bell stifled a giggle, leaning near me. "You know - if you get caught…"

"Don't worry," I whispered. "He'll never notice. And we've got eyes everywhere… even better, Gunner sees everything."

The game was subtle. Dangerous. And absolutely addictive.

We ate… we watched while Aman did his usual. He would usually wrap up some unfinished meal into a napkin then reported back to the command center for any requests – for any translations. We were all playing the game, and we – obviously… got the CID investigators involved.

Bell went to work while we trailed Aman back to his tent in the contractors' village, trying to stay casual of course. When I suggested calling him in for an interpretation, I knew we were about to see which twin we were really dealing with.

Captain Worthen from CID chuckled "Good Idea." And he made the call.

A few minutes later "Salam" wandered back over to the command center – right past me and Gunner, and he gave him a smile and a pat on the head… Captain Worthen just smiled… and when 'Asad' walked closer to the light…

No mark on the back of his neck.

"I think this tells me all I need to know." As Captain Worthen saw what he needed. Worthen turned to me and asked me real nice if I'd go back to the "Salam's" tent… take a squad and make an arrest.

"Arrest?" Asad questioned.

"Yes Mr. Salam – if that's even your real name. We have reason to believe you have a twin brother, and want to know why the two of you have been switching around on us." Captain Worthen… wasn't smiling as he placed the handcuffs onto Salam's wrists. Worthen motioned to me – to go find the other one.

Wade was by my side before Gunner even got into position.

A small squad made up of mostly Military Police Privates followed Wade, Gunner – and me… as we got close to the tent. Gunner got to it first. I raised my hand to keep the squad hushed, and I tried to listen. I couldn't hear anything other than Gunner's sniffing – before he sat… on point.

"Does that mean – what… I think it can mean?" Wade said in a muted voice.

"It could… but I don't know how we'd have missed it in our detection patrols" I answered.

I thought to myself – for those seconds – how anyone could smuggle explosives into the camp. We had security at the entrances – checks of our perimeters, but had we… had we *really* focused on the contractors coming from the nearby town of Najaf five miles to the east of us? Had we focused on the right things?

We were about to find out.

The tent was silent – I snapped my fingers and Gunner took a ready stance. The MP's stood prepared sidearms at the ready.

Wade opened the flap to the tent and all I could see through the shadows of the afternoon – half hidden toward the back of the tent was Aman standing wrapped in a vest packed with plastic explosives.

In his hand was a 'dead-man' switch – his eyes glued to Gunner with sweat dripping from his face. In his broken English he stuttered "If I let go – bomb will explode."

From the corner of my eye I could see Wade carefully checking out the make-up of the device blanketing Aman.

"You free my brother – you take me to him" he continued as he inched his way toward us – as if he wanted to walk out in one piece.

We backed away slow – guns drawn, our aim direct, but we didn't dare fire and risk him letting go of the switch he held tight in his sweaty hand... setting-off the explosion.

The procession inched toward the command center, slow and tense. Aman shuffled forward, sweat dripping, his thumb clenched around the switch as if welded to it. We had him ringed in – in a corral of sorts: like a staggered, but moving perimeter. Our weapons fixed but fingers steady, every man afraid of even the slightest twitch.

We had to pass the hospital tent on the way. The doors opened, and Bell stepped out. She was still holding an armful of patient charts – but they fell to the ground and she froze at the sight of Aman in his vest, and the squad around him.

Her eyes locked on mine.

I shook my head sharply, motioning her back. She didn't move. Instead she started following, careful, silent, a shadow behind us. My pulse spiked hotter than the desert sun. I couldn't protect her from this, not here. Not like this at least.

Aman muttered in broken English as he walked, "You bring me brother. You let him go."

Worthen's voice carried calm like steel. "That can't happen, Salam. Your brother stays where he is."

Aman's steps faltered, his hands trembling. The dead-man switch wobbled. Wade leaned close to me, his voice barely a whisper. "That grip's not gonna hold long."

"Can you disarm it?" I asked.

Wade let out a nervous chuckle. "Yeah. But… it's never just the red wire."

We drew closer. The command center loomed, canvas flaps stirring with the wind. Worthen stepped closer, holding his hand up. "This is far enough. Stop right there."

Aman hesitated. His eyes darted, desperate, and then caught movement as another officer pushed through the tent flap behind Worthen. For the briefest second, his focus slipped.

That's when Gunner launched. No command. No hesitation. Just instinct. He clamped down hard on Aman's wrist, teeth burying into both flesh and the metal switch. Aman screamed, jerking back. The switch tilted.

I dove, grabbed onto Gunner's bite – and Aman's hand still in Gunner's grip. I tried to shove Gunner clear before his bite pulled too much. I'm not sure how I got my hand on the switch as my hands wrapped Aman's, crushing them around the trigger, pinning it tight. **"Wade! Now!"** but I wanted Gunner out of the way… I didn't want him hurt.

But the fight was on. Aman struggling to break free – Gunner now releasing and falling back while I was wrapping everything I could around his arm – his hand – the grip that was slipping away from the switch. I shouted again…

"Wade – where are you!!!"

But Wade was already there before I could finish shouting. His eyes narrowed, fingers moving with sharp precision. I held my breath, sweat pouring as the seconds stretched like hours.

Wade tried to hold Aman still so he could disarm the bomb, but Salam kept fighting. Several of the group jumped onto his legs – we were all trying to hold the screaming suicide bomber as still as we could, and then…

Click.

Wade jumped back and pulled out his knife – Salam still fighting. Wade lunged back into the fight again and cut away at the straps holding the explosives.

I grabbed Aman as hard as I could to roll him – and the others – away from the vest of explosives as Wade grabbed the bomb and pulled it away. Wade slid the vest away from us – skidding across the dirt, and he jumped up – and exhaled – then shouted "**Safe**."

Aman Salam was now crying – shouting something in Arabic as Captain Worthen and the MP's were restraining him. I could hear several choppers winding up their engines, and I knew – somehow – that they were getting ready to haul the Salam brothers away to a more secure facility.

Bell ran toward me – with Gunner greeting her like a pup, and we hugged. As the vacant grounds around the command center started to fill with the camp that had been evacuated – cheers and praise found its way back to the base.

Wade walked over to the explosive vest still lying on the ground – Gunner followed him – as if to protect the others from it. Braxton had called for Wade's disposal team to remove it – so it could be detonated a ways off from us… safely.

As we watched them walk away with it… Wade – calm now – simply said "Real… Very real, by the way."

Relief came in a rush so fierce it nearly left me weak. Wade let out a sigh… kind of smiled and said…

"You know – it actually was… the red wire."

For a long moment, no one moved. Gunner sat beside me, chest heaving, muzzle flecked with blood and sweat. His eyes had never left Aman, but now… showed the relief we were all feeling.

Braxton walked over to us – now silent – simply held out a half-pack of Marlboro cigarettes and simply smiled "I think you earned this one."

By the time it was crushed out – we were at the mess tent. Ray met us and somehow knew we'd want to sit for a few minutes, and decompress, and eat. He had a table waiting for us, and his team brought our food to us.

I knew we'd be filling out our written reports – describing the events of the day, but for now – we just needed a quiet moment to relax.

Father Pat walked in. He saw us at our table and sat down with us.

"Anything you guys feel like getting off your chest" he asked calmly.

None of us wanted to speak. The reality of it all starting to sink in. finally – I turned and looked at Wade. I could only shake my head, but I think he could tell what was going through my mind. And I finally found the words I wanted to say:

"I should have caught this."

Gunner rested his head on my lap – looked at me with his caramel eyes and an understanding I can't explain… Wade finally said "It's not your fault – it's not anyone's fault – all of us trusted… all of us didn't think to check, but it's over – and we'll never make that mistake again…"

After we gathered our thoughts – our composure maybe… we walked Bell back to work – and we headed to the CQ office so we could finish our paperwork.

I met with our newer K9 teams, and gave the instructions I knew we'd be getting from Captain Knight – even Colonel Nettleton.

"We're going to start sweeps on everything. Every inch of this camp is going to be included in our daily patrols… **Everything**." I drew out a makeshift map of the camp in the dirt, and assigned the teams to have our working dogs at every entry gate – we'd patrol and inspect every, and any individual coming in.

I knew they wouldn't want the extra time spent on shift – considering the season, but I told them that I'd been doing most of this with Gunner – without any help.

Before any of the new guys could complain… I stood up, Gunner stood with me… and I simply pointed to the "Wolf-Pack" motto posted above the exit door…

"We are the Wolf Pack: Suffer in Silence - Quietly Endure - Patiently we will Wait - We are Warriors - We Will Survive."

I clapped my hands, but smiled… "Let's go to work."

Gunner and I left our meeting, and walked back to the hospital. I met Bell, but she had about an hour before she was off shift. I told her Gunner and I'd grab a shower, and that we'd wait for her… at home.

**

Our little Family walked into the mess-hall… again.

It was lively – yet all the faces I could tell… wanted to be home. Our Chef – now friend, who became a part of our little family… met us and told us tonight's dinner menu, and that they even arranged for a movie. Bell tugged at Ray's arm – the crusty rugged cook looked puzzled when Bell led him toward the makeshift tree – all decorated with whatever could be found in a combat zone – and with pictures of soldiers and their families from all over the US…

Wade handed Father Pat his Polaroid camera, and he took a family picture for us… Ray, Wade, Gunner – Bell, and me… so now Master Sergeant– Ray Collins had a picture for the Christmas tree he'd made.

Bell looked at our little group, and quietly said: "Blood makes you related… Loyalty makes you family."

We all ate together. Watched a movie together… "It's a Wonderful Life". . .

Amid the flickering lights of the movie, and the glow of chem.-lights of our home-made Christmas tree… I leaned over – kissed Bell…

"Merry Christmas."

Chapter 13

Silent Prayer

The next morning the camp felt different. It seemed lighter somehow. Like maybe Christmas had stolen a piece of the war away for one night. But the desert doesn't care what day it is, and neither do the people trying to kill us.

I'd grown up, and learned early on… complaining about it wouldn't make it any easier.

Sgt. Collins arranged for a nice Christmas Day breakfast, but it almost seemed like the nicer things became – the more I missed life at home. But our little family ate in silence. We looked at each other with a calm that felt empty. Hollow.

Sure – I'd grown accustomed by now – to life in uniform… working holidays, long hours, and missing family, but this was different. I kissed Bell as we went to work. And as usual I could hear the words she'd say under her breath as we would turn to walk away.

"Dear God… let them come home safe."

We were ordered to clear a stretch of road leading up toward Karbala. It was nothing out of the norm, but it had to be done. And even though we hadn't found anything for Wade to blow-up… it almost made it even more surreal when we didn't find – anything.

Bell never told us to hurry – she didn't want us making any mistakes. But I knew she wanted me to attend Father Patrick's Christmas Day sermon later on.

Gunner and I kept walking.

I couldn't tell what kind of vehicles they were off in the distance of the desert, but I knew they weren't ours. We kept 'eyes' on them as long as we could – until they disappeared across the horizon, and the cloudy sky hid them in the shadows.

I'm not sure what's worse – the fight, or waiting for the fight that never comes.

**

Father Patrick stood at the makeshift pulpit, his voice steady, carrying over the camp even in the desert stillness. Soldiers shifted in their seats, some leaning forward, some fidgeting, and some staring at nothing at all.

His Christmas Message carried the traditional story of the Nativity – the life of Jesus, and then the words that meant the most that afternoon. To me at least.

My hand brushed the upper left pocket of my uniform. I slipped my fingers in and they closed around the little Bible my mom had sent me. The leather was worn now, and the torn pages frayed at the edges, and I traced my finger across the page where bullet stopped.

John 10:11 "I am the good shepherd. The good shepherd lays down his life for the sheep."

I smiled, just a little, remembering the day a bullet had gone through my Kevlar, and the point stopped against the passage on that page.

A little gift from home that spared my life. And right there, in that moment, I looked down at Gunner, sitting faithfully at my side. My Shepherd. My friend. My partner.

He tilted his head, eyes warm, trusting, loyal. I scratched behind his ears and he leaned into my hand. The sermon droned on in the background, but I barely heard it. All I felt was that silent, unshakable connection.

I whispered under my breath, a small prayer I didn't need anyone else to hear: "Thank you… for this one."

I could see rays of light creeping through the breaking clouds as I looked through the opening of the 'mess-tent' turned Chapel. The sunlight was now higher, glinting off the horizon, warming the camp. For one quiet morning, the war felt just a little farther away.

I tightened my grip on the Bible and Bell placed her hand on mine. I didn't have to look up to know she was looking at me with her warm smile. But I looked anyway. Then with my hand in hers – we both glanced at Gunner, and knew that we'd walk through all of this… together.

For the next few days we kept a watch out for the mysterious sightings – the distant little vehicles that seemed to follow our movements out in the desert. We wondered if they were 'locals' doing geotechnical work for the petroleum industry? Maybe they were 'smugglers' or black marketers from nearby Najaf who wanted to use the roads we'd cleared? None of it made perfect sense.

Wade didn't think they'd be with the oil well cleanups – since we were a ways from that area, but then he thought again… "You know Jack – I think we should bring it up to command – and maybe start looking at re-scanning the areas we've already hit… could be they are planting things along these roads… after we've cleared 'em."

By the next morning we passed it up the chain. Command didn't like surprises, and neither did the battalion's Intel shop; they ordered a priority re-sweep of our sectors and increased the 'fly-by' patrols along the roads.

That afternoon we started running the dogs along the grid again, slower this time, while Wade's team stood by. Gunner and I walked point and watched the horizon for any new sightings.

At dusk one of those little vehicles crested a dune three clicks out - stopped - and didn't move. It wasn't quite local traffic anymore. Wade pulled his Humvee up to me. We just watched.

Off to the south, a small Toyota pickup crested a rise, stopped, and just… sat there. Three klicks out. Too far for detail, close enough to notice.

"Could be surveyors," I muttered.

"Or smugglers," Wade said, squinting through binoculars. He lowered them, jaw set. "Or someone seeding behind us."

We finished the sweep without incident, but as we were loading our gear the same truck reappeared - this time from the east. Different dune, same distance. Watching.

That night command doubled the watch along the perimeter of the camp. Every few hours, headlights winked on and off at the horizon, never approaching, but never leaving entirely. A pattern. Almost like they were timing us and our response…

By the third day Intel sent a liaison down. He didn't say much, just asked if we could log exact bearings and times of every sighting. He seemed more interested than concerned, which put my nerves on edge.

"Jack," Wade said quietly as the liaison's Humvee rolled away, "we might not be the only ones cleaning up out here."

"What ya mean?"

Wade scratched the back of his neck – climbing into the truck: "I've heard about some of these guys using old mines as 'IED's'… saving 'em for later."

"Well – let's log it… and head back for dinner." Gunner liked rides. It didn't matter what kind.

**

Father Patrick joined us for our evening meal. Gunner licked at his paws a little. Bell could tell something was on my mind. "What is it?" she smiled.

I told her I was concerned about Gunner – walking in the rocky sand all day – even though his paws were tough… it concerned me. I mentioned the little trucks shadowing us, and how that was bothering me too.

Bell had some medicine to help with Gunner's paws, but I wished she had an answer for our desert shadows.

That answer would come soon enough.

At first light we rechecked a lane we'd cleared two days before. This time we brought a couple more K9 teams with us. The dogs detected and this time – like the last… they found what we'd suspected. I motioned for the new guys to pull their dogs away to a safe distance.

Before I walked away – thinking Wade would just 'blow' this one… he knelt down, then crawled up to where we'd flagged it. And we weren't about to leave him. I whispered "please God don't let Wade blow us up."

Wade turned his head a little – huffed out a slight laugh – "thought you weren't that religious."

"I'm not – so don't get any ideas… and don't mention any of this – to Bell."

Wade dug with gloved hands, and then used a paint brush to sweep away the sand spilling away in dry flakes, and there it was: fresh wiring, insulation still bright, a thin scrape of disturbed sand around it like someone had just shoved it back into place.

Gunner and I stood by – almost watching over Wade's shoulder, his breath shallow. "That ain't old." He pointed to the charge: commercial blasting cap, wired to a new switch assembly we hadn't seen in the Iraqi piles before.

Tracks ran in a shallow arc away from the device. Tire marks that hadn't been there the last time we were through. I looked up and saw a Toyota pickup cresting the nearest ridge, engine idling, and then accelerating away before we could get a clear bearing. The same small truck we'd logged twice before.

"Someone's been right behind us," Wade said. "They're planting after we clear."

We reported it. Command went from cautious to urgent. The liaison radioed back that the pattern matched other sectors. Devices were also turning up in recently cleared lanes, and that vehicles had been seen loitering on the same bearings. It was no longer rumors. Somebody was watching our routes and reseeding them.

Wade's jaw hardened. "Game's changed. We don't sweep and leave. We sweep, and then watch."

"Yeah but – but won't they notice if we 'don't ' blow something up?"

Wade turned – raised his brow, and then smirked "you're right… I've got an idea."

He turned back to look at his team in the "BAT" – or Bradley Armored Transport M2 – and then looked at me as if "you gonna stand there and get blown up?"

I heeled Gunner around the back of the transport – Wade gave the signal and "his" gunner let loose with a couple of short bursts from the 25 mm M242 Bushmaster chain gun.

No matter how many times you brace for it - you feel it. It still rattles you when the blast goes off like the shock-wave punches straight through you. And then Wade – every time – does his celebratory stomp on the ground and hums the famous line from "Queen…"

"Bump – bump, bump – bump… another one bites the dust!"

The echoes of the Bradley's cannon still rattled in my chest as the smoke settled. Wade clapped the side of the turret like it was an old friend, and then turned back to me with that lopsided grin. Gunner shook the sand out of his coat, ears still flat from the blast, and looked at me as if to ask if we were finally done here.

We weren't, but the lane was clear enough for today. We logged the grid coordinates, and command ordered us to mark it for follow-up disposal. Wade gave one more theatrical stomp in the dirt, humming the line again, and we started back toward camp.

The ride 'home' was quiet. I could tell the others were running the same math I was: someone out there was reseeding behind us, and sooner or later we'd catch them too close.

Back inside the wire, the air felt heavier, the routine of camp folding over us like a blanket you didn't ask for. First stop was the ops tent. Wade and I laid out the evidence: new wiring, fresh tire tracks, the Toyota. The First Sergeant – Braxton - scribbled fast, already calling in the Intel by radio. Higher command wanted full re-clears logged and extra patrols on standby. No one liked the idea of ghosts moving in behind us.

Gunner limped as we walked out. I noticed it before Bell did, but not by much. She was waiting near the mess tent, arms crossed, brow tight. The moment she saw the hitch in his gait, the soldier in her melted into something softer. She knelt, pulling him in like a child.

"Poor boy," she murmured, checking his paws. She had the balm and gauze ready, like she always did, pressing it in with gentle fingers. Gunner leaned against her chest, eyes half-closed in trust. I could've sworn she was more worried about him than me. Truth be told, I was grateful for it.

Later that evening we were called into CQ for the planning session. The next assignment wasn't close. An old caravan trail west of Tullaiha. It was fifty miles out, too far out to keep a convoy safe. The brass wanted us flown by Blackhawks at first light, dog and all. The idea was simple: re-clear the trail, map any finds by GPS, flag for disposal. The subtext was clear: if someone was reseeding, that trail was the perfect testing ground.

The room buzzed with map overlays and radio frequencies, but I found myself tracing the line west with my finger, thinking about the emptiness of that desert and the feeling of eyes we couldn't see.

By dinner, the tension eased into the usual gallows humor. Wade couldn't resist. "Bell, you'd have been proud. Jack here actually said a prayer over me while I was elbows-deep in wiring."

Bell's eyes widened. Father Patrick nearly spilled his coffee, chuckling. "Careful, son. Silent prayers have a way of being heard."

I rolled my eyes, but their laughter softened the edges of the day. Tomorrow was New Year's Eve. No parties, no countdowns, just another sweep in another stretch of sand. Still, for one night, it felt almost enough to just sit together, to eat, to breathe, and to know we weren't alone in it.

Chapter 14

Luck Isn't Enough

I never liked that feeling… that feeling of time standing still…

Bell woke me up – wiping away Gunner's wakeup call from her face.

"Good morning to you too" I said now looking at an eager Gunner staring at me – Bell simply stroking his fur with a smile.

As we got dressed Bell laughed a little "Happy New Years' Eve."

"It would be – if we could have a party… but I'm pretty sure Ray isn't going to find any beer in his supplies for us."

"Yeah it would be nice if he could" as she finished buttoning her uniform.

I opened the 'door' for her, but Gunner rushed out before her – she laughed again "I guess he really needed to go…"

We stood holding hands – waiting for 'our' boy – then he trotted back – right to my side, and we walked toward the mess-tent.

As we strolled down Wolf Street – Wade joined us and Bell giggled a good morning – then we began to swing our connected hands and walked like school kids expressing a mutual crush.

Breakfast was quiet. And then it became almost too quiet. Ray had managed to scrounge up something that looked like real eggs and hash browns… we were all too happy that it was a far cry from what we used to get… the food that used to taste a lot like cardboard.

But after a year in the desert you don't get picky. The guys even joked about how MRE's peanut butter had more calories than the meal itself. Wade swore he saw a date stamped on one of the boxes that went back to Vietnam. Nobody laughed too loud. We all knew today was going to be longer than most.

Gunner stretched out under the table, paws twitching, and his tail giving an occasional thump against my boot. I bent down and checked his pads again. A lot less raw than yesterday, the ointment Bell smeared on them was really doing its job. He gave me that steady look of his, the one that told me he was ready, no matter how sore. I scratched behind his ear and whispered, "We'll take it easy today, buddy." His ears perked like he believed me.

Wade, Gunner, and I walked Bell to work – I gave her a kiss, and told her we could celebrate New Year's Eve Army style… with nothing.

Morning briefing. Maps laid out across the table in CQ, pins stuck where today's trouble waited. Fifty miles out, west of Tullaiha, old caravan routes that hadn't been walked in a while. Not by anyone we trusted anyway. JTAC was already on the line, cool and steady, telling us that air cover had been coordinated. Not the routine flyover kind, but A-10 Thunderbolt's - or Warthogs - were on call. That meant somebody higher up wanted us protected in case this got ugly.

The squad was set: me and Gunner, Wade, three privates who were still figuring out which end of the rifle to point, and Corporal Sanchez, another EOD man with nerves of steel and too many tattoos for his own good. Seven of us in all. That is… if you counted Gunner, which I always did.

We checked our gear twice, and then checked it again. It was always 'check – double check, and then re-check' – the rule that keeps us alive. Wade hauled in extra ammo boxes for controlled detonations. His philosophy was simple: if in doubt, shoot it until it doesn't exist anymore. I gave Gunner's paws one more once-over before we boarded the Black Hawks. They looked good enough for the day.

Right before Gunner and I climbed aboard – there she was. She just wanted one more kiss before we left. I loved it, but somehow – it gave me a surreal feeling. It was warm – yet… why she wanted to… today of all days. She hugged me tight, and then Bell kissed her fingers and touched Gunner's nose like a mother sending a kid off to school. He wagged, clueless about the weight she carried for him.

We loaded heavy on water. December wasn't punishingly hot, but the desert floor threw sunlight back up at you like a mirror. The kind of heat that cooks the back of your neck even when the air feels cool.

The flight out took maybe thirty minutes, wind roaring through the open doors. Below us the desert rolled out in all directions, endless sand broken only by rock outcroppings and dry riverbeds. I tried not to think about how far fifty miles was if we ended up on foot. Gunner pressed against my chest – strapped in tight, head resting on my arm, unbothered by the chop. I envied him that.

After a half hour – I sort of expected our pilot to play us something right before touchdown… he shouted "two minutes" and then… another AC/DC… this time… "TNT"

We set down hard, rotors kicking dust into our faces, the smell of fuel mixing with sand. The birds lifted and suddenly it was just us and the silence again.

Work started quick. Gunner went nose-down, sweeping the caravan trail. Wade and Sanchez flanked him, eyes on the ground, rifles at the ready. Within twenty minutes he flagged, pawing at a patch of earth we'd supposedly cleared weeks back. Wade's curse cut the air. New wiring, fresh sand. Somebody was following us for real.

We marked it, called it in, and then detonated it. The blast rattled teeth, a sharp echo across the flat land.

"Not leftovers," Wade said flatly. "They're reseeding."

We found two more like it within the hour. Each one set where an old device had been. Each one newer than it should've been. And then, in the distance, the telltale glint of sunlight off a windshield. A pickup, maybe Toyota, sitting on a ridge, watching. By the time we raised 'eyes' it was gone, dust trailing east. Even with our binoculars – we couldn't see 'em anymore.

The privates muttered about bad luck, how we'd drawn the short straw for New Year's Eve patrol. I wanted to believe it was only bad luck. Deep down I knew better.

We moved north toward Al Hajj Road, a line on the map that promised faster egress if things got hairy. Problem was, the terrain didn't care about maps. Ravines cut the land like scars, forcing us to pick careful paths. Each gulch meant bottleneck, it meant exposure while we were in a 'fatal-funnel.' I didn't like it. Neither did Wade. His jaw had that grinding look. Again.

We were skirting one of the deeper cuts when the first shots cracked. Small arms, sharp and close. Instinct dropped us flat into the dirt. Gunner pressed against my chest, like he was covering me. He was alert – a hint of a low growl, but still silent.

Rounds chipped stone around us. Someone had us dialed in.

Private McAdams, too green to know better, lifted his head to fire back. Gunner lunged, teeth catching his sleeve, dragging him down just as an RPG shrieked in and detonated against the lip of the ravine. Dirt and fire erupted overhead. My ears rang, the world tilting sideways. McAdams stared at Gunner like he'd just seen God.

"Stay down!" I roared, shoving him lower.

I couldn't tell if the sound of thunder was our Air Support – or the machinegun fire we were under.

Return fire crackled from Sanchez and Wade, short bursts keeping the shooters cautious. I could see muzzle flashes dancing along the ridge opposite, half-hidden in the rock. Whoever they were, they knew the ground.

A younger private shouted over the noise, panic high in his voice. "What's plan B?"

"There is no plan B!" I yelled back. **"It's do or die out here!"**

The words tasted like iron.

Sanchez crawled up beside me, map case under his arm. He stabbed at it with a dirty finger. "Old concrete plant, five clicks east, near the highway. We could make it."

Wade snapped a glance at the open expanse between us and that plant. "No chance. We'd be fish in a barrel. Better to stay in this cut. At least here we've got cover."

I grabbed the handset from the radio man, barked for command, gave our grid. JTAC's voice came steady in my ear, calm as if he were ordering coffee. "Stand by. We've got **A-10's** inbound. ETA five."

"We don't have five – we need them NOW!"

JTAC repeated "Stand by Wolf Pack – War**hogs** inbound!"

Five minutes can feel like five years. Time stood still. But Wade? I never loved that man more…

Wade's grin split through the dirt and grime. He threw his head back and bellowed like he was back home on the farm.

"It's **HOG** callin' time!   Suuuuuu - ^{eeeeeeee}!"

The guys laughed, tight and desperate, clinging to it. Even I cracked a smile through the dust. Gunner's ears flicked at the sound, confused but steady, pressed against me like he understood how thin the line was.

Fire still raked the ravine, chips of stone biting at our helmets, sand stinging like needles. My heart pounded so hard I thought the enemy could hear it.

Rounds came in from the side now – I shouted "They're flanking us!"

I draped an arm over Gunner when a mortar landed too close, showering us with burning grit. He didn't move, just steadied me the way he always did.

We took more fire. I heard one of our boys scream. I brushed off the dirt and rocks that pelted me – while firing into the direction of the muzzle flashes coming just up from us in the gulch.

He couldn't have been more than 18, but crying in pain – shot… he looked like he was twelve. He was breathing hard, panicked. I returned fire while grabbing my bandage pack from my vest.

"Hold on – we're gonna get ya out of here!" I shouted – returned fire with one hand while trying to stop his bleeding with the other.

Wade and the others were firing over our heads – Gunner barking every time he could see someone shooting at us – like he was seeing the threats before we could. Pointing at them so we could see them.

They were a lot closer than we imagined.

The boy started to close his eyes – I slapped his face "Stay with me – don't you go to sleep dammit!" as I slipped more bandages onto his chest – then shouted again "JTAC – we need med-evac – call 'em – get 'em here – NOW!"

I was working hard – firing in several directions – firing wherever I thought a threat was. I was trying to remember whatever I could from our first-aid class in 'Basic' – I was trying to think of anything Bell would have said – that could help in a situation… like this.

I don't know how he held it together, but Wade looked like he was firing rifles with both hands – shootin and scootin like no other. Every time a burst of incoming fire came in – he kept it back so we could keep this kid alive.

"Call 'em again – get 'em here NOW!" I kept shouting… "tell 'em we're surrounded and we're taking heavy fire!"

I could hear the thunder – I could feel the ground shaking before I could hear the unmistakable growl of turbofans. The A-10 Wart**HOGS** had to group into attack formation – Wade tossed a smoke grenade toward the main group of attackers – to let "*the hogs*" know where the main threat was.

The sound of salvation, of the ugliest birds ever built. A-10s. Wade shouted – smiled "**Here Come Da HOGS!!!**"

I tilted my head skyward, couldn't see them yet, but the hairs on my arms lifted. The squad huddled lower, clutching weapons – still firing.

The ground shook – dirt and rocks caving onto us like a landslide. I grabbed for Gunner – but he jumped onto the wounded boy and covered the young soldier with his body. I slid down and covered them as best I could also.

The ravine lit again with enemy fire, trying to break us before the cavalry came around with another pass. Wade reloaded, teeth bared in a grin that looked half-mad.

I whispered into the wounded soldier's ear, "Hang on, boy. Just a little longer."

And then the sky roared. Again.

The Warthogs – flying Low and slow – firing 65 rounds a second from the 30 millimeter Gatling guns as the planes made a second pass. I returned fire up the ravine while sitting tight by Gunner – who was covering the boy who trusted him with his life.

For a second it was quiet. I raised my head just enough for a quick peek. Gunner stood – shaking off the dirt. I rolled slow so I could still protect the boy, and aimed my rifle toward the last place I saw incoming fire from.

We all kept low – backs toward each other keeping eyes out for more threats…

I could hear the beats of chopper blades. Rhythmic and in concert with each other. I could tell – there was more than one.

I could hear the separation – like they were covering each other and then…

The heavy beats of the M240 door guns from one of the Black Hawks. Short bursts – like they were finishing the job from the WartHogs.

Wade jumped up – flagging the medical chopper to land as I was lifting the wounded soldier – Gunner trying to help.

His eyes heavy – his breathing slower… I kept shouting at him…

"Stay with us – you're going to be fine!

Chapter 15

You Never Know

Sometimes it's better not to know. It makes saying good-bye easier.

Wade and I pulled the boy up out of the ravine. We were nearly running with him as the Black Hawk gunships kept firing. Flight Medics met us only feet away from the bird, and began assessing him as we loaded him on board. Its blades never stopping. The medics with IV bags – shouting over the sounds of the engines – the slapping of the blades – "I've got him!"

It was a rush of dust, dirt, and sand – a blast of hot air as the Black Hawk spun toward camp as it lifted off. Wade and I ran back toward the gully and found our team. Wade shouted:

"Where's Gunner?"

I looked around – he wasn't by my side. There was a moment of panic – the way a parent would feel when they can't find a lost child.

My throat – already dry and cracked called out for him. Silence. I choked but called again – then I heard the bark. It was Sharp and insistent – like he was calling me too. I ran up the ravine and found Gunner – on point holding an insurgent to the ground.

Before I could retrieve some zip-ties to restrain the combatant and call Gunner away – he pulled out a pistol – aimed right at Gunner. Like I said before – there is no worse feeling than time standing still. I wasn't holding a weapon in my hand. And in that instant when eternity is half a heartbeat away… I thought – no – I prayed… "Wade – where are you?"

Maybe that silent prayer was louder than I imagined. In the time it takes forever to last a split second – a single shot rang out. An enemy lay still and Gunner was saved.

I stood and embraced my partner – and from behind me a voice called out again…

"I'm here!"

His look was solid - firm, and focused, and for a moment of silence that sliced through the terror… all Wade could say was:

"This time… **I** shot the Cougar."

There are moments in every life that create bonds. But there are bonds that cannot be explained to those who haven't experienced the trust one has – when your life, or someone you love is in someone else's hands.

In the moment I thought would be an expression of that bond… Wade simply walked closer to us – looked at the insurgent… we all stood silent – maybe even reverent, but then - in a 'mock' Arabic voice – Wade coughed out…

"I – do – not – thin – he – will – be – home – for – dinner."

I looked at Gunner and shook my head. Then we stood… and hugged Wade.

I told Gunner "we're not done yet boy – let's check the others" and he turned – led us back down the ravine toward our remaining team. It wasn't far – but far enough for us to have to walk past the bodies of so many men who tried to kill us. We didn't even count.

As we walked up to the guys – Sanchez was trying to comfort the other two – still stunned by the firefight they just survived – and seeing one of their friends hauled-off… injured. But comfort wasn't what they needed. They just survived an attack with insurmountable odds, and all I could say was:

"Sometimes it's better to be an unleashed monster – than a well behaved coward. You boys just grew-up to be men… welcome to the Wolf-Pack."

I looked at the kid with the radio – "tell 'em we'll mop-up a little – then we'll need a ride home."

We scoured the area our attackers ambushed us. There wasn't much left. Three small trucks were destroyed beyond recognition, light weapons and explosives were gathered… and we tried to count the casualties. We tried. There are no words that can describe the smell of bodies burned – torn apart by 30 millimeter rounds firing 3900 rounds a minute… the sight of remains destroyed beyond recognition.

Yes they were trying to kill us. But they were husbands, fathers – brothers… but when I saw the worst… I wanted to throw up. A boy.

He couldn't have been more than ten years old. Laying in the impact of the cannons left by the A-10's. His body torn – his lifeless arms still clutching to a Kalashnikov AK-47... but what will haunt me forever is looking into his eyes... yes...

He was just a boy.

Sometimes we laugh in the shadows of death because that is the only means to survive the fire. But in that moment... we stood there in those shadows. Silent.

I pat Gunner on the head – turned to the team... and being the ranking soldier told them "Let's finish this."

I told Gunner to 'stay' while I stepped into the crater. I picked up the rifle the little boy held and tossed it. Wade picked it up and placed it into the pile with the others – and nodded back at me like he knew what I had to do. I looked up at Gunner – told him to go to Wade.

I knelt by a boy who tried to kill me. I looked to the sky – I looked for God. And at that moment – I couldn't see Him.

They say there are no Atheists in fox-holes – so there on my knees I reached down, and closed the boy's eyes. I couldn't have cried if I wanted to so I did the only thing I could.

I recited the only real prayer I knew – The Lord's Prayer.

I stood. I turned so I could climb out of the hole. Gunner never left. He never would. As Wade and Sanchez finished wiring up the final charges to neutralize the cache of weapons... I turned for the last time to look...

He was just... a boy.

In the distance we could hear the choppers coming so we could go home. Wade turned the key to the switch so he could detonate the explosives and destroy the insurgents weapons.

I didn't know at that time – this would only be one of many days that would haunt my memories – and slip into my dreams on sleepless nights. But this was a day... When strangers became friends, where bonds were forged in fire, and brothers walked side by side.

Wade lit a cigar with his left hand, and raised his right hand holding the detonator then clicked it. The percussion – the impact of the explosion never made us flinch. We just walked through the cloud - through the dust – dirt – and the debris of that explosion… and emerged into the light as warriors.

We walked up to the waiting choppers – the pilot shouted out – "are you Duncan?" I shouted back… I answered loud enough for the <u>dust</u> to hear…

"NO… WE ARE THE WOLF PACK!"

My team climbed into the Black Hawk first. Gunner stood with me one last time as we looked back toward the cloud we survived. I felt a hand on my shoulder. I turned to board and grabbed onto Wade's waiting hand.

The sun was finding one last beam of light sinking into the horizon as we approached the landing pad. Just enough light for me to see Bell waiting at the edge – then running to greet me. She held me tighter than I'd ever been held. I never felt more safe than at that moment.

It was the first time I ever heard her cry.

"How is the boy?" I asked.

Bell fumbled with her words, but finally could say "he's on his way to the Navy's hospital ship down in the Gulf. We got him stabilized…"

I could tell she didn't want to talk. We just wanted to hold each other. I wanted to be home. I wanted all this to be over.

Gunner turned quick – my heart nearly stopped, but it was only Wade…

"Where's mine?" he said smiling as he was motioning for us to include him in our family group-hug.

And for a moment amid chaos and the winding down of the engines of the helicopters… it was finally quiet.

We started walking, but we really didn't know where we wanted to go. I knew I was hungry, but didn't feel like eating. I knew I was dirty, but didn't feel like doing anything. Bell just looked at me with that look of hers, and when she told me that I'd feel better after I got cleaned up… I knew I should at least shower.

At first it was funny – Gunner playing in the water. He turned from sandy grey ash color – back to his shiny black and brown. If I had to guess – he must have had a hundred pounds of dirt that washed away.

Then it wasn't so funny. As the water poured over my body I looked down at the planks of our canvas shower room. Seeping through the cracks and the drain… was the dirt, the ash, and the blood of the boy who stood with me and fell in combat. I looked at my hands… still stained with his blood. For the first time I felt regret that I didn't even know his name. There would never be enough soap to clean that away from my conscience.

Bell handed me a towel – she could tell it was bothering me. She smiled.

"Carter. His name was Private Ben Carter."

"Any relations to you?" I asked… Bell said no – that Braxton already asked. In the short time we've been together – Bell seemed to know what I needed… when I needed it. She continued…

"He was 18 – only a few months out of basic – and he volunteered to come here."

"I bet he never volunteers for anything else" Wade's voice booming in.

"Really Wade?" I laughed… "You want to shower with us too?"

We waited outside for Wade to finish… I smoked a cigarette, and Bell just stood there shaking her head – still laughing.

I looked at her and asked "You can still find out how Private Carter is doing can't you?"

"I'm sure I can" she smiled.

Wade came out of the showers with nothing but a towel and a smile. "Ready for chow?" he blurted…

"Not until you're dressed – Sergeant." Bell chuckled.

"Well – OK there Lieutenant – Maam…" he smiled with a makeshift salute… the towel almost falling from his waist.

I think Gunner even shook his head.

Once the four of us were all put back together – we headed for the chow hall… I still wasn't in the mood to eat, but… my wife told me to at least try.

We walked back down Wolf Street – passing a couple of new Privates complaining that New Year's Eve wouldn't be fun without fireworks. We just stopped – stunned… thinking these kids would never like fireworks again… if they'd gone through what we just went through.

Father Patrick met us at the door to the chow hall. He didn't have to say it, but I knew he wanted us to talk about it – when we were ready. Ray sat to eat with us – it was our little family together again.

First Sergeant – Braxton entered – and walked to our table. We offered him to join us, but he declined politely – however…

"I gave the order – well… Colonel Nettleton gave the order I'm all too happy to pass along… that tonight is going to be quiet. No shooting – no… nothing…" as he looked around at all the disappointed faces in the room… but he continued…

"You guys have been through enough – you don't need any reminders… so – the order is out – quiet time tonight."

Then he turned to me and in more hushed tones so only our table could hear… "I know what happened out there today… been there myself, and it Ain't pretty… so if ya ever want to talk…" as Braxton's eyes said the rest for him.

We ate in silence for a few moments, but then Wade couldn't take it anymore. He stood – his face solemn and stoic… and then he spoke…

"I suppose you're wondering why I called this meeting? My name is Wade Callahan, I'm from Utah, and I'm not a Mormon… is anyone else here from out of town?"

There was a pause – then a giggle… then our table erupted in laughter. It was what we needed after the day we just had.

Father Patrick told us he was from Austin Texas… Ray said he was from Glasgow… "Scotland?" Bell choked…

"No – Glasgow Montana... it's such a little town – no one knows where it is – hell... neither do I anymore... I've been in the Army so long I wouldn't recognize it if I saw it..."

Through the chuckles Bell told our group I was from Utah also – that Wade and I were friends as early as Kindergarten... I took a sip of soda and while laughing said "hell yeah – in fact the first time I met Wade – we were playing in the sand-box at recess... and look at us now – we're still playing in the sand."

And Bell still laughing said "and no – he's not a Mormon either."

And then – Father Patrick asked Bell where she was from... and she looked at me with a grin "I told you before that I was from Grand Junction – Colorado didn't I?"

I nodded my head yes, but then I asked her... "I just don't know My Love..."

"When's your birthday?"

Chapter 16

Hints and Hope

I don't know why, but when I could hear the faint shouts in the distance counting down the final moments before the New Year… I thought of Charlie. Bell could tell I was thinking something, and she asked.

"I was just remembering a trip my old friend Charlie took me on. I was sixteen, and we drove to his brother's ranch in Wyoming. I learned a lot on that trip – even rode a million-dollar stallion – Smokey Joe, and it just got me thinking…"

We sat for a second listening to the hushed happy New Year cheers, and then she hummed at me… "Go on…"

"It just got me thinking that – it always seemed like the longest part of a trip is the last little bit of it… does that make sense?"

"Yeah – it does." As she cuddled into me – Gunner pressing his nose like he was reminding us he was there.

"Babe – it's like… how do you forget all this?"

I looked deep into her eyes, and all she could say was "Hope."

I could tell she wanted to say more, but words wouldn't erase today. We fell asleep wrapped in the love we found in a foreign country… and wool Army blankets.

As the last whispers of love were fading from her lips, she turned into me a little closer and in near slumber sighed "what happens to Gunner when the war is over?"

I kissed the top of her hair. "We'll figure it out," I whispered. I wanted her to believe it; I wanted myself to believe it. She sighed again, drifting away, and I held onto her like the answer might come if I just stayed still long enough.

But it didn't. I didn't sleep all night.

I was dressed for the day – I got ready as I watched Gunner sleeping at Bell's feet. Neither one of them stirred – not really… and so I sat. I just sat watching them sleep – the thoughts that were troubling me all night running through my head.

By the time my wife began to wake – Gunner climbed onto the cot and rested his head onto her thigh. I wish I'd taken a picture. Priceless. Bell turned to look at me just sitting there… watching. In her morning voice and stretching asked "what ya doing – just sitting there?"

"Yeah… couldn't sleep. I've been thinking all night about what you said."

"Remind me… what did I say?"

"You asked about Gunner – I mean – what happens to him when the war is over."

"Oh – that's right…" she whispered with a sleepy sigh. "So – what does happen?" her voice turning to a little concern.

"I don't know" as I paused – remembering some of the rumors I'd heard the past few years… "But whatever it is – I know it isn't good."

"What do you mean?"

"I've heard rumors the military does away with them – or sometimes leaves them behind when the deployment is over… not good either way."

Bell sat up from the cot – Gunner sat and stretched – the blanket still half covering him. I handed her some clothes, and as she dressed she turned and saw Gunner watching her, but she laughed "um – do you mind?" and Gunner laid his head back down toward the blanket.

"I'll go talk to Braxton" my voice cracked. Bell stood and we hugged, and I could tell the unease about our boy was sinking in. Bell pulled her head back a little so she could look into my eyes… "Yes – Braxton will know – he always seems to know."

Wade could tell something was on our minds, and as usual – tried to keep things lively. But a cloud shadowed any attempt he made to lighten our mood. But he did share his scrambled eggs with Gunner.

Gunner and I walked Bell to work. Silent. She hugged Gunner tight, and then me. "Go talk to Braxton... see what you can find out."

"I will... I'll see what I can do."

**

Gunner's claws ticked softly against the plywood floor as he shifted at my feet. Braxton's office smelled of coffee and gun oil. Gunner and I waited patiently while our First Sergeant finished up some business. He looked up from his table – saw it was us, and then motioned with his head for us to enter. I asked, and he told me what the strict policy was... although he wasn't expecting this conversation... for a moment it was silent. A fan hummed, slicing the silence like a blade. Braxton rubbed his thumb against a paperclip before he finally spoke.

"Jack – the Military Working Dogs are technically 'owned' by the Air Force – that's why you did your training at Lackland." As Braxton continued – he confirmed my fear. The cloud – the dread I'd felt all night now loomed even darker.

I tried to make the arguments – Gunner the hero... Gunner the protector... "You've seen him out there, First Sergeant," I said, my voice cracking. "He's saved more of us than any man could count. He's not equipment. He's family."

But Braxton couldn't give us any comfort, and he couldn't give us any help. And his face somber, formal... yet compassionate did tell us...

"The only thing I can do – or request for you is... that we make this as easy on him as we can..."

"What do you mean?"

Braxton looked down at Gunner like he was looking at his own dog back home. His hand hovered for a moment, and then dropped it back to his desk. "Jack... what I mean is... when his time comes... we can make it peaceful, quiet, and as painless as we can. We can have medical give him the 'sho...'" as he stopped before he could finish the word, and paused – then swallowed hard... "The medicine that will let him go to sleep."

I stared at the floor. I was speechless. Gunner shifted and leaned against my leg. The career soldier who has seen a thousand battles showed us a side of him not many have seen. But he stood, walked around the table he used as a desk – knelt down by Gunner. His hands, scarred and calloused, softened as they stroked Gunner's fur. Then, almost like he couldn't stop himself, he pulled Gunner into a rough, awkward hug.

"If there is anything I can do – I will, but what you have to come to grips with is…" again he paused – looked Gunner in the eyes… "Is spending as much time with him as you can."

Gunner may not have understood the words, but I believe… Gunner knew what we were saying.

Braxton told me he'd give us some time off – especially after our day out in the sand…

The first place I took Gunner was… to see Bell.

She was brave. She was strong… but I could tell her heart was breaking.

"So – it's just – like that?" her voice showing her feelings… "There's nothing we can do? We just stand back and let them…" she couldn't even finish her words either.

There is a feeling of love and loyalty one feels when one of your own is threatened. It is a feeling that reaches so deep inside you that anger mixes with determination. It burns inside you and… I told Bell a saying I'd heard: "Courage isn't having the strength to go on… it's going on when you don't have the strength." I looked at her without the words that would comfort her, but what I said next surprised even me…

"It's not over when you lose… it's only over… when you quit."

Strength doesn't lie in the ability to avoid challenges - strength is your ability to rise above them after someone has pushed you down. I looked at Bell – then felt Gunner lean into me. "I hope they don't underestimate me because – they haven't survived half of what I've been through…"

I knew my next stop would be… Colonel Nettleton.

Nettleton leaned back, studied me for a long moment, and then looked at Gunner. "You know, Sergeant… most men here wouldn't last a week without a partner like him. That ought to count for something. I'll make sure your concerns don't stop here on this base. It's not much, but… it's a start." He leaned back in his chair – then continued: "Sergeant, I'm not going to lie to you. The policy is bigger than me - bigger than this camp. But men who survive long wars know one thing: policies change. Sometimes slow, sometimes too late… but they change. If you believe in this fight - for your partner - then don't quit. That's an order I *can* give you."

I'd spent the day talking to everyone I could. I didn't stop for lunch – I didn't stop for anything… except Bell.

Gunner and I went to find her so we could get some evening chow. We walked quiet – deep in thought. Deep with concern. Bell stopped for a second – paused… "You know that boy – that one you saved – Ben… Ben Carter?"

"Yeah – I remember." Thinking she was about to give me some more bad news…

"Well" she said with a slight smile… "He's going to make it. He went through surgery – he's going to make it. He'll be going home now… but you saved him."

The news was good, but still hollow at the moment… I may have been able to help that boy… but if it weren't for Gunner… Ben wouldn't have made it.

If it weren't for Gunner… I wouldn't be alive – I wouldn't have met my wife. He had touched so many lives – done so many things. How could the military think he was merely surplus property? Like he was something to be disposed of when they were through with him.

Bell and I walked into the mess-tent and there was Wade sitting at our usual table. Bell asked "what ya doing?"

"Just catching up on some letters – you know – writing mom and dad and such."

"Anything interesting you're telling them?" I asked…

"Naw – just about what's happened the past few days… about the combat – how Gunner kind of saved the day for so many people…"

Wade went on for a minute – he'd told his parents before how Gunner saved him the day wind blew away the flag we'd marked – how Gunner tackled him – to save him from the hidden land mine… he told us how much his parents loved Gunner for that – even though they never met him… how his parents would love to thank Gunner… in person.

That gave me an idea. Letters. Lots of letters.

"Wade – do you think your parents would help us?"

"Sure – they love you too Jack – what kind of help you asking for?"

"Wade – we need help saving Gunner."

Bell and I got Wade up to speed on everything I'd been doing today – the conversations – the disappointment… and Wade?" there wasn't anything Wade wouldn't do… for Gunner.

When he nodded, I knew we had the first real crack in the wall. One spark of action - letters from the people who had seen him in action, and the loved ones at home who appreciated what Gunner had done for them… And maybe, just maybe, it could start a fire no one could ignore.

Back at our tent – Bell started writing her family back in Grand Junction: "my dad owns a bike-shop – and maybe we can get all the guys there – even bikers from all over… to write letters too!"

"You're dad? Owns a bike shop?"

"Yeah – he sells motorcycles – builds 'em from nothing too."

Bell never ceased to surprise me. And right then – I knew I'd spend the rest of my life learning… and loving her.

I wrote home – hoping my family would appreciate how much help Gunner has been… hoping that they'd know… how much Gunner meant to me.

Father Patrick said he'd help. He knew 'dog' lovers all over the US who would think the military policy was not only inhumane, but ridiculous since these wonderful animals save so many lives.

I turned to Bell and smiled: "I'm determined to fight with every word, every letter, until no one can ignore us. Not now. Not ever."

We spent the day amid a shroud of darkness… and thanks to Wade sitting at a table – writing home… we now have a spark of hope… a single candle shining through the shadows… giving us hope that one little flame…

Becomes a burning firestorm.

Chapter 17

A Reach for The Stars

How does someone describe combat to someone who didn't want you to join the Army? It was never easy to tell my family back home what it was like every time I survived another combat mission. But every time I did – I gave all the credit to Gunner.

The dust hadn't even settled from our New Year's ambush when I put pen to paper. It wasn't easy for me to write about it. And it was hard reading mom's response – I could tell reading about combat and danger wasn't easy for her as well.

Mom wasn't long on words – she never has been, and I think I could tell she was thankful I had Gunner… thankful I had Bell to watch over me too.

With mom – you always had to read between the lines – she was seldom outright, and most often shy. But when she heard we may lose Gunner… Well… I think something in her may have changed. Quiet as she was, I could feel it even in the spaces between her words.

**

Every day the cargo planes would come and go. Deliveries. Everything from supplies to the daily mail – from our beans to our bullets. Deliveries that included our weekly supply of kibble for Gunner. I could count on it all… like clockwork. The quartermaster office made sure we had everything we needed.

Gunner's food and 'regulation' treats usually came on Wednesday, and when I went to pick up our weekly order… it wasn't there.

My stomach sank. Not just because he was hungry – Thanks to Ray that was fixable. But because it was the first real crack in the routine that told me how fragile this all was. One missed shipment? Could it mean delays? Was it confusion? Or was this something worse…

Was this – the something beyond my control that could hurt him? I rubbed his head, and he looked up at me, eyes wide, trusting, like he always did. I hated that I couldn't promise him anything.

For several months we'd all been writing home – rallying support from everywhere we could, but our voices weren't being heard. Our cries for help went nowhere. The heads of the Army – The Air Force… even the Pentagon… it seemed no one cared what would happen to our Gunner.

It was that one moment – the moment I feared the most. Looking into Gunner's eyes as he sat looking up at me. I sat on the edge of my cot holding a pad of paper – pen in hand… I looked into those eyes "I'm doing all I can – boy… I'm doing all I can…"

Gunner sat up straight – almost like he was 'coming to Attention' - like he was ready to follow any order… sharp – direct… obedient. But that moment his eyes softened and his stare into my eyes straight… I could almost feel him saying "*It's going to be 'ok' – I'm ready… I'll make this easy for you.*"

I put my writing aside and gave him a hug. My heart was breaking. I whispered into his ear "I wish I knew what to do – I wish I knew who to talk to."

While I hugged him – I looked over at my 'ammo-box' night stand and saw the letter. Gunner turned his head to watch me reach for it. And so it was… I opened the envelope from my mom – as few words as it was…

"*Son: I always told you to reach for the stars, but to keep your feet on the ground. So Jack, Son, reach high – higher than you have. Write to the one who has touched the stars – who is in a position to help. He is a God-fearing man. Write to Senator Garn… Mom.*"

Her words were short, plain, but they burned into me: reach for **the stars**. Not as a dream, but as a direction. She was pointing me straight at the one man who had actually been there.

I handed the letter to Bell – silent. She read it… and smiled. We all started to write again… and this time – we'd flood our Senators and Representatives offices with so many letters… we could only hope they wouldn't ignore us.

Wade took pictures of Gunner – with Bell, and me too – even the wedding picture with Gunner giving Bell away as a Bride. Wade's dad told us to make the letters as personal as we could… and we did.

We stayed up late – writing… we ate at the chow-hall – and kept writing. We talked with everyone we could – everyone who met Gunner, and fell in love with him too.

I think what surprised me the most was… stumbling onto Colonel Nettleton and Captain Knight – at their desks… writing letters also. They were getting their families, friends – even neighbors from home – hell – we all were… writing letters to our Senators and Reps. so we could save… our Gunner.

It felt like a storm building… one letter, then ten, then hundreds, and each envelope was another drop of rain. And maybe, just maybe, we could make it pour… and make a river become a flood.

I could tell Bell was tired – it was late… her hands stiff from writing, fingers smudged with ink. I told her we could go over and get some coffee – she thought that was a good idea. She gave a quick whistle – Gunner hopped up from the cot… she looked at him with so much love… and told him "We're doing all we can boy… we just can't wait for this storm to pass…"

I smiled… I may have even choked a little, but then – looking at them the fire ignited once again in me… and all I could say at that moment was "You don't need to wait for the storm to pass… when you are the storm."

I think Sgt. Collins – Ray – could tell we needed a break. And he smiled. And I was curious… he told me that he contacted some relatives in his old home town of Glasgow Montana… that even they were writing our Congressmen… so we all sat down and had some coffee.

Sleep wasn't easy, but exhaustion and worry began to take its toll on us. We all finally drifted off to sleep. But when I felt Bell's arm tugging at me I opened my eyes and saw it was Gunner tugging at Bells arm… making it move… I couldn't help but laugh… he told us it was morning.

Our day began like most – but breakfast was a surprise I wasn't expecting. As we were eating Wade boomed into the mess hall with a huge bag. You know – one of those huge duffle bags soldiers use… but this wasn't filled with gear, or uniforms… it was letters.

Letters from all over – from friends, family, from strangers who heard about our fight to save Gunner. Wade just smiled his huge farm-boy smile… and told us his dad – Lieutenant Callahan from the Sheriff's department… hung a sign on the interstate with the information… and a huge "Save Gunner" that even made our local news, and our Governor's office.

I looked at Wade who could hardly contain his smile and I asked him "are you crazy?"

He burst out laughing "Roses are Dead - Violets are Rotten… I **am** freaking crazy - or have you forgotten?"

He handed me one of the letters from the stack he'd poured out onto our table… "Jack – I thought you'd really like this one…"

I opened the envelope, and read… and was touched beyond words… Ben Carter – a young 18 year old boy who became a man in combat had written the President of the United States petitioning him… to save Gunner.

He told us that it was a dog who came to his aid without any concern for his own safety – that when he was most vulnerable… it was a dog who protected him from the fire and frenzy of hell. He told us it was a dog who comforted him when he thought he would face his last moments on earth. He wrote us and told us… that when he needed help – he reached for a hand… and found a paw.

I was always told "Big Boys Don't Cry" – but it was hard in that moment – reading the testimony of that – that man… for me to hold back the tears that were trying to escape.

And the letters from all over kept coming.

I sat alone in our tent while Bell took Gunner for a walk. I reached for my pad of paper, and wrote one more letter. I wrote to an Astronaut – the only Astronaut who was a sitting Senator – a Navy hero and Veteran who – if anyone could understand – he would. So I wrote him again, but didn't address the letter to his official office this time… Wade's dad thought it might mean a lot more… if he read it at home.

I included in the envelope a picture. Yes – it was a picture of Gunner, but it wasn't what you might think. I didn't know it at the time, but there was a moment when the heat and flames of combat calmed, and the reality of life and death were more evident than ever – that a dog showed the humanity and respect – who bowed in reverence alongside his human partner as he prayed for a ten year old boy who died… even after that little boy was trying to kill them.

"This – Senator Garn… This is the life we are trying to save. This isn't 'just a dog' – this is a soul worth saving. Senator Garn – we have no more time… you are our only hope."

Alone – with pen in hand… my tears fell as I finished these words because… Bell and I just received our final transfer orders… and discharge approval. We were going home, and the medical office informed us… they received Gunner's final package. "The Shot."

"How do you fight an enemy you can't see, can't out-shoot, and can't outrun? Bureaucracy was the cruelest battlefield yet."

Bell was walking Gunner – she wanted some time alone with him. We were leaving in two days, and Gunner had an appointment – that we were putting off as long as we could. But time ran out, and everyone could feel it…

It was Buddy all over again, but this time it wasn't a gamble – it was real.

The afternoon dragged. Every tick of the clock echoed like a drum in my head. Gunner now lay at my feet, ears twitching at the distant hum of the camp, and I couldn't shake the feeling that every second we waited was a second too long.

I only had two hours until we would walk our final patrol. It was only two hours we had together until Gunner would walk his final walk down Wolf Street.

Bell stepped into the tent – we didn't need words… they wouldn't come anyway. We just wanted to be alone and sit in silence… with our Gunner.

It was quiet… it was reverent. Until…

We heard a knock on our tent post. Then the company clerk appeared at the tent flap, looking flustered. "Sergeant Duncan? Senator Garn is on the line. He asked for you personally."

I froze. For a second, my brain refused to process. Garn? The Senator? On the phone? Now? Would this be the horror – the worst news we could get – that there was nothing he could do?

Bell stayed with Gunner – and the company clerk walked me to the office.

I picked up the handset, and a calm, familiar voice came through. "Sergeant Duncan? This is Jake Garn. I understand there's a matter regarding your dog…"

I swallowed hard, words lodged in my throat. "Senator… I… yes, sir… I… thank you for calling…"

"There's no time to waste, Jack. I've reviewed everything, and I can tell you this – Gunner's orders will be ready in a couple of hours. You and Bell will be able to adopt him. He's coming home with you."

I felt the air leave my lungs. My legs nearly gave way.

"You heard me right," Garn continued. "You've done everything right. You've fought for him, written, gathered support, and most importantly… you never quit. I'm making sure no one overlooks that now."

I nodded, barely able to speak. "Senator… sir… I… thank you… I… I don't know what to say…"

"Say you'll keep reaching for the stars, Sergeant," he said with a laugh. "You've already saved one hero. Keep making sure others get the chance."

By the time I hung up, my hands were shaking. My legs felt weak, but I ran.

I opened the tent - Bell sitting on the cot holding Gunner, eyes filled with tears… I simply nodded toward Gunner, still lying at her side, his tail wagging slightly. I smiled.

"So we get to keep him?" she laughed.

I could only nod, but then found the words I thought would never come. "He's ours. Gunner's ours. The orders… they're coming."

Gunner leapt into my lap, and I hugged him tighter than I ever had before. Bell's laughter, her relief, filled the tent, but I couldn't stop staring at him, wondering if I'd ever feel this way about anything again. We did it. Against all the impossible odds… we did it.

Wade… of all things… was waiting just outside and couldn't help but hear… it was a moment words cannot describe – that only a heart can feel.

I wrote a little note home – quick, short, and to the point:

"Mom, we reached for the stars… and this time, they reached back… I thought I was out of fight… but maybe fight isn't what saved him. Maybe it was love. Maybe it was all of us."

When we walked into the mess tent for dinner… with Gunner's orders in hand…

The whole camp cheered.

Chapter 18

Home

The last few miles of a trip… are the longest.

Gunner may not have known what this new word was. It was something we've said before, but now it meant something different. We kept saying it – not quite foreign yet now? Comforting. He could, however; tell something was changing.

A bustling city of canvas and plywood began to disappear – the planes delivering supplies were now taking away the remnants of a place that would soon be nothing more than a mark on a map…

What was once a hive of noise and movement with convoys grinding through dust, and generators humming, and even voices calling over the rattle of aircraft… was now unraveling at the seams.

But for us it was a life where we met, fell in love, and survived. The place where holidays were cobbled together from scraps, where losses cut deeper than we knew possible, and where strength revealed itself in ways we never expected.

I paused in the doorway of our tent, watching Bell fold the last of her few clothes into her duffle bag. Gunner nosed at the bag, sniffing, tail thumping, and then glanced up at me as if to ask, "*are we really leaving?*"

"We are, buddy," I whispered, rubbing his ears. "We are."

He leaned into my hand, trusting, like always.

Our life together fit into two large bags. We sat together for just a minute longer with the last of what little we had… we sat on empty cots holding hands – holding onto the memories… good and bad…

Gunner would tilt his head and listen every time we said it. We could tell he wondered what it meant, because soon we would be…

Home.

Our orders told us we'd be back at Diego Garcia for a week for out-processing and final discharge orders. After that… the big leap. Wade was scheduled to leave earlier than us. That morning he was double-checking his duffel, humming something off-key. He looked up and caught my eye.

"You know," he said, grinning, "for a guy who doesn't talk much, I'm gonna miss hearing your voice."

I smirked. "You never stop talking, Wade. I think you'll be fine."

He laughed, but when he came over and pulled me into a bear hug, the humor fell away. Bell hugged him next, and even Gunner pressed his head against Wade's leg like he knew this was goodbye.

"Don't you worry," Wade said, his voice thick. "I'll be waiting on the other side."

And just like that, he was gone.

The last few miles had begun.

The flight out was quiet. Not somber, not heavy… just quiet in a way none of us were used to. No incoming chatter on the radio. No gunfire in the distance. Just the hum of the engines, steady and constant, like a lullaby we didn't trust yet.

When the wheels finally touched down on Diego Garcia, Gunner was the first to stir. He pressed his nose to the tiny window, tail thumping like he'd just discovered a whole new world. And maybe he had.

Palm trees swayed against the breeze, the air thick with salt instead of dust, and for the first time in months the horizon wasn't an endless sea of dirt, rock, and sand – or even jagged with mountains or cloaked in smoke. It was open, endless… and blue.

Bell stepped off the plane first and laughed - a sound I hadn't heard in a long time where she didn't have an edge of fatigue behind it. She bent down, pulled her boots off right there on the tarmac, and said, "If I have to wait one more minute to feel sand between my toes, I might lose my mind."

Gunner beat her to it. The minute we hit the beach, he seemed to remember our time here before. He bounded forward, paws sinking into white sand like it was made just for him. He darted in circles, nose down, tail high, then froze when a wave rolled in and licked his feet. He tilted his head, and gave it the side-eye, barked once, then jumped straight into the foam like he'd been waiting for this moment all his life.

We stood there. We were three silhouettes on a shoreline that didn't know our names, or didn't care about our scars, and didn't ask for our stories. For the first time, the sky was filled with stars that no one was shooting at.

Bell slid her hand into mine. "Do you realize," she whispered, "this is the first time since we met that I don't feel like we're counting down?" She paused again – and with eyes wide and an even bigger smile… "This is the first time since we met – we've been anywhere other than the desert!"

I squeezed her hand, still watching Gunner chase waves. "Yeah," I said. "Feels like… maybe time finally stopped trying to kill us."

And under that vast sky, with Gunner racing free, and Bell beside me, I believed it.

The week on Diego Garcia felt strange, like living in two worlds at once. On one side, there was paradise with palm trees, beaches, food that didn't come from a mess line, and stars we could finally admire without flinching. On the other side, there was paperwork, lines, signatures, and the endless shuffle of a system that wanted every box checked before it let you go.

Bell and I carried folders thick with forms that seemed to multiply overnight. Medical evaluations, equipment turn-ins, final clearance briefings – and questions why Bell's name changed while she was deployed… but we had the documents… It was like someone took our entire lives, broke them into pages, and asked us to sign off on every moment.

Through it all, Gunner followed close, tail wagging like he didn't care if we had to wait in line for three hours… as long as he was still with us. And that made all the difference.

The first real jolt came when the clerk at medical tried to separate him from us. "The dog goes over there," she said, pointing toward another door.

I felt my throat tighten, but before I could speak, Bell squared her shoulders and cut in. "No, ma'am. He's not 'the dog.' He's Corporal Gunner. He's with us."

The woman blinked, opened her mouth, and then shut it again. She glanced at our paperwork, saw the fresh adoption orders signed and stamped, and finally waved us through. Gunner trotted beside us like he'd won a medal. Maybe he had.

He'd found us on that little island. Wade came by our quarters to say goodbye. His orders had him leaving for The States earlier than us, back to his family. He slapped me on the back with that grin of his, but his eyes gave him away. He was going to miss us. He crouched down to scratch Gunner behind the ears.

"Take care of them, buddy," Wade said softly. Gunner licked his hand, like he understood. Maybe he did.

When Wade walked off, duffel over his shoulder, Bell slipped her arm through mine. "It feels like we're leaving pieces of ourselves everywhere we go," she whispered.

I nodded. "Maybe that's how it works. We leave pieces... and bring others home."

The morning of departure came quicker than either of us wanted. Our duffels were packed, paperwork stamped in triplicate, and Gunner had a brand-new set of tags clinking softly against his collar.

The transport sat on the tarmac, engines whining, heat shimmering off the runway. We climbed the ramp slowly, each step feeling like it carried the weight of a thousand memories. Gunner trotted ahead, tail wagging like he was the one leading us home.

Inside, the rows of seats lined both sides of the isle. Bell settled in by me, Gunner curling up at her boots. I reached down, scratched his ears, and whispered, "No more goodbyes, boy. Only hellos from here on out."

The crew chief gave the signal, and the doors clanged shut. The vibration built under our feet as the engines roared to full power. Bell slipped her hand into mine, and for the first time in a long while, I felt the future rushing toward us instead of away.

As the plane lifted off, Diego Garcia shrank into a strip of green in a sea of blue. The island, with all its scars and secrets, slid behind us. Ahead was home, family, new beginnings, and the promise that Gunner would be with us through it all.

I leaned back, feeling the weight finally begin to lift from my chest. For the first time, I believed it: we were really going home.

The wheels screeched against the runway, and the cabin erupted with cheers and nervous laughter. Bell gripped my arm, eyes wide and shining, and Gunner sat up as if he knew exactly what those sounds meant. He gave one sharp bark that made half the soldiers laugh. "Yeah, buddy," I whispered. "We made it."

When the ramp dropped, the cool mountain air rushed in, carrying with it a smell I hadn't realized I missed. I could smell the dry sage, pine on the wind, and something that just said home.

The hangar was packed. Flags waved, signs lifted above the crowd like Welcome Home Daddy! We Missed You! - And the noise of families reunited hit like thunder.

And then I saw them. My mom. My brothers and sisters. And standing right beside them, a little nervous but smiling big, was Bell's family, all the way from Grand Junction. Wade was already there too, standing with his folks, then spinning around to hug Bell's mother like he'd known her for years.

Bell froze for a second, taking it all in. "Jack…" she whispered, voice breaking. "They… they came."

I squeezed her hand. "Go to them."

We walked forward together - Bell, me, and Gunner prancing between us like he owned the runway. My mom's tears ran freely the second she laid eyes on us. Bell's mother stepped forward, arms wide, pulling her daughter into a hug that swallowed them both.

Bell's dad shook my hand while her mom hugged me - like I was already part of the family, then they bent down to scratch Gunner's ears, grinning through tears.

And for the first time, all the lines that used to separate us - my family, Bell's family, Wade's family – they all blurred together in one messy, joyful reunion.

"They've been waiting a long time to meet you," Bell said softly in my ear.

She looked around, laughter spilling out between tears. "I feel like we're bringing them all together… like Gunner really is our child, bringing families home."

I smiled. "That's because he is."

Gunner barked once more, tail wagging so hard it nearly knocked over one of the welcome signs. Everyone laughed, and in that moment, I knew: this wasn't just a return. This was a beginning.

Gunner leaned into me as we watched our families come together. I can't explain why, but through the crowds I kept looking. I knew he wouldn't be there, but still… I was looking to see – if I could see Charlie.

Bell's dad was there. Wade's dad was there… I didn't have one. And maybe that's why I missed seeing him.

I felt a slap on my back – Wade's dad – Lieutenant Callahan – smiled, and without words knew what I was thinking. "I know son – I knew you'd want to see him, and later on – I'll take you there."

I've known Wade's dad since I was in kindergarten. I'd learned how to tell when he was keeping a secret. There was a beat in his step I'd only seen – the times before when… he wanted to surprise someone.

But maybe it was we'd returned home – or maybe it was we all had a little more light in our steps, but I could feel something. And I was right.

We walked through the maze of military one last time, and weaved our way through traffic down the Interstate. I had an hour on the last stretch of road… to home.

Sixty minutes may not seem like a long time. but in those sixty minutes I had time to reflect on the people back at camp "Wolf Pack" like Father Patrick, Colonel Nettleton, Captain Knight, Sgt. Braxton – and Ray… all the people that became a part of our lives… that made our lives a little better in a place where we faced the worst, and came out smiling.

Gunner rested his eyes, Bell held my hand, and my throat tightened a little – I may have coughed trying to hide my thoughts as we passed by the old ranch…

It was now empty – boarded and dry. It looked lonely like it missed having a family… like it missed Charlie.

It was sixty minutes of mixed feelings and blended memories – of both war, and home.

Wade's dad just smiled when we passed by the little road that led to my childhood home.

Our little convoy cruised on paved roads – the dirt and dust of the desert now behind us… these roads now led us to our local High School… and in the distance – I no longer heard the thunder of war… but the rush of cheers from the stadium… and saw the banners…

WELCOME HOME – WE SAVED GUNNER

Bell couldn't believe her eyes – neither could I. We both hugged Gunner as we drove into the stadium – with a dog that brought us together…

And united a community.

Chapter 19

Homestead

Wade and I were childhood friends turned soldiers; Bell was the light who met us under desert stars halfway across the world. Gunner was the four-legged soldier turned partner… and became family.

Together, we found purpose again - whether in uniform or at home. But peace… that feeling of peace never seemed to last for long.

You can almost forget the sounds of battle… when the wind moves through the pines and the sun catches the porch rail just right. My wife says that's what peace looks like - that quiet stretch after the noise of war is finally gone.

We were new to a life we thought was long gone, and our dog Gunner was adjusting to a life without the fear of being left behind. The community came together to celebrate saving him, and when the excitement calmed – quiet filled the night air.

Wade and I grew up, went to war, and somehow survived. Through the rigors of military life, I held onto what I knew as a boy, and found something new along the way. A partnership. A purpose. Not just with the dog the Army assigned to me, but with the woman who became my anchor… my wife.

Isabel - or Bell - wasn't just another partner. She was my life. A life my best friend Wade and I met among chaos, war, and we endured together until the noise of that war finally fell silent.

The quiet stirs memories of a life before we survived combat, and then – the quiet reminds me to be cautious… since tranquility is temporary.

But old habits die hard. Even back here at home, I still scan the tree line before I sit down. Still park the truck facing the road, and I still reach for the sidearm that isn't there.

That's when Gunner growled - low, quiet, deliberate.

He was standing at the edge of the field, eyes locked on the tree line. I couldn't see what he saw, but I'd learned to trust that dog's instincts more than most men I'd served with. Bell called from the porch, asking what it was.

"Not sure," I said. "Could be a deer. Could be something else."

We were only kids still, but we grew up fast in the shadows of combat. Coming home should've meant peace. Instead, it felt like a layover between wars. One was fought out in the Deserts of Iraq, and the other was the one that waited quietly inside us… not sure of what the future held.

After my wife and I left the Army, we needed a place to start over. For a while, we stayed in my old room at my mom's house. It was the same room where I'd grown up. The gun rack still hung on the wall, and the scuffed floorboards still carried the faint sound of my old dog Buddy pacing in the night. It was a room full of memories, and of the quiet longing for Bell and me to build something of our own.

Even though Gunner was making new memories where Buddy used to sleep – it still felt like there was something missing – something more to come. It felt like home, but then again… It didn't feel like home anymore. Maybe it never would again.

Bell had just finished her shift at the hospital, and I was driving her back to my mom's place when we passed the old farm where I used to work. "Ol' man Hawkins," Charlie, was more than just a boss - he filled in for the father I never really had. He seemed to know what I needed before I did and taught me lessons that should've come from the man who should have raised me.

As we rolled by, I slowed the truck, staring out across the weathered fences and empty corrals. That place wasn't just land and barns - it was where I'd learned what it meant to grow up, to work, and to become who I am.

She'd heard me tell of the stories – the memories of this place… but now? The fields were gone. They were carved up by survey flags and half-poured driveways, but the old house where Charlie lived still stood. It looked lonely - gray and stubborn, like it was holding its ground.

I slowed the truck even more as we passed by the old ranch, and we stopped. Developers had been circling it for months, waiting to flatten the last bit of history. Bell looked at me and said, *"It doesn't deserve to die like that."*

She was right.

Bell didn't know Charlie the way I did. Not really. She'd heard the stories, though. Everyone in our town knew *something* about him.

He wasn't blood, but he treated me and Wade like we were his own. We spent every summer and after school baling hay, fixing fences, and learning the kind of lessons no school ever taught. Charlie didn't talk much about God or war, but he believed in work, and in keeping your word. That farm was his proof of both.

When he passed, something in that land went quiet too. Wade and I promised we'd keep it alive, but life had other plans. Then came Iraq and the long days, the noise, and the heat that could peel the skin off a tank. We thought we'd seen everything there was to see. But what I learned out there wasn't about killing; it was about *losing*.

You don't come back from that kind of lesson the same.

Maybe that's why I can't stand seeing Charlie's place die like this. He built it with his hands. The least I can do is fight to save it with mine.

We stopped alongside the road and got out of the truck. Bell simply watched as I kicked a few rocks where the pavement met the gravel driveway. I stood in silence remembering the ranch that used to be – feeling the nose of the future now sniffing at my hand. Gunner…

Gunner looked over toward the now ragged barbed wire barely clinging to the fence post. He started sniffing like he was trying to find the memories of my youth somewhere in the weeds.

"What ya lookin' for boy" I chuckled… then I stepped over to the fence post and kicked away a few weeds and found that old weathered plank… with the wood-burned writing…

"Ol' Charlie Hawkins Place"

I felt a hand on my shoulder as I held that memory in my hands – turned to see a smile that silently said 'I want to know your history as much as you want to remember it.' I reached for her hand and we walked up the drive – the gravel where each pebble told a story, and past the trees that clung to the life of a thousand tales.

I stood by the kitchen Window. I peered through the foggy glass… As if I could still see Charlie talking to me – and my childhood friend Wade… as we would sit with Charlie at the table – a memory playing out in my mind like watching a movie… like I was there – all over again.

The old kitchen door creaked the same way it always had - like it was clearing its throat before letting you in. The smell hit me first: dust, cedar, and something faintly sweet, like old apples left too long in a cellar.

I used to know every nook and cranny of this place. I could sneak in without a sound, and through the kitchen door that stuck halfway, or the side window near the tack room, where the latch never quite caught.

Wade and I once thought this house was a castle. Every creak was a secret passage. Every shadow had a story.

Gunner trotted ahead, tail low, sniffing like he was tracing ghosts. It was like he could tell… I'd been here before. Bell stood in the doorway, taking it all in - the rustic beams, the sunlight slicing through gaps in the ragged curtains, the quiet weight of years.

I ran my hand along the old stair rail - the one Charlie made himself from a fallen cottonwood. He used to say, *"If you build something right, it'll outlive you - and that's the point."*

In the living room, the floorboards still groaned in the same spots. My boots remembered where to step, and where *not* to. I knelt down near the old stone hearth of the fireplace and pried up the loose board that hid what I once thought was treasure.

There it was. It was still wrapped in oil-cloth and dust: the old **Colt .45 Peacemaker**. I remembered the day Charlie first showed the old 'Cowboy Six-Shooter' to me. He said it wasn't about what a gun could do, but about the kind of man who carried it. "Respect it, or don't touch it," he'd told me. "This one's seen more years of peace than war - and that's how it oughta stay."

Bell knelt beside me, eyes wide. "You kept this secret all these years?"

I smiled. "Didn't have to. The house remembered for me."

She laughed softly - that kind of laugh that says she understands more than she lets on.

Gunner lay down by the fireplace; head on his paws, like he'd already claimed the spot. He looked natural – resting beneath the mantle where the folded flag that once draped across Charlie's son still sat – displayed with pride – reminded me of all that was lost, and all that Charlie wanted to remember. Now more than ever – this place held me in a cradle of love – of memories…

For the first time in a long while, I felt like I was home. Not the kind you inherit - the kind you *earn back*. Bell and I held onto the memories I'd lived as we held each other – Gunner at our feet. It was quiet – it just felt right. It was one moment of peace that wrapped us in the warm blanket of comfort I knew as a child, until…

Gunner stood sharp – intent, and that low rumble from his deep chest told me – **no** – warned me in the language I learned to listen to… then he started slowly toward the old kitchen door.

I could see shadows cast onto the half opened door – Gunner breaking into a near frenzy – a man in jeans, an orange safety vest - now falling back in fear – his hard-hat bouncing onto the wooden porch.

"Gunner — **on me**. Heel!"

Gunner – ever true to his Army training - came instantly to my left side, hackles still raised. Bell caught her breath, eyes wide from the surprise. Call it instinct – or call it reflexes trained through surviving combat – I don't know… I was still holding Charlie's old Colt .45 at a low ready when the man threw up his hands and hollered, "Don't shoot!" He froze, half sitting from falling back onto the porch - his eyes as big as dinner plates.

I scanned quickly for any threats while Gunner's eyes locked onto the construction worker – his low rumble still echoing against the porch. I slid the Peacemaker into my belt, along the small of my back, and asked who he was.

He said he was with the construction company - just making sure no one was in the building before demolition started.

I tossed Bell the truck keys. "Go find help. Call Wade - maybe his dad. They can't… they *shouldn't* do this."

She didn't hesitate. Isabel turned and ran down the path toward the truck. I heard the gravel crunch, then the distant roar of the engine fading down the road.

I turned back to the man, still trying to collect himself on the porch. "You're not demolishing this house," I said flatly. "I know the former owner's family - up in Wyoming - and I know damn well they wouldn't sell this part of the property."

He said nothing. Just stared, uncertain.

I wasn't leaving until I knew for sure this old place - run down as it might be - was safe. I wasn't about to let this memory collapse into dust, not while I could still stand for it.

Gunner stayed tight at my side as we watched the man walk back toward the ridge where the equipment sat idle. Gunner and I watched from the kitchen window – as all the construction workers seemed to be watching… us.

For a moment - and only a moment - old Charlie's place was safe.

I could feel the longing in my chest, the kind that settles heavy when you realize some ghosts never leave. The air smelled of rain and sawdust, and I wished my childhood friend - my brother in arms, Wade - was standing here beside me, the way he always used to.

I stayed like that for what felt like hours - maybe it was only one, maybe two - just watching. The hum of crickets faded into the low creak of the porch boards beneath my boots. I was still staring out across the field when I heard tires crunching gravel again.

At first, I thought the workers had called in reinforcements, but when I turned, I saw Bell driving my old family pickup, dust trailing behind her like a comet's tail. Right behind her came an SUV from the Sheriff's Department.

Gunner's ears perked up - and before I could say a word, he bolted through the door, his tail high and he barked sharp.

"Gunner! Heel!" I called out, but his excitement was already justified.

Wade climbed out of the passenger side of the truck, that same half-smirk spread across his face - the one that always showed up when the world was trying to tell him 'not to.' **"I'm here** for ya bro" he yelled out - Bell was right beside him, calm but determined, her hand brushing dust from her jeans.

Then, from the Sheriff's SUV, stepped Lt. Callahan - Wade's dad.

He hadn't changed much from when Wade and I were young, and the time since we'd gotten home from the military. He still carried himself like a man who expected the world to answer when he spoke. He was another who… took me in as his own – when he didn't have to.

His voice was even, and steady. "Son," he said, glancing between his son Wade and me, "I hear we've got a bit of a misunderstanding about this old place."

"Misunderstanding's one word for it," I said… my voice low.

Callahan looked over the roof of his SUV toward the workers still loitering near their truck, then back at me. "Developers don't own this parcel yet," he said.

"The paperwork's tied up. So until they can prove this parcel is part of the development, nobody's tearing down a damn thing."

Relief hit me slow, like rain after a drought.

Bell smiled softly, resting a hand on my arm. Wade clapped me on the shoulder. "Guess we just bought ourselves a little time, brother."

I nodded, looking back at the old farmhouse - paint peeling, roof needing some repair, but still standing proud against the wind.

"Time," I said quietly, "might be all we need."

**

The following week, Wade and his dad took us for a ride to see Charlie. We met Calvin Hawkins at his ranch - north end of the Big Horn Mountains in Wyoming. Charlie's brother – well… he looked older than I remembered. It had been more than five years or so since we'd last met, but he had the same quiet strength that lived behind his eyes.

Calvin led us to the small family cemetery on their ranch, and the moment felt sacred in a way I'll never forget. I knelt and carefully placed the flag – the one they had given Charlie when his son was laid to rest after Vietnam, beneath the inscription on the stone:

Charles J. Hawkins, Sr.

"Old Charlie"

I stood there a long moment, looking at his name, thinking of the man he was… and the son he lost. Then I came to attention and offered a silent salute. Before I stepped back, I noticed Bell, Wade, his father, and even Gunner beside them…

All standing at attention, returning the salute.

Calvin – I believe… appreciated how much we loved Charlie. He took us into his big ranch house… He didn't waste words. "I figured one day you'd come back," he said, handing me an old envelope. The deed, worn and yellowed at the folds. "Charlie told me, before he passed… "If that boy ever comes home, the place is his - so long as he's got the heart to make it live again."

I couldn't find words. Bell slipped her hand into mine. Gunner sat between us, tail thumping lightly against the porch boards.

Calvin smiled, looking out over the pasture. "Land's not just dirt, son. It remembers who loved it."

We signed the papers right there at his kitchen table, over coffee that tasted like campfire smoke and a hundred good memories… yes – the memories of a boy who learned lessons from a horse, and…

Before we left to come home – I walked once more down the corridor of stalls in Calvin's big barn, and I leaned against the half-door of a stall and I smiled. The horse turned slightly with the simple shifts of his hoofs, and our eyes locked one more time.

We stood in silence. No words were needed. The stallion inched his way to me, and hugged me with his neck. We remembered each other, and in those memories – the connection I made with Smokey Joe filled my heart once more. And one more time the dust and wind from the trail we rode together blurred my eyes.

It was a moment and a memory that will live forever. I slid my boots against the barn floor – the planks creaking slightly. And before I could walk away, Joe turned his head one last time… gave me that smirk, and we smiled.

I walked out to our truck – Calvin was giving Bell one last hug, and Gunner a final scratch behind the ears. Bell smiled – and I could tell she knew what Calvin did – that my moment with Smokey Joe was something I needed… alone.

It was only a couple of days later, and we stood in front of the old house - our house now. While the sun dipped low behind the trees. Bell leaned against the porch rail; Gunner trotted through the weeds like he was already on patrol.

The place still smelled of dust and pine, and somewhere deep inside those walls, I could almost hear Charlie's laugh.

"For the first time," I said quietly, "it feels like we're not just coming home… we *are* home."

Bell smiled. "Then let's make it live again."

We watched the last light fade over the field, the same light I'd chased as a boy. It felt like the past had handed me one more chance - and I wasn't about to waste it.

Chapter 20

Dads And Fathers

I was alone in my thoughts… but only for a moment. I glanced over to see Gunner's head resting on Bell's lap while the open road stretched across four hours of open sky. My wife stirred and then leaned her head just enough to gaze out the window taking in the picture – the stillness… the silence that said more than words.

The mountain passes, desert – even the highway itself – all had that kind of quiet that wasn't empty. It was alive in its own way – wind chasing tumbleweeds, the smell of sage, and the faint hum of the tires against the road like a soft heartbeat beneath us.

We didn't say much. We didn't need to. Every mile east toward Grand Junction was like shedding another layer of the war – the noise, the discipline, and the ghosts. Bell had her roots in this land. I could see it in the way her eyes softened when the red cliffs started rising in the distance.

Gunner gave a low sigh and adjusted himself, his muzzle sliding off Bell's knee onto the seat. She smiled, brushing her hand over his ears – a small gesture, but it said everything about who she was. Steady. Gentle. Capable of healing just by being near.

"Dad's probably out back, covered in grease," she said, breaking the long silence. "Then it's a good thing I wore my old boots," I answered, and she laughed. It felt good to hear that sound without any weight behind it.

By the time we rolled into the outskirts of Grand Junction, the world had shifted from open desert to small-town edges – faded billboards, old pickup trucks. The kind of place where time never felt in a hurry. We turned off the main road, and gravel popped under the tires as the old sign came into view: Bell smiled, a little wistful. "He never did change that sign."

When we pulled into the gravel lot beside her father's shop, the old sign still read *Carter's Motorworks – Custom Harley & Repair.* The place smelled like oil and leather, and the sound of an "oldies" rock station drifted faintly from the open bay doors. It was the kind of place where work and art were the same thing – where a man's hands told his story more than his words ever could.

I put the truck in park and stepped out. The shop looked the same as the last picture Bell had shown me – corrugated metal walls sun-bleached to silver, a row of bikes out front like sentinels at attention.

Gunner jumped down from the cab and stretched, his nose working the air. He trotted a few feet ahead, ears perked, tail slow and curious as if he knew he was on new ground but could sense we were safe here.

For a moment, I just stood there – taking it in. This wasn't war. This wasn't survival. It was life – loud, ordinary, and somehow… beautiful.

Bell slipped her arm around mine. "Welcome to my world," she said softly.

That's when the sound of a socket wrench clanged against a lift inside the open bay doors, Bell's father stepped out from under a raised bike, wiping his hands on a rag. "Well, I'll be damned," he said, grinning through the beard he never quite managed to trim evenly. "You brought that old war dog too?"

"Wouldn't have it any other way," I said. Gunner barked once, tail thumping against the truck bed.

He reached out, shook my hand, then looked me all over again the way only a man who's seen years can – not judging, just knowing. "You look like you've been carrying too much."

I shrugged. "Guess I'm still learning how to set it down." He nodded, and then gestured toward the garage. "Maybe a good ride'll help."

Inside, he uncovered a gleaming Harley – black and chrome, but with age in its bones. "This one's been waiting for someone who'll ride it right," he said. "Consider it a wedding gift. She's got spirit – you'll know what I mean when you fire her up."

Bell rolled her eyes. "Dad, you can't just *give* him a bike." He smiled. "You think I don't know a rider when I see one? You marry a man like that, you better expect him to come with horsepower."

I ran my hand along the tank, feeling the cool metal under my fingers. The smell of fuel, oil, and old leather was grounding. For a second, I wasn't lost anymore. I belonged to something more – family. It may have been the gesture of being accepted through something mechanical, alive, simple.

Bell's dad gave me a slap on the back – nodded to Bell "how about we let him ride it – mamma's probably got some dinner ready – he can follow us home…" as he now looked down at Gunner… "You think he'll let me ride with ya Bell?"

"He'll be fine dad – so will you – I think he can tell you're ok."

Gunner looked at me like I needed to give him permission to ride with Bell's dad – I nosed toward the truck as I carefully swung my leg over the saddle – it was almost like it was made – just for me. It felt like home. Gunner sat between Bell and her dad… I just chuckled. Then…

The sound of thunder echoed through the garage – I saw Gunner jump a little. The smile on Bell's face told me more than a thousand words could have… like she was happy… that I was happy.

The smell of something home-cooked met us before the screen door even swung open. Bell's mom stood there with a dishtowel draped over her shoulder, that easy kind of smile people get when they've learned to live through storms and keep right on loving anyway. The kitchen light poured out into the dusk like a welcome sign.

"Come in, come in," she said, wiping her hands. "So good to see you Jack – and how is our little Gunner?"

Before I could answer, Bell stood in the doorway with a pleasant smirk "Um – well hello mom…" as Bell's mom chuckled then turned to give her a hug.

Gunner had already claimed his spot near the table, tail thumping on the floor. Bell's mom laughed softly. "He knows where the heart of the house is."

Dinner was simple… meatloaf, mashed potatoes, green beans, the kind that sticks to your ribs and calms something restless inside you. Bell sat across from me, barefoot, her hair loose – relaxed. The talk drifted easy: stories about her growing up out here, her dad's old bikes, the year the water line from the City froze and "ol man" Carter – or "J.D." as some would call him – he had to haul water in from town. I didn't say much. Just watched and listened, trying to take in the rhythm of it all - the easy laughter, the little looks between them that said *this is what home sounds like.*

When the plates were cleared, Bell's mom poured us coffee. She sat down beside her husband, then looked at me the way only a mother can – straight through. "You've seen some hard things, haven't you, Jack?"

I hesitated, nodded once. "Yes, ma'am." She reached over and patted my hand. "You don't have to talk about 'em tonight. Just know you're safe here. That's enough."

I swallowed hard and nodded again, but the lump in my throat didn't move.

The next morning – the sun crested the horizon and the fields were turning gold. Gunner made sure I knew that the aroma of coffee that whiffed through the house meant he was about to get some breakfast too.

Army life meant breakfast was usually 'rushed.' I was about to 'chow-down' and start eating – remembering that old Army adage – "if you can taste your food – you're eating to slow" – but was kindly reminded that "Grace" always comes before a meal…

After my polite apology – and Bell's laughter – Bell's dad told her mom not to be too hard on me. Bell chuckled looking at the two of us sitting together and told her dad – "he's just like you pop – hiding faith behind leather and war stories."

We enjoyed another meal. Bell's dad looked over at me and said, "Ever ridden a Harley like that before?" I grinned. "Not since last night." "Well," he said, finishing his plate – "that wasn't a real ride – how about the girls babysit Gunner, and we let ya open her up…"

He fired up his own bike, an older one that still showed the miles of a man who fixed things with his hands instead of replacing them. We rolled out side by side, the wind tugging at my jacket, the world opening up in front of us. For a while, neither of us said a word. The road did the talking. Its hum - steady and forgiving.

Halfway down the road just outside of town, Bell's dad slowed, turned toward me, his voice cutting through the engine noise. "You remind me a lot of myself at your age," he said. "Difference is" as he paused with a welcoming smile - "I had a father who helped me find my footing again. You didn't, not right away at least." He let that hang for a beat, then added, "Sometimes life hands you another one along the way. Doesn't mean the others – or the old ones didn't matter - it just means the story keeps building."

Something in me eased then - like a knot loosening. I looked over and saw him smile, the kind of smile a man gives when he's not trying to fix you… but - just to walk beside you for a while.

The Harley rumbled steady beneath me, that deep, living heartbeat of the road. Every mile felt like I was shedding something… grief, guilt, or maybe even the ghosts.

When we finally rolled into the driveway, I cut the engine and sat there a second, watching the dust settle around the tires. Bell walked out and stood beside me, leaning on my shoulder with that familiar grin. "Looks like you handled the Harley like you were born on it," she said. I shrugged. "Maybe I just needed the right road." She smiled, softer this time. "Well… it suits you. You look better in motion than standing still."

Bell's dad came up beside us, wiping his hands on his pants, eyes bright in the sunlight. "Keep her a while," he said, nodding toward the bike. "I think she likes you."

As Bell walked with her dad, and they headed inside the house, I stayed – sitting on the bike a moment longer, listening to the breeze play its melody through the trees, and whisper through the fields. Gunner came to sit beside me, tail brushing the gravel.

I looked out across the valley, that old ache stirring again - but softer this time. For the first time in a long while, I didn't feel I was missing what Wade always had. Maybe that's what another dad really is - someone who meets you halfway and lets the road carry the rest.

A week passed in a blur of grease, laughter, and quiet lessons. I learned how to balance a bike on its stand, how to read the tension in a chain, how to coax stubborn engines into life, but it wasn't just mechanics. It was about bonding. It was watching Bell in her element, confident and steady, moving through her father's shop like it was a second home, and seeing her parents' pride in the small things she did, and the accomplishments she conquered. It was like I was getting to know the woman I fell in love with by seeing her in the world she came from – and I was a part of it.

Evenings were spent around their worn kitchen table, sharing meals, telling stories, and listening to the hum of the town settle outside. By the end of the week, I'd picked up more than skills... I'd picked up a rhythm, a sense of safety, and the quiet reminder that there was a place I could belong.

Maybe this is what having another dad feels like, I thought. Not replacing Charlie. Not replacing Wade's dad. Just... someone else to lean on – to learn from... and to love.

The ride back to home was quiet, except for the steady hum of the Harley beneath me. Bell drove the truck ahead, and sometimes she followed. But we were together even if we driving separate. All along the way Gunner's head was hanging out the window, ears back, eyes sharp, watching me like he was making sure I hadn't lost my mind. The sun dipped low behind the distant ridges, painting the valley gold and rust, and for the first time in months, I felt the tight knot of war inside me loosen - just a little.

When we turned onto the old Hawkins drive, all I could do is smile. Boards leaned against the porch, half-finished steps awaited paint, and the smell of fresh-cut timber mixed with dust and old earth. Wade and his dad had already been working, wanting to surprise us. They were shoving boards into place and measuring, and the sound of laughter and quiet orders mingling. For a moment, it felt like the house had been waiting for us, holding its breath.

I swung the Harley into the gravel and cut the engine. Gunner hopped out of the truck and nudged my boot, looked up at me with the old knowing in his eyes, and I knew for the first time in a long while we were exactly where we were meant to be. Home.

We spent the evening moving boards, dusting shelves, and fixing the floorboards that had borne the weight of generations. Wade was a whirlwind, laughing and joking as he guided me in - where to hold, where to lift, what to repair. His dad – was quiet, but precise. He offered pointers that reminded me of Charlie: patience, pride in the work, the kind of hands-on teaching that spoke without words.

By nightfall, we'd cleared the porch and stacked tools in neat lines. Wade leaned against the doorway, wiping sweat from his brow, and I realized I'd been holding my own breath all day. The house had felt heavy, like it carried the memories of my childhood, but now, with Bell's hand brushing mine and Gunner at my side, the weight had lifted just enough to breathe.

"It's looking good, Jack," Wade said, a hint of mischief in his voice. "But you know, there's more than one way to put your skills to work."

I was puzzled. "What do you mean?"

He glanced at his dad, then back at me. "The Academy. You've got the right instincts, the training, and the head for it… and you've been itching for more purpose than just fixing up old houses, haven't you?"

I shook my head, half in denial – maybe from being half tired. "I don't know, Wade. It's… it's a big commitment. But... it is something to think about."

I looked over at "dad" smiling – putting his tool belt down… he'd been quiet about the whole conversation of joining the Police Force, and I could only think he wouldn't want me to feel pressured into it, but Wade?

Wade smiled, the same one he'd had in Iraq knowing I was the kind of guy who needed a challenge. "You're ready. You just don't know it yet. Think about it. The work here, the dogs, the people who need someone who can keep them safe… It's a chance to do more than patch walls."

I looked out at the farmhouse, the valley beyond, the first stars coming out, and I felt the old ache in my chest. It was softer now, tempered with hope.

Charlie. Bell's dad. Wade's dad. Men who taught me about strength, about loyalty, about stepping into a role you didn't even know you were born for.

"Yeah," I said finally, breathing in the evening air. "I think… I think I need that."

Gunner nudged my boot again, and for a moment I thought it was him letting me know he thought it was a good idea, but… he just wanted me to throw his ball for him. He sat staring at me – waiting. I looked into his eyes – bright… thoughtful. Maybe I was looking for confirmation in small gestures because I still needed reassurance. But that look – whether it meant something or nothing – felt like permission.

Gunner had seen more than most men in his short life. And even though he didn't say any words… that look in his eyes was almost as if he was telling me – we were on the right path.

And for the first time in a long while, I believed him.

Chapter 21

Big Boys In Blue

Wade was always talking me into something. This time? It was Wade who may have planted the seed for the Police academy, but I really couldn't disagree since… we were going from "now what?" to "where our road would lead…"

I stood firm by Wade's side as the commandant of the academy pitted Wade and me against each other – not as enemies, but as squad leaders of the two different groups of cadets that joined the Law Enforcement Academy… He wanted to see who would rise victorious… Tradition demanded a winner, a champion squad. But Wade and I had already fought real battles, the kind where no one walks away clean. We looked at each other and knew: no ribbon, pin, or banner could ever come between us. Surviving had already taught us everything we needed to know.

Wade and I survived the real world of combat – we stood together – we looked at each other and we knew… that there was nothing more important than teaching by example – that survival meant standing together as a unit, that success meant we were all winners – or no one was.

Once again – we would get through this… together. It was nothing like 'boot-camp' – or anything like the Army. It did smell of polished boots, gun oil, and the crunching of gravel after springtime rain… it was lots of law, procedure, and preparation… but it was still nothing like living through… the real thing.

We didn't allow the usual pranks – jokes, and typical teasing other cadet classes did. We demanded excellence, attention to detail, and performance. Competition wasn't about who did worse, or who we could beat, but who could do better. And 'better' meant – surviving as a cohesive unit.

And our squads ended up – in a tie. Go figure…

Maybe it was because we learned – and lived by one of Charlie's old sayings: "Knowledge will give you power, but character will bring you respect."

When we graduated the academy – we were 'badged' by "dad" – Wade's dad. He was the only dad I had that wore a badge. We celebrated in the barn that we worked on for over a year. We worked in the evenings and weekends, and made it a place worth the commemoration and tribute that we needed. It was the old barn behind our house – Charlie's old house, and now… it was done… and so were we.

It wasn't long after all that – I stood once again at Wade's side. The pianist played a traditional "Cannon In 'D'" as Wade's childhood sweetheart walked – arm in arm with Wade's dad…

Charlotte Spencer – still young and in love – walked down the aisle with a dad who has been by my side most of my life… she smiled as she walked knowing she was about to become the wife of a war hero… and her best friend.

I looked across the podium at Bell – one of Charlotte's 'brides maids' – and smiled. But I had small regrets that this wedding was the one I wished I could have given her. The look in her eyes as hers met mine said it all… that hers was the wedding she'd always wanted – as long as we had each other.

I watched her eyes, the way they shone, As if the stars were hers alone. And in her gaze, of hopes and tears, of longing held through lonely years… Each look she gave, a gentle flame, that whispered softly, that spoke my name.

In that moment – in that glance – her smile… I knew… how we met, and how we started our lives together… was how it was meant to be.

As the blushing bride stepped up to her husband to be – she giggled softly and whispered to Wade – barely loud enough for me to hear "I'm glad you could make it today."

Wade simply smiled that 'corn-fed' farm-boy smile and softly choked…

"I'm here."

We were all still so young – yet all so experienced with the hand life had dealt us. And as I 'toasted' the bride and groom according to tradition… I couldn't help but remember the childhood story we'd read… I raised my glass, feeling a lump in my throat - but I couldn't let them see it. So I smiled and said…

"I see Wade today – the man I knew as a boy – who… I guess I'd always known he'd get caught in… Charlotte's web…"

Yep… it got the laugh I'd hoped for.

We had a good time celebrating. Wade and I had a few minutes to reflect on our lives together – a beer – some laughs… we looked back on the open roads that led us to this moment. It was a moment he thought would end up right where it did.

We reminisced looking back on how much Charlie's ranch has changed. It went from sprawling acres – to a few that would always remain untouched… but loved.

The fields Wade and I worked now weren't farms and ranches – the way we did when we were young. Now it was police cars, uniforms, keeping the peace, and the weight of the badge. Peace was swallowed by progress, and our community is now growing from a rustic college town with farms and factories into something louder – into a small metropolis that is finding its voice.

Sure – we'd always have those family farms where the reins of tradition would resist the future, but the city no longer slept. The hum of new construction, the glow of streetlights, and the steady pulse of traffic told us that where we lived now was awake - and hungry for more.

Wade took a deputy's job with his dad at the County Sheriff's Office. I found myself inside the city limits, but always knew Wade would never be too far away.

The county was still stretched wide with open roads, mountains, canyons, and farm gates, the kind of place where folks waved when they passed you. Wade fit there. While he was still full of energy – always with a smile and a joke - he was steady, patient, always taking his time to think things through. He'd grown up under his dad's badge, and now he wore one of his own.

Me? The city was different. The lights stayed on all night, and the calls came fast. It wasn't the quiet kind of law enforcement we grew up admiring. It was restless, raw, and loud. Fights outside bars, traffic stops that went sideways, and the kind of trouble that never seemed to sleep.

I always thought we'd be working side by side, like old times. Our jobs did overlap as I thought they would. And we still worked together on a number of calls and cases, but the County handled the wide-open miles; I took the streets that never cooled off. Still, on weekends or late nights after shift, we'd end up at the old barn. Gunner would sit at our feet while Wade, Bell, and I would compare notes, share stories, talk about the things we'd seen. We were always 'there' for each other. Even though our badges, our uniforms, or the worlds we worked in were different – the job was all the same.

That first year taught us more than the academy ever could. The law was written in books, but life out here? It wrote its own rules.

In spite of my friend and me wearing different uniforms – different departments – we found ourselves working together more than we would have imagined. We didn't mind.

Our 'rookie' year was coming to an end, and we would be working the streets and alleys on our own. It wouldn't be long before I'd be getting my own police car. Even though the 'new' guys always got the leftovers, I was glad I was getting something…

A car meant trust. It meant I was part of the machine now - the hum of the radio, the call signs, and the endless chatter of the city that never slept.

After the end of that first year, I found a rhythm between work, Bell, and Gunner. It was the life I'd always wanted I guess. I was needed, valued, and our family began to grow. We'd finished fixing up our old place long ago – but it still kept the memories, and the reminders of Charlie.

I came home one evening and found Bell had purchased some paint, and she said she wanted to remodel one of the upstairs rooms – I asked "why?"

She said the room was nice enough, but… she wanted to make it into…

A nursery.

Life was changing – not only for our home and family, but I found myself swapping four doors for two wheels. The motor unit had a way of getting into your blood. The feel of the bike, the throttle, the growl of the pipes, the way the road rolled beneath your boots.

It was freedom with a badge attached. There was nothing like rolling through town before dawn, the streets still wet from the night before, steam rising off the asphalt while the world was just waking up.

Winters were rough on the bikes, though. Most of us went back to patrol cars once the first snow hit. Still, whenever the air bit cold and the clouds hung low, I missed that wind cutting across my face. It was always the silence between the gusts that made a man think.

That's when Wade called. His voice came through rough and low, the way it always did when something serious was happening.

"Jack, we've got a situation up near the canyon. Avalanche took a hiker off the trail. Search and Rescue's on scene, but they can't find him."

I didn't have to think twice. "I'll bring Gunner."

The road up the canyon was half-iced and slick. Snowflakes hit the windshield like sparks. Gunner sat in the seat beside me, ears perked, eyes fixed out ahead. He knew the tone in my voice. It was the same one I used overseas, when men needed him and time was thin.

When we got there, the wind had carved the drifts into sharp ridges. Deputies and volunteers were scattered along the slope, digging where they thought the man might be. I stepped out, then I un-clipped Gunner's lead, and pointed toward the ridge.

"Find him, boy."

He lowered his nose, circled once, then twice. Within minutes, he stopped, pawing hard at the snow, whining low in his throat. We dug like madmen. A glove appeared, then a hand. The man was cold, but alive. Barely… but he was alive.

Wade looked at me, snow stuck in his hair, eyes wide and shining.

"Damn, Jack. I knew Gunner could do it."

I just smiled, ruffling Gunner's ears as he leaned against my leg, tail thumping slow and steady in the snow.

"Yeah," I said. "He's got a nose for it."

That night, after the medics took the man down, Wade and I stood by the cruisers, breath rising in white clouds. The canyon was quiet again.

Wade nodded toward Gunner. "You know, you might've just started something."

Maybe he was right. The department would talk about that rescue for months. By spring, there was word about starting a K9 unit, and I had a feeling I knew who they'd call first.

As I looked down at Gunner, still alert, still watching the mountain like there was more work to be done, I felt that old pull again - the one that told me this was where I belonged. Not just behind the wheel or on a bike, but side by side with a partner who didn't need words to understand.

Chapter 22

Legacy

It didn't take long after the avalanche rescue before word started to spread. I tried to downplay it, but Wade had already filled half the department in before I even got back to town. By the time I turned in my report, the Chief was waiting in his office with a grin that told me something was coming.

He motioned for me to sit. "You and that dog of yours made quite an impression, Jack."

I shrugged. "Gunner just did what he was trained to do."

"Maybe so," he said, leaning back, hands laced behind his head. "But I've been thinking… maybe it's time we made that kind of training part of the department."

I raised an eyebrow. "You mean a K9 program?"

He nodded. "You've got the experience. Lackland, right? With your Military K9 and your Police training? I want you to help us build one."

That's how it started. There were no big announcements, no ceremonies, just a quiet conversation in a small office with the faint hum of a coffee pot in the background. I walked out of there with a new assignment and a sense that something important had just taken root.

Shadow

They called him Shadow before he ever set his paws in the city. He was American-bred, broad-shouldered, smart, inquisitive, and already showing the dark saddle and mask that made him look almost black in certain light. He was young, raw, and full of that restless energy I recognized from a hundred dogs before him. The difference was, this one was ours. Shadow was the city's first official K9.

Gunner met him the first day. The old boy stood at my side, head tilted, sizing up the newcomer with that calm, confident look that only seasoned dogs have. Shadow circled him once, twice, then gave a low bark as if to say, *"Alright, old man, teach me something."*

I laughed. "You just met your first mentor, kid."

Gunner took to him quicker than I expected. Shadow followed him everywhere. He watched how Gunner responded to my voice, how he waited for a signal before moving, how he worked the wind when we were out in the field. You could almost see the gears turning in that young Shepherd's head.

Training came easy. Shadow had the kind of focus you couldn't teach. He loved the challenge, loved to please, and even loved the routine. By the time we'd finished the first few weeks, he was already responding to hand signals, scent cues, and recall drills better than most veteran dogs I'd worked with in the service.

The Chief dropped by one morning to watch. He leaned against the fence as Shadow cleared the six-foot wall, circled back, and came to a perfect sit at my side. Gunner barked once, as if proud of his protégé.

"Looks like you've got something special here, Jack," the Chief said.

"I'd say we do, sir," I replied.

Shadow became more than a success story. He became the symbol of what could be done when training, trust, and purpose came together. Over the years, he worked searches, rescues, narcotics cases, and crowd control. He loved every minute of it.

Bell would often sit on the floor with our babies – and the 'Shepherds' would sit nearby and sneak a scratch behind the ears – and our kids learned to love and grow within the life of working dogs.

And when his time came for him to retire, the Chief didn't hesitate. He took Shadow home himself, and I couldn't think of a better ending. Every officer knew that the first K9 the city ever had didn't just serve… it set the standard.

Max

When the next dog arrived, he came with a passport. Max was German-bred, all the way down to his tattoo and pedigree. The Chief said, "If we're going to expand the program, we might as well see what the Germans are doing right."

Max was a specimen. He was big, muscular, and mostly gray with streaks of black and tan. His eyes carried that sharp, calculating look that made rookies nervous. He was the kind of dog that didn't hand out trust easily; you earned it, and you earned it slow.

His drive was unmatched. He hit every track like it was a mission, every search like it was life or death. At home, though, he was quiet – maybe even a little aloof, but always near and never needy. I understood him – so did Gunner. Some souls, human or canine, just preferred the edge of the circle rather than the middle.

Training Max was different. He was textbook German. He was precise, methodical, and a little stubborn when he thought he knew better. But once he bonded, he gave you everything he had. During one call, we were clearing a warehouse when a suspect jumped from behind a stack of pallets. Max didn't hesitate. He intercepted midair, drove the man down, and held until I gave the release. It was clean, fast, and professional. He was everything a handler could ask for.

The Captain on scene looked at me afterward and said, "That dog just saved your life."

I nodded. "That's his job. And he loves it."

Max served his years solid before that Captain – the same one who'd seen what he could do that night... adopted him after retirement. I could tell Max approved. He wasn't much for goodbyes, but when I knelt down and scratched behind his ear one last time, he leaned in just a little longer than usual. That was all he needed to say. That was all I needed.

Ajax

By the time Ajax came along, the K9 unit wasn't an experiment anymore - it was a cornerstone. The city had three full-time teams, and other departments were coming by to watch our training methods. It felt good, seeing something we built from nothing turn into something respected.

By now, Gunner was getting older. His muzzle showing signs of silver, and his step was slower, but his spirit hadn't changed. He'd watch the younger dogs over the years from his favorite spot near the fence, that same steady gaze he'd once given Shadow. It was strange, thinking how much had come from one avalanche and one loyal friend.

When Ajax first met Gunner, he approached slowly, tail low but confident. Gunner sniffed him once, then twice, then gave a small approving huff and walked off toward his shade. That was his way of saying he passed inspection.

Ajax was the last of Gunner's "recruits" that would become my partner… and when that final day came, when the sleep well-earned by a Soldier – a teacher, and a mentor for the other K9's… it was Ajax that came to let me know…

That Gunner – sleeping at my feet… would finally rest…

Where Heroes Run Free.

Ajax was another German import. Like the others he was large, strong, and steady. He carried himself like an old soul even when he was young. His coloring was a beautiful blend of gray and tan, almost like smoke over sand. He bonded quickly, not just with me but with the families who came to the training field. Kids could tug his ears, and he'd just stare at them with that quiet patience that spoke volumes about his temperament.

He worked hard and played harder. He loved the job, but he also loved lying in the shade, watching the other dogs work. Sometimes I thought he was grading them in his head. When it came to scent work, he was unmatched. His nose caught traces no one else could. We closed some tough cases thanks to Ajax's instincts. For the years he walked by my side I could see every day – the influence of Gunner…

When it came time for Ajax to retire, one of the department's other Captains - another believer in the K9 program… took him home. I made sure Ajax's final day on the field was quiet, just the two of us. No ceremony, no applause, just a walk under the old cottonwoods where we used to train. He sat at my side, where Gunner would - his tail brushing the grass, and I said what I always said: "Good boy." He looked up at me, and I swear there was understanding in his eyes. Some dogs just know.

Then came Tina.

Since she was smaller than the other "German's Shepherds" – the breeders in Germany named her Tiny – or Tina. She wasn't "that" much smaller, but she was lean, quick, muscles tight as coiled steel. Her coat shimmered between black and tan, and her eyes had that spark I'd seen only a handful of times in my career. Sharp. Focused. Curious. Like the others, she was smart. She didn't bark much at first, didn't need to. She sized up everything in silence before making her move.

She was almost a complete package of all the others… wrapped in bright eyes and warm fur. From the moment we met it was as if she'd always known me. She had a way of looking in my eyes that told me… she understood.

As I watched her move, whether it was on a call, a search, or across the training field, she was light on her feet, fast, and concealed a hidden strength hidden somewhere in her small frame. I knew right then she wasn't just another partner. There was something else… something I couldn't name yet.

A connection waiting to be written in the long hours ahead, in the chases, the searches, the moments when instinct mattered more than words.

Every dog before her had built the foundation. Buddy taught me how to talk to animals, and Gunner taught me how to train. Shadow, Max, Ajax. They'd each leave a mark, a lesson, a piece of the story. But Tina? She'd be the one to carry it forward. It started with an eight year old boy hugging a puppy at a grocery store, and grew through years of serving with loyal partners.

I looked at this 'little girl' as we ate at our favorite hamburger drive-in, sitting in my truck with me… looking deep into her eyes I never realized how loyalty and devotion would be re-defined, and how much my world would change because of her.

And as I watched the sun drop behind the horizon, painting our yard in gold, I'd sit with Tina on my patio after a long day, and felt it deep down - the road that started with Buddy, and with Gunner, it wasn't ending. It was only turning toward the next chapter.

It would be Tina that would open the door to a future I never thought was possible.

Chapter 23

Big Boys Don't Cry

Whoever it was who said "big boys don't cry" - never lost a partner...

I was still in pain when I walked into the conference room, surrounded by my department's leaders, friends, and my family. But the one I wanted - even needed the most, wouldn't be there.

I was celebrated for a life of service, and courage under fire. I'd seen it all. The best humanity could give, and the worst nightmare a cop could survive. It was still difficult to hold back my emotions knowing my partner, Tina, would never know the freedom of retirement.

After the celebration - my wife - Isabel, and my family were walking with me - still walking slowly through the station lobby. Then, I saw our picture on the wall...

As I stood before the memorial wall, of fallen officers, and heroes, the memories overwhelmed me. In an instant, I was back there...

As if frozen in time, I stood and looked at the picture of my partner and me standing by the 'police truck' we'd spent so much time in, both of us smiling. But this time - I wasn't smiling. I tried to hold them back, but tears rolled down my face, as the memories of that day played again in my mind. I was terrified, yet proud...

The bullets were flying, and I was hit, my partner dragged me to safety - ignoring her own injuries. Together we faced the fire of the suspect until my team took him into custody...

My partner died in my arms.

I kept telling her "you're going to be fine girl" as I stroked her hair: "we're going to get you taken care of."

Her breathing slowed, and her eyes closed as we looked at each other for the last time… it all came back to me standing there.

She wasn't "just a dog" - she was my partner. And I **loved** her.

**

I was angry. I was sad. My body was healing, but in my mind I was still living in the adrenaline - dispatch on the radios, the sounds of sirens - the urgency of every call. But now, all of that was replaced by silence.

Sitting on my patio, I saw the shadows of our life together. Her toys, her dish, her leash – her empty leash and collar, and her little tag inscribed… "Tina." I gripped that leash tight, as if holding onto it could somehow hold onto her. And with every step I took alone, the anger returned.

I looked up at the sky, wondering if God was hiding in those clouds. How could He take something so loyal, so selfless, and so young? I tried to pray, but my heart was lost in the darkness.

The world felt colder, quieter, as if it knew she was gone.

**

My wife Isabel – or Bell – suggested I talk to someone. She suggested I talk to Father John, a Priest at her church. I had been through so much already; I figured what could it hurt? Isabel had known him for years, and even though I'd met him on only a number of occasions - I knew if my wife could trust him, I could at least try.

My first meeting with Father John was uncomfortable and I told him that I was ashamed that my family had seen me 'tear-up' like that. I told him it was hard for me to reconcile tears with the badge I'd worn for decades. All my life I was told not to show emotion, because…

"Big boys – don't cry."

"I feel like I've failed them," I admitted, my voice low. "My family doesn't deserve to see me… like this. Weak."

Father John raised an eyebrow. "Weak?" he repeated. "Jack, let me ask you something. How many times have you run toward danger when everyone else was running away?"

I shrugged, feeling a little uncomfortable. "It was my job. You don't think about it - you just do it."

"Exactly," Father John said, leaning forward. "You don't think about it. You rely on your training, on your instinct. You rely on an inner strength most people don't have, and it takes incredible courage, doesn't it?"

I nodded slowly, somewhat embarrassed, never accepting complements or praise very well, and I was unsure where this was going.

"Now think about this," Father John continued. "What you're facing right now - this grief, this guilt, this pain - is no different. It's another kind of danger, another kind of fire. But instead of running from it, you're standing your ground, facing it head-on. That's not weakness, Jack. That's courage. And not everyone has it."

I looked down at the floor: "But it doesn't feel like courage. It feels… messy. Out of control."

Father John smiled gently. "It is messy. But that's the thing about emotions - they don't come with a manual, and they don't follow orders. That's why most people bury them. But not you. You're doing what you've always done: you're showing up, even when it's hard. The same strength that kept you running toward gunfire is what brought you here, working through this. And that, Jack, is bravery most people will never understand."

I looked down at the coffee Father John handed me as he continued.

"Grief doesn't make you less of a man, Jack," Father John said, his voice steady. "It doesn't make you a 'cry-baby' - It makes you human. And letting yourself feel it - letting others see it - doesn't take away from your strength. It proves it. Because it means you're not running away.

"What you're feeling now, this grief over Tina - it's not the end of your strength. It's the proof of it. Strong men **are** allowed to cry, Jack. They have to.

Because if they don't, they lose the very thing that makes them strong - *their heart*."

Father John suggested I join his local support group for veterans and first responders - people who understood what it was like to stand between danger and the innocent, to carry the terror, the pain, and the nightmares that society expects us to bear silently. "This group is full of people who, like you, were told to suppress their emotions,"

His words struck a chord. We were the ones paid to shoulder society's pain, the ones expected to endure the unbearable. Some couldn't handle the pressure and simply walked away. Others, tragically, succumbed to the echoes of what they'd seen - the weight of the memories, the relentless nightmares. They slipped beyond the reach of mortality, lost to the shadows of life behind the badge.

So I started going to Father John's group meeting also, but I didn't say much at first. After a few sessions, the minister, Father John Forsythe - pulled me aside. He said something that stuck with me: "Sometimes the best way to heal is by helping others heal."

At first, I didn't know what to think. How could I help someone else when I couldn't even help myself? But I trusted him. And I opened up - just a little.

I was with people going through their own hardships, losses, and internal battles. We related to each other because – we lived the nightmares, yet we hid behind the appearance of being normal. In some ways it was harder to open up, since I was already friends with some of the group's members... and I didn't want to appear weak.

One day, Father John asked me to speak at Sunday service. Me. A preacher? I laughed. I told him "I don't know how to preach." But he said that's exactly what the congregation needed. "They don't need perfect, Jack - they need real." I was terrified. But after some coaxing, I reluctantly agreed.

The day before church, I was having coffee with some of my friends, and I mentioned I was going to speak in church. Wade nearly choking with a laugh..."You're preaching now?" he joked. "I've gotta see this."

When the service started the next morning, Father John spoke beautifully. And then he called me up. He introduced me, shared a bit of my story. Then… it was my turn. I didn't want to "Preach." I wasn't trained for helping others like this. But Father John said, "When the time is right, you'll know what to say." I had my doubts, but in that moment I had to believe him.

I stood there, looking at the faces of people who had no way of understanding what I had been through. I started talking about my doubts, my anger, and my loss. And then **I** told them about my partner. About the day she saved me.

I talked about how I blamed God for taking her from me. I saw tears in the eyes of people I didn't even know. I felt my own tears well up, but I held them back. And then I noticed my wife standing beside me, smiling as she took my hand - knowing that the words coming to me - were just as much for me, as they were for the congregation. And after I finished speaking, we embraced. There was a love in that moment that only a partner could offer.

**

I kept going to the group sessions that Father John led, but I still struggled. I just… didn't want to talk about these things in front of others. But my wife kept me going.

Father John could tell this struggle within was bothering me. He could see me wrestle with doubt, and my questioning a belief in a 'divine' being. I mean, who could allow so much darkness in the world. I'd lived with this darkness for so many years - looking evil in the face. I was trying to live in a normal world where so few could understand how 'we' have to hold a line of defense - how 'we' were the thin line that tries to keep society from harm… this was a struggle where not all of us survive.

How *was* I supposed to feel? My partner was the victim of such senseless violence.

"My brother" Father John said: "seeing you struggle like this is, well - in a way like seeing a fish out of water."

"What do you mean" I asked.

"You lost more than a partner that night" his voice steady but somber... "You were a victim too" he said.

Father John continued "you have a message, and the message - the words you need to say to others like you, are just as important to you as they are to the others - in group, or wherever you can find them."

Father John told me that I wasn't the kind of guy that was meant for speaking in church. He said the lessons I learned through my experiences were meant for those who were avoiding church. He wanted me to find a little light in my life by helping others who needed "the light" - but maybe not religion.

I wasn't sure what he meant at the time, but he said "in time - I would"... then he just smiled.

**

My friend Wade told me about a 'rally' some of the motorcycle clubs were holding. This meant we would meet at the motorcycle shop, and take a ride around the lake. He invited me to join in - knowing how much I still like to ride. Although I was still healing – I thought it might be good for me to get back out on the bike, and ride with some friends.

The following Sunday I met my friends at one of our favorite hangouts – a local café, so we could grab some coffee and some breakfast. After that, we rode to the motorcycle shop together. As we pulled into the parking lot - a couple of members from one of the biker clubs recognized me as a cop.

"I smell bacon" a couple of voices shouted out... all I could do is chuckle. I knew that it was all in good fun - the way bikers like to joke with each other. I parked next to my friends, and shut my bike down. Wade commented to the others that "he became a Preacher!"

Several bikers chuckled while one hollered out "hey Preacher - Where's your Bible..." all I could say was "I'm really not a **preacher** - I spoke **one** time in Church - and believe me that doesn't make me a "Preacher?"

We all laughed...

191

As more arrived for the 'shop ride' - one of the other members of a club recognized me from a news article he'd seen... "Hey - aren't you the one who lost his K9 partner in that shoot-out a little while back?" he said respectfully... I nodded my head.

Some of the guys teased a little – "hey Preacher - why don't ya give us a Sunday sermon!" as they all laughed...

"You really want me to 'preach' to you?" I said with a chuckle, as I began my 'makeshift' sermon - I continued... "As we ride around the lake today – we all pretty much know where to go. So if you know where to go, and know the way to get there, you don't need anyone to tell you what to do. When one of us is in trouble, or when someone needs help, we band together to lift each other up... when one of us is hurting - we all hurt together... That's the code we live by - when one of us is lost, the others are there to show them the way. So I don't need a Bible, and I don't need to be a "preacher" - what I need today is to be here with you all."

Several more 'bikers' joined us - then a voice from the back of the pack shouted "now that's a Preacher I can listen to!" We all laughed...

Before we left the shop, a young man approached me. His father had been diagnosed with cancer, and he was afraid of losing his mentor and best friend. I told him, "Son, you need to be strong for him. He's going through tough treatments and will feel weak... he needs your strength."

"But what if I'm not strong enough? What do I do then?" he asked.

"You'll never know how strong you are... until strength is all you have."

As we talked, I realized these words came from a time when I was at my weakest - when I had to draw upon my own strength, and Bell's.

I shared some of my struggles, and the loss I recently faced, telling him that I doubted God. But I also told him that when doubt creeps in, we need someone to show us how to be strong.

The young man asked, "Do you think God tells you what to say?"

"I don't know," I replied, lighting a cigarette. "I'm not going to feed ya a line of 'bull-shit' and say I have all the answers. Maybe it comes from somewhere deep inside, from what I've been through… I just don't know."

He smiled. "You sure as hell don't talk like any preacher I've ever heard…"

"Well, I'm not a preacher," I said, seeing his puzzled expression. "I'm just another lost traveler, trying to find the right path. It's not about being a preacher – it's about helping each other find the path to where we want to go."

The rest of the day's ride was enjoyable - it was good for me to get out on the road. Even though the memories of loss, and recovering from the pain is still fresh, it felt good to be with others.

Throughout the ride, and the gathering for lunch afterward, the only thing "they" called me that day was… "Preacher."

I knew it was all in good fun… and my wife, Bell - even Father John, saw the humor in it.

Chapter 24

Tina

A couple of days after I went out with the bikers, my wife and I were talking at breakfast, and she mentioned that Father John had asked about me when she went to church. She had told him what I'd been doing that Sunday, and he thought it might be good for me to talk about my experience. She passed along the message, but I was reluctant. I didn't even like talking about it in group – so maybe talking with Father John *could* be a better option, though I wasn't sure that was the right approach either. Sharing anything, whether in a group or one-on-one, felt difficult. But maybe Father John's invitation was something I needed to consider.

Later that day, while I was sitting on the patio, I was lost in thought, remembering Tina. I was still holding onto her leash, and her memory. Isabel told me I had a phone call. When I asked who it was, she said it was Father John.

I picked up the phone, and his voice was warm but steady. "Would you come by my office for a quick chat?" he asked.

I didn't know what to expect, but I knew I needed to go. I kissed my wife, slipped on my leather jacket, and rode down to the church on my bike.

I pulled into the parking lot, and the kids playing in the church-school playground all ran up to the fence to see what the thunder was, and it was only me. I got off my bike to see all the smiling faces and gave them a little wave of greeting.

Father John met me at the door - "it looks like you've attracted some attention" he said smiling. I smiled too, and thought to myself "I guess I wasn't the usual kind of 'parishioner' that shows up here at a church."

We sat in his office, and briefly discussed my day at the bike rally last Sunday. That's when I told him they were calling me "Preacher" – he thought it was funny. I told him that in spite of how good it felt, it didn't help - it didn't ease the pain as much as I thought it would.

"Acceptance" Father John spoke with a stoic voice with authority - "accepting what happened won't heal the pain, but it will open a path so you *can* heal… what we need to do is get you to be able to keep the fond memories, accept that you will have sorrow for her loss, understand that all the things you have experienced are a lesson, and that the pain you feel now, is not a life sentence." He went on: "the feelings of sorrow are normal, and I believe the anger isn't just about losing Tina, but the culmination of all the darkness you've seen through the years."

His words cut deep, and at that moment I told him that I'm not sure if I really do want to heal. I told him that healing might mean I don't respect her sacrifice - the sacrifice she made for me.

"I understand that my son" his face now turning back to his comforting smile… "So how about we start with you telling me a little about your partner - Tina."

**

"I remember the day I met her… I mean - I've had several dogs over the years – Shadow, Max, Ajax – not to mention Gunner from my Army days, but the police dogs were always adopted by my superiors when it was time for them to retire. They liked how well I trained them, and how well they were adjusted to 'home' life… my wife said it was because I was a dog "whisperer." I believe it was because I'd learned how to speak to them - and to love them on a level of understanding - that could only come from a life where dogs were the only ones I could trust. It seemed like through my life - dogs were the only ones who could understand me too.

"I needed my next assignment to be a partner that could understand this as well… a partner who understood me as well.

"We were told that we'd be getting three new K-9's - and I would be getting my new "Partner."

"I was the Sergeant that supervised the K-9 crew - but the assignments were already made by our superiors. When the truck came from the airport, that the German based training company sent - the first dog to come out of the shipping crate was "Aries."

"Aries is a black Malinois (*Mal-In-Wah*) – lean, mean, and lightning fast: right out of the crate he was ready for work… Aries was assigned to my corporal Stan - the football player – the Quarterback and track star, who needed a dog who could 'keep-up' with him… smart and athletic - they were a good match.

"Next, out came "Thor" - another large mix between the Malinois, and a German Shepherd - black and brown - stocky and lean… living up to his namesake: powerful and commanding… assigned to my other corporal - Nick. Thor needed a handler who could 'pack the weight' - like the weight-lifter Nick was - who could carry a heavy load, and tackle big jobs… Thor was the right match for him.

"My anticipation was building - knowing what should come next would be another amazing specimen of German breeding… And out of the crate - stretching from the long trip… "Tina"

"She was sleek - smart, and had a look in her eyes as if she was wondering what kind of handler I would be. As if she was interviewing me for the job. We looked at each other - and she smiled at me, it looked like she said I'd be just fine. She was tan and reddish-brown with a black saddle - her black muzzle graced her face with elegance, and she had a hint of grey across her back. From the start - I could tell we were destined to be together for a long time.

"She was different from the others - even Gunner, who I'd served with in the Army.

Right out of the 'crate' - she seemed like she knew "she was the boss"…

"She graduated from her training six months early - as if she knew what she was meant for. I discovered she could track, sniff, and it seemed she could find whatever it was I was looking for - even before I knew I was looking for it. It seemed like she had telepathy - a sixth sense - a "nose" for being a real cop.

"I told her to come, and instead of standing at "attention" like the other "military" trained dogs - she came and leaned against me as if she knew me from her beginnings. It was almost surreal - yet comforting… something about her made me feel at ease. Like a long lost friend coming home - something in my heart made me feel like she was home.

"I would learn so painfully later - how truly special she was.

"We all took a few minutes to 'get to know' our new assignments, and Tina was all too willing to get in my face, showing me the love from the start. She sniffed and licked me like we were 'old friends' reuniting.

"I asked her if she wanted to 'go for a ride' - and she paused, then looked around and started sniffing again. She jerked the leash out of my hand, and sniffing the ground - ran toward the K-9 Police truck that was mine. She jumped into the open door I'd left, and sat in the driver seat - smiling at me as I walked over – not too far behind her.

"Hey Princess" I laughed - "don't' you think I should drive?

"All the other officers laughed too - Stan said - "well Sarge - I guess she knows who's boss."

"On the way driving back to our home - I stopped and got myself a burger at a fast-food drive-in. As I was ordering - Tina, sitting in the passenger seat (instead of the kennel in the back of the truck), looked at me as if I should order her one as well… So I did. We sat in the parking lot and had our first meal together.

"As I introduced her to my family – it was like she knew what to do, because of what I was thinking. Tina slowly approached my wife, and as if she knew how to show Bell she wasn't a 'threat' - she lowered her head and nuzzled up against her feet. It was love at first sight. She immediately fit in to our family.

"Even the grandkids loved playing with her - and she was gentle, nurturing - and had the demeanor of a puppy. She could match the temperament of any situation, and as I would discover… she could bring fear to the Devil himself - when one of her 'own' was threatened.

"It wasn't too long after we got home that I took her outside with me, and I sat on the patio. I watched her play while I opened up the "personnel" file we got from the breeder, and trainers. I looked over at her, and then back down at her history page: the notes from the breeder *really* told the story…"

"Tina" the breeder wrote – "was the smallest of the litter, and showed from the start she was extremely intelligent." He wrote "I named her Tina since I knew she would be going to America, and because of her size being tiny - I thought Tina would be a good name for her."

The breeder - Hans - was bilingual, and noted further: "as I began her initial training before the Schutzhund (protection dog) course she would be going to, I noticed that she needed very little training in the basic commands. She seemed to watch the others and know what to do. She was agile, intelligent, and very clever. She appears to have a good heart, and protective of her surroundings. She will make a good candidate for protection. In spite of her size she is muscular and strong."

"I read through the many pages - the notes from the advanced trainers, all of them amazed how special she was. Even they were amazed that she finished her training six months early… six months before her peers.

"I was lost in the reading, and before I knew it, she was sitting before me with a "what-ya-doing" look on her face. I smiled and told her that I was just getting to know her. The smile on her face said it all. She rested her head on my lap, and I stroked her fur, and I knew she truly was something special.

"She seemed to watch everything - and everyone - like she was always learning. She had her place in the house - her food and water dish - but she'd watch my wife get ice or water from the fridge door, and soon enough, she figured out she could get an ice cube to play with… or a cool drink of water… just by pressing the lever.

"It seemed like all she wanted was to be like us. I'd find puddles of water and half-melted ice cubes on the floor by the fridge… nearly slipping on them more than once. I wanted to scold her, but I couldn't. I'd call her name, and she'd look at me - you know, with that 'I'm guilty' look with those big eyes…

"It was one of the best years of my career - and yes, I'm angry that it was all taken from me."

Father John interrupted gently, "How about we focus on Tina… not the anger."

Reluctantly, I agreed.

"I just feel so guilty Father - that I survived, and she didn't"

"I understand son - but tell me more about Tina"

I went on saying: "Her first day on the job was nothing less than what I'd read about her. From the 'get-go' she discovered drugs, and just her presence - when we needed a show of force, she could diffuse the tension – I guess suspects could tell that dynamite comes in small packages.

"Tina may have been smaller than a lot of her peers, but it seemed that she wasn't any smaller than a lot of the American-bred German Shepherds - anyway…"

Father John smiled and told me that 'it's all a part of remembering, and honoring her memory…"

I went on… "She didn't like riding in the kennel in the back of the truck - every time we would go to get in the truck, she'd walk over to the cab, and 'nose' toward the handle letting me know where she wanted to sit. Every time we got a call, it was as if she knew my call sign, and would give me the 'look' that she knew it was time for us to go to work…

"In all the time I've spent with these dogs - I'd never seen one like her. There was something about her that was - well - almost human. Not that I'm trying to put human traits on her, but she really seemed to know - to understand…"

"It really sounds like she was special" Father John said respectfully.

"Yes - she really was… the year I spent with her was more than remarkable - we grew to love each other. Not like a pet, but as a real partner. Every time we did anything - I knew I could trust her, and she knew she could trust me. I guess that's what hurts me the most. I feel like I let her down!"

Father John leaned back in his chair, his voice calm yet weighted with meaning. "It's clear Tina wasn't just a partner; she was a gift. She lived her life for you, gave you everything she had. What do you think she'd want you to remember most about her?"

I stared at my hands for a long moment before finally speaking, my voice low. "I guess… she'd want me to remember the way she lived, and not the way she died."

I leaned back in the chair, a faint smile tugging at my lips as memories surfaced. "Every morning, she'd nudge me awake before my alarm, like she couldn't stand the idea of wasting a single minute of the day. She was always so full of energy - she'd bring me her leash and look out at the truck, as if to say, *'Come on, we've got work to do.'*"

I chuckled softly to myself "On patrol, she'd tilt her head whenever I talked, like she was hanging on every word. Sometimes, I swear she was more attentive than my team. And she had this thing with tennis balls…" My voice trailed off as I shook my head, smiling at the memory. "Didn't matter where we were or how serious the situation was - if she saw a ball, I knew she wanted to be all over it. It was like she was a pup again. But her training and dedication to her duty – kept her strong, but she knew - when she had the chance – she'd get to play ball…"

I paused again, my smile fading slightly as another memory came to me. "There was this one time I caught her sleeping in my chair - head back, paws dangling like she didn't have a care in the world. I thought about scolding her, but when she wagged her tail, I knew she had me wrapped around her paw. And she loved watching TV - especially when animals were on the screen. She'd perk up, ears forward, like she wanted to be a part of the show."

"One time – she heard an officer say the word 'drugs' on the radio, and she grabbed the mic, and started to talk – almost as if she wanted to make the call to respond – or the time we walked into the squad-room for pre-shift meeting, and she stole my chair from me, and sat in it like it was hers… she truly had the 'cop' sense of humor… and she knew it."

My voice softened again, as the weight of her loss came creeping back in. "Tina loved our little traditions, too - like sharing burgers and fries. She'd always try to steal a bite when I wasn't looking, but it was a game. She'd give me this look, like she was daring me to catch her. And then, there was that smile…" My voice broke slightly - "I'll miss that smile. She had this way of looking at me, like she knew exactly what I was thinking - and like everything was gonna be okay."

I fell silent, my gaze distant. Father John waited, letting the quiet settle between us. Finally, I spoke again, my voice barely above a whisper. "She gave me everything. And now she's gone, I let her down – like I let her go… just like that."

Father John leaned forward, his voice steady. "No, Jack. You didn't just let her go. She chose to protect you. That's what love does - it gives everything without hesitation. Tina wouldn't want you to carry guilt; she'd want you to carry her love."

I nodded slowly, the moisture in my eyes trying to escape - as I did my best to hold them back: "Yeah," I murmured. "She would."

The chat I had with Father John was more than a few minutes. It ended up being several hours, and when I walked away that day…

I was still angry.

Chapter 25

Acceptance

Father John and I would talk for hours about Tina. He told me that moving past losing her didn't mean I should forget about her, but instead - keep her memory close... "She was loyal, she was courageous, and she protected you when you needed her" Father John continued... "Wouldn't the best way to honor her be to live the way you did when you were with her?"

"I don't know Father - if I didn't feel so bad, wouldn't that mean I don't respect what she did for me?"

Father John continued... "The pain and anger you feel, the feelings of sorrow - you don't need to hang on to all this to keep her memory – and her love for you... you see - your suffering doesn't come from the pain - it's coming from your *attachment* to the pain."

I disagreed with him... I realized that there are steps to healing like: denial, anger - acceptance, but I refused to accept that some 'scum-bag' took such a beautiful soul away from me.

Father John continued "it's common for different people to 'jump' around the different phases of grief" as he leaned back into his char - "like you holding onto her leash while you're out on your patio - in a way you are hoping to hold onto her - in a way denying that she's gone...

"Obviously you're angry, and I suppose it's okay for people to experience these different emotions at the same time." Father John leaned back in toward me: "No one can blame you for the way you feel - Jack, I just don't want it to consume you"

"I will never accept what happened" I blurted out.

Father John calmly replied "acceptance doesn't mean you approve of what happened, it just means you understand the reality that it *did* happen - it was a situation - a call that you couldn't control - it only means you can feel the sorrow, the loss, without letting it become suffering."

I told him that part of my anger comes from knowing that the world will never know how special she was - her selfless sacrifice - her true love for service. I told him that *he* may understand how special she was, but in the short time she was by my side - she touched the lives of so many… and I continued:

"A week into us being partnered - Wade called from the County Sheriff's department. They needed a K9 unit to help find a lost child up in the canyons. Tina heard our call sign, and she gave me the look, and I knew she was ready…

"At the campground where the Deputies were with the family of the lost child – we were handed some articles of clothing that they knew we'd need for Tina to track on…

"Tina could tell that the situation was urgent. Before I could get her leash on she acted like she knew why she was there - like I said - I believe she had a sixth sense about being a cop.

"I gave her the scent; she sniffed around the clothing, and pulled me over toward the edge of the campground. Wade said that 'wasn't the direction' they last saw the child' - but I trusted my little girl to do what she was trained to do.

"I had a hard time keeping up with her, and as we'd climb the hills in the steep canyon - she pulled me along, never breaking her pace. She would stop and lift her head - maybe even sniff the ground, and off she'd go - but all I could sense was the smell of fresh pine, and the damp woodland ground we'd been trudging through.

I was tired - it was starting to get late in the afternoon. Tina could sense the urgency, and I knew she wouldn't stop until she found what she was supposed to.

"We'd been hiking – running actually - busting through the trails and brush for a couple of hours - she stopped again, and raised her head again sniffing the air. Her ears started focusing on something - I could tell she heard something… we started to walk again toward a small clearing and then I heard it too.

"I could hear the soft crying of a child, and I told Tina she was a 'good-girl' as we walked closer to the sounds. We found the young boy huddled up against the base of a tree.

I didn't want Tina to scare him, but before I could hold her back - she started licking his face, and nuzzled him affectionately around his neck. He stopped crying and asked me if I was going to take him to his mom and dad…

"I told him that 'we' were going to take him to his mom and dad, and I asked him if he was hurt - he said no, that he was just scared."

I continued to tell Father John that I radioed the others - that '*we*' found the boy, and that we were headed back. I took Tina off her leash, so I could carry the boy through the rough spots on the mountain side, and that Tina never left us - rather - guided us back down the mountain so I wouldn't get lost either." Father John smiled.

"When we got back down by the edge of the campsite - the boy's mother ran to greet us, and took the boy in her arms. The dad wasn't too far behind, and when he got to me - he threw his arms around me and told me that I was his hero.

"I told them that Tina was the hero. There was no way I could have found him - it would have been impossible for even a helicopter to see him… it was Tina that was the hero. The three of them hugged and pet Tina, and told her how much they appreciated her for finding their little boy.

"Tina got the reputation pretty quick around the department, that whenever they needed a dog for the tough calls - that Tina was the answer."

Father John said he remembered reading about this in the papers, and how impressed he was that the 'police dog' was able to find the kid in such open, and rough terrain.

He also understood why it was so hard for me to 'accept' her loss - but he wanted me to look at 'accepting a loss' in a different way… Father John said:

"Jack – you seem comforted when you talk about and remember Tina. You may not be able to change the facts - of what happened to you and Tina, but try to view it in a different way. If you can focus on the things you can control now, and use the logic in your mind to analyze what happened as if you are an observer" as he motioned his finger toward his eye… "Maybe it can open the door to 'not blaming yourself' for what happened - for not feeling guilty in surviving - when she didn't."

I sat in silence for a moment trying to understand… Father John broke the silence and said "you chose a life – a life where you are the protector, and Jack – that life comes with risks. Look back and think – what led you up to wanting to live a life where you knew you'd be in the middle of taking those hazards?"

"What made me want to be a cop? I guess I've always been drawn to protecting others, even if I didn't fully understand why. It's always been something I can't explain – like I was drawn to it. But something happened when I was barely a teenager – it's what made me become a good cop. You see Father - I had a secret spot - a hollow in the scrub oak between two hills we called 'pheasant hill.' It was the perfect hideaway for me and my friends to smoke, a place no one else could ever know about.

Getting caught would've meant the worst - my freedom, gone. But one day, while we were in our spot, we heard someone breaking through the brush. I was stunned to see a local cop, Officer Porter, standing there with a grin on his face. He asked what we had, and before I could respond, I handed him my pack of cigarettes.

"He took one, lit it, and smoked while handing me the pack. I thought, 'this guy's all right,' until he told me to crush the remaining cigarettes. He'd deal with the other boys later. Then he motioned for me to follow him to his car. I was scared now, as he gave me a ride home. I knew I had to think fast.

"When we got to my house, I walked to the driver's side and shook his hand. I thanked him quietly, but he nodded and told me to go talk to my mom. I told her I'd been riding around with him, avoiding the truth. She was suspicious about the cigarette smell, but I quickly blamed it on him – because I knew I could.

"A few days later, I saw Officer Porter's car again. He pulled over, and with a look, he asked if I wanted a ride. I got in, and we spent hours talking. I confessed what had really happened, when I talked with my mom - and he laughed. He knew I didn't have a father, and for years, he became that figure in my life also - teaching me, guiding me. He even bought me my first leather jacket for riding my dirt bike.

"Through him, I learned that enforcing every rule wasn't always the priority. It was about building trust with the people you protect. One day, though, in the car, he turned serious and warned me: 'If you ever touch the *bad* stuff, you won't make it home to your mom.' I promised him I wouldn't, and I never did.

"Over time, Porter became another mentor to me. It was because of his example that when I decided to become a cop - I'd want to be a lot like him. After Wade talked me into the idea - I knew I wanted to be a good cop too. To protect, to be there for others - just like Porter had been for me."

Father John listened intently with a half crooked smile of his own then said "Jack – these are good memories for you; they carry meaning, and they can carry you forward. If you can reach into the past and remember some of these it can help soften some of the harsh. You may never fully 'accept' what happened to you, and Tina - and no one would blame you. Like I said - you have every right to feel angry" as his hands landed firmly on the rests of his chair - "we just need a way for you to feel peace as well, so the anger doesn't consume you. When you were young and in the 'infancy' of wanting to become a cop, you may not have realized all the dangers you'd face, but when you did, and when you faced the 'fire' – Jack – you never backed off… you rose to the challenge, and the challenge you face now is allowing yourself to live in peace. You did everything right, and you are not to blame."

I could understand what he was telling me in my mind, but my heart still hurts, and I refuse to 'accept' that she was taken away from me. I told Father John that I can logically 'accept' the reality that it did happen, but not the sorrow and grief of missing her.

I was walking back out to the parking lot thinking about what Father John was saying. I thought "maybe he's right"… if I thought of my anger as a hardship, I could commit to making positive changes in my behavior - something like "fake it 'til I make it." But how… how do I pretend to be what I had a hard time accepting? What is it like to be a 'normal' part of the society - when all I've experienced is the worst of humanity?

I guess I would have to learn how to take small steps - and see each moment as an opportunity to overcome a challenge. I'm beginning to see that whatever it is that 'triggers' my feelings isn't the real problem. The real problem… was me.

While I was riding back home on my bike - I tried to think about the things Father John was trying to teach me. My thoughts kept creeping back to Tina, and how she was a comfort through the things we'd see, and how she was able to be a comfort for so many of the things I'd already seen. Maybe losing her also meant - losing a way to heal from a lifetime of darkness.

I was alone in my thoughts - thinking "I've lived so many years mired in the filth of the world, and so many of them were lived with a dog at my side. How can I be expected to accept these things? Things that aren't normal for most - were the experiences I could only hope to forget. I'm glad that I had so many good K9 partners to help me through these times, because I would never have wanted my wife to bear the burden of my experiences - even though she never would have complained about it."

I came home to an empty house, the silence thicker than usual, while my wife was on her shift at the hospital. I walked out to the patio; I lit a cigarette as I settled into the quiet with the memories of my youth still on my mind, and the longing for my partner still in my heart. In my hand, I held her empty leash, feeling its weight as if it held all the memories we shared.

Sitting alone, I let the silence wash over me, my thoughts circling back to her.

"I know, little girl… I miss you so much." My voice was barely a whisper, words dissolving into the evening air. "If there's any way you can hear me… please, help me through this. I know you're gone, and - God, if you're listening…

Let me feel her here with me just once more."

Chapter 26

The Rock

I was becoming more comfortable with Father John. And I was glad that Isabel had me talk to him. I still had reservations about letting anyone "in" – to see what was really happening inside me, or maybe I was having a hard time trusting anyone at this point… so – Father John, in his usual way of getting through the hardened walls I've built… asked me how my wife – Bell – how she was doing… even though I believed he already knew, he wanted me to think about all I'd been through and picture it in my mind – to see how it has been affecting her…

"I'm not sure if I understand Father – she's solid, and she's, well, she's always been there for me, and…"

Father John stopped me, and asked me to back up a little… "Jack, think for a moment – think for me, and tell me what it was like when – well – when you first met, and how you two became a family."

I paused – took a breath, and while I looked out his window – past the tree and into the school play yard – my mind wandered back to that day… I smiled and chuckled, "I met her in a foreign country. I was a sergeant on a K9 bomb searching squad. My partner – Gunner, excited about 'the job' - jerked me as I held his leash and we'd jumped from a helicopter a little too soon, and I landed on my foot - just a little wrong. 'They' said I'd have to report to the medical unit before I could return to duty.

"Amid the organized chaos of a makeshift hospital, the smell of Army canvas protecting us from the dust we could never seem to escape… And there she was - blonde and beautiful. She looked at my sprained ankle, and as she moved it around, I winced in pain. "Don't be a baby about this Sergeant," she said with command - yet compassion - sporting a half smile and a slight chuckle "It only hurts for a minute…"

"I let her treat me, as if I had a choice, but as she fixed my hurt, she captured my heart."

"You're little friend here is beautiful" she said looking at my partner 'Gunner'… "He looks like he can 'hold his own'" she said with a smile.

"My K9 at the time was "Gunner." He was a large German Shepherd with muscles like steel. He - like most 'Shepherds' had a sense of loyalty unmatched by other breeds… He stood firm and stoic at the side of the bed where I was sitting, and watched her work on me with an intent look on his face - but still trusting, as if he knew - this 'person' - this "human" was someone - that if I could trust… so could he."

I smiled at Father John remembering Gunner: "he tried to help Bell when she was wrapping my ankle with an 'Ace' bandage, and she looked at him chuckling *are you trying to do my job for me too?*"

With a chuckle of my own **I** said to my Nurse, **Bell** "You know - '**Gunner**' would like you to join us for a cup of coffee…?" I said with a questioning smirk, and a half smile…

She smiled back with a wink in her eye. "Yeah - I bet '*Gunner*' would really love that" This was a smile that I would learn to love for more than 40 years…

"We had that cup of coffee, and a lot more. We learned that we could lean on each other in a place where trust, loyalty, and love were a luxury… and that finding that love in the dirt, dust, and sand of a foreign country… well - I knew that somehow… this would be a bond that would last forever…"

"Well Lieutenant" as I smiled at her - "Um - does this mean I have to salute you when we go out on a date?" I chuckled…

"You bet - Sarge…" she laughed. You better know who's boss over here" she smiled…

"That 'cup of coffee' turned into a lifetime together, and that mug of 'mess-tent sludge' turned us into a family. When we finally got the approval for the Chaplain to perform the ceremony – it was the three of us… Lieutenant, Sergeant, and 'Corporal Gunner' . . .

**

"It was a while after we met, and after we'd left military service - I joined the Police force, and Bell started working in the local hospital's ER. I worked my way to become a motorcycle officer, and Bell worked her way into supervising other Nurses.

"Every morning when I would 'fire-up' my bike to go to work - she would pray - 'dear God - let him come home safe...' and of course - I would, but that never stopped her from worrying about me. All throughout the years there were times when I'd get home – well..." I paused for a moment, and then continued "there were those times, I would go to each of my kids' rooms, and make sure they'd be ok... my wife seeing this would ask - "how was your night...?"

"Do you really want to know?" I'd ask... and she'd calmly say - "no." Even though she'd seen so much over the years - as a nurse in the Army, and as an ER trauma nurse... I knew that she didn't need to hear about it all over again.

"If anyone would think for a second that the wife of an officer doesn't feel everything he goes through - is wrong!

"I could tell that every incident - every experience I went through, she felt - and somehow, she knew that every sight of a tragedy - the smell of death - the life I tried to hide from her, she experienced, and felt as much as I did.

"She didn't want to know, but I could tell she knew, and even felt what I was going through - she was right there with me. All she could do was hold me, and tell me that things would be all right.

"I would wake in the middle of a night with a bad dream, and she would simply hold me - comfort me - not knowing that the screams of a mother watching me put an eight-month old baby in a body bag still haunted me. That the smell of blood, and the sight of broken bodies still appear in my mind every time I closed my eyes...

"Somehow in the shadows of her mind - she experienced the same horror of my world, and the terrible things I would see - or feel, and even the memories I wish I could forget...

"Even though I don't want to talk about these things with her, my wife somehow knows - that the world I live when I walk out the door - is just as much a part of her life, as it is mine...

"When the call comes, and I don't know what I'm going to face when I get there - I have split seconds to make decisions, and keep control of uncontrollable situations. I have to make choices that will be scrutinized in reviews, courts, and opinions for months and years to come, but I have to do it in a half of a heartbeat.

"So when I'd come home after a shift, and she asks how my day - my night - or whenever it was I worked… I ask her if she really wants to know… and the look in her eyes tells me that she already knows."

**

"When I transferred to become a K-9 officer, I thought the horrors would end - that my new partner, Shadow, and I would just be finding drugs, contraband, and backing up other officers. But I was wrong. I ended up deeper in the world I thought I was escaping.

"Sure, there were rewarding moments - times when Shadow and I made a real difference in people's lives - but still, I had gained a reputation. When my partner and I showed up, it was because we were the ones called to solve the 'unsolvable' situations.

"No matter how hard the day had been, we'd come home to Gunner. It was like he had a way of teaching his new friend what to do - how to protect me, how to be 'on duty.' I've always been amazed by how dogs seem to learn from each other, as if Gunner was showing Shadow the ropes.

"I loved being a 'dog-cop,' and I loved working my way up to supervising them. Life at home was good, even with the weight of the real world pressing in. Our house was well lived-in, and the dogs adjusted beautifully to our growing family. They weren't just working dogs - they were part of our family, our protectors, and they were deeply loved."

"It was a sad day when we finally put Gunner into memoriam, resting forever with us - as if watching over us… like the friend, protector, and family member that he was. He had been there when our family began, and now, in spirit, he would always be with us - a quiet guardian, still standing watch."

**

"Our years together only brought us all closer – all of us. We learned how to balance our lives – with work… so I thought."

"When I would come home from a shift – like all the others before her, I would take Tina's vest, her collar, and all of her gear from her, and let her know she was in a safe place… she would spend a few minutes out on the patio with me, and sometimes my Rock - my wife, would join us, and just sit with us… she would ask if I wanted to talk about it, and I would, but I knew she didn't really want to drag all the darkness of the world into our home. Even I didn't want to think about what we'd seen just hours before.

"I would say something like - it was a hard day, and she'd know that the horror's I saw would haunt her too. So I would sit with the 'girls' in my life, and appreciate that they both knew I just needed some time to decompress before the nightmares of my life would appear in the dark - when I closed my eyes in the embrace of my wife, and with the partner that slept at the foot of my bed, who was there too - to protect me as I slept."

"Keeping our work separate from home was never easy."

**

"My wife was my 'Rock' - she was the foundation I needed for me to keep my sanity. Even though I'd spent so many hours now in the 'group' and talking with Father John - it was the constant knowing - that the one who was there with me in the darkest of times, and through the darkness of the night, she was there to feel my pain - even when she didn't know the details of what I was going through.

"She had been through enough too, as a Nurse in the Army, in a combat zone herself. She worked in the ER at the hospital, and I knew - that she knew, and shared my nightmares with me."

**

Father John sat in silence, his face lost in the memories of his own… "I'm glad you have a foundation - a 'rock' that you can lean on" he said, "In many ways - I know how you feel."

I thought to myself - and I wondered how *he* could know how I felt… losing a partner was not something someone could understand… I asked him, but he already knew I needed to hear what he had to say… then Father John started to speak…

"My childhood buddy and I joined the Army on the 'buddy' program, and we went through basic training together, then we were assigned to the same unit when we went to Viet Nam. The jungles weren't like the fields we used to play 'Army' in back at home - it was a nightmare all our own.

"We were assigned to 'dig-in' to set a perimeter, and kept the enemy at bay for a week. One night we sat in our 'fox-hole' through the rain and the mud when the mortar shells started landing all around us." Father John, scratching his forehead, leaned back in his chair… "We tried to fire back, but it all kept coming. Gunfire and shells kept hitting us hard, and we did our best to keep them at bay.

"A mortar shell hit near our fox hole, and machinegun fire kept us pinned down. Some of what I'm about to say was told to me by the men who were there with us… but,

"Both my buddy and I were hit - and hit hard. Everything went black. He tried to stop my bleeding - he did everything he could to save me. He held my chest wound tightly, and kept me from bleeding out. He couldn't move well through the mud, but he still kept me alive until the 'choppers' arrived to take us to the hospital."

Father John, was looking down at his feet, he paused, then returned his gaze into my eyes. "He ignored his own wounds, and kept his hands on my injuries. The medics wanted him to let me go, but he wouldn't. He kept his hand on my heart knowing that if he let go, I wouldn't survive. All through the flight to the hospital - he kept his hand right where it needed to be, so I could be saved.

"They rushed me into surgery, and they saved me. When I woke from it all, I asked about my buddy." Father John's eyes now staring off into the distance… "They said he didn't survive. He kept me alive in spite of his own wounds - he'd been hit in the femoral artery, and after I was cared for… he'd already lost so much blood… that there was nothing more they could do. He refused to let go of my chest wound - he sacrificed himself.

"I didn't just lose a partner that night - I lost a hero. I lost a friend I'd known since my childhood. It has taken me more years than I can count to realize I was not to blame for his death. He chose to live his last moments to save me."

As he spoke – my right hand tried to scratch away some moisture from the corner of my eye – then slowly as I lowered my hand to my chest – I could feel my own scars through my shirt – then I moved my hand down to my right leg, and I felt the scar through the cloth. As I felt the scar on my thigh through my pant leg – I realized now - how close I came that night Tina saved me.

"Yes - I felt guilty that I survived," Father John continued, "and he didn't. Yes - I felt the anger, the denial, I felt the grief that I'd never be able to say thank you… I've been there Jack - I've seen and felt, and known the loss that you are feeling.

"It may not be the same as what you are feeling, but Jack, it's as close as it can come…"

I sat there in his office stunned. We looked at each other for what seemed like an eternity. I could only say - "I didn't know what you've been through…"

Father John said that he doesn't like to talk about it either, but this would be a moment that he thought would be appropriate. He knew that I'd seen and been through a lot of similar actions when I was in Iraq and on the streets as a cop - he felt that he could share his experiences with someone who could understand.

As the hours passed that morning - we both cried together, and remembered our pain together. We both talked about the foundations - the Rocks that we leaned on when the pain of our pasts haunted our thoughts - the thoughts that become nightmares when the silence of the nights become the canvas that terror paints its indelible pictures, and the images we could only hope would go away - the images that reign heavy.

I knew from that day forward that Father John wasn't just looking to see me through my own fight, but looking in the mirror of his own past, and needing a friend that could understand the same things he was going through.

"Jack" Father John said softly as I approached the door to walk out... "The pain may never truly go away, but the thought I hold onto - similar to yours - is that my friend, my partner... will forever hold in his hands... *a little piece of my heart*."

**

When I got home from talking with Father John, I was met at the door to see the familiar silhouette of a woman with a smile standing in the doorway, and I knew by the look in her eye that she could tell I needed a quiet moment to just sit, and contemplate - to hold a hand. I looked deep into her eyes as she smiled that smile; the smile that said it all as she said "now you know why I'd needed *my* talks with Father John."

She seemed to know <u>what</u> I needed at the right time I needed it.

So we sat on the patio in silence together - both of us holding onto the end of an empty leash - a link that tied us to our memory - a lifeline that also, held us to each other - and to a love we *both* lost. It was as if the leash tied us to our Tina.

So many thoughts rushed through my head - Father John, Viet Nam, the night in the alley and the look in Tina's eyes... but - in that moment what I needed most was... the solace, and comfort of...

My Rock.

Chapter 27

Forgiveness

For several months - my meetings in 'group' went well, and my 'chats' with Father John continued. Every Sunday I'd go out for coffee or on a ride with my friends, and yet, slumbering still within – somewhere deep - I still felt the anger…

One evening sitting alone in my memories - on the patio… holding a leash… I heard the phone ring… my wife came out and handed me the phone - it was the Chief of Police. He told me that he wanted me to join them at the department headquarters for a memorial tribute for my K-9 partner. I was silent for a moment, as the flashback of that night hit me.

As I spoke to the Chief, the memory caught me off guard, clawing up from somewhere buried deep, surfacing in a flash. My heartbeat stuttered, and then slammed against my chest, fast and unsteady. Each beat feels like a hammer, jarring my insides, a sudden awareness that everything around me is both too real and utterly unreal. My skin prickled as if I was burning up, a hot flash that sends beads of sweat rolling down my neck. It felt like I was drowning, gulping for air that won't come, my chest a locked cage, I felt the scars of the bullets once again tightening around my lungs that just won't expand, and my gut - and the pain in my leg. I was there in the moment - yet watching myself as if from afar…

My mind is no longer in the present - it's back there. The images are too vivid: the sound of the gunfire, the yelp, and then the silence. Guilt wraps around me, whispering that it was my fault, that I should've done something differently. My stomach twists, and my hands shake, my fingers numb and useless. I try to press my palms together, to press the trembling away, but my mind is in freefall, scattered between past and present. I can't ground myself, I can't find solid ground. Every instinct screams to run, to escape - only there's nowhere to go.

Years of training tells me to breathe, to center myself, but my body betrays me before my mind can catch up.

The world around me blurs, voices and faces melting away as if I'm looking through thick glass. My vision tunnels, darkening at the edges, and I fight to stay anchored, I fight to remind myself where I am. But the fear swells, thick and suffocating, as if all the air is being sucked out of the room. Just as my breath starts to ease, a tremor of shame washes over me, deeper than the fear, telling me I shouldn't feel this way – and that I'm supposed to be stronger than this. And yet, I'm paralyzed, caught in the grip of a memory too painful to bear.

Seconds seemed like hours, I fought hard to ground myself. I could hear my old 'boss' talking, but the words seemed like a blur… I had to interrupt him… I had to ask him to repeat himself… I lit a cigarette so I could regain my focus…

I was told the details for when I needed to be at the station. After I hung up the phone… It felt like I'd been hit in the gut.

I walked around the patio quietly - not knowing my wife had just called Father John. She'd sensed something was wrong as she overheard my conversation with the Chief, and… as always, she knew what I needed. She brought her phone out to me - told me who it was…

"Jack - I'd like to come over - you got a minute" as I thought Father John's conversations never lasted anything like a minute. I told him I'd be here, and he continued… "We have a couple of tough things I'd like to talk about."

"Great" I thought - the last thing I needed was anything 'tough', but I'd come to trust his judgment.

I opened the door and greeted Father John. Bell, ever gracious, cordially offered him a cup of coffee, and he - graciously accepted - then he asked if we could sit outside on the patio so we could - 'chat'.

"Isabel told me about the phone call," he said… "And I kinda knew it would be a tough one for ya Bud" his voice steady and calming. And he was right. I told him about what happened to me on the patio – how it felt like the world was caving in around me…

"I think you were having some sort of panic attack - and it's completely understandable. What you're going through, you need to share with those who understand.

"Jack, the world may not understand the pressures, the split-second decisions, or the constant threats of losing your life… but those you've served with do… and I really do think you should be there at the police station to honor Tina…"

I wasn't sure of myself again at the moment, and I didn't want all the cops I'd worked with to see any of my emotions. Father John said - "that's exactly what 'they' need… they need to see someone strong - **like you**, to show them it's ok for strong people - like *you* Jack, to be able to show emotions. That's what's kept you alive - your ability to show emotion, even though you've hidden it from others for so long…"

I knew that - like the rest of us who tried to live as "manly men" who could stand tall, and face the fears no one else could - that by holding back and not being able to release the emotions - sadness, fear, anger… that these could build up, and for some, could be dangerous. For me - it felt good to be able to let some of these things go, at least when I was talking with Father John.

"Jack, I think your next step is to learn how to forgive…"

I interrupted him - "I'll never be able to forgive that son-of-a-bitch for shooting us" the anger in my voice heating… Father John putting his hand on my shoulder simply said in his soothing voice: "I'm not telling you to forgive 'him' - I want **you** to be able to forgive yourself."

"Forgive myself? How can I forgive myself for what happened to my partner. How can I forget that look in her eyes as she lay in my arms - her life slipping away, and there was nothing I could do to save her… she trusted me - she needed me, and… she died saving me…"

Father John continuing softly said "You don't forgive yourself for being alive. You forgive yourself for thinking you *could* control what you never had power over in the first place."

"I should have protected her… I could've done more" I thought as the images in my mind, and pictures of that night rushed through my head… again.

Father John seemed to be able to see that I was remembering the thoughts of that night… and he continued… "You did everything you could, Jack. She knew that. The question is - when will *you* believe it?"

I sat quietly while I stared out at the horizon, lost in thought.

Father John took a deep breath and continued: "You aren't honoring her by carrying this guilt. She gave her life to save yours, and I'm sure she wouldn't want this to be the only thing you carry forward... Wouldn't she want you to live without all this weight on your shoulders?" Father John repositioned himself, settling back into the chair he was sitting on - a slight sense of him being uncomfortable... but he continued.

"Jack, do you remember when I told you about that night in 'Nam? About how **I** carried that weight for years, thinking it *was* my fault? It's not easy to let go, and I don't expect you to do it today... or tomorrow - but you owe it to yourself to start trying."

I shook my head, the anger still simmering "But how? How do I let it go when I can still see the look in her eyes, cradled in my arms - her life slipping away?"

Father John again placing his hand on my shoulder: "By accepting that you did everything in your power... and by honoring her sacrifice, and by living, and not by drowning yourself in this guilt."

I remained silent, my jaw clenched, fighting back the tears...

Father John went on - "Jack, I know that place you're in. But it's a prison we've built for ourselves. And forgiveness? That's the key to getting out. It wasn't easy for me either, but Jack... you're not alone in this..."

**

I arrived at the police station, feeling a knot in my stomach. I see my former colleagues standing in formation, their uniforms sharp, and faces somber. As I walk up to the podium, my heart pounds in my chest, feeling that familiar grip of guilt. It was how I remember standing in front of the congregation that Sunday morning. How I felt the pain of my memories, and how the guilt began to resurface then too. My wife sensing my hesitation squeezes my hand, and Father John, and even Wade joined us to stand by my side, offering a quiet presence of strength.

The Chief of Police takes the microphone first, his voice steady but emotional. He talks about my K-9 partner - her loyalty, her bravery, and her sacrifice. He speaks about how she saved countless lives through her service and how she gave her life protecting her partner… me.

As the Chief speaks, my mind drifts back to that night, the memory vivid and painful - my partner's eyes, the feeling of helplessness. But this time, the words of Father John echo in my head, pushing through the fog of guilt. "You owe it to her to live."

After the Chief finishes, a ceremonial tribute follows - a wreath placed before a memorial plaque with my K-9's name etched in brass. My hands are trembling as I'm called to speak. I don't know what to say. All I can think of is how I failed her.

I step to the microphone, the crowd - my community: neighbors, bikers and friends - strangers all watching expectantly. My voice is low at first, barely audible, but I force myself to speak.

"I… I didn't just lose a partner that night. I lost part of myself. And I've spent every day since then wondering if I could've done more. But standing here today, seeing all of you here today to honor her the way she deserves... maybe it's time I stop asking what I could've done differently."

My voice cracks, and I grip the sides of the podium as I gather myself "Maybe it's time I start remembering her for what she was - loyal, brave, and always by my side."

As I speak, tears well in my eyes, but I hide them. I know I should forget the adage that "Big-boys don't cry" – but I wasn't ready… I know this was for her – and maybe this was for me - the relationship we had, and the love we had for each other. At that moment, nothing else mattered, but I still held it in.

I look at the plaque, at my partner's name, her statue shining in the sunlight, and I feel the weight lift ever so slightly from my shoulders. For the first time, I allow myself to let some of the tears fall - not just for my loss, but for the release of all the guilt I've carried. I did my best to hide them behind the shade of my sunglasses, but only those closest to me could tell…

Father John watches me closely, knowing this is a pivotal moment for me. My wife, standing nearby, takes my hand again, and this time I squeeze it back, feeling her support.

The final tribute is a salute, the officers all raising their hands to a gesture of honor. I stand straighter; I salute back, and let out a long breath I didn't know I was holding.

Afterward, as the crowd disperses, Father John walks over... "It wasn't easy, but you did it, Jack. And that's the first step toward forgiving yourself."

My voice still hoarse: "I'm not there yet, Father... but maybe, just maybe, I'm starting to see a way forward."

**

The drive home was quiet - words could not break through the feelings in my heart, and the silence now became a comfort. My Rock - my wife, never breaking her gaze upon me - simply smiling in a comforting way...

Entering the house - before I could even change from my uniform... my wife - Bell... gently took my hand, and as we walked past the refrigerator near the back door, I looked at the floor – hoping just one more time, to see the puddles of water, and half melted ice cubes Tina would leave us... my wife sensing my nostalgia, held my hand tight and led me outside to the patio... she placed the end of a now vacant leash into my hand... and said softly... we'll hold onto this... all of this... together... forever...

As we sat in silence - there was a hint of comfort in knowing that there really wasn't anything else I could have done that night. I didn't know how to forgive, but I knew that by telling myself what happened wasn't my fault... was the first step.

I sat still, my back against the patio chair. I looked deep into Bell's blue eyes as the shadows stretched longer now, wrapping the landscape in a quiet that felt almost reverent. The ache in my chest hadn't gone, not entirely, but something else was there now - a flicker of peace, fragile but real.

For the first time in a while, I wasn't running. But I was still searching. In this moment, I was simply here, and that was enough - for now.

And then it struck me: the world I chose to live in had never promised certainty. The promise of safety? That promise falls on the shoulders - and hearts of the strong.

In that instant, I realized I would have to reach deep, into a place I thought was lost, to find the heart, the courage that...

Tina wanted to save.

Chapter 28

Trials and Testimonies

At times I look at my life - the same way a writer gazes at a blank page… wondering what words, wondering what thoughts, or what deep contemplations should be shared… and not sure of what the outcome will be.

But this page was different - the words and the message was clear. The time had come for me to appear in court. I read the court subpoena again - realizing how important it is for me to testify, so no one else would be hurt. It was my duty once again… to protect.

Many times I related the feelings of loss, of guilt, and anger - to those who could understand, but this was different. This time I would be telling about what happened to Tina – and to me - to total strangers. Firefighters, EMT's, Soldiers, and Cops - at least they could get a sense of what I'd experienced, but Judges, Lawyers, and Jurors may never know - or feel, the terror of being shot… of losing a loved one who served by my side.

I knew I needed some help.

My wife suggested I call Father John. She could tell that my actually having to relive the events of 'that night' would be different. I had to think…

I stepped out into the sunlight and sat for quite some time thinking - "this isn't about my feelings - this is all about the facts. This is about putting a criminal away for a long time."

**

I sat in his wooden chair, and I gripped the armrests, nervous - knowing that what I was about to talk about would be the hardest thing I could do. Father John sat across from me - close, so I could feel the comfort he was there for. Although Isabel was my 'Rock' - my soft place to fall - Father John was a comfort that only a trained counselor could provide.

"Jack - I know this will be hard, and hard times call for tough men. We've talked a lot about this, but in a way - danced around the details of what actually happened that night."

"I know" I said looking deep into his eyes, "and I don't know if I'm really ready to do it" as my eyes now drifted toward the trees - the playground outside Father John's window... looking at the innocent children - the lives that should never know horror...

"How about you tell me what you were doing as you were getting ready for your shift that night" he said peacefully, yet commanding. And all the memories of that day – the day that turned into the darkest of nights... began to play like a broken film reel, scenes flashing out of order. Pictures in my mind overlapping, pulling me in without warning.

Father John gently rested his hand on my knee: "Jack – how about we start with the simple things... take a deep breath, and describe your routine of getting ready..." and I began again...

I looked around the room - then back out the window, and the pictures I saw in my mind, it was a beautiful day. "I was outside sitting on the patio. I can see my wife walking out to the patio with Tina by her side – they were both smiling, and they joined me for coffee."

"Then" I continued... "It started like any other day. Working the swing-shift always seemed exciting - and we got to see both daylight - and nights... and it gave us the time before we went to work to play with Tina for a few minutes... I wish I had those minutes back...

"It was a quiet routine, the familiar motions. I knelt beside Tina, securing her vest, checking the straps, making sure everything was in place. She always stood still for me, patient as always, her dark eyes watching me with that steady calm I'd come to rely on. My hands moved from buckle to buckle, more out of habit than thought, but tonight felt different. I would always put her duty collar on last - like I was putting on her necklace. I called it her 'pretty'... she would smile.

"*You ready, girl?*" I said in a low voice, giving her a light pat on the side. She responded with a small pant, her eyes full of loyalty and focus. She knew the drill. This was what we did. Day in and day out, we prepared for the worst, knowing it could come at any moment – praying it never would.

"I went out to warm-up the truck, while my wife sat with Tina on the patio, and when I walked back to them they were getting in one last 'hug' before we all went to work…

"*You look after him*" she told Tina standing up to kiss me good bye. "*You take care of 'our guy' Tina*" she said with a bit of nervousness in her voice. We all walked toward the truck, I opened the door and Tina jumped in with her usual joy of 'going for a ride.'

"It's hard to explain how you can have a 'routine' day and yet feel a kind of heaviness in the air, something I couldn't quite place. We'd been on several searches for drugs, a number of traffic stops, and stood ready to back up some officers on a domestic violence call." I chuckled slightly: "Tina had a way of diffusing a situation, just by her being there."

"Tina had her favorite burger joint, and she loved French fries. I radioed into dispatch that we'd be stopping for our 'lunch' break - even though it was approaching 8pm in the evening. We picked up our food, and pulled through the parking lot where we could eat under the lights, as the day drew on becoming darker.

"I turned my radios down so we could eat in peace for a minute, when my Corporal - Nick, pulled his truck up to mine - so his driver side window was next to mine. He told me that he'd heard on the radio there were a couple of fugitives from the next State over, 'that they were armed and dangerous,' and that their last know direction was up the Interstate toward us. I turned up my radio so I could hear the "attempt to locate" call - I wrote down the description of the suspects and their vehicle. Everyone on my team let dispatch know that we 'copied' – in other words, we received the message.

"Tina - alert as ever seemed as if she knew what to be on the look-out for too…

"I thought I'd take a slow drive up by the foothills overlooking the city, just to see if I could see anything out of the ordinary. "Bell called me from her work at the hospital just to see how things were going: I knew she felt a sense of nervousness, and was curious if anything was out of the 'norm' - I joked with Tina while I was on the phone with my wife, asking Tina if she "saw any 'bad-guys' and Tina would get that 'excited' look on her face. My wife laughed, and I told her I'd call her back in a while.

"Tina and I parked on a hill overlooking the city. I turned off the truck and lit a cigarette, watching as Tina wandered around for a few minutes. The radio was turned up just enough to catch any calls, but for now, it was just the two of us, sitting under a cloudless sky as the stars brightened above. If there was ever a moment to hold onto forever, a night meant to etch itself into memory - this was it. Or at least it should have been.

"Tina eventually came and sat beside me while I finished my smoke. We didn't speak; we didn't need to. For a few fleeting minutes, the world faded away, leaving only…

Tina and me.

"Not seeing anything up in the hills - we made our way back down toward the city lights. By now we heard several officers in another division call out on the radio that they thought they saw the suspect vehicle down in the industrial district. So I told Tina that we'd go take a look with them. She looked excited.

"We didn't get too far before the other officers called out that they confirmed it was the suspect vehicle, and now a possible visual on at least one of the suspects. I used the "car-to-car" mode on the radio to let both Nick and Stan get their dogs Thor and Aries ready to respond. We pulled into a warehouse complex, as more officers arrived. I was the ranking officer so I directed some to set up a perimeter to block anyone from leaving, and the others to block off the alley-way where they spotted the suspect. I motioned for Stan to follow me over to where the suspect vehicle was…

"Tina and I pulled up and got out - Nick and Thor not too far behind us. I told Stan and Aries to set up on the entrance to one of the alley ways thinking if anyone were to 'run' they'd be the best at catching them. Stan looked at me and smiled saying *go get 'em Sarge - you two make an awesome team*."

Nick and I parked our trucks so we could block anyone from leaving also, and more officers began to arrive. I told them to hold their position at the entrance.

"Nick, Thor, Tina, and I started to walk slowly up into the dark alley. Nick commented quietly '**most people wouldn't go in here for a million bucks… we do it for a whole lot less**' - and he is right. We continued to walk slow - quiet - the dogs panting in anticipation. Out of the corner of my eye I saw movement, I ordered the individual to '***STOP!*** *Get on the ground*' but he didn't. It looked like he was reaching for a weapon and Nick let Thor loose. I held Tina back - in full attack mode - while Thor made one huge leap and tackled the suspect, who did have a weapon in his hand at this time.

"I immediately called out on the radio 'roll medical' so we could have an ambulance on hand to treat any wounds Thor might leave on the suspect. I could hear Thor's excitement and the suspect's pain. Nick told Thor to stop, and for the suspect to get face down on the ground. Nick kicked the pistol away and Thor stood close as Nick started to cuff…

"I told Tina to 'sit-ready' - while ordering a couple more officers to help take the suspect into custody, and walk him out of the alley - Thor still ready and watching the suspect, bearing teeth… Tina ever more vigilant, scanning the darkness for any more threats.

"I looked deep into the darkness, then down at Tina, the hair on her neck raised and her teeth ready - I knew she could tell something was down the alley hiding in the dark.

"The first suspect was in custody" some officers said over the radio - I could hear them talking to the suspect as they walked him back toward the opening of the alley - asking him where the other guy was - he just laughed. Tina, and now Thor, both gazing off into the darkness - the only lights coming from our vehicles parked a hundred feet away.

"I asked Tina - *'what do ya see little girl'* and she started tugging at her leash. *'Hold tight girl'* my hand slipping down to the clip that restrained her on her leash. Slowly releasing her - she stayed at my side - I told her to 'heel'… we took a few steps, slow and steady - and I drew my pistol from the holster as we inched further into the alley.

"I was in the lead, and hearing Thor panting in a near frenzy, I knew Nick wasn't far behind me."

I told Father John - still listening intently, that it is impossible to describe the surreal - to see, hear, and feel - even smell everything going on - to describe the indescribable…

"Do your best Jack" he whispered…

"Tina and I take a few more steps - I'm trying to make sense of the shapes - the shadows - can I see any movements? A few more steps… I hear nothing but my heartbeat - dogs panting furiously… I see the brilliant flashes from the muzzle of a rifle. I fire my pistol at the flashes. It feels like someone hit me in the chest - then again in the gut, like getting hit with a baseball bat - my right leg feels like it's on fire. I feel the concrete on the back of my head as I hit the ground… but I turn toward the flashes from the rifle and fire my pistol again and again while I feel Tina dragging me by the collar of my ballistic vest - tearing my shirt - I see Thor rush through hail of bullets. I can hear the screams of a man amongst Thor's growls.

"There's a torrent of radio calls - shouting, while a lot of officers now rush to help. Tina lay across me - then I sat up against a building - behind a garbage dumpster, Tina now in my lap. I could tell she was hurt - I started removing her gear. I moved my hands up and down her - now covered in her blood. I couldn't breathe - it hurt. I grabbed Tina and held her close, her breathing was fast and I could tell she was in pain.

"I kept telling her *"you're going to be fine girl"* as I stroked her hair: *"we're going to get you taken care of."*

More and more officers came, and I could hear some of them saying they needed several more medical teams – *"Officer down"* and *"the suspect is down"* – but I ignored them. My mind was focused on Tina, I couldn't breathe, but I kept talking to my Tina - '*I love you girl - mamma loves you - hang in there baby, you're going to be Ok!*' I struggled for a breath - I looked deep into her eyes - once dark - yet bright, now fading into the darkness that surrounded us. Her breathing slowed, and her eyes closed as we looked at each other for the last time."

As I spoke my eyes were closed envisioning the moment.

**

As I opened my eyes – I was now sitting in a chair that has no arm rests. The pictures of that night were still flashing before me in my mind. I look across the large room to see Father John and my wife Isabel – even Wade – all sitting in the audience. Tears in their eyes - tears in the eyes of the jury… my heart pounding - I knew that I had to be at my best. There was too much at stake. And all I could hear was the Judge saying…

"Answer the question sir…"

"No" I said: "there was no one else in the alley that night. After the first suspect was in custody - there was no-one else, but the other officers, and (me pointing at the defendant) him."

I looked at the defense attorney - my heart still pounding, and he stared back at me. I could feel my anger, I could feel the loss all over again, but I wasn't going to break. And all he could say was… "No further questions."

**

We walked out of the courthouse that day - silently, in near reverence. Now standing in the sunlight, Father John said "I know it wasn't easy, but I'm proud of you." Father John turned to my wife Bell and said: "I know this wasn't easy for you too."

Bell looked at Father John with a faint smile, "Thank you for being here, Father John… for him, for both of us." She took my hand as we walked - her touch a steady reminder that through all the trials, the darkness, and the loss, she was my anchor.

Bell was at work that night - she was there to see first-hand what had happened to me… she was the first one at the hospital - to treat my wounds.

I could tell this was a nightmare she had to relive as well. But she stood at my side quietly and embraced me, and said "you were so brave - I'm proud of you too."

As we reached the parking lot I was able to take a deep breath feeling the weight lift from me - even if ever so slightly. The trial was over, but the memory would never fade. The sacrifice Tina made was one that I would carry with me forever, her loyalty etched into my soul.

For the first time since that night, I felt a bit of peace knowing that justice was served, even though it came at a cost I'd never fully heal from. I looked up at the sky, and with a faint whisper on my lips I said, *"Rest easy, girl… we did it."*

Father John was right - I wasn't walking this path alone. With us at the courthouse were so many of the Officers who were there with Tina and me that night. All of them in their 'Dress' uniforms - pressed and polished; a testament to the unity that brought me through that dark night.

Before I could reach my truck to drive home, they formed a line for us to walk through, and in unison as my friends Wade and Stan shouted "Present-Arms" they snapped to 'Attention,' saluted sharp, and remained steadfast as we arrived at my truck.

I turned… and with the moisture from my eyes hidden behind my sunglasses – I returned the salute as they snapped their arms back to their sides. I *shouldn't* have cared at that moment - to even *try* to hold back the tears, bit I did - because…

"Big boys - aren't supposed to cry."

Chapter 29

Sheepdogs and Wagon Wheels

The days following court – and having to relive that once bright day that turned into the darkest of nights - were filled with a mix of emotions, swirling through my mind, and landing in my heart. Anger, sorrow, guilt - confusion, all spun together cementing the indelible picture in my mind - of my last look at Tina.

I tried to shake it all off - I struggled to process it logically, but nothing seemed to work. Isabel, always intuitive, suggested we take a ride together to help clear my mind.

We ended up in a small countryside town hosting a Border Collie competition. We watched herding trials, obedience tests, and agility courses. I watched these magnificent animals, listened to them bark - laughed at their playful antics and endless energy. They seemed to enjoy the open air and sunshine as much as me.

I looked at Bell; I said "The dogs - they move with precision, focused and unrelenting, their eyes never leaving the flock. It's like a dance of instinct and purpose." The hum of the crowd, and dogs barking all seemed to fade into the background as the moment shed a spark - a flash of clarity. As if by some sort of inspiration on why Bell brought me here today… it hit me. I wasn't just impressed by their ability, but it struck a nerve about my own life. The dogs I watched that day weren't just moving sheep from one point to another - they were protectors.

I sat there, reflecting: *I'm a Sheepdog.* I've spent most of my life guiding the flock, keeping them organized, helping them get to where they need to go. I was just like them - I had a duty to watch over my community - my flock… standing between them and danger.

Sometimes, I would have to bare my 'Sheepdog' teeth, and fight the fight; I had to deal with things the flock - my community - couldn't handle. But then I would quietly retreat to my safe place, my Rock, and like - how a sheepdog would lick their wounds, I would prepare for another day.

My wife seemed to sense the thoughts deep in my mind, and asked me softly if I'd ever thought about getting another dog. The idea brought a pang of fear - of losing another partner. It nearly sent me into a panic. Then she said quietly, "You know… you weren't the only one who lost a partner that day."

Her words hit me like a blow. Bell had been going through the same pain I was, and it should have brought us closer - like Father John's understanding had - but it didn't. She may not have been in the line of fire, but she had been my foundation, the one pulling me through, treating my wounds. And when she needed my strength, I wasn't there for her.

For Bell, that night wasn't just about losing Tina. She almost lost me. The realization struck me deeply. She had saved my life, and treated my wounds - all while knowing Tina wasn't coming home. I couldn't imagine how unbearable that must have been for her.

"I'm sorry," I said at last. It was all I could manage. All this time, I'd been mourning Tina, consumed by my own loss. Maybe it wasn't selfishness – maybe it was, but I had been so caught up in my grief that I'd missed the signs - missed what my wife was going through.

**

Meeting with Father John was more than therapy. He was not only curious about my going out on rides with my 'biker' friends, but also how I was doing with the anger, the guilt, and blaming myself for what happened. He knew some of my friends were in the same PTSD meetings I was going to. I told him that I didn't feel ready to share *all* the things I'd experienced to them - the way I was sharing with Father John.

I told my friend - my counselor, that my wife mentioned getting another dog. I told him that I was afraid of loss - getting attached and missing another relationship… I told him that I now realized that my wife too missed and mourned my partner… our partner. I told him my heart nearly 'skipped a beat' when she asked me about having another dog. I told him that thought made me feel like I would be replacing Tina… replacing her memory. And all those feelings – and, well - they brought back the memory of the pain.

Father John said "it's normal for innocent comments to 'trigger' emotions – feelings and such, and there are probably a lot of other things too… things that can spark some of those memories – experiences of your life 'on duty' – that you're trying to forget. Jack… there are lots of things, and even combinations of things that can 'trigger' you back to that night."

I nodded my head – because in my mind, and as I thought - I wasn't just agreeing with what he said, that it wasn't just simple words or comments, but I was remembering things like sights, or sounds, and even the smells… and for a moment, and before I could break the silence - as I paused - my voice cracked a little: "The wail of sirens that echoes in the distance, sharp and insistent, those sounds pierce through the quiet of my time out on the patio. It seems like the sounds of the sirens snap me back to that day - the day everything changed. The bullets, the shouts, the blood - my partner, gone in a flash of violence. The loss always fresh again, like an open wound I can't stitch closed… Father - I can still feel the heat of that moment, as if it were happening all over again."

Pictures in my mind flashed again – even the pain I tried to ignore as my partner closed her eyes… I felt it all over again, and it was hard to speak, but I went on… "The sirens… whenever I hear them in the distance – they still take me back to that night. They trigger me back to the smell of blood. Even now, I can almost taste it, thick and metallic on my tongue. You know Father - they tried to prepare us when we were in the Police Academy - for the sights and sounds… they showed us pictures of shattered glass and twisted steel, and even pictures of crime scenes and such… but no one could ever prepare us about the smells, no matter how hard they tried. These smells are what worm their way into my nightmares, creeping into my senses when I least expected it. You can't escape it."

The priest nodded with understanding in his eyes. "'Triggers' come in many forms, Jack. Sometimes it's what you see; sometimes it's what you hear. And for you… it's all this, and much more – it's also about what you smell. We can't run from it. But we can learn to live with it."

Father John leaned back into his chair and gave me that smile of his and continued: "Jack – let's take a step back, and think about your day at the Sheepdog competition. You were enjoying the sunshine, the dogs – just having a good day with your wife. I'm sure you were thinking about Tina, but you had moments where the memories weren't as painful – didn't you?"

"Yes Father – I guess so" as I thought back… "It really was a good day for me…" I went on and told him how sorry I was for not realizing how much Bell was going through. I felt bad it hadn't dawned on me.

Father John wanted me to focus for a minute, just on me though… "Jack – I know it's not easy, but let's go back and talk about some of these things that 'trigger' you into the memories that cause you pain…"

Father John said that "it's normal for comments – or other sounds to trigger memories, and that one trigger – as simple or 'innocent' as it may be, can set off many others…" he went on… "Trauma - PTSD, and other feelings, are like the spokes in a wagon wheel, leading back to you Jack - the hub, the same place where all the pain lived. Everything connects" - his voice was steady, his hand tracing a circle in the air as he went on…

"Memories, trauma, fear – they're all part of the wheel. And right now, you're stuck in the center of it, with all those spokes pointing inward. But healing, Jack, it's about finding a way to deal with each spoke - each trigger, one at a time - and isolate them from letting 'em consume you."

I sat quiet, my imagination painting a picture in my mind - me standing in the center of a large wagon wheel - the spokes pointing inward toward me - sharp and threatening… I didn't like it… I forced my attention back to listening to Father John as he continued:

"The memories of loss, of any - or even all of your experiences will never go away, but what we need to do is keep it from dominating you, controlling you - damaging you. We need to find a way to turn your focus on the things preventing the trauma all around you from getting to the center - to you."

He leaned forward slightly "Jack – I think I have an idea that may help…"

As he spoke, I was deep in my thoughts - I couldn't help but reflect on how many jumbled memories flooded me… the pictures during my academy days - crime scenes, mangled cars, and lifeless bodies - enough to think I'd be prepared for the real thing. But what no one warned me about, what no training manual could explain was the smell. The copper tang of blood hanging thick in the air, mixing with burnt rubber and gasoline. It was a smell that clung to me, that soaked into my skin and followed me long after the scene was cleared.

No textbook mentioned how the scent would latch onto my memory like a vice, showing up in the most unexpected moments, even years later. Nothing I could do - would, or could, let me escape the sensations that haunted me. Memories and nightmares that lurk in the shadows of "our" minds, that all too often drown those of us who haven't sought the solace of a lifeline…

My thoughts drift back to that night – every time one trigger 'hits' me – others follow. And it seems that these triggers – lead to me remembering the smell of blood – and keeps "that night" fresh in my mind.

"I'd learned and experienced, and I even thought I was prepared for the worst - and in many ways - I lived through it all." It was hard, but I tried to keep my thoughts focused. "I'm sorry Father - I'm having a hard time focusing…"

"It's Ok - believe me - I understand…" Father John smiling in an understanding way…

"How do I get past all the 'triggers' - how do I keep from alienating Isabel - I know she's paying the price for all this - how could I even make it up to her?"

Father John looked deep - studying my face "One step at a time Jack – you're not going to be able to make anything up to Bell, until you learn how to help yourself."

"I feel so bad - I feel so angry - angry that - that 'ass-hole' shot my partner…" I could feel the anger welling within me… Father John went on and explained why losing Tina - in a way 'broke' me… when I'd been through, seen, and survived so much. "I don't know Father - maybe losing Tina was the final straw that broke the proverbial camel's back?"

Father John spent a few minutes going back over how losing Tina was the pivotal moment that brought a lifetime of trauma to the surface. The look in Father John's eyes told me he had an idea… but he told me to continue – he wanted me to 'get it out' in the open – for me to express feelings I'd held inside… for so long.

"I don't blame the gun - I don't blame the bullets that ripped through my body - I blame HIM - he shot my Tina" my voice raising… "He is alive - I am alive, and my Tina - she'll never see another sunset. She'll never play with her toys, or feel our love! Father - she is gone! Father - my Tina - she's gone" as tears began to well-up from my eyes… "I was able to save Gunner, but I couldn't save Tina!"

Father John was able to understand as no other could in the moment. And as we talked - he was able to relive his own pain as he'd shared with me before… he wasn't just an educated, trained counselor and therapist… in this moment, he was my mentor… he was my friend.

As he was able to calm me - we talked further so I could identify and then isolate the triggers… triggers that could be something as simple as **me** complaining about idiot drivers on the road, to the sights, the sounds… and the smells that bring back vivid images of horror… how many searches found lifeless bodies – how many rescues had failed.

There are too many crashes – too many homicides, and so many times a routine day becomes a nightmare '**we**' have to bear the burden for. I told Father John that I couldn't even watch a mother stroll a baby down the street without remembering the screams - the memory of a crash, and having to take a lifeless baby from a young mother's arms… and place it in a bag…

As we talked, we painfully remembered so many 'trauma's' that surrounded me, and that they may never go away, but we could at least deal with each one independently.

"You see Jack – you've been trying to deal with all of these triggers at once – whether you realized it or not. This is why I want you to be able to identify each one as separate, so we can find a way to replace each of them with something good – like how you could remember Tina without the pain while you were watching the Sheepdogs out in the countryside."

Father John's words sank in deeply, but what hit hardest was his analogy - the wagon wheel. Each trauma, each trigger, was like a spoke connecting back to the hub, to me, to my core. It was all connected. But his calm voice carried hope, even when I felt overwhelmed by the weight of everything.

I sat in silence for a moment, thinking about the Sheepdogs I had watched that day in the countryside. They weren't just herders, guiding the sheep from one place to another; they were protectors. They stood between the flock and whatever threat might come from the wild - watching, waiting, always alert. That's what I had always been - a Sheepdog, standing guard, baring my teeth when needed. But it hit me then: just like those dogs, I wasn't just protecting others. I had to **protect myself**, too.

Father John had traced those spokes of trauma back to me, to the hub. But maybe part of being a Sheepdog wasn't just only about fending off the wolves. Maybe it was about finding a way to shield myself from the things that threatened to break me down. I realized it wasn't just about the bullets that nearly killed me, or the blood or the horrors I'd seen.

It was the triggers, the things that kept gnawing at me - the sounds, the smells, the memories that were a constant reminder of each day on the job could be my last. These triggers – they'll never go away. They're always around, and they're a constant reminder that brings back the pictures in my mind… They were the wolves at my door. And if I didn't find a way to fend them off, I'd be overwhelmed.

Father John leaned forward - his face turned from the stoic understanding stare back to his slight grin, and he simply said: "The Sheepdog stands firm, protecting the flock, but even the Sheepdog needs moments of rest, moments to recover and heal. It doesn't mean they stop protecting. It means they become stronger, more resilient, prepared to face the wolves again tomorrow. Jack – the Sheepdog knows the threats, knows the danger, and knows that each day could be its last, but it also knows how to celebrate each day as a success – how each day is a victory over the adversary. Jack, that's where you are now."

I needed to become that kind of Sheepdog again. Not just for the flock, but for myself - and for my wife, my Bell. Father John was right. I couldn't protect her from my pain, or from our loss, until I found a way to protect myself from it first.

"I'll keep fighting," I said softly, more to myself than to Father John. "I'll find a way to deal with it… the triggers… the memories."

"You will," Father John replied. "One spoke at a time, Jack. I want you to come by tomorrow – you've made a lot of progress in conquering your pain and your fear of loss, and even the anger… I'll see you tomorrow."

As I left his office, I thought again of the dogs in the field – watchful, steadfast, and protective. And for the first time in a long while, I felt like I could be a Sheepdog again.

I walked in the door and saw my wife in the kitchen, and I looked at her - I paused… I held her close, feeling a new resolve settle in. I wasn't alone in this - she was my strength, my purpose. I needed her - so - together; I'd find my way back.

I felt a surge of pride I thought had been lost forever. Yes, I had been broken. Yes, I had been beaten. But as we stood there together, I understood - survival wasn't just about enduring. It was about recognizing my victory, and reclaiming my life, one step at a time… one spoke at a time.

We stood side by side, our words unspoken but clear in the quiet connection between us. My thoughts of how she not only cared for my wounds, but how she - in many ways…

Has held my heart in *her* hands.

Chapter 30

Hands

The following day when I met with Father John, he asked me about my day - handed me a cup of coffee, then had me sit in a chair unusually close to his. I wasn't totally surprised, but not sure what he had in mind. Father John asked me what religion meant to me. And I told him that I wasn't sure if religion *was* really meant for me. I reminded him of my doubts – "I mean, how could God let so many bad things happen…?"

"Ok Jack" Father John said with a smirk - "I can understand that. I know - well - knowing that you've experienced a lot in your life, I'm not going to give you a 'Sunday School' lesson, but I want you to think about something…"

I still wasn't sure where he was going to go with this, but I said "I'm listening…"

Father John continued: "as you think about *you* as the hub of our imaginary wagon wheel, and the spokes bringing all of the trauma you've experienced - the trauma that's surrounded you - directly to you… if we can replace each of the spokes - each bad memory with a good one – that's where I'd like to start…"

I was interested - and yet doubtful, and Father John went on… "Let's take a look back at the day you and Bell were watching the Sheepdogs – this was something that brought you joy - instead of the something that brought you pain. Even though you could still think about Tina – it didn't remind you of the anger you feel…"

We sat for a few minutes - my mind swirling with memories, both happy and sad. Moments that made me smile - even laugh - drifted through my thoughts.

"It's kind of funny, Father," I said with a small smile. "She'd lose one of her favorite balls and come tug at me, almost trying to tell me to follow her so I could fish it out from behind a cabinet or somewhere she couldn't reach - how she would almost try to verbalize that she wanted me to follow her." I paused, my smile fading. "It's hard sometimes… the things that make me happy are the same things that remind me of what I've lost."

"Jack," Father John said quietly, "that's normal. But what we've got to do is focus on the happy parts - it's all right to feel the loss too."

Father John continued, leaning in slightly, his voice calm and reassuring. "Jack, it's normal for the happy memories to also carry a sense of loss. It's part of the human experience. But here's the thing - those moments of happiness still have value. They shaped you, and gave you strength. We can't erase the pain, and the anger may never completely go away, but we can make sure it doesn't overshadow the joy. Just like you did the other day."

I nodded slowly, but the doubt still lingered in the back of my mind. "I get what you're saying, but it feels like every time I try to think about something good, the bad creeps in. I don't know how to separate the two."

Father John smiled softly. "It's not about separating them, Jack. It's about learning to hold them both at the same time. Life is a mixture of joy and sorrow, and one doesn't cancel out the other. Think of your hands... one holds the joy, the other holds the pain. You don't need to choose between them, but you can learn to let the joy shine a little brighter."

Father John reached over from his chair across from me, and took me by the hands - I felt a bit uncomfortable, and yet at the same time, comforted... and he went on...

"Jack, you've told me now, so many stories of 'Tina' - and how you'd play with her in your back yard - throw the ball, take her for walks - spend the quiet time in the evening - drinking your beer, smoking a cigarette... you've mentioned how you'd stroke her fur, and I'm willing to bet – you would even sit and hold her hand" as he smiled...

In that moment, I pictured her lying on her back - paws in the air - reaching for my hand. That ball clenched in her mouth, her tongue hanging out, and a smile shining in her eyes... as Father John continued:

"Jack - she wasn't just a dog - she was your partner on, and off duty... she comforted you, and she saved you... even though she sacrificed herself for you - and you feel the loss... think about the times you just sat with her..."

For a moment I may have even smiled. For a moment I may have even felt a sense of joy. Then, the thoughts of her not being here brought back the pain... I could hear father John as he was still talking...

As I listened I felt my throat tighten. "She wasn't just a dog," I muttered, barely above a whisper. Father John nodded. "No, she was more than that. She was your companion - your partner in every sense. When the world felt like it was in chaos, she was there. She protected you. She understood you in a way that no one else could. And even though she's gone, Jack, those moments still belong to you."

I looked down at my hands, at Father John's grip. His words were starting to break through. "Sometimes I still feel her there, like she's sitting beside me," I said, my voice cracking. "But when I remember those good moments, it's like it just brings all the pain back."

Father John squeezed my hands gently, grounding me. "That's because love and loss are intertwined. But you can choose what to focus on, Jack. You can choose to honor those moments with Tina - the times she brought you peace, not the pain of her loss. She gave her life for you because that's who she was. She wanted you to live, to be here in this moment. Jack – healing, it's all in your hands."

The memories of that night in the alley flooded back - gunshots, and the look in her eyes as they drifted away across the rainbow bridge. She lay in my arms. I could feel her fur, her blood, the slow rhythm of her breathing... the sights – the sounds, and even the smell - all of it, right there, in my mind, and in my hands. I remembered my own pain - the radio calls, the ambulance - and then the bright lights of the hospital, where the confusion turned into a thick fog. I remember waking up after surgery, but it didn't feel like waking at all.

I remember the grip of my wife's hands on mine - almost as if I could barely feel them, yet they held me tight. The sounds of the machines keeping me alive... I wasn't holding onto memories anymore. I was holding onto life. The life my partner saved. The life my wife saved - and wanted me to keep. In that moment, it was all in my hands.

My breath caught as the memories gripped me, so vivid, so raw that they might as well have been happening again. The alley. The gunshots. Tina's eyes locking with mine as her strength faded - her look drifting away like a shadow into the dusk. Her last gift to me was her life.

Still sitting across from Father John, I closed my eyes. In my mind, I heard the faint echo of the hospital room - the cold, sterile beeping of the machines that kept me breathing. I wasn't awake, not fully. But I remember her hands - my wife's hands. Gripping mine as if she was holding me to this world. Her silent plea, begging me to fight, to stay. To live.

"I wasn't just holding on to memories," I murmured, barely recognizing my own voice. "I was holding onto life. The life Tina gave me. The life my wife wanted me to keep... It was all in my hands."

Father John remained quiet, letting the weight of my words hang between us. I could feel his presence - steady and warm - grounding me like the earth beneath my feet.

"You're right, Jack," he finally said. "It was in your hands. But you weren't alone. Your wife, even Tina in a way - they were there, holding you, carrying you when you couldn't carry yourself. And now, it's up to you to keep holding on. To honor them by choosing the path to heal."

Father John knew what I was going through - I remembered what he told me - what he went through in Viet Nam... he lost a partner - he lost a childhood friend - he knew what it was like - to have someone literally hold them onto life... at the expense of their own...

Father John held my gaze, and I saw something in his eyes - a reflection of my own pain. It wasn't pity, it was recognition. He didn't say anything right away, but I could tell he was remembering. The lines on his face softened, "I get it, Jack," he finally said, his voice low and steady. "I know you think no one could understand. But *I* do. I've been where you are." He softly lowered his hand to his chest - as if feeling the pain of his own wounds all over again. "My friend gave me his life, Jack. Just like Tina gave you hers. I've had to live with that... with the weight of it. You're not alone in this," Father John said softly. "It's heavy. But you don't have to carry it by yourself."

"He gave me his life, Jack, and I'll carry it with me until the day I die." I swallowed hard, feeling my chest tighten, knowing Father John's story mirrored my own. The look in Father John's eyes seemed to say 'helping you - Jack - is helping me bring closure to my own story.'

My thoughts returned to Tina's sacrifice, and it echoed in my mind - the way she stayed with me until the end, until I was safe. And just like Father John, I would carry her with me forever, her memory woven into every beat of my heart.

Father John continued: his voice now somewhat raw with emotion. "I've made peace with it now. Because my friend didn't save me to live in guilt or regret. He saved me so I could live. He gave me life, and that's what I hold in my hand – so the pain of his loss isn't shadowed by the weight of him not being here…"

We sat in the quiet of the office – two men who have, and are now facing the challenge of grief… working on mending the pain, and growing past the hurt… Father John leaned back in his chair, his eyes fixed on something distant, as if searching for answers in the cracks of the ceiling. "You know, Jack," he said after a long pause, "there's an old line from a poem, from John Greenleaf Whittier that I've always carried with me. 'Of all sad words of tongue and pen, the saddest are... it might have been.'"

I let the words settle, their meaning curling around my thoughts like smoke from a dying fire.

Father John looked back at me, his gaze steady, filled with both sorrow and resolve. "The past is full of those words, isn't it? But here's what I've learned: we can't let the 'might have beens' keep us from the 'what could still be.' Healing... real healing... starts when we let go of what we can't change and choose to step forward, even if it's just one small step at a time. Jack – in this case… one spoke at a time."

For the first time in a long while, his words didn't feel like a platitude. They felt real - earned through pain, struggle, and a journey not unlike my own.

"Jack… Tina didn't give her life just to have you drown in grief. She saved you - so you could keep living… hold her in your hand, see her in your heart – feel her when you're lonely… and accept her sacrifice as a gift of love. Know that when you hold her memory – that she isn't ever far away. Jack – if you can see the light hidden in the shadows of loss, you can feel the peace of what true love is. Love isn't always without pain, but love is knowing sacrifice… and love is a gift that sheds light on the future. And **that** is what you hold in your hand.

"The world around you is like the rim of our wagon wheel, and you can choose which spokes reach you. What you choose is what will bring you joy – or pain… Jack – this is all in your hands."

I couldn't move… I couldn't even breathe at the moment. Father John's words cut me to the quick. I was speechless. Father John went on…

"The day you and Bell spent in the countryside watching the Sheepdogs – you held in your hand a moment of peace while you could think of Tina without the pain. Jack – that is how you have to think about the spokes of the wagon wheel – to find a moment of peace – a light that can erase each shadow of darkness – each spoke of the wheel that wants to hurt you. I can't promise it will be easy, but with each ray of sunshine you can find, the memory of Tina will brighten, and the bond you and Bell have will be even stronger.

**

I walked away from Father John feeling humbled - again. The weight of his words settled into my chest as I rode home in the quiet of the night. The hum of the bike beneath me was steady, almost meditative, but my thoughts were anything but still.

When I pulled into the driveway, the soft glow of the porch light flicked on. I sat there for a moment, just breathing. The night was calm, but inside me, emotions churned - fresh, raw. Slowly, I climbed off the bike, feeling the gravity of the evening in every step as I approached the house.

Before I could reach the door, I heard the familiar sound of the latch turning. The door creaked open, and there she was - my wife. The one who had held me by the hand during the darkest of times. The one who stayed by my side.

The one who kept me alive… She was the one who had encouraged me to keep going, even when I felt like I couldn't.

Our eyes met, and in that moment, we didn't need words. We both knew. The loss, the pain - the shared love of someone we both cherished - it all hung in the air between us, unspoken but understood.

She reached out, taking my hand in hers. Her touch was soft, familiar, grounding. We stood there on the threshold, wrapped in a silence that said everything we needed to say. I didn't want the moment to end… I swore to myself I would learn to – no – I would *force* myself to… cherish every moment with her - forever.

For the first time in a long while, I felt a small sense of peace settle into my heart. My heart that she'd held and protected… and in spite of her own loss… she remained strong… reminding me of the famous words…

"The most beautiful things in life are not seen, but felt by the heart."
Helen Keller

As I sit on my patio - I can still feel my partner sit with me in the quiet of the evening. I now cherish every moment I thought would never end – even if it is only the memory of every touch of her paw in my hand.

I feel the presence of my wife standing behind me, as she quietly takes a seat beside me… in the silence of the evening we just sit…

And hold hands.

Chapter 31

The Protector of Heroes

They told me once - that I was a hero. I didn't feel like one. I just felt angry. With every step I walk alone - I remember the companion I wish I could have saved.

My mind realizes the logic, but my heart still aches.

Sometimes I sit alone on the patio - I still see the toys she would play with… sometimes I can still hear her steps, and feel her by my side. Bell will talk about the moments she shared with her, and I'm hurt all over again knowing that she feels Tina's loss ever as much - maybe even more… than I do.

I sit and look at pictures in the album - of so many dogs I've served with. Each having their own special memories. From the deserts of Iraq - to the jungles of the city – I always knew I could stare into the eyes of the devil, or face the unknown and know that I was safe…. With them by my side.

I didn't feel much like a hero. I was just doing a job. I was simply lucky enough to be the partner to the real heroes - the dogs that kept me alive. I was the partner that was lucky enough to have served with Tina.

Father John reminds me that the sorrow, the anger, and the guilt may never fully go away. I guess in time I'll learn how to replace these feelings - with joy, with laughter, and maybe even peace.

I can only hope.

**

Father John once asked me "Why do you think losing Tina was harder on you than - let's say - moving on from your other K9 partners, or the many other hard things that haunt you, Jack?"

I fumbled with my words: "I don't… I don't really know… maybe it was the way I lost her, maybe it was the relationship I had with her… I don't really know."

I sat deep in thought - knowing my other K9 partners went to good homes, living comfortably in retirement. Even Gunner was able to come home to live with us after he served.

Maybe it was the years of nightmares and haunting images that had piled up - one on top of the other. In a way, not having a direct or personal connection with the strangers I was sent to protect made it easier - at least sometimes - to detach from the memories… those mental snapshots of everything I'd seen and experienced on the job.

But detachment doesn't mean forgetting. Those memories still waited - tucked away in the corners of my mind - surfacing when I least expected it. Faces I didn't know, cries I couldn't stop, moments I couldn't change… they stayed with me, no matter how far I tried to push them away.

It's hard to say. The only way I could explain it to Father John why losing Tina was so hard - was that, somehow, it all came down to the bond I shared with such a remarkable creature.

"She wasn't just a partner," I said slowly. "She was part of my family. Tina wasn't like the others. Tina had something really special about her. But like the others - she came home with me, slept at my feet, and loved my kids… My wife, well, she looked at Tina like our own – just like Gunner."

Father John gave a knowing nod. "So maybe, for you, it's not just about losing a fellow officer. It's about losing part of your family."

I blinked a few times, not sure how to respond. He was right. It wasn't just the job this time - it was family I couldn't protect.

I wasn't just angry at a man, who shot a dog. I was angry at the man who took a family member…

"My wife keeps her pain quieter than I do. She doesn't say much, but I see it in the way she carefully walks past the empty dog bed or how she keeps some of Tina's old toys tucked away in the drawer we swore we'd clean out months ago, but always knew we never would. It's always little things - like how she still makes the same amount of food for dinner as if Tina were still around for 'her' share…

"Sometimes, I find her sitting on the porch, sipping her coffee, staring at nothing. I know what she's thinking. The silence between us has grown familiar, a kind of shared understanding that words can't seem to touch. We both feel it - this gaping absence Tina left behind. But we're so wrapped in our own ways of coping, it's like we're each carrying the weight - and comforted that we aren't alone.

"Our kids come by more often now, bringing our grandchildren. They've always been close to us, but lately, it feels like they're trying to fill in the gaps Tina left behind. They never say much about it, but I know they feel the loss too. They grew up around the dogs, even pretended to train with them when they were younger. Tina was more than a partner to me - she was part of the family. Father, I know Bell misses Tina, and when she suggested getting another dog, well - I just don't know…"

Father John listened, silent with his understanding way. His gaze direct, but filled with compassion. When he finally spoke, he said softly:

"Jack, bringing another dog into your life doesn't mean you're replacing Tina. It means you're honoring her. It means you're taking all that she taught you - the loyalty, the courage, the bond you shared - and sharing it with another. Tina wouldn't want you to walk this path alone. A new partner doesn't erase the past; it helps you carry it forward. And Jack… both you and Bell – you deserve to keep walking, to keep living, with someone special by your side."

**

One day, my granddaughter Izzy came bounding into the living room, her feet tapping against the hardwood like Tina's paws used to. It was a comforting sound, and I half-expected her to drop a ball at my feet, the way Tina used to do, but instead, she had something behind her back. She stood there, grinning, the way kids do when they're about to reveal a secret they've kept for too long. "Grandpa," she said, her voice full of excitement, "we have a surprise for you."

I looked at my son, who was standing behind her, arms crossed and a knowing smile on his face. He nodded, giving her the go-ahead. Slowly, Izzy pulled out a small framed photo from behind her back. It took me a second to realize what I was looking at - the picture of me with Tina, from our days on the force. Next to it was another photo, one that I hadn't seen before.

It was a picture of a German Shepherd puppy - tiny, with those big upright ears - and bright eyes that seemed to sparkle with energy. At the bottom of the photo, written in bold letters, was the name: *Athena*. I felt my heart catch in my throat. "What is this?" I asked, my voice rougher than I intended.

My son Jason stepped forward. "Dad, we've all been feeling Tina's loss. We know how much she meant to you, and to all of us. Izzy and I… well, we talked with the department and with Mom. We also reached out to the breeder in Germany." He paused, and I could feel the weight of what he was about to say.

"We've raised the money, with the help of the community, your colleagues, and… we've arranged for another Shepherd. **Athena** is from the same parents as Tina. We contacted them, and they remembered Tina, and thought '**Athena**' wouldn't just be the right tribute to her, and being her 'sister' – would continue her legacy." Before my son could finish – my granddaughter Izzy interrupted with a burst of energy "She's waiting for you, grandpa. She's yours if you're ready."

I couldn't speak. The mixture of emotions - grief, hope, guilt - all swirled around me. I looked at my wife, who was watching me carefully, her eyes reflecting her own feelings. For the first time in a while, there was something in her expression other than sadness.

"We thought it was time," she said softly. "But it's up to you."

I held the photo of **Athena** in my hands, staring at her curious little face. It was like looking into the future while remembering the past - one filled with both the pain of that past and the possibility of healing. The weight of loss was still there, but for the first time, I felt something else creeping in alongside it.

Maybe Father John was right. Maybe the sorrow and guilt would never fully go away. But maybe, just maybe, there was room for something else - something that Tina would have wanted for me.

"I think… I think it's time," I whispered, my voice breaking.

Jason clapped me on the back, and Izzy threw her arms around my neck. Even my wife smiled… her eyes moist with joy.

Athena - named after the goddess of war and protector of heroes - would soon be by my side. Not that she would replace Tina, but come to honor her. And maybe, in time, she'd teach *me* how to heal.

**

It wasn't hard for me to figure, I knew something was going on. The surprise from my granddaughter Izzy – of her 'spear-heading' the fundraising - and my family - the police and all - arranging it… I thought that around every turn of the corner – they would try to surprise me.

Yes - I could tell something was going on… Wade, and even Father John were 'tight-lipped' about it all. I had been to a few of the department "events" - expecting something - but it all ended up being all the usual stuff… the "smoke-screens" I thought would be their surprise… yes… I kept waiting.

I was sitting on my patio - the morning coffee, the lonely memories of Tina. I could hardly bring myself to move - or put the toys away. In some ways I thought it would betray our last moments in the back yard together. Something I didn't want to - or couldn't bring myself to do.

My dear wife… Bell could tell I was feeling a bit nostalgic, and she suggested we go out for a bit of brunch at our little café we all know and like. It's the same place where I like to meet my biker friends.

I suggested we ride down on the bike, but she said "she wasn't in the mood" to ride the bike, so we hopped in the truck, and drove the few miles down through the neighborhood - a nice day, and not a lot of traffic. I thought it would have been a perfect day for the bike… As I pulled into the parking lot - I could see a lot of the big motorcycles of some of my friends from "group", and a couple of police cars. "Nothing out of the usual" I thought…

My wife and I walked into the café and we were greeted by the staff that we've come to know - big smiles on their faces. I should have known something was up. What I didn't see - were the cars of all my kids hidden behind the building…

We were escorted to the back room of the seating area where they could accommodate large groups - parties and such - where we were greeted again by… a lot of my cop friends, biker friends, Father John - my kids and grandkids… and breaking through the group was my oldest granddaughter Izzy with a beautiful little girl…

She couldn't hold back her excitement, and for nearly a half of a heartbeat - I thought "**Tina**?"

This beautiful little girl was nearly a mirror image of my Tina. Born and bred from the same parents. She had the same look in her eyes - bright and beautiful. Izzy let her loose and this little girl came prancing right up to me and my wife.

Nearly everyone present said together: "Jack - meet '**Athena**'!"

I bent down to greet her - and as if it were Tina herself - her mannerisms - her smell… it was as if she was the reincarnation of the savior that pulled me from the line of fire… and sacrificed herself for me.

She leaned into me in such a familiar way, and as if she already knew - the look in her eyes seemed to let me know she could feel the pain - the loss… the memories…

I whispered softly in her ear - "*You have some pretty big shoes to fill, little girl*" - and she tilted her head ever so slightly the way German Shepherds do, and she looked deep into my eyes. In that silent exchange, it was as if she was saying, "*I know, and I'm here. I'll do my best for you.*" Her gaze was steady, full of warmth, trust, and an unspoken promise, as if she understood the weight of what she was stepping into. Her youth never hindered her brightness; her love was truly a comfort…

It seemed like a celebration for newness, and **Athena** never strayed from me. There was something so familiar about her - something we've missed. Father John simply smiled.

**

We walked Athena out to where we were parked. She seemed to know what to do when I let her off from her leash and nosed at the handle as if she tried to open the door to my truck… She hopped into the driver seat - proud and perky - and looked at me as if she wanted to drive… I remembered the day I first met Tina… how this was also a near mirror image of - not only what I saw, but what I felt as if **Tina** were still here with me.

I looked at her - smiled… and told her "*Don't you think I'd better drive…*" My wife chuckled, and Athena was more than happy to share the passenger seat with my wife as we drove home. I looked over at Bell, and I chuckled… "So that's why you 'weren't in the mood' to ride the bike down here."

My wife just smiled at me.

Athena seemed relaxed on the short ride home - her typical German Shepherd nose as active as ever. She is big enough that she could sit comfortably, and still see out the windows - taking in all the sights along the way. I think she could tell she would be loved.

As we got out of the truck - she hopped out and stretched again. We unlatched the front door, and she walked right in. She didn't seem to have a nervous bone in her body. She is curious, alert, and yet comfortable.

We all walked out into the back yard - onto the large patio, and I stopped for a minute - looking at Tina's old toys - the ones we didn't want to move in hopes we would remember our last moments - forever. Athena walked around - and sniffed each of them, and we looked at each other in surprise that she didn't touch them… until…

Athena walked up to one of Tina's old balls - stopped and looked at us… I told her - "*it's Ok girl - I think Tina would be proud to share with you.*" Athena carefully picked it up walked over to where we now sat, and placed the ball in my lap… she looked at me as if to ask permission.

We sat there for a few moments - once again in near reverence, the three of us... as if we all could remember - the little girl that brought us all together... the one who saved my life.

Tina

Chapter 32

Moving Forward

Father John's office has become a place of comfort - a place of solace, where the surroundings invite a sense of hope. "I'm still angry," I admitted, though the words felt different this time. Less sharp, maybe. More tired.

Father John nodded, always the patient listener. "Anger has its place, Jack. But it's how we carry it that matters. We can let it eat at us, or we can find a way to let it be a part of our healing."

I stared at the window, watching a bird land on the sill. "And how do I do that?" He smiled, knowing the answer wasn't a simple one. "You've already begun, Jack. You just don't see it yet."

"I feel like I failed" shaking my head – "I let her down Father, I still feel like I let my team down!"

"Jack, you were the supervisor, and you took the lead. You took control, and protected your team, and took two dangerous fugitives into custody. You were there to make sure those two didn't hurt anyone else, and Tina paid the price for it. Jack, you don't need to keep reliving the pain, you've already paid a heavy price. You were shot, and you lost your partner. What more can you expect? You *can* expect to live in peace knowing you and Tina did what you were supposed to do.

"You Jack, didn't stand behind anyone – you were in the lead. You didn't ask anyone to do what you weren't willing to do yourself. You knew the risks, and you did it anyway. Even when you were hit – you didn't stop. You kept firing at the suspect. Through the hail of gunfire Tina was there to drag you to safety. Tina died protecting you, as you were protecting your team."

Father John continued: "you have made so much progress and done wonderfully about replacing harmful emotions with good ones."

I hadn't realized - maybe I **was** healing. Father John's words and lessons not only made sense, but made a difference. The triggers that once haunted me seemed less daunting. It wasn't yet peace, but it was a start.

I rode home deep in my thoughts, hopeful - yet confused. I felt pride in how far I've come, but a little sad that I haven't recognized the pain my wife was going through. So I decided - this is all about to change.

**

My wife and I sat down for coffee with the familiar faces of my biker-cop friends. There was always laughter with this crew, and today was no different. They still got a kick out of calling me "**Preacher**," a nickname that seemed to have stuck like glue.

"I spoke in a church '*one-time*' - and now look at what I'm stuck with!" I chuckled, shaking my head. Wade jabbed me with his elbow a little and teased, grinning at my wife. "Careful," he laughed "We might see him up there again someday."

The banter flowed easily, and I found myself relaxing more than I had in a while. My wife joined in too, laughing along. It was good to see her smiling again. After a while, the conversation shifted. One of the guys leaned over, looking at me with a smirk. "So, Jack, how's it going with your new girl, **Athena**?"

My wife and I exchanged a glance, her eyes twinkling. "She's a smart one, that's for sure," I said, pride slipping into my voice. "Already reminds me so much of Tina."

"Yeah, we've heard she's sharp. And I'll tell you what - if she's anything like your old girl, well – we can't wait until you get back in the field." He paused, letting the idea settle. "Why don't you bring her down? We've got some tracking drills lined up. See how she handles herself." Another one of my friends gave me a gentle look and said: "we really miss your experience too Jack."

I looked at my wife, expecting hesitation, but instead, she smiled. "Why not? It could be fun." I wasn't sure who was more surprised - me or the guys. "You're coming too?"

"Of course," she said her smile widening. "I want to see what all the fuss is about with Athena. Besides," she added with a wink, "it'll be good for both of us."

Soon after, we were getting Athena ready for the training field. As my wife and I stepped outside, Athena bounded toward the truck, her ears alert and her tail sweeping. Her energy was contagious, and I couldn't help but grin. Watching her, I was struck by how much this moment reminded me of Tina - preparing her for a day in the field. But this wasn't the past; it was something new. As I opened the truck door and Athena leapt in with eager confidence, I realized this wasn't just about her proving herself. It was about all of us - me, my wife, and Athena - stepping into a new chapter together.

As we pulled up to the training field, our friends were already there, running drills with their dogs. I could see the seriousness in their eyes, but there was also a camaraderie that put me at ease. This wasn't just a job - it was something we all loved. Athena was alert but calm. My wife looked over at me, raising an eyebrow, and then back at Athena "You ready for this?"

One of the guys waved us over, a grin spreading across his face. "There they are! The dynamic duo. Jack, we've got a tracking course set up for you today. Let's see what your girl's got."

I'd already taught Athena to "find your ball" – since she had the habit of losing her ball the way Tina did – and like her sister, had the knack of finding what she wanted… all we had to do now is sharpen what she'd learned.

Athena was already focused, her nose twitching as she took in all the scents. I could tell she was eager to work, and a surge of pride filled my chest. We started with basic commands, and Athena nailed them like she had done it a hundred times. The work I'd done with her while I was healing – it was paying off. But there was something more, and at the moment, I couldn't put 'my finger' on it…

My wife stood beside me, watching with a smile. She had always loved Tina, and seeing her so involved with Athena just felt right. She even called out a few commands herself, and Athena responded without hesitation. Athena seemed be able to anticipate what to do - much like Tina.

The first day went smoothly, better than I expected. Athena impressed everyone with her natural ability, but it wasn't just her instincts - it was her bond with us. That bond, the unspoken connection, I believe... was what made all the difference.

Maybe there was something from beyond - a connection Athena has with Tina... that they were sisters... Athena has a spirit that seemed to ground us - connect us... something special...

**

Over the next few weeks, we settled into a routine. Athena grew sharper with each session, taking on more advanced drills - tracking, detection, even agility. The guys started calling her "the prodigy," half-joking, but I could tell they were impressed. She wasn't just another dog; she had something special, just like Tina before her. We found joy in watching Athena learn and grow, in seeing her step into the role she was meant to fill. What I thought I left behind didn't seem as heavy as it once was.

One afternoon, after a particularly challenging scent-tracking drill, Athena trotted back toward me with her usual proud strut. "She's incredible," my wife said, shaking her head. "I didn't think it was possible, but she's really living up to Tina's legacy. It's almost surreal that she's so instinctive..."

I nodded, feeling the same. But it wasn't just about living up to Tina - it was about moving forward. About building something new while honoring what we had lost.

**

The field was quiet except for the occasional commands and the steady footfalls of dogs working the course. I watched Athena weave between obstacles, her focus sharp, her body coiled like a spring ready to snap into action at any moment. She had taken to the training like it was second nature, but every time we worked together; I saw the same drive in her eyes - the need to please, to understand, to do the job well. Athena seemed to learn from the others as she was simply watching – as we were performing even more advanced drills in the Schutzhund course...

We had fallen into a rhythm during these sessions. Athena mastered all the drills. It felt good to be out here again, to be part of something bigger than myself. My friends had embraced Athena, my wife, and I, treating us like family, and their dogs had become Athena's playmates.

"She's something special, Jack," one of the guys said as he walked over, tossing a tennis ball in the air for her to catch. She caught it before it hit the ground. We both smiled. He smiled too and said "I know she can find anything, and I know she'd even be great at search and rescue, and... how long before you get back into the field?"

I blinked, taken aback for a moment. "I don't know... I mean – I need a doctor's release, and she's still pretty new to all this."

He smiled. "You'd be surprised how quickly you guys can get back into working, especially with a nose like hers. We're assisting with some contraband searches in a few days. If you're up for it, we could use an extra set of paws."

I looked at Athena, and I tossed her ball. She whipped around at full speed to chase it. Her reflexes were lightning fast and she leapt into the air to catch it on a bounce. She was prancing toward us, tongue lolling, but eyes still sharp. I knew *she* was ready. But was I?

Bell got me into the doctor... and they agreed... I was ready.

**

A few days later, Wade called while we were on our way to meet our friends to do the searches we had arranged. Wade wanted us to report to the canyon instead. A hiker was missing, and our friends were in need of some real special help. Like Tina before her - Athena seemed to know that there was urgency from the call. I told Bell that I was glad she was going with us – a lost hiker might need medical assistance.

We reported to the campground, and soon we found ourselves getting ready to work. The dense forest undergrowth was thick with the scent of pine and damp earth. It had rained earlier that morning, making the conditions less than ideal for tracking, but I could see Athena's tail wagging, her nose twitching as she caught onto something in the air.

The missing person was a local elderly man who was reliant on medication, and had wandered off the trail several days ago. The clock was ticking, and every second mattered.

I crouched down beside Athena, running my hand along her back. *"You ready, girl?"* She looked up at me with those intelligent eyes, as if to say, *I've got this.* I clipped the long leash onto her collar and gave her the command to start searching. Instantly, her demeanor changed - nose to the ground, focused and driven. She looked at me with that look, as if to say *"trust me."*

That look! – Just like Tina. A narrow sliver of caramel with pupils open wide - blackened to take in every detail… her nose in a near shudder - ears like radar listening… as if she'd done this before. She moved with purpose, zigzagging through the trees, following a scent that was invisible to all of us but vivid to her.

The team followed close behind, watching as Athena led the way. My heart pounded in my chest, a mix of anxiety and pride swirling in my gut. This was it. All the training, all the preparation - it all came down to this moment. Her movements, her strength - all reminded me of that first week with Tina. She reminded me of that lost little boy and how Tina was the hero. As Athena pulled me along - each step was a reminder of the past - as she pulled us into the future. But it was more…

We moved deeper into the forest, the trees closing in around us. I could see Athena picking up speed, her movements more deliberate. She was onto something. I exchanged a glance with my wife, who was walking - even running beside me, her face tense but hopeful.

Minutes passed, feeling like hours, until suddenly, Athena stopped, her body rigid. She let out a sharp bark, like a signal to let us know she found something. My heart leaped as we rushed forward, following her lead.

There, lying among the underbrush, was the missing hiker - alive, but weak. He looked disoriented, but when he saw the team approach, relief washed over his face. Athena sat like she was trained to do when she found something, but eased her way next to him, calm but alert, as if to reassure him that help had arrived.

The rest of the team moved in, Bell checking his vitals and calling for a medical chopper. But I couldn't take my eyes off Athena. She had done it. She had found him. I knelt down beside her, scratching behind her ears. *"Good girl,"* I whispered. *"You did good."*

My wife's training sprang into action, her medical training taking over as she assessed the hiker's condition. "Thank you," he whispered" his voice hoarse. "I didn't think anyone would find me."

"You can thank her," I said, motioning to Athena, who was sitting proudly by his side, her tail thumping against the ground.

My wife still attending to her patient, looked at me, her eyes focused, then she looked at Athena. "She's amazing," she said softly. I nodded, the weight of the moment settling in. This wasn't just about the training anymore. Athena had become more than just a companion - she was a partner, a lifeline for someone in need. And in a way, she was helping me find my own path forward, one prancing step at a time.

We stood in silence for a moment, letting the weight of what had just happened sink in. The hiker was in good hands now, the helicopter lifting him away to the hospital. Athena had not only stepped into Tina's shoes, but also guiding us both through this journey of healing. But she commanded the scene. As if somehow connecting with the past, she made the future her own.

My wife rested her hand on my shoulder, her voice barely a whisper. "She's more than just a dog, Jack. She's part of our family." I nodded, swallowing the lump in my throat. "Yeah, she is."

The woods were quiet again, the urgency of the search fading into the background. But inside, I knew something had changed. Not just with Athena, but with me. The anger that had simmered inside me for so long was still there, but it no longer controlled me. There was room for something else now - hope, pride, maybe even peace.

As we made our way back to the truck, Athena trotted faithfully by our side. I glanced at my wife and couldn't help but smile. Our girl hadn't just found a lost stranger today - she'd uncovered something for me, too. Maybe she understood what I didn't yet realize: that maybe I had something more to give.

Maybe I have a purpose waiting - if I was ready to reach for it. Perhaps Tina, in her own way, had brought me Athena to help guide me through the healing. And as we walked down that mountainside together, it was clear…

We were all finally moving forward, together.

**

That night, as Bell and I sat on the patio, Athena sprawled at our feet; I couldn't help but feel a shift within me. The pain of the past was still there, but it was no longer the only thing I carried. In its place was something new - hope, pride, and a renewed sense of purpose.

Bell reached over, resting her hand on mine. "I'm proud of you" she said softly. "We did good," I said, looking down at Athena, who lifted her head at the sound of my voice. "All of us."

As the stars began to dot the night sky, I thought about Father John's words. Maybe I was healing after all. And maybe, just maybe, moving forward didn't mean leaving the past behind. It meant carrying it with me, but in a way that allowed me to keep walking, step by step, toward something better.

I looked down at Athena still resting at our feet… I smiled. I looked toward the heavens, as if to see my Tina, and silently said…

Thank You

Chapter 33

Echoes of the Past

I started back working with the department – Athena at my side. It was a great part-time job at first. Bell was concerned that I would push myself too much – too fast. I assured her I wouldn't. But even as I said it, I knew she could see the weight I carried - those old shadows that followed me every time I put the badge back on, even on 'light duty.'

"I think about that night Tina was killed... every day - the bullets that almost took me out too. I know you're worried." Bell nodded slowly, with understanding. "Just promise me you'll talk to me. If it ever gets too much, even if the past starts creeping up again... we'll face it together."

**

Bell was working a late shift, and 'we' had nowhere to go for the evening. Athena and I played ball for a while, ate some dinner, and then went to the living room to relax. I picked up an old photo album and sat on the sofa; Athena sat at my feet and rested her chin on my knee. I began to look at the echoes of my past. The pictures that captured moments in time – memories of a lifetime ago that somehow seemed like yesterday.

I flipped through the pages, smiling as I recalled the many days of training in the military. I looked at pictures from my basic training graduation, and then the photos from K-9 training when I met Gunner as a pup at Lackland Air Force Base in Texas. We did our advanced training at the 341st Training Squadron at Joint Base San Antonio, where all military working dogs are bred and trained. It was also where K9 handlers, like me, were taught how to become trainers, and K9 instructors.

I showed Athena a picture of Gunner: "He used to be my partner, just as you are now."

More pages filled with memories of the dust, dirt, and heat, and the love I'd found amid the chaos of a combat zone. Pictures of Gunner and me, and I chuckled at the snapshot showing us standing in front of our tent – where my friend Wade (Sgt. Callahan to some) made a funny sign that said "**Dog House.**"

I showed Athena so she could see the picture of Bell, Gunner, Sgt. 'Wade' and me, all in our Army clothes. As *if* she could truly understand. She seemed interested for only a moment, and then placed her chin back on my knee.

I sat in the quiet as my mind returned to the adventure, to the sights and sounds – the smells of the camp. I sat thinking and remembering. I could almost smell the dank canvas, and hear far off shells exploding. The sounds of the soldiers clanking their gear, and I could almost feel again where the straps of my pack would leave their mark after a long day on patrol.

I looked at the pictures of me and Gunner, and then looked down at Athena thinking "These two are so similar, and yet so different." He was so large and muscular, and she is so slender and sleek. I told Athena "*I loved, and still love every one of you*" as my hand left holding the page for a moment to stroke her fur. The motion brought back memories like I could feel Gunner's fur again, as I would remove his gear, and the familiar damp scent of dog filled my mind – recalling the times I would 'sneak' him into the outdoor canvas showers with me. Athena sensing my nostalgia moved to sit on the sofa with me, and now rested her head on my lap.

My mind raced back to Gunner and how every patrol, and every mission I'd worry about keeping him safe, but I did. Whenever he would 'indicate' the presence of a bomb or an explosive I'd pull him back so he wouldn't set off an explosion. We'd mark the location so the Explosive Ordinance Disposal team could remove them. Day after day we'd walk the paths of danger, and we learned to trust each other like no other.

I remembered the day on patrol. Gunner had detected a number of explosives and we'd flagged each of them so the EOD team could dispose of them.

I told Athena that One of the 'flags' must have blown away in the breeze, and left an anti-personnel bomb undetected. The ordinance disposal team was in danger. Gunner and I were "standing by" to confirm the explosives in the area were in fact clear for troop movement. Sgt. Callahan – Wade – was approaching one of the other 'flags' and before he could reach that threat…

Gunner broke free from my hold and lunged toward Wade. In a leap, Gunner tackled Wade and pushed him away from the undetected bomb that was buried beneath the ground. Gunner immediately pointed toward the hidden explosive "on point" and wouldn't release his warning until we 'flagged' the threat – as he'd been trained. My friend – Wade... never forgot that. Gunner truly saved his life that day.

I thumbed through the pages and smiled at the photos of Bell and Gunner together – both smiling. It brought back so many good memories. I tried to focus on the happy moments from way back then - maybe in a way to help, so I could focus on the happy memories with Tina.

I remembered the day Gunner and I met Bell at the hospital and how she immediately fell in love with him too. How the three of us became so close. The three of us were almost like a family.

I closed the album and thought back about how hard it was when our time in the combat zone was coming to a close. I petitioned the Air Force to adopt Gunner, and my Attempts fell on deaf ears. Both Bell and I wrote letters explaining that Gunner wasn't just 'surplus' equipment to be disposed of when his service came to a close... that Gunner deserved to be treated like a true Veteran, and treated with respect... but still... our plea went nowhere.

Bell and I would stay up late at night writing letters – we called our families back home – and we all started a campaign to save Gunner. **Wade** even began a letter writing campaign to save the one who saved him – telling the story of a true hero – a true soldier who risked his life to save his own.

It wasn't until Bell and I both petitioned our Senator from back home – Jake Garn, a US Navy hero and the first sitting Senator who became an Astronaut... Bell and I were sure that if anyone could save Gunner – he could. We both knew that we were Gunner's only chance to live. K-9 Veterans were destroyed after service, and I couldn't bear the thought of him being 'put to sleep' after he'd saved so many lives.

Gunner was my partner in service – he was my friend, he was my family, and became a living symbol of Bell's and my bond in a war zone. We had to save him. Gunner was a life worth saving... and we were determined to save him. But time was running out. Both Bell and I received our transfer letters to go home... Gunner didn't.

Two days before we were to leave the camp and return to the States, my company's administrative clerk called me in to receive a phone call. He motioned for me to pick up the phone, and I said 'hello.' I was prepared to hear the worst. I was prepared for the news that Gunner would be 'put down' as surplus equipment. My heart was in my gut, and my mind was a blur of heartbreak. I remember the despair. I remember the hurt.

The voice on the other end announced himself as Senator Garn from Utah – I was speechless. All I could say (again) was 'hello' not knowing what to expect next.

The conversation was short. He said within hours we would have Gunner's transfer orders, and that he was proud to inform us we would be allowed to adopt our companion. I didn't know what to say – I could barely muster the words –"Thank You Senator" my voice was thick with emotion, or maybe it was choked by the 'dust' in the air…

As I reminisced - I looked deep into Athena eyes as if I remember looking into Gunners – or even Tina's eyes. I was thinking – then saying… *"You know girl – there isn't anything I wouldn't do for you – either…"*

I remember after receiving that phone call from the Senator, that I immediately ran to let Bell know – I ran into my tent and found her with Gunner. She could tell by the look in my eyes I had good news. I didn't have to say a word…

"So we get to keep him?" she said, almost laughing. I could only nod. We both hugged him tightly - we couldn't let him go. He was coming home with us. Gunner was no longer just a war hero or a K-9 partner. He was ours, and we were his.

We called everyone so we could to give them the good news. The next couple of days were a blur of excitement and anticipation. We were **finally** going home. **All of us**.

We arrived at the Air Force Base in Utah met by so many of the friends and family that helped in our letter writing campaign, and Gunner took it all in, amid all the hugs and congratulations.

✱✱

Later that week, I sat with Father John and shared stories of Gunner – the celebration, and how Gunner helped both Bell and me transition to civilian life. We chuckled at his constant sniffing – always on the lookout, ever the soldier, trained to protect us. We reminisced, and I told Father John that Gunner lived his retirement years, healthy and happy.

As I transitioned to working with dogs on the Force, we had two German Shepherds, and it was almost like Gunner had helped train my new duty partner, Shadow. I loved how they got along. Our work to save K-9 heroes gave me a deep sense of purpose. We kept writing letters, and seven years after we saved Gunner, our efforts – along with the efforts of countless others – culminated in the passage of Public Law 106-446 (10 U.S.C. 2583), better known as "Robby's Law," enacted in the fall of 2000. This law prioritized former handlers for the adoption of their K-9 partners and, finally, recognized the unique bond that forms between them during service.

Our chat stirred something deeper within me. Father John must have seen it in my eyes as we talked. His expression softened, solemn but kind. "Jack," he said, his voice steady and understanding, "maybe that's why losing Tina was so hard? You fought so hard to save Gunner, but you couldn't save her?"

Father John's questions lingered in my thoughts, but there was a small smile growing inside me - in the memory that came next. One time, my childhood friend Wade, who'd joined the County Sheriff's Department, stopped by our house on his way to the department's office – so he could pick up some evidence bags I had for him. As he came in, I thought Gunner might have remembered him, but when Wade walked through the door, Gunner started sniffing him all around and then sat. Wade looked at me, and I smiled. "You've got something on you, don't you?" I said.

Wade grinned back, reached into his pocket, and pulled out a bag of cocaine he'd been carrying to 'book' into evidence. We all laughed, but Gunner? He just thought he was doing his job.

I sat in silence for a moment – with the fond memory, but then his words hit me as I thought of Tina, and, I hesitated – knowing I'd said those words before – now it became a reality. I didn't know what to say… "Maybe," I finally admitted, my voice barely above a whisper. "Maybe that's why losing Tina - maybe that's why it's been so hard."

As we talked, I sat in reflection, the deep pain from Tina's death lingered like an open wound that would heal slowly. I was physically healing, yes, but there was a gaping void inside that no search mission or rescue operation could fill.

I realized that part of my need to return to work was a way of facing my fears - the fear of losing control again, the fear of feeling helpless like I did that night. Every time I donned the uniform or took Athena out for a search, it felt like I was daring myself to step closer to that edge.

**

One evening - the three of us came home from working at the county fairgrounds. I'd been working security for the rodeo, and Bell was at a "Nursing aid station." It was a long day, and we all grabbed some dinner at a fast-food drive-in on the way home. We settled in for the evening, and sat down on the sofa to watch some television. We were watching the news, and they were showing the people in Florida affected by a hurricane. I'd mentioned to "my girls" that I was glad we don't get those kinds of storms here in the mountains…

We watched the images of people evacuating, something stirred deep inside me. The chaos, the fear - it was all too familiar.

Shortly after, the phone rang, cutting through the quiet. Something told me this wasn't a social call. I glanced down at Athena, noticing something I hadn't expected. She had lifted her head, ears perked, her eyes focused on us with an intensity that I had learned to trust. Athena knew. Somehow, she knew.

"Our department said the Red Cross is asking if we could assist with the hurricane relief effort in Florida. They know that they'll be overwhelmed, and... They need people with search and rescue experience."Athena stood up, coming to my side as if she understood that her time had come again. I ran my hand over her fur, feeling the strength she carried. Bell watched us both, waiting.

"Looks like we're needed," I finally said, meeting her gaze. "All of us." Looking down at Athena, I could feel her anticipation. She knew something was coming, something bigger. It was as if her own instincts were guiding her - like she was ready to face whatever we'd find.

I smiled, grateful for her strength, and for the silent bond that connected us all. "Together," I agreed. "We'll face it together."

Athena watched intently as we began to pack our bags, then turned around and ran out of the room. It wasn't but a few moments when - she proudly pranced back in dragging her leash and harness - with a 'cheesy' smile... I chuckled and thought - yes - she knows, she always seems to know.

**

The next morning, we loaded the truck with everything we'd need for the long trip. Athena could tell there was an excitement in the 'air' - and of course, she loves going for rides in the truck. We were told the hurricane would likely have weakened by the time we arrived - but that's when the real work would start.

We had to wait at the Red Cross camp in Alabama while the Interstate 10 could be cleared. FEMA officials said they were re-assigning us. As soon as the roads opened up we could proceed to Tyndall Air Force Base - where all the K-9 crews would set-up for search and rescue operations. And it didn't take long. The news could hardly describe the devastation and debris that remained even after the winds had died down.

The Air Force Base brought back so many memories of military life. For both of us. These were the echoes from my past I'd thought were long gone. My wife joked around - remembering the military food, but I told her that we'd get used to it again. And we did. Athena didn't seem to mind either. I wasn't sure if I missed this life or if I'd just never fully left it behind.

For days we traveled into the disaster zone by boat - up through the "North Bay" area up into Deer Point Lake. We were surprised at how much flooding there was - it was as if the entire area was a lake. Water had swallowed up whole neighborhoods, turning them into ghostly canals where only rooftops and treetops broke the surface.

Most of our searches merely confirmed that evacuated areas didn't have any remaining people. The days were long though, and the few searches where we did find people – so far had happy endings - no serious injuries. It seemed everyone we met enjoyed meeting Athena.

At evening 'chow' we were told they had reports of heavy damage and possible casualties up in the Wausau area - about 40 miles north of the Base. They needed a crew to investigate, but there wouldn't be any open roads. They requested that anyone experienced with "aerial" travel and K-9 searches report to the communications tent.

Before I knew it - my wife was there volunteering us for the job. She told them that she used to be an Army nurse, and part of the current K-9 rescue team. They were happy to have us on board. Athena could tell she was about to embark on a new adventure - her eyes sparkled with that familiar gleam. She knew this was her moment, her mission. As we packed up, I could feel it too...

This was why we were here.

Chapter 34

Healing By Helping

The following morning at the base brought the renewed sense of urgency. Reports were finally streaming in with the numbers of people still unaccounted for. We could hardly eat our breakfast - I was slightly apprehensive since it had been a long time since I'd been aboard a helicopter. Athena had never been aboard one.

We were told we'd have to fly in since there was too much debris along the waterways further north, and we'd have to land in one of the few 'dry' areas around Wausau. A military van drove us out to the helicopter pads, Athena hopped out ahead of us and sat proudly as we got out and began to don all of our gear. She smiled her big grin as I clicked her leash onto her, and she immediately took the "*on-me*" position and "*heeled*" at my left side as the three of us walked toward the 'chopper' we were assigned to.

It all came back to me as I heard the winding-up of the engines, and the rush of the blades - Athena took it all in - in stride. She jumped a little while laying across my lap when we lifted off, but smiled again when she saw us smiling back at her.

The 20 minute flight went quickly, and the pilot began to circle an area he was supposed to land. He kept looking for an open area that wasn't flooded with water. He shouted back at us and told us the only dry area was in the trees, and that we'd have to be lowered down since he couldn't land. I had to think for a minute. We didn't bring a harness for Athena that would let us lower her down. So I thought…

"If the tool 'ain't' right - the man ain't bright" as I remembered the saying from old Charlie… I asked one of the crew members for some of the carabiner clips they had, and some spare nylon webbing material. I fashioned a harness - threading the webbing through Athena's protective vest. All the training and experience came back and I began to secure Athena to my rescue gear.

I told Bell that I'd go down first - then I asked the chopper crew if they would make sure she was safe and secure. I knew they would, but it made me feel better to ask… We were attached to the cable to let us down, I grabbed onto Athena tightly and said *"OK girl - you ready!"*

We swung out of the door into the blast of air from the chopper blades. I chuckled as the rushing air flapped Athena's chops back and forth. It was hard to tell if she was smiling, or not. The look in her eyes clearly showed that… she was.

We were lowered down through the trees slowly - the one hundred foot drop seemed slow, and the branches of the trees were bending and swaying in the gusts of the powerful rotors, and kept hitting at us as if trying to keep us away…

I felt the earth under foot, and the slack in the cable, and used the radio to let them know we were on the ground. I quickly released the rigging, and told them we were free from the cable. As I was undoing the makeshift harness I'd made for Athena, a man rushed up to us. It looked like he'd been through hell. He was ragged, bruised and bloodied, but told us the real injuries were nearby in a storage shack they'd taken shelter in.

I radioed back to the hovering chopper that my wife needed to bring her advanced medical bag, and I asked the man if he knew of any more people in the area that could be missing. He said he didn't know, but - probably, a lot of people could still be missing.

As Bell was being lowered down Athena took refuge near the base of a large tree, and as soon as the cable went slack again, I immediately unhooked my wife, and the three of us followed the man back to the shack. I told the chopper we were all safe on the ground, and that we would apprise them of the injuries…

It all went quiet for a moment as soon as the helicopter headed back to the base. We opened the door to the shack and there were several people with broken bones, a compound fracture, and lots of deep cuts and bruises. Bell used her radio to apprise the hospital on the base of the patient's conditions, and she began to treat the victims. She told me I should begin to search for any others.

Athena and I began to look through the many damaged buildings. I had to take her off of her leash to prevent it from snagging onto the many branches of broken trees in the debris. She kept looking - sniffing the air for clues. She could get into the areas I couldn't, and would return without indicating the presence of any people. Over and over - she would pause, lift her head, she'd check the ground - and as she was following the unseen path of scent - she would turn back toward me to make sure I was behind her. It wasn't easy - I did my best to keep up.

We would mark each place - to let others know we'd already confirmed there were no casualties in that building…

House after house - sloshing through mud and swampy water, she never backed off from searching. She was relentless. She began to push through into an area that soon got too deep for her to walk. I bent down, and placed her on my shoulders, and then we proceeded to wade into an area she seemed to get excited for. The depth of the water was nearly up to my chest, but we kept walking. As soon as I could let her down back to the ground, she began to run toward another broken house… meanwhile, in the distance now - I could hear the repeated arrivals and departures of the helicopters attending to the others where my wife was treating the injured.

Athena pushed ahead through the twisted mess of broken boards and debris, her nose low to the ground, tail held high, every step calculated and focused. I stayed close behind, watching her ears twitch and her head tilt as she assessed each new scent and sound.

At one point, Athena stopped, lifted her head and sniffed the air with intensity. Without hesitation, she glanced back at me, as if to say, *"This way."* I nodded, trusting her instincts, and followed as she forged a path through the wreckage. Despite the mud and the risk of sharp debris, she pressed forward, unwavering, guiding me to what lay hidden ahead. It was clear her determination was as fierce as mine, if not more so.

Athena tried to get into a heavily damaged house, but couldn't. She indicated that she knew someone was inside. I got to the house and started to call out to anyone who could be inside.

There was no answer. The doors seemed to be locked. As I looked through windows I thought I could see an individual on the floor. I took a nearby branch, and broke the window so I could crawl through. I did my best to remove as much glass as I could so I wouldn't get cut. The smell of stagnant water - moldy with a hint of wet wood hits me and I can't help but try to clear the smell from my throat as it gagged me a little. I was already waterlogged from wading through the swamp, the humidity after the hurricane, and the late summer heat. It made our physical exertion even worse.

I approached the individual on the floor, and he appeared to be unconscious. I tried to revive him while I radioed my wife for help. Athena was looking through the broken window watching me - she still looked like she was detecting something. I started CPR on the victim - I kept telling the radio that I needed help. Athena finally jumped through the window and began to sniff through the house. I kept working on the victim… I kept thinking - *"come-on dammit - you gotta live!"* I know I'd been in tight spots before, but the weight of the life in my hands made it feel like the first time.

Athena announced with her "I found it" bark that she found something – and she sat like she'd been trained... I knew she found something. I asked *"what is it girl"* and she started barking again. I dialed "911" on my cell phone and placed it on the ground so the dispatch could zero-in on my location, and as I kept working on the unconscious man - I would tell the voice on the other end what was going on.

In the distance I could hear the sound of another chopper, and hoped it was headed my way… it was. It wasn't long before another rescuer came through the window and took over CPR. I was exhausted, but I rushed to where Athena was on 'point' and I broke through another door, and found a couple of small kids huddled together.

I asked them if they were hurt, and thankfully they weren't. They said their mommy went to find help for their dad, but hadn't come home yet. They said the storm broke their house and that they couldn't leave the room.

I radioed again: this time for another chopper with a lift gurney, and hopefully it would be a medical helicopter with an advanced trauma crew that would come… I got the children out of the house, and they were comforted by Athena;

I told her to keep an eye on the kids while I went in again so we could work on saving the children's dad.

I felt an enormous relief when I could hear the sounds of another flight coming in… we were exhausted. The chopper that arrived was in fact a medical team with advanced training. They lowered the paramedic and then retrieved the kids in the gurney. Athena sat proudly, her fur blowing in the rotor gusts, as she watched the kids being lifted into the safety of the helicopter.

By the time the paramedic could transport the dad - there wasn't enough room aboard the next 'rescue-bird' that arrived, since the first 'chopper' had already left with the two children - and so, Athena, the other man who came to help with the rescue, and me - all sat in the quiet while we watched it fly away.

I stood there and watched - opened a little water-proof bag where I had my cigarettes, and lit a smoke. I held the pack in my hand, and tilted it slightly toward my 'new-found' partner, and offered him one… Athena came and leaned up against me and I softly stroked her behind the ear. I told her she was a good girl, and she smiled.

I turned to the man standing to my right, and reached out my hand and said "hi - I'm Jack…it's a pleasure working with you." He shook my hand and said his name was 'Bob', and that he was one of the FEMA volunteers. He said he was an EMT from Las Vegas. I joked with him: "hey - we're nearly neighbors, we're from Utah…"

We sat there in the heat and humidity for a while - joking… about how so many of us came to work together, yet we hardly had the time to get to know each other. For a moment standing with him in the quiet, we laughed together… wondering when they would come back for us…

After what felt like hours, the sound of another chopper's blades broke the stillness. The exhaustion was bone-deep, but there was relief in knowing the kids were safe, the father stabilized, and the storm's aftermath was being handled, piece by piece. We never did hear back on what had happened to the kids' mother.

When our ride finally arrived - I used my makeshift harness for Athena and tied her tight to me. We were lifted the hundred or so feet into the chopper - tired and hungry.

When we got back to the base, my wife was waiting. She was covered in mud, her face a mix of exhaustion and determination. She'd been tending to the injured who had taken shelter in the storage shed, working as tirelessly as we had on the other rescues. "You okay?" she asked, her voice low. I nodded, and for a moment we just stood there, not needing to say anything more.

**

The next few weeks blurred together, filled with more rescues, more broken lives trying to piece themselves together in the aftermath of the hurricane. We pulled people out of flooded homes, patched up the injured, and brought hope where we could. Bell, Athena, and I worked flawlessly together, I couldn't have been more proud.

As things began to quiet down, the weight of it all hit me. I looked at Athena, who was resting at my feet, her job done. Isabel caught my eye, and we shared a tired smile. It wasn't just the hurricane that had battered these people, but life itself. We couldn't fix everything, but for a moment, we were part of something bigger, and that was enough. Although we helped so many shattered lives, I felt a sadness that I never got to know any of the victim's names. This was a time where introductions and pleasantries had no use.

I'm pleased that I could help, and more so that we could be an anonymous force that even for a fleeting moment - touched the lives of strangers.

We had a couple of quiet days at the base - waiting around for any unforeseen reports that hadn't been addressed. Athena was quite the attraction - making friends with all the other K9 teams, rescuers, and even the military personnel… she enjoyed the attention… Bell and I relived memories.

Isabel had been in contact with Father John - who had been back at home organizing relief projects through their church. She said he'd been asking about me - and that didn't surprise me at all.

As we packed up to leave - I felt a sense of pride, and yet, a sense of sorrow. I knew we did our best to find everyone - to help everyone we could. I was sad though - that there were some who didn't survive the tempest of the hurricane.

Finding and helping victims was rewarding, but locating and recovering those who perished, was always going to be inevitable.

As sad as it is – I'd always known it was going to be a part of the job. Whether an avalanche, an accident, or flood – bringing closure to someone else's loss is always going to be a part of the life I chose. But like the protector – the Sheepdog in me... I'll lick my wounds, and prepare for another day...

Although Tina had been on my mind, and I still missed her - watching Athena work made me feel different. I remembered the words of Father John, and how the sorrow of Tina's loss - and even the anger of losing her, might never go away completely. But through these past few weeks, I started to realize that Father John may have had a point: helping others really did help me...

I can't help but wonder – if that was his plan all along.

Chapter 35

Facing Fear

Like I've said before - unless you have experienced it, you don't know how alive you feel, until you look death in the face.

The life our family has come to know all too well is a life of service to others. It is a life of serving without recognition. It's a life of duty that demands much and often offers little in return. Like the sheepdogs - we serve from a sense of duty… because that's just what we do.

The thin line I have walked a thousand times didn't come from the safety of an office or a routine job, but from stepping into the unknown. I'm driven by a duty that's as much a part of me as breathing. For my family, facing fear isn't a rarity; it's the path we chose, and it's one we walk without applause or reward. It's that moment, standing between chaos and peace, where purpose sharpens, and everything else fades away.

Father John once said that courage - bravery, isn't the absence of being afraid, but being able to conquer it. "It's how you hold your ground - when everything inside you tells you to run."

I'd held onto those words, letting them remind me of why we do this, why we step into the unknown - time and again. For so long now, I have walked in fear. It wasn't the fear for my safety - it was the fear I couldn't save what I loved.

For more than a year now we have been facing the challenges of searching, rescuing, and serving from the shadows - we have done the things that make our world a little safer, and brought people from the depths and darkness of disaster, into the light of hope. But that's just what we do. Athena has risen to every challenge without fear, and I could only hope I would never let her down.

**

Even though we had some down-time at the Air Force base before we came home - we took a few extra days to relax while we unpacked all of our gear. Athena loved the attention we'd been giving her - she really did 'shine' while we were in Florida.

I took Athena with me when I went to meet with Father John, and she greeted him warmly like he was an old friend. We sat in his office and chatted about how good it felt to help, and how I wasn't thinking about the pain - or sorrow, as much as I had been.

We talked about fear… we talked about facing the things that brought us pain… facing the memories that we avoided in order to stay away from hurting. It wasn't easy, but he told me I was ready. "Ready?" I asked… Father John smiled – "yes Jack, you're ready to heal."

When Athena and I walked out to the truck - she hopped in proudly, and looked at me with that funny look as she sat in the driver seat… *"Really little girl"* I chuckled - *"we're going to play this game again: I think maybe I should drive"* as I remembered the way both her and Tina did the first time we met. She hopped again over to the passenger seat… and smiled at me.

I started the truck, and put it into gear. I looked over at her and asked her *"you hungry girl"* - and I swear I could see her nod her head - yes.

We pulled out of the parking lot and drove down the familiar street - approaching the 'burger joint' that Tina loved so much. The place I'd avoided for so long now, because - I was afraid. It was kind of like - being afraid to face the past. I had to tell myself again… "I'm ready to heal."

I slowed the truck - I looked over at Athena, I swallowed hard. But I did it anyway. I pulled into the drive through, and ordered the same things that I used to order for Tina. They gave us our food, and I drove into the same parking spot where Tina and I shared our last meal together. We sat for a few moments in silence, as if Athena knew…

I handed her a burger, and she reached over and snuck a few fries out of the container between us. I couldn't help but see Tina doing this in my mind's eye... watching Athena was almost as if Tina was sitting in here with me - her presence filling the silence in a way I hadn't allowed myself to feel in a long time.

When we got home, I told Bell what we did. She looked proud. She looked at me with kind of a stare, and right when I thought she was about to say something meaningful and profound - she said *"and you didn't bring me anything?"*

We laughed.

As we started back into our routine - Isabel would go to work at the hospital, and I'd take Athena out with the team and work. Bell would go out with us at times - and when we'd get home, we would play in the back yard together... it felt good to laugh again.

**

It wasn't long after that Bell and I had our kids and grandkids over to play in the sprinklers and have a backyard picnic. The summer was nearly over, and we thought it would be a fun day before school started again. Everyone was having a great time. The grandkids were laughing and squealing - splashing through the water, and Athena was running and playing alongside with them. Athena truly was a part of the family. Izzy had a very special connection with Athena - almost as if Athena knew who it was that brought us all together.

We all had fun throughout the morning and into the early afternoon. We ate hotdogs - played games, and had fun throwing the ball for Athena. No one wanted to go home when it was time for grandma Bell to go to work, and for me to take Athena back to the shadows of the city jungle.

My son and granddaughter were the last to leave - they stayed and played with Athena while we got ready. We both came out to the patio where Izzy had dried Athena and brushed her, and made her look pretty. The sunny and clear noon-day sun began to take its occasional cover behind the veil of afternoon clouds. I knelt down and began our routine of fastening the vest and collar - stroking her fur as the shadows of the cloud darkened the afternoon sky for a moment.

I felt a hollow feeling in the pit of my gut. Bell looked at me with a worried look as if some kind of premonition warned her. I continued my routine… as we all began to walk out to the truck, Izzy knelt down by Athena one last time and gave her a hug and said: *"you take care of my grandpa - you pretty little girl."* No sooner than when she said this - a ray of sunshine peered through the clouds, and we all looked at each other with a sense of comfort.

Bell and I drove down to the hospital. I drove up to the ER doors, and kissed her. As she stood up from the passenger side, before she closed the door, she held Athena behind the ears, and then hugged her. I thought I could hear her say, softly under her breath as she held Athena close *"you look after our guy Tina."*

I knew she really said "**Athena**" - but the reality of that instant and the feelings going through me made the moment even more surreal.

**

As we approached the station - we met Stan outside, and began to walk in with him. He said it was probably going to be a slow night, and that they might not need us. We walked into the squad room, and Athena sat down at my feet. We all chatted for a few minutes - drank coffee, and the lieutenant walked in and said they had a 'routine' bomb-threat call, reported to be at a local school. Stan's K9 'Aries' was at the Vet for a cut he'd received, Nick was on vacation, and so - Athena and I were the only K9's on duty that night.

We reported to the school, and walked through every room, passed every locker, and we even patrolled around the entire outer areas… it seemed like we walked for miles… and nothing. She never picked up on anything out of the norm. I knew that even though most of these reports are fake, I wanted to make sure nothing would happen to the school – that there would be nothing dangerous in the building for the upcoming school year. We searched for hours, and I was happy that we found nothing.

When we got to the truck - I let Athena play with her ball for a minute - her 'special' reward for doing a good job. We'd spent most of our shift so far working on clearing the school - so I asked her if she wanted to get some dinner. I knew she wouldn't mind.

Almost, as if testing fate - we ended up at Tina's favorite burger place. We ordered - and Athena barked happily, and we ended up parking in the same usual spot under the evening lights to enjoy our meal. I called Bell at the hospital, and told her that she need not worry, our big 'call' for the night turned out to be nothing. She seemed relieved.

I turned down my radio so we could have a few minutes of quiet while we ate. She ate the burger, and loved 'sneaking' the fries. It was a game she liked to play - even though she truly knew I'd give 'em to her anyway.

Before we finished - like he knew we'd be there… Stan pulled his truck up to mine so our driver windows were next to each other… "You're not going to believe this - Sarge… an inmate at the County Jail slipped away from a highway work crew, and hasn't been seen for hours. The Deputies called for a K9 team to see if we could narrow down the area he might be."

Words cannot describe what went through my mind in those moments - in the words Stan was saying… as if the past came back to haunt me - as if fate was *now* - tempting me…

To face my greatest fears.

We followed Stan to the last known location, the work site on the freeway where the inmate was part of a highway garbage crew. The Deputies from the Jail smiled as we pulled up "we sure are glad to see you two…"

As Athena started sniffing around some of the inmates unwashed clothing the Deputies brought so Athena could track him…

I said *"you guys know what's black and brown, and looks good on prisoners?"* They all just shrugged their shoulders…

I looked at Athena and said… ***"German Shepherds"***

They all smiled, some even laughed a little as I tried to lighten the mood, and Athena, well…

She seemed more than excited when I asked her *"you want to find the bad guy."* I put her on the 20 foot lead, and watched her weave back and forth until she honed in on the invisible trail.

It was now quite dark, and I was already a bit tired from our hours of searching at the school, but I knew we were the only way to get a lead on where this guy went. I tried to focus on the task at hand, putting the memories aside. We started out through a wide open alfalfa field, crunching under foot from being nearly dry now at the end of the long summer. In the distance I could see the lights from some farm houses, and from the silhouette of the lights - some fenced off fields where dairy cattle were kept.

I'd learned early in my younger years to watch the animals. Their behavior could reveal more than tracks ever could. As we got closer, the cows' unease was clear - they had bunched up tightly, their usual calm broken. It was a telltale sign, honed by centuries of survival as prey animals. Something wasn't right, and they knew it.

As we approached the barbed wire separating the livestock from the hayfield - I stopped Athena short of her getting tangled in the fence. I reined her in on the long lead, and lifted her carefully so she wouldn't get hurt. I told her to "hold up" while I crossed the fence. But…

Before my feet hit the ground, I slipped. My left leg snagged onto one of the barbs. It slashed through my pant, and cut into my flesh. Athena immediately came to me, as if to attend to my wound. I told her *"it's not bad girl - I'll be all right."* It stung a little, but I knew I could walk on it. I radioed what had happened, and that we were approaching some farm buildings. Athena was on point as she regained the scent trail.

I was happy to see a gate we could go through as we came to the farm compound. I told Athena to heel, and then attached the five foot lead onto her. *"Quiet girl"* I said - *"let's be quiet if we want to find him."* Athena seemed to know exactly what I was saying.

We walked slow, although there was an excitement in Athena's steps - nearly breaking my command to heel. I told the team where we were, and that *'my little girl'* was close to something… my heart was pounding in my chest, and I thought I could hear a little prayer in my heart as I thought - "dear God, please let our back-up get here soon."

We walked closer to the farm buildings - I saw an old Ford pickup, and I nearly panicked as I saw the driver side window was broken out, glass all over the seat and floor; and the empty gun-rack in the back window.

That told me everything I needed to know. Yes! I was scared! But I knew that by this time - the fugitive inmate was armed, and that the farmer's family could be in danger.

Athena was leading me toward a barn. An older gentleman poked his head out the door of the farmhouse. I motioned for him to be quiet, and then he pointed toward the old barn. I radioed again - that we have a possible hiding location on the fugitive. I tried to ask quietly if anyone else was here on the farm - he whispered back that he thought his wife was out on the grounds somewhere, but he hadn't seen her for a while. My heart nearly stopped, and I radioed the team we may have a hostage situation... I could hardly hear anything but the pounding of my heart in my ears. But I had to focus. I had to be the force that would protect my little partner... the force that had to come between good... and evil.

I remembered my "combat breathing" - in slow and out slow, and it helped, a little. Athena inching me closer and closer to the barn. I looked down as we walked slowly, and all I could see for a moment was... Tina.

"Focus Jack" I thought to myself: "I'm not going to let this happen... again." I wasn't afraid for myself... I was afraid to lose another partner. My silent thoughts turned into an unspoken prayer: "please God, let her be safe." I watched - and I could tell her ears were zeroing in on something. I said to myself "Focus Jack" as *I* tried to hear what Athena was listening for.

I followed Athena's lead, my grip tightening on her leash as she crept toward the barn door, her muscles coiled. The air was thick with the smell of dust, stale hay, and something else – fear. My hand hovered near my holster as I pushed the barn door open, only to freeze at the sight in front of me.

Through the dimly lit barn I could make-out that the inmate had his arm around the elderly woman, pressing her close in front of him as a human shield. His other hand gripped a shotgun, barrel pointed right at the door. My heart thudded in my chest as his eyes locked onto mine, cold and desperate. I pulled my pistol from the holster holding it at a 'low-ready' – and before I could say anything... the inmate interrupted...

"Drop your gun," he spat, his voice tight with panic. Athena's low growl rumbled at my side, her stance stiff and ready. I didn't move, didn't even blink.

"That's not happening," I said calmly, keeping my voice steady, trying to ignore the tremor in my gut.

The woman's eyes were wide, terrified. Athena, sensing the danger, tensed further, her anxious energy making the inmate's hand tremble on the gun. The situation was unraveling fast.

"Back off! Or I swear I'll shoot her!" He tightened his hold, now pressing the muzzle hard into her side. I could feel time slowing down, the echo of Tina's memory still pulling at me. The consequences, the risks - losing another innocent life, another partner - it all rushed through my mind, but I forced myself to focus.

"*Athena, easy,*" I whispered, trying to keep her calm. I needed to buy time, and I needed him to look anywhere but at the woman. "You don't want to do this," I said, taking slow, deliberate steps closer, hand still steady on my gun. "Let her go. You don't want to make this worse for yourself."

I was scared that I would *do*, or that I would *say* something wrong. I'd never been trained as a hostage negotiator. Athena's focus was intent, and direct. When she saw the inmates grip falter for a fraction of a second, it was all she needed. She sprang forward, lightning fast, slipping past the woman and launching herself straight at him. The woman fell to her knees, crawling away as Athena latched onto the fugitive's arm, her teeth gripping firmly. The shotgun fired, but his aim was wild, missing by inches as Athena's weight brought him down.

I closed the distance in an instant, kicking the gun away as I took hold of his wrists. Athena was holding him in place, her body tense and ready. I was comforted when I heard the sound of the ratchet from the handcuffs.

"*Good girl, Athena,*" I breathed, steadying her while securing him. The woman scrambled up, dazed but appeared to be unharmed, and as I glanced back, she met my eyes with a look of silent gratitude. I could finally exhale, the tension in my chest slowly releasing as Athena held her place, unwavering and steadfast now by my side.

I stood quietly for just a moment, gathering my thoughts. Athena remained on point, her eyes locked on the inmate now frozen with fear. I clicked the radio and broke the silence. "We're 10-82," I said - Prisoner in custody.

Cheers broke out over the radio, and I shared directions to our location in the barn, requesting a medical team for the farmer and his wife, and to check for any other injuries.

The inmate started to speak, but I cut him off. "Don't even try," I said. Athena's low, menacing growl kept him silent.

In the distance, I heard the rumble of team vehicles approaching, and only then did I feel a measure of relief settle in.

We could finally breathe easy.

Chapter 36

After the Storm

Deputies from the County Sheriff's office rushed into the barn. I was still at the ready, my gun still drawn, and Athena on point. Her gaze on the inmate locked solid on him and her body tense and set for action. As the Deputies took control of their prisoner, I holstered my pistol, and we exchanged a subtle nod of gratitude as they walked him out to their patrol car. My friend Wade gave me a pat on the back – and a proud look… that meant more to me than any other look of approval - silent but profound - reminding me that some bonds never fade, even in the line of duty.

Then - for just a moment, Athena and I were alone in the dim light of the barn. I sat down on a bale of hay, and Athena calmly came to my side. I could only think for that moment, as I looked deep into the eyes of this little girl - I was looking into the eyes of Tina. I wiped away only a hint of moisture from my own eyes - stroked her behind the ears and kissed her forehead… all I could whisper to her was…

"You're safe… you're here girl - we made it."

In that moment of silence she rested her head on my knee still looking at me - as if to say *"yes - I'm here, we did it."*

Athena and I gazed into each other's eyes - brief as it was, and her eyes never closed. "Never again" I thought and then I whispered into her ear… *"Never again little girl - I'm never going to lose you."*

**

Athena and I walked out of the barn into a sea of flashing lights. More deputies had arrived by now, and their supervisor came to thank me.

"You're little girl here sure did a fine job! - she sure is well trained for this" he said with pride.

We shook hands, and I smiled back at him saying: "yes, she did really good… she's a natural."

We walked over to the porch of the farmhouse so I could sit for a minute - I could hear the investigators' inside interviewing the farmer and his wife. It was a couple of hours past the time our shift should have ended, and I knew Bell would be worried sick. I reached for my cell phone from my chest pocket, and Athena nosed at it like she knew who I was going to call. I smiled at her and said "*girl - maybe I'm getting too old for this…* " I swear I could hear her laugh.

Bell answered my call, and she was relieved we were ok. Wade had already told her what was going on, and that I may be a little detained coming home. I let her know I got cut climbing over a fence, and she asked me if I was ok to drive. I told her I was, but I'd need to find a ride back to our truck. She said Stan was on his way to pick me up.

My wife - always the nurse, told me to meet her at the hospital as soon as I could. Reluctantly… I agreed.

I could see Stan's truck making its way through all the other police vehicles. I chuckled and told Athena - "*look girl, we don't have to walk back through that big field.*" She smiled.

Stan hopped out of his truck with a pleased look on his face. I knew by now he'd heard all about what happened in the barn. He blurted out "way to go Sarge" as he clapped me on the back.

Before I could give Athena all the credit - he kneeled down and gave her a big hug - fluffed and scratched her all over and told her how proud of her he is. She loved the attention…

"**You got 'em Sarge**" Stan said with a grin – "**The two of you sure make an awesome team**"

My heart skipped a beat. He'd said those same words, right before I lost Tina. I knelt down, pulling Athena into another hug. My voice failed me as I struggled for words, and I felt the warmth of her fur against my face, the quiet loyalty that needed no explanation.

"You okay, Sarge?" Stan's voice was soft now, steady.

I managed a half-choked laugh. "Yeah… yeah, I'm fine. Must of been some dust in the air – blew into my eyes, or something."

Stan tilted his head, a gentle, knowing look in his eyes. "Sarge… there's no wind. But it's all right. You're safe here."

I forced a smile, and Athena, as if reading the moment, nuzzled me softly, her eyes holding steady then licking at my face.

Stan reached out his hand and helped me to my feet. We exchanged a look, one of those silent understandings, and then he cracked a smile. "How about we get you back to your truck? Pretty sure Bell's been worried about you." I nodded and looked down at Athena. *"Come on, girl - Uncle Stan's giving us a ride."*

The drive was quiet, the darkened fields slipping past, softened under the dim wash of Stan's dashboard lights. Athena lay at my feet, resting her head on my lap, eyes half-closed in a familiar, shared fatigue. Her steady breathing seemed to mirror the rhythm of the road beneath us. Each time she closed her eyes, I found myself drifting back, seeing that same darkness that had once held Tina.

I wondered if, in some unseen way, Tina was here - allowed, maybe, just this once, to stay close. My thoughts traveled back to the barn, where the shadows and silence had held Athena and me, and somehow, it felt as though the shadows tonight were kinder. In this quiet, I could almost sense Tina alongside us, a reminder of the path that had led me here.

**

After Stan dropped us off at our truck, Athena and I followed him up to the hospital. We pulled up to the hospital entrance, the fluorescent lights casting a soft glow across the lot. Bell was waiting outside, her eyes instantly finding me as we stepped out. The worry melted into a relieved smile, but I could see her nurse instincts kicking in.

"Jack," she sighed, looking at the makeshift bandage on my leg. "And here I thought tonight might be routine for once."

"Guess I keep it interesting, huh?" I grinned, though my voice was softer than usual. Athena leaned in close, her head nudging Bell's leg as if to say…

We're all here.

Bell laughed and knelt to rub Athena's ears, glancing back up at me. "Looks like *somebody* kept you safe." She stood and, in one quick motion, pulled me into a hug, whispering, "I'm so glad you're all okay."

She stepped back; eyeing my injury with the no-nonsense look that I knew meant I wasn't getting out of here without a check-up. "Alright, tough guy," she said, gesturing towards the ER doors. "Time to patch you up properly."

I smiled a little and said "it's really nothing - just a scratch" and before I could finish Bell piped back: "look here bud – don't you give me any excuses - I'm the one in charge here now." Her warm smile said more than her words, and I couldn't help but chuckle, looking down at Athena, whose tail wagged in agreement. I followed Bell inside, feeling the weight of the day start to lift as the three of us - my wife, my partner, and I - stepped *forward* together.

Bell led me to a treatment room - Athena never leaving my side. She smiled at the two of us "you two - always together." She put me on the treatment bed, and I lowered my hand knowing right where a cold nose and nudging head would be. My wife continued "let's take a look at this leg." She used some scissors to cut open my pant, and was somewhat surprised - "oh my" she said - "you might have to have a couple of stitches."

The ER doctor stopped by, looked at me, nodded his head, turned to my wife and told her "well nurse - I think you can handle this."

"Wait - Doc…" I blurted out, "you're going to let her stitch me up?" he looked at me… and just smiled… and walked out.

Bell left the room for a minute to retrieve the suture kit, and as I lay there on the bed - leg throbbing, my thoughts drifted back to the last time I had to go to the hospital. I was shaken, even haunted, but I was safe… she was safe. I stroked her head remembering the feeling as I stroked Tina… that one last time.

The room was quiet, the smell of antiseptic hanging in the air as I reflected on that night. I hadn't noticed Bell standing in the doorway, allowing me this moment of solitude, as if she could read the thoughts going on in my head.

Bell smiled gently as she knelt beside me, her eyes filled with warmth. "You've come so far, Jack. You're so strong now. I've been thinking about her too."

My wife - my nurse - not only tended to my wounds but more so, cared for my heart. It felt like a reverent moment; the weight of my fears lifted, if only for a breath. Deep within me lay the shadows of sorrow I knew would never fully fade, but with each stitch, I felt my body, and my heart healing. The brightness in Athena's eyes as she gazed at me, glimmered, with a promise of a bright future ahead.

Bell could tell I was exhausted. She knew today hadn't just been about the physical hurdles we'd tackled; she knew I'd finally faced and conquered a fear that had haunted me for so long.

"I bet you two are starving by now," as she chuckled with the warmth of relief in her eyes. "How about we grab a bite?" I knew there wouldn't be any fast-food places open. By now, it had been more than twelve hours since I'd dropped her off for her shift. She had spent a little more than four extra hours at her 2 to 10pm shift at the hospital – and I could tell these were four hours of worry and concern. But Bell had that look. As the lines of worry had slowly changed into relief, she smiled her smile, and said "The kids are back at the house, and they fixed us dinner."

I swung my legs off the treatment bed, ready to stand, only to be met with a wheelchair. I shook my head. "No way I'm riding in that... I'm walking out of here."

"It's hospital policy," another nurse replied with a grin. And despite my protest, I let them wheel me out the doors, Athena never straying far from my side.

At the truck, I reached into my pocket for the keys, only to have Bell take them from me with a knowing smile. "I think I'll drive. You've had a long day," she teased, but I knew her day had been just as long.

Settling into the passenger seat, I felt Athena curl up at my feet, her head resting against my knee. As we drove through the quiet, darkened streets, I gently stroked her, unsnapping her duty gear. Her gaze was steady, a deep satisfaction in her eyes. We shared a long, knowing look; she seemed to sense the memories surfacing in my mind.

"Never again," I whispered to her. *"I'll never leave you. I'll always protect you."* And in that moment, the dust that had blurred my eyes back at the farm, and like the ride from Smokey Joe... it all returned in a moment of relief. I felt the weight of the day - the closeness of how things could have gone. Without hesitation, this loyal girl had stood *ready to defend me, ready to protect me,* as if it were all that mattered to her. I started to realize in that fleeting moment – that is what Tina wanted too.

And that is what Tina did.

The fear I once felt transformed into pride, swelling inside me. I felt honored, blessed, and incredibly lucky to be loved so deeply by this dog and by so many others in my life. It started to sink in, the risk we all took, the uncertainty we faced every day. We couldn't control everything, even if we wanted to.

Passing the streetlamps that lit the way home seemed to cast away a piece of the fear, the guilt, or maybe even some of the sorrow. Looking down at Athena, I was overcome with a deep love that eased the last of the shadows. I thought of Tina then, and a bittersweet feeling washed over me - honor and pride for her sacrifice, for the protection she had given me.

For the first time in a long time, I felt at peace.

Chapter 37

A Path to The Light

There comes a time in everyone's life, where they have to cross a river. When that time comes - we have to decide whether to cross through the torrent, or find the calm.

My choices were never that clear. I was always forced to cross through the darkness… and violence. It has taken a lifetime for me to find a small token of hope, where I can find a quiet place for me to rest… with a ray of sunshine. But for me it seemed the beams of sunshine were always skirting the clouds – always something more. It was always… something more…

**

Springtime came, and with it, the warmth of pleasant memories. I woke this morning with a nudge from a cold nose - letting me know it was her time to play. She sits quietly as the coffee drips, and then we walk to the patio knowing the world is a safer place as she has become a force that stands between the quiet of the day, and the darkness of the storm.

I sit. I watch. Athena prances up to me and places Tina's ball in my lap. I smile. Athena smiles… and looks at me like *"are you going to throw it - or, what?"*

I feel myself chuckle, and I toss the ball. Reflexes - lightning fast catch and snap - before the ball even reaches the ground. It all comes back to me. The flurry of memories and feelings - the pictures of Athena still vivid in my mind - lightning fast, a leap of faith rescuing a hostage, and apprehending a suspect. The picture in my mind of Tina - choosing to save me. Dragging me through the hail of gunfire… ignoring her injuries - sacrificing herself. For me.

A lifetime of memories - walking through the shadows, always skirting the darkness, the danger, and coming close to death. I sit in the light of springtime remembering the sorrow, the joy, and the thrill of living at the edge. Few can know how alive you are until you come as close to death as we have been.

I couldn't help but chuckle, even with the moisture I held back from my eyes - remembering the past, and loving the future. Sometimes, tears carry more strength than a thousand unspoken words. For those who've faced life's hardest edges, tears aren't weakness - they're proof of everything we've endured, every loss honored, and every love remembered. They're the tears of quiet moments that remind us we're still human, still connected to the people and memories that shaped us. And maybe, just maybe, letting those tears fall makes room for a little more light.

Over and over I would throw the ball for her, this morning was more than the routine we created... in the cool of this bright morning, it was an epiphany of hope, a beam of sunshine that shed light on a future of healing.

She laid her head on my lap, and I stroked her fur... I looked deep into her eyes and I chuckle *"ya think I am getting too old to keep up like this little girl?"* As if my thoughts were swimming through her head, her gaze piercing me - looking as though I were once again comforted by the presence of Tina; it seemed like she was telling me *"it's ok - you've already done so much."*

It was a surreal morning. It was a flash of memories. From living a lifetime at the threshold of survival, to the sight in my mind's eye of a selfless sacrifice; the memories of altruistic love split between the past, and the comfort that was sitting at my feet.

This was a morning I had waited a lifetime for. The thoughts of so many partners, and now - so many retired leashes. Each special creature willing to pay that ultimate price, and the one who ultimately did... I looked up to the sky and tried to see each of their shapes in the clouds. And through a heart healing from all my hurt, and tried to tell them all...

"The honor was mine... I always hoped I was good enough for each of you..."

I don't know if it was closure... I don't know if it was how far I've come to conquering the darkness with a hope of light... but I do know that **I** was the one lucky enough - even blessed... to have been the partner to all of these heroes who protected me.

So, as this past winter has given us time to reflect on the past, spring offers me a light - revealing a new direction. In the quiet of that morning, it was clear: maybe it was time to pass on to others everything these incredible creatures had taught me…

The years of jumping from planes, hard landings in helicopters, the miles of walking - searching for bombs: even the daily life of riding motorcycles, the duty equipment and sitting in police vehicles - it all takes a toll on our bodies. This is something we don't think about when we enlist - or volunteer to serve the public - it just what we do… it's what the Sheepdogs do…

I asked my little girl *"how about we try something a little different… let's go talk to mom…"*

My wife Bell and I talked about slowing things down for us, and maybe start doing something a little different. "What kind of 'different' are you suggesting?" she said with a puzzled look on her face.

"I've been thinking, and I believe we can make an even bigger difference by creating a new division in the department specializing in K9 training. We could even expand it to offer training classes for all the departments - all throughout the state!"

She thought it was a wonderful idea, and we began to come up with a plan. My wife, Stan, Nick, and several other members of the department - well, we all got together, came up with a proposal, and we let my granddaughter Izzy - make the initial pitch to the department, and with our city leaders - with Athena at her side… and they loved it.

Not only did the Chief, and even the Mayor love it, but they suggested we take the plan to the Governor to help with state funding.

At times, it was a whirlwind of activity. We felt a newness of excitement… and maybe even a new sense of purpose. We would be doing the training of the K9's ourselves instead of simply purchasing them - and teaching the officer's how to be handlers – and trainers.

My wife and granddaughter rallied support from school kids all over the state, organizing bake sales and art contests to raise awareness for our cause. With the pictures Izzy had taken with Athena, each poster and social media post added a gentle look to the face of public protection.

Izzy's passion was infectious, sparking conversations about the vital role K9 units play in our community and reminding everyone of the bond between humans and their canine partners.

At the time of my life I intended to slow things down, well, we were busier than ever. We continued to search, to rescue, and to serve. We did our best to keep up with the demands of duty life, and to keep training new K9 officers, and their human handlers.

The training field we had spent so much time at was busier than ever. The selection process was tough, with each candidate required to prove they could meet the demands of temperament, intelligence, and strength. Opening a new training division for K9 officers meant establishing a commitment not just to their duties, but to a lifestyle. Every officer had to be prepared to live with their K9 partner 24/7, understanding that this relationship was built on love, trust, and unwavering loyalty.

Training a K9 was more than teaching a dog to obey commands; it was about fostering a deep connection where teamwork and mutual understanding prevailed. A K9 duo needed to operate as "one," anticipating each other's movements and instincts. Not every officer was cut out for this role; it requires a special temperament, one that could embrace the challenges and joys of sharing their life with a K9 companion. This commitment to serve with a K9 partner is a promise to live with and love your partner. An assurance – a realization even, that you can't just 'put this dog in a cage' like a child would put a toy away on a shelf… this is a life of true partnership.

Similarly, not every dog was destined to become a K9 officer. Only those with the right disposition would make "the cut." Only those who could work seamlessly with other officers and K9 teams, and possessed the innate ability to sense human emotions and detect potential threats – they made the cut. This line of work demanded the proverbial "best of the best," both in human and canine partners.

I found comfort in knowing that my legacy could continue through Athena and the future K9 teams trained in our approach and values. Together, we would cultivate a new generation of dedicated officers and their loyal companions, ensuring that the bond we cherished was passed down and honored for years to come.

Father John came out to watch us during one of our training sessions. Even he stood proud while watching my little protégé, as my Izzy was working on beginning obedience drills with the K9 candidates… and how we were continuing Athena's training to include them both to help teach the "schutzhund" course – since her natural instincts made her perfect for it.

Father John smiled as he watched my granddaughter "She sure takes after her granddad" he said with a slight chuckle - admiring the bond I have with her. I couldn't hold back my pride either: "Yea, but I'm glad she's got her grandmother's looks… I think that balances things out."

"It's inspiring to see the two of you working together like this. It's clear you've made significant progress, Jack."

I nodded my head slowly "Thanks, Father. Some days it feels like a battle, but with Izzy & Bell - and Athena by my side, it's easier to push through."

Father John, with his 'I told you so look' said "The strength of family and companionship is a powerful thing Jack. It reminds me of how we all need a little support in our journeys. You've done so much, and - Jack, you've made great strides in conquering your fear - your guilt. I've noticed that you feel more at peace now… I'm proud of you man, you're learning how to calm your anger by embracing something special."

"I never realized how much I needed that focus, Father - to see the light. Thank you for that. I hadn't understood how much I needed your support until recently. It feels like I'm finally finding my way back from the darkness."

Father John smiled his knowing smile… and said "Yes Jack – and before long… you can be the light for someone else."

I felt a sense of peace – knowing I was finally on a path toward the light.

***

I had just gotten off the phone with my wife. Bell let me know she would be working late. She would be covering part of a shift for a nurse that had 'called-off' sick.

I was on my way to do a routine search at one of the local schools when my cell phone rang again. It was the central dispatch for the State Law Enforcement system... she asked me to respond to the county just north of ours – to a different school where a suspected cache of unlawful drugs was held. This was a school in an affluent area where a number of the State's political leader's children attended.

I told the dispatcher that I could possibly respond – but she insisted that this was a priority situation – where a judge was already to sign a warrant, but he was reluctant to allow the search unless the best K9 unit would indicate contraband was present. The officers and the judge were hesitant due to the delicate nature – with the possibility of political repercussions if they did a search on one of the children of an important figure of the State.

I told them I would respond. A moment of pride filled my heart knowing that Athena... was considered... one of the best.

I called our dispatch – I informed them I would be doing the scheduled search I was originally assigned to – later. I told them that Salt Lake County needed me to help with something pressing...

I arrived at the High School, and the judge was actually on scene – the officers had the warrant request in hand – the judge ready to sign. I looked at Athena – she looked at me... she had that look, and that drive... I think she actually liked doing... what she was meant to do.

We walked through the halls of the school – not knowing the 'target' area the other officers wanted us to search. Athena stopped by a section of the hallway lockers... and sat.

She pointed her nose toward a single locker, and just sat. The Sergeant radioed out to his team that 'we' got a 'hit' on the locker they'd suspected... the judge signed the warrant, and when they opened the locker... they found a weapon, and a stash of 'drugs.'

We walked out of the school – the officers, and the judge thanked us – that being such a sensitive situation... they needed to be sure of that what they suspected – and that what they were informed of... was in fact... correct.

Athena and I began our drive back south to our home county, and as we were listening to the radio-calls for the area we were passing – we heard something...

I wasn't expecting... like I've said... it's always something more. The life I chose rarely gave me – or should I say 'us' – the luxury of knowing what to expect. One moment of duty can change in an instant, and just as the Sheepdog can snap and adjust... so do we.

We heard a call-out on the radio before we reached the narrow stretch of highway where our two counties meet – that the State Prison had an inmate attempting to escape. Athena's ears perked as if she knew what the call meant.

I slowed the truck and hit my emergency lights. I moved the truck over to the right hand lanes and headed off the freeway so we could assist in case there was a need for a search.

We arrived to find the Prison Police units already on site – the inmate caught between the double fence-line. He'd been cut badly by the razor wire, but secured from escaping.

Athena was anxious to help, but by then – there was really nothing we could do to help – other than keep a strong presence for the other inmates in the prison yard.

We stood vigilant watching as the Special Operations extraction team secured the prisoner from within the double fence line. Athena watching everything closely. Officers from the prison housing unit were attempting to clear the recreation yard only to find some of the inmates reluctant to comply.

One by one – the housing officers escorted the crowd in the yard into the doors to the building. We just stood and watched as a number of the men jeered and poked fun at the 'dog-cop' while Athena would growl and attempt to lunge from my hold on her.

The yard was nearly cleared – empty from the group that enjoyed the afternoon sunshine. Athena took particular attention to one... as if she knew.

A straggler – an inmate holding back from going into the building – stood there as if he recognized me. As if he recognized Athena... he stood... he watched... his focus was on me... and Athena.

I couldn't help but wonder why, until it hit me. I looked closer, and I looked again. I looked until I recognized his face... the face I looked at when I testified in court... the face of the man...

Who shot Tina.

I felt my blood beginning to boil; I felt the anger welling inside me. I tried to hear the words of Father John in my head…

"Jack – it's time for you to heal"

For the first time since that day – I was less than a hundred feet from the man who tried to take my life. I was so close to the man who took the life of the little girl I loved so dearly.

What do I do? How was I supposed to feel? At that moment I had to reach deep inside – I had to be the Sheepdog – I had to be the protector… I knew he was no longer a threat to my body, and that he was no longer a threat to my partner… all I knew was I had to protect myself from the feelings – the anger… I had to protect myself from whatever control he thought he had over me.

What did I do? I stood there holding Athena – remembering Tina. We stood together holding the line – the line that I knew I had to protect myself from – the hold he thought he had, but no longer could control. I reached down as if I were going to release Athena from the leash – maybe a way – a way of showing force, but I didn't. My hand lowered, and as I felt her fur – I felt a sense of peace. As if she grounded me in the moment – as if Athena was saving me… from my anger – from my fear.

I stood strong – holding my stare, while I was fighting the anger. Athena stood strong – with a look that could frighten the demons of Hell. She was panting – nearly frothing… and all I could do was to tell her… *"yes little girl… that's the one"* as if she didn't already know.

Two officers finally came to escort him into the building, but before he could reach the doors – he broke from their grip on him, and he turned toward us… and simply motioned with his hand in the makeshift imitation of a pistol, and pretended to 'fire' at us…

Athena let loose with a ferocious growl and bark that made him jump as the housing officers re-secured their grip on him… while all I could do is maintain my constant glare at him…

Athena and I could go home… that poor 'son-of-a-bitch' would spend the rest of his life… walking around in a short circle… of a prison yard.

Eleven minutes. From the time the fence alarms activated to when the prison yard was cleared... eleven minutes. A lifetime of trauma and a moment of clarity... all in eleven minutes. It was those eleven minutes where I realized I could walk away knowing my past no longer held me captive – that this is *my* life to claim, and my healing to pursue.

I stood strong. Athena was ready, and... I wasn't going to allow myself to succumb to the intimidation of someone who would never again be allowed to walk the streets again freely.

Athena sat on the seat next to me on our drive home. As the truck hummed down the long stretch of highway, the low glow of the setting sun painted the sky in deep oranges and purples, like a bruise healing after the day's battles. Athena rested her head on the center console, her chest still rising and falling with the rhythm of hard-earned calm. She was tired but satisfied, her eyes half-closed, as if even **she** understood the weight of what we'd faced together.

My hands gripped the wheel, not out of tension, but as if anchoring myself to the present. Pride swelled in my chest as I glanced at my partner - my companion - who had proven once again why she was considered the best. But beneath that pride was something quieter, something deeper. A whisper of Tina's laughter echoed in my mind, her memory as vivid as the streaks of light on the horizon.

I thought about the fragility of life, how easily it could be shattered, and how, even in the pieces, I found strength. Athena had stood beside me today, unwavering, and in *her* steadfastness, I saw a reflection of the protector I once was - the protector I was still trying to be.

As we drove on, the past and the present seemed to merge, not in conflict, but in a quiet understanding. The road stretched ahead, and I let myself feel it all - pride, sorrow, healing, and...

Hope.

Chapter 38

A Ray of sunshine

Athena sat at my feet while I drank my morning coffee. The little patio table offered her the right amount of shade from the sunlight - a shadow of solace from the crisp embrace of autumn's first light. Her ears twitched at the faint sounds of children chattering while walking to school, and I could tell she was relaxed but ever alert, as always.

I stared into the swirls of my coffee, the steam curling up like a lazy ghost – nearly dancing with the smoke from my cigarette. The quiet moments had become something I cherished more than I'd expected. They weren't common in my life – at least not before Athena, not even now. I thought about the training session we had just wrapped up the day before, her precise movements, her unyielding focus. She was a marvel.

But as I sipped my coffee, there was a nagging feeling I couldn't quite shake. Life had a way of throwing shadows across the sunlight. Maybe it was the quiet that made me restless. Or maybe it was just the sense that calm never stayed for long. Bell had already left for a long shift at the hospital, and the quiet of the morning left me wondering... thinking... "It seems like there's always something more."

The ring of my phone broke the stillness. Athena's head snapped up, ears perked, her eyes locking on me as if she knew. I reached for the phone, already bracing myself for the disruption.

"Jack? It's Wade!"

The voice on the other end was familiar -Wade Callahan, my childhood friend, Army buddy, and Deputy with the Sheriff's department. His tone was tight, urgent, and I knew this wasn't a social call.

"We've got a situation out here. Could use a hand!"

"My grandson is missing – we can't find him anywhere!" Wade nearly shouting! "We've searched everywhere!" Wade's voice cracked, panic bleeding through every word. Athena's ears twitched again, her muscles coiling as if she understood Wade's desperation.

I asked him where he was – and where we could meet. **"I need Gunner"** – "I need you to find my grandson!" I felt a pang at the mention of Gunner.

It had been years since my old partner passed, but there was no time for grief now. Wade needed me – and he needed Athena. Wade rattled off the address, his words rushed and uneven. I scribbled it down, my mind already racing through the possibilities. Athena watched me intently, her amber eyes reflecting my urgency. "*Let's go,*" I said, grabbing my keys. There was no time to waste. I knew that Wade was aware Gunner had passed away years prior, but I also knew what he meant. He was in a state of panic, and I wasn't about to correct him at a time like this. Athena was alert as if she could tell - she was ready to help.

I told Wade Athena and I were on our way. We left so quickly that I hadn't put Athena's 'gear' on her. Like Tina – she seemed to have that instinct – that natural ability to know something's up.

We started driving and I called Isabel. "We're on our way to help Wade. He's lost his grandson and needs our help." I told her I wasn't sure how long we'd be and that I'd keep her updated. I called Wade back – instructing him to remain calm, and to have his daughter and son-in-law gather some unwashed clothing for Athena.

Athena and I pulled up to Wade's daughter's house, and there were already some of Wade's Sheriff's friends vehicles parked outside. Athena nearly knocked me over as she jumped from the truck, she could sense the excitement. I called her back to me, and we were greeted by Wade – his face pale - washed with fear as he grabbed my arm, his hands shaking - as if he was holding on to dear life.

I could see through the front room window Wade's wife Charlotte and his daughter were pacing – the other Deputies trying to comfort them. I knew by now that Wade's Deputy Partners had already asked where the toddler was last seen, but out of habit I asked Wade anyway.

"They - they said he was playing in the back yard, and when my daughter went out to call him for a morning nap – she couldn't find him!" Wade's voice cracking with stress…

I assured him we were going to do everything we could – "We'll find him Wade – trust me" as I did my best to hide my own fear of knowing the possibilities, the many things that could happen.

Athena walked close by my side as we walked into the front room of the house. The child's mom and grandmother's faces were red and their eyes moist – while Wade's son-in-law sat on the couch holding his head in his hands – bent down to his knees. I told Wade to sit down as I began to question again to see if there was anywhere the child could have gone.

One of Wade's officers handed me a small bag of clothing "This is from last night," he said, his voice cracking. Athena sniffed the fabric, her body tensing. Her sharp, searching eyes flicked to me as if to say, *"I've got this."*

I placed a hand on her head briefly, grounding myself in her calm confidence. *"Let's find him,"* I said, and then… she sat. Athena simply sat for a moment as if she had found him, and then she raised her head – nose twitching, her head pointing toward a nearby hallway.

It might not have been the best thing for me to say, but I had to ask – "you all searched the house didn't you?" Frustrated by my question - they all said they looked everywhere…

Wade just looked at Athena with disappointment – the Deputies were puzzled and Athena… she slowly stood, her eyes scanning and carefully stepped toward the hallway. I looked at the group, but was focusing on Wade, and by now I could tell his confidence in Athena was failing fast. I started to follow Athena toward the hallway.

Wade stood back up – it looked like he was about to say something, but I stopped him before he could speak. "Wade – you have to trust me – you have to trust Athena."

I turned again toward my partner as she led me down the hall. I couldn't help but wonder if a family member... then I thought again – "No - not Wade's family" as my suspicious mind tried to wipe away a lifetime of darkness. "Please God – let's find him safe…"

Athena passed by a couple of open doors to vacant bedrooms, and then sniffed at the door to the master bedroom. Not far behind us was the curious group obviously wondering what my 'girl' was going to do. I asked if it was 'ok' to open the door, and Wade said "yes."

I unlatched the handle and slowly opened the door. Athena sprang up onto the king-sized bed – disheveled and unmade, and she started to nose at the blankets that appeared to have been tossed between the wall and the nearby bed. She 'indicated' she found something by sitting – pointing her nose toward the space between the wall and the bed – and then she let out a bark.

"Wade?" I said with a question... with Athena now digging at the blankets – "did anyone look behind here?"

Wade's daughter sprang up alongside Athena and helped her pull the blankets away from the wall. Athena let out another bark – a smile beaming from her face.

There napping peacefully was the little rascal – who decided to take a nap on his parent's bed, and probably rolled off wrapped in the blankets during his slumber. The mood in the house was turned to elation – smiles now replaced the stress, and Athena was hugged and loved. The boy's mom sobbed with relief, Wade exhaled – near exhausted... but smiled tearfully as his fears were calmed.

Knowing the trauma Wade has from his years diffusing and disarming explosives – bombs – *that* alone can tear at someone's nerves. But compounded with his life in Law Enforcement, and the thought of losing his grandchild . . . ? I gently escorted him away so we could have a quiet moment on the front porch. Wade shifted uncomfortably on the porch step, avoiding my eyes. Athena rested her head on his knee, her quiet presence offering the kind of comfort words couldn't. He stroked her fur without thought, his rough hands trembling less with each pass.

"I'm sorry you had to see me like this, Jack," he said after a long silence, his voice raw and uneven. "It's not like me to... to cry."

I lit a cigarette, taking a slow drag before responding. "Forget what you've always been told, Wade," I said, my voice calm but firm. "Forget the notions of what the world expects of us. We're human. We're allowed to feel."

He glanced at me, the vulnerability in his eyes barely masked by his pride.

I leaned back against the porch railing, looking out at the street where the Sheriff's cars had just left. "You know what Father John used to tell me?" I asked, my voice softening. "He'd say, 'You can't carry the weight of the world if you're not willing to share your own.'"

Wade's grip on Athena tightened briefly, and then relaxed. "I don't know how to… let it out," he admitted, his gaze fixed on the horizon.

I turned to face him, my tone gentle but insistent. "You just did. It's okay to cry, Wade. It's okay to feel scared, overwhelmed - even broken. It doesn't make you weak. Hell, it makes you human. And it's what makes us stronger in the end."

In that moment I felt the guilt – this time, for how often I'd hid my own emotion. Sure – when I was with Father John, or alone, I could, but now… I felt like a hypocrite. But I continued…

"You can't always control emotion – and letting it build, well Wade – letting it build up – can kill us! We don't hide laughter; we let it out – because that's what we've been taught. Wade, you can't let what the world expects – you can't let it control you."

His shoulders sagged, the tension slowly ebbing away. He let out a shaky breath, and for a moment, we just sat there, the quiet of the porch broken only by the distant laughter from inside the house.

"Today wasn't easy," I said after a while. "It was a trigger - brought back memories you've been trying to bury. But burying them doesn't make them go away. It just makes the weight heavier."

Wade nodded, his jaw clenching as tears welled in his eyes again. "I've been fighting this for so long," he whispered.

"And you don't have to do it alone," I said, placing a hand on his shoulder. "Come to our meetings. Share your story, your struggles. It's not weakness, Wade - its survival. And it's a hell of a lot easier when you've got people who understand."

He exhaled deeply, wiping his face with the back of his hand. "I'll think about it," he murmured, his voice steadier now.

Athena nuzzled him again, her tail wagging softly, as if to say she was proud of him too.

We sat there for a while longer, the weight of the day slowly lifting as we talked. For the first time in years, I saw a flicker of hope in Wade's eyes - a glimmer of the man he used to be and the strength he still carried within.

Time wasn't important - not now. This moment wasn't about anything other than being present, about being the friend Wade needed. I made a quick call to Bell to let her know I'd be a little longer, but beyond that, nothing else mattered.

As the evening deepened, the porch became a quiet sanctuary, the kind of place where words weren't always necessary, where the simple act of sitting side by side was enough. Wade's breathing slowed, his shoulders loosening as if he were finally letting go of a weight he hadn't realized he was carrying.

"I don't know how to thank you," he said softly, his voice still rough but steadier now.

I shook my head. "You don't need to. That's what friends do, Wade. We show up."

The storm clouds on the horizon crept closer, their dark edges brushing against the fading orange sky. But even as the sun dipped lower, it made one last, defiant attempt to break through. A single ray of light pierced the clouds, casting a warm, golden glow over the porch.

Wade noticed it too, his lips curling into a faint, almost reluctant smile. "Guess that's a sign, huh?"

"Could be," I said, leaning back against the railing. "Maybe it's telling us there's always light, even in the darkest places. We just have to look for it."

He nodded, his hand resting on Athena's head as she leaned into him. And for the first time, I felt it too - the beginnings of healing he hadn't realized… and a real feeling like *my* healing…

Was truly possible.

Chapter 39

They Called Me "Preacher"

Although it felt good - the long day with Wade was exhausting. I truly believe emotional exertion is much harder than physical.

Athena and I hadn't eaten all day. I knew she was hungry. I knew I was. We drove to our little burger place, and as if they knew by the sight of our truck – we would want our usual.

The sunlight had faded into the darkening clouds, behind the horizon, and now it was the glow of the streetlamps in the parking lot that cast its light on our evening meal.

The night shadow of the growing clouds was nothing unusual for the beginnings of a Rocky Mountain autumn. In the distance we could see the flickering of light nature shared. We could hear the faint rumblings of thunder… I told Athena *see – I was hungry.* She let out a huff – as if she could really laugh.

We ate in silence, listening to the natural world around us. There was a strange kind of peace in it - the kind that comes just before something breaks. I could feel it building. The storm on the horizon was no longer distant; it was drawing closer, and nature was about to unleash its fury.

As we finished our meal, the flashes of lightning were now brighter, the thunder louder and more insistent. My phone buzzed on the seat next to me, pulling me out of my thoughts. It was Bell.

"Jack, the power just went out - and the generator at the hospital isn't kicking on," she said, her voice edged with worry. "The ER's gone dark except for the battery backups on critical systems. None of us knows how to start it… we called maintenance, but he's over an hour out." She paused with a sigh in her breath, and then added, "I figured you'd know what to do."

I looked out toward the storm clouds looming over the city, their ominous swell matching the weight in my chest.

"I'm on my way," I told her, already grabbing my keys. I tossed the last of my fries to Athena. She caught them mid-air, tail wagging - still unaware of the chaos brewing.

We hit the road, the headlights cutting through the early darkness as the first heavy drops of rain began to splatter against the windshield. Athena, ever alert, shifted her focus to the storm outside, her ears twitching at each crack of thunder.

By the time we reached the hospital, the storm was in full swing. Bell met me at the side entrance, her face illuminated by the dim emergency lights. "It's worse than I thought," she said, her voice steady but edged with worry. "Half the systems are offline, and the rest won't hold for long."

Athena stayed by my side as we worked. Her presence was a quiet reassurance in the chaotic moments that followed. By the time the generator roared to life, I could feel the tension easing, though the night was far from over.

My radio began to chatter with calls – all over the city, neighborhoods; entire sections of the area were losing power. The lightning triggered power substations all over the valley to shutdown. Dispatch was calling for any – for *all* available officers to respond to the growing darkness all around.

I kissed Bell – she 'wished me luck' as Athena and I ran through the intense rain. I closed the door to the truck and felt a brief moment of being dry as Athena shook her coat and scattered drops all through the truck. I could smell that familiar smell of wet fur, and it too was a comfort knowing she was by my side.

For a moment my thoughts were to drive to my house and retrieve my foul weather gear – heavy rain-coat and hat that could help in a moment like this, but as we pulled out of the hospital parking lot – the rain began to 'let-up' – but the lightning didn't.

The storm had worsened. The flashing of lightning, so intense it painted the entire valley in white-blue hues, had now become a constant barrage. The clouds rolled in thicker, a churning mass of gray-black fury.

I told dispatch 'we' were back 'in-service' – then we were told to report to a shopping center immediately. "Multiple reports of looting in progress. All available units, respond."

I let out a low growl under my breath, knowing this was the kind of situation no one wanted to handle - especially not in this weather. Athena's ears perked up as the urgency in my voice sunk into her senses. Her paws shifted uneasily on the truck's seat, but I knew she was ready.

As I pressed the accelerator, the truck surged forward into the storm once again. The shopping center was only minutes away, but with the grid down and streets flooded; I knew it would take longer. I activated my overhead emergency lights and could see people standing in the storm – confused, curious, yet cautious. The flashing of my lights seemed to dance with each burst of lightning.

The thought of what we might find there - people desperate in the face of a storm and a city in darkness - sent a chill down my spine.

The storm had a way of amplifying things, turning the simplest sound into an ominous threat. I tried to push aside the unease, focusing instead on Bell, and what I might be walking into once we reached the shopping center. She'd be fine - I knew she would be - but that didn't stop my worry. Streetlights were out, leaving long stretches of blackness between the occasional flash of lightning. I pulled into the shopping area parking, and the scene in front of me made my heart skip a beat.

There were figures moving in the shadows - dark silhouettes dashing between storefronts, the sound of breaking glass slicing through the booming thunder. My hand instinctively went to the pistol holstered at my side, though I wasn't sure how much good it would do against the chaos unfolding before me.

"*Athena, stay close girl,*" I muttered, my voice thick with resolve.

She gave me a low growl, her alert eyes scanning the scene as we parked the truck a little off the main street, out of sight for the moment. We'd need to move quietly - discretion was our best option here.

I grabbed the radio, reporting in again that we were on scene. I Requested backup for looting. I didn't know if the many suspects could have been "armed and dangerous."

I could hear the commotion grow louder in the background as more officers responded, but I knew help wouldn't get here fast enough. Athena's low growl rumbled again as we began moving toward the first storefront. My senses were heightened, every crack of thunder feeling like an announcement of the chaos that would follow.

This wasn't just another storm. This was a test of patience, of resolve, and of survival. And it wasn't over yet.

As more officers converged on the shopping center I started directing the growing team to cover as many of the entrances and storefront windows as they could. There was the sound of even more law enforcement units from all over rolling in. It filled the air with a comfort only a Cop could understand. Deputies from the Sheriff's department were joining in to help, adding to our growing presence.

Stan and Aries said they'd cover the other side of the complex, and I told Wade to come with me – as the crowd of looters began to flee from all the 'cops' showing up.

We were clearing one of the stores when I caught a glimpse of Wade's hand twitching. It was subtle - he tried to hide it, but I knew the signs. Not a lot of us could do this job without carrying something heavy in our hearts. We all had our ghosts.

Wade stood at the end of an aisle; scanning the darkness where only the faintest light from a dying flashlight flickered. His voice broke the silence. "Yeah, tomorrow this'll all be a bad memory, right?"

I raised an eyebrow as I glanced over at him. "Kinda like 'crisis + time = humor?'" I couldn't help but smirk, trying to lighten the mood.

He chuckled weakly, but his smile didn't quite reach his eyes. It was a small thing, but it was a step.

I moved closer, checking the store's back room, making sure he was still with me. Not that I expected him to break, but after everything we'd talked about earlier, I wasn't about to leave him hanging. His progress didn't need a spotlight, but it deserved recognition.

I'd seen too many men - too many of us - forget that just because we couldn't see the scars on the inside didn't mean they weren't there. But scars and all – we kept going. Our presence kept the property safe, and a number of arrests were made. We had a number of the Officers set a perimeter at the shopping center - before Athena and I were off again to help elsewhere.

The storm had passed quickly. One minute the rain came down like a wall, relentless and pounding. The next, it had stopped, as if nature had decided it was done. But the damage was already done. Lightning had taken out the power grid, sending it into a blackout that felt unnatural.

The city felt like it had been erased. All the streetlights were down, leaving behind a void of pitch-black silence, broken only by the occasional flash of light in the distance from a still-flickering transformer or the low hum of radio calls.

It wasn't the rain that would keep us busy - it was the damage from the lightning. The City had taken a beating, and the repairs would take hours.

Athena stayed close, always by my side, keeping me grounded as we drove through the darkened streets, scanning for anything out of place. The flickering of lights on the horizon seemed to mock us, reminding us that everything was still broken.

The hours stretched on. We cleared more stores, kept the peace, and watched the city sleep in its chaos. By the time the storm had completely blown over, the power grid was still down. But there was something about the quiet after a storm - it was an eerie calm since the system wasn't fully restored. The world around us was still dark, but there was a softening in the air, a sense that the worst was behind us. I checked in with dispatch once more. They said repairs would take time, but we had it under control.

The next morning, the sky was clearer. Not completely bright, but at least the sun was making an effort to peek through. The damage from the storm would take longer to fix, but the most pressing concern was keeping order, and we did. I soon found myself outside the church after that long, restless night, seeking Father John's guidance as the city began to stir again.

**

"It was quite a night – huh Jack?" Father John said with a tired grin – probably from the lack of sleep from the storm... "It sure was Father – for all of us."

We 'chatted' for a few minutes – about the storm, and about Wade. I told him that I invited my friend to the meetings, and that he might benefit from "visits with Father John."

Father John smiled... and I continued:

"It felt good to help someone – like I'd helped – not by sharing my story, but really getting close to someone who needed it. I was surprised at what I was saying, but it felt good."

Father John leaned in with encouragement "And that's something worth sharing Jack. It's not only your *story* that could inspire others in '*our*' community, but the insight you've gained. Jack, what you have inside needs to be shared!"

I sat in silence within a myriad of thoughts – the emotions, the pain... yes – still there. But I now felt more in control this morning... more so than I have for a very long time. Then Father John gave me that smile – that dangerous smile that told me something else was coming...

"Jack - I'd like to invite you to speak at church this Sunday. What do you think?"

"Really Father, again?" I said with a smirk. "Well - I'll think about it - when can I get back with you?"

Father John went on: "I'd like to know soon Jack, you have a unique perspective, and your experiences could resonate with many who are facing their own struggles. You don't have to have all the answers - I just want you to speak from your heart."

"I guess I could try. I just hope I don't trip over my words, or say something stupid... I'll let you know soon"

Father John grinned warmly "Just remember, you're not alone. We're all here to support you."

I went to turn away for a moment, but stopped... "Father - <u>you</u> know what I was always told from a young age – about strong men not showing emotion – well... thank you... these past visits with you have taught me I can do, what I was told I couldn't... you've really helped me..."

Father John stood stoic, and somber, he looked deep into my eyes. He said: "you know Jack, Tina - may have saved you, in more ways than one."

His words hit me, as if hit by a train... as I thought about it, I thought again and again... it's true. If it weren't for losing Tina, I may never have been able to understand the sorrow that allowed me to feel the pain I didn't know I was hiding, and a way to find my way out of the darkness, and be able to walk into the light.

**

I hadn't called Father John back yet. Truthfully, I was still mulling over how I could find the words - or even the courage - to stand up there and share my story again... And I was in no rush to make a decision.

A few days later, Bell and I sat at the diner with our usual crowd of cop and biker friends, each of them cradling a cup of coffee. The morning hum was alive with chatter, and I was beginning to relax, enjoying the comfortable, familiar rhythm of the place. I had my back turned from the doorway, and didn't see him coming. I was surprised to see Father John walk up to our table. I glanced up, only to realize the good Father was looking straight at me, wearing that grin... that spelled trouble.

"Jack," Father John announced loudly enough for the whole café to hear, "I'm so glad you've decided to speak at church this Sunday!"

The whole Diner went quiet, and then erupted into laughs and whistles.

"Oh, is that so, **Preacher**?" Wade jeered, giving me a good-natured shove. Another one chimed in, "Well, we wouldn't miss this for the world!"

I gave Father John a long look, one that could only mean, *"You're going to pay for this."*

But the good Father just smiled knowingly as he sat with us to have coffee. And somewhere beneath my reluctant grin, there was a spark of warmth. It seemed like the right thing to do - even if I wasn't ready to admit it yet.

**

The following Sunday, my wife and granddaughter walked me into the church, and Bell made sure I was sitting on the front row. I wanted to sit in the back - just in case I needed to make a 'hasty' retreat… I really didn't want to do this.

I can't say why I was so afraid to speak, I sat quietly thinking, and then my thoughts were interrupted by Father John calling my name…

I took a steadying breath as I stepped up to the podium; Father John gave me a gentle pat on the back as he started to step away. He made a final nod with his head while looking toward the stand, and smiled. I stood scanning the familiar faces in the congregation. Neighbors. Friends. My community. They were the people I'd spent my life protecting, and now they looked at me with an expectation that made my hands feel a little heavier.

I gripped the edges of the pulpit, fumbling at first, feeling the weight of my own story. "I… uh…" I cleared my throat, stammering a bit before looking out again. "A while back, I had a dream."

The room was quiet, the kind of quiet where you know every word matters.

"In the dream, I was standing by a river, facing a choice: to cross at the rushing torrent - where the current was fierce and I might not make it - or to search for an easier path. I felt the pull to step into that raging water, though I knew it wouldn't be easy. I could feel the danger. But I also knew…I wouldn't be crossing it alone."

I paused, scanning the faces in the crowd again, feeling the support in their eyes, though I wasn't completely certain that I could go on, but I did…

"You see, at that river, I had to ask myself two questions – two questions I think I heard from a movie: *'Had I found joy in my life?'* And *'Had I brought joy to others?'* I looked back at the years - the darkness I'd lived through, the tough decisions, the friends and family who had stood by me - and finally, I could answer the first question with a 'Yes.' Only now, after all this time, I can say that I have found joy."

A soft murmur rippled through the crowd. I nodded, steadying myself again.

"But that second question…" I let the words linger. "That question…*'Have I brought joy to others?'* That's one I'm still working on, friends. "I have looked the devil in the face. I have walked through the fires of hell. And through all that, I've tried to bring a little safety, a little comfort, and a little peace. I don't know if that's joy, but I hope it's enough to make a difference."

I paused again, letting the honesty settle between us. The silence gave room for a deeper truth I hadn't always acknowledged.

"But I know this - I couldn't have survived by walking alone. I had my wife, Father John…" I nodded toward him, and then looked over at Izzy and Bell. "I had friends" as I looked at Wade and his wife smiling at me, and then continued: "and I had loyal partners who stood beside me, men and women and dogs who served selflessly. I lost a partner, my Tina, who sacrificed without hesitation, without any thought for herself, and that, my friends, is what love truly is."

Heads nodded; I felt their understanding in that shared silence. And so, I kept going.

"Love," I continued, feeling the weight of the word. "The very essence of love is that willingness to serve others – to sacrifice for others - without thinking of ourselves. And I've had the privilege of serving with people, and even my K9 partners - who have done just that. That's a gift - a calling, and it's what's kept me going through my darkest days."

I finally looked down at the polished wooden surface of the podium. The grain caught the light, but my focus shifted to what rested there. Father John's Bible lay open, its well-worn pages gently curled, the passage highlighted as though waiting for this moment. John chapter 15 verse 13:

"Greater love hath no man than this, that a man lay down his life for his friends."

I paused; I took a breath, and then read the passage out loud. It was hard for me to utter the words, but said "true selfless sacrifice – true love, whether it is human, or even if it comes from a dog! It doesn't matter… it's still true love." I paused, and then caught my breath again… "For so long I hadn't realized that my partner – a dog – truly lived what Father John has been preaching to you all – to serve – to sacrifice – to love…"

For a moment, the room blurred as emotion welled up. But with it came a strange and comforting clarity.

I took another deep breath, feeling it move through me, carrying away the heaviness. Then I let the words flow, confessing what had been locked inside for so long: my journey from anger and blame toward God.

"In those days of blaming God for my loss, of facing down that darkness alone, I thought I'd lost myself. But somewhere along the way, I realized it was my own heart I was wrestling with. I was the one keeping myself from the light. And it's only now that I see this…that my course has been a path from confusion to clarity, from shadow to light."

My gaze swept across the room, landing on familiar faces and strangers alike, and I felt the calm settle over me like a steady hand on my shoulder.

"So I stand here to tell you…I survived. And I survived because of every hand that's helped me, every hand that's lifted me up when I was down, and every person who's stood by my side. If I can leave you with anything, it's this: Be that hand for someone else. Because none of us are ever really walking the path – alone."

After I finished speaking, I began to turn so I could take my seat. "Hold on there a second Jack" Father John pulling my arm and turning me back toward him… "There's a little something more we need to do up here…"

Right as he was saying all this - Izzy had walked toward the back of the audience, and opened the big double doors. The click of the latches seemed to echo through the hall. The doors opened with a hint of a squeak, and I saw Stan, with about a half dozen of my friends from the department, all in uniform.

Stan handed Izzy a large package, probably 18 inches by 24, wrapped in brown paper, and she led this procession up to the stand, where Bell, Wade, and the rest of my family were now standing at my side… all with huge smiles.

I was now surrounded by friends and family - supported by my community… Father John, beaming with pride as he announced: "Jack - you've been through a lot, and I know you have made great strides in overcoming these challenges… we'd like to present you with a little token of our appreciation… Jack - this will forever be a little symbol that represents your journey - the sacrifices both you and your partners have made…"

I began to tug at the paper - I began to tear at it a little, reluctant at first… maybe even a little embarrassed… but as I unwrapped I began to see… I could hardly breathe at first, and then felt the reassurance of Bell's hand on my shoulder. Father John smiling - Izzy beaming with pride… Stan, and the crew – even Wade, all stood fast, a hint of moisture in their eyes. In that moment, in that fleeting instant… I knew I could accept that my journey - my struggles could now make way for a ray of sunshine to brighten my path.

I now know that I can commit to embrace a future with hope, and honor, and a renewed sense of purpose. I felt a sense of closure from grief - while looking to the future…

There I stood - looking at the familiar sight of me, my police truck - the picture with Tina at my side, and professionally photo-shopped at my other side - was Athena… both of my little girls - as if looking at each other… in the clouds behind us were the fond memories of my partners past – ears perked, and ready to defend me – as if somewhere beyond the rainbow bridge. Centered in the images of my memories – shadowed in the clouds of artistry, was Gunner… my first – but not the last.

I tried to hold back my emotions, but I felt safe being surrounded by those who care about me…

Yes – I finally felt the healing, the release, and the courage. I stood there with the tears in my eyes falling freely, and I didn't care anymore, because… sometimes…

"Big boys can cry."

Chapter 40

Father John

My wife told me that she would meet me a little later, and wished me luck as I went to my group meeting. I walked out the door – still sad, but with a new determination to move forward.

I pulled up to the back of the church building, and before I met the group in the recreation hall, I walked slowly up the stairs to the office. The door creaked open with a familiar greeting, and I walked in.

I stood there for a moment looking – staring at the familiar sites and remembering the many conversations. I walked over to the desk and looked down at the many papers and notes... and the Bible.

I took a seat in the big leather chair, and thumbed through the pages, and found the passage that meant so much to him.

John Chapter 15 verse 13... and next to the highlighted passage was the little 'sticky-note' he'd wrote... "For Jack and Tina. It's hard to forget a dog that has given us so much to remember." I was all by myself, but I didn't feel alone. I could still feel him in the room with me – still coaching me... still comforting me.

I closed the book, and held it to my chest. I sat quiet and looked at a picture he still had poised and proud on his desk. Old and now faded – a picture of two soldiers in a small frame. Scribbled at the bottom of the picture was that same passage that meant so much to him... John 15:13.

It was hard, but I stood – I didn't want to leave, but duty now dictated what I had to do. I placed the little picture atop the Bible before I walked back down the stairs and met the men and women who have relied on him so heavily, and they all stood there waiting to greet me. The banter and jokes were now quiet, a faint shadow of the lively conversations we usually had before our meetings. Now the mood was reflective, tempered by a feeling of loss. Our jeans and jackets now replaced by suits and dresses, and even still – many of us wore the uniforms he had grown to love.

Veterans, First responders of all sorts; even dispatchers, doctors and nurses – any and all who witness the tragedies of life now gathered together to honor a man who helped us all through the struggles to remain normal. I poured a cup of coffee, and we all took our seats and took turns remembering our friend, our mentor.

It was me now – leading the group's discussions. It was me now who was relating the story of loss – of trauma, and of fear… it was my turn to share, and it wasn't easy.

Isabel walked in as we were finishing our conversations, and she whispered… "It's time."

We all walked across the hallway and stepped quietly into the chapel – reverent, solemn, and respectful. I choked back my feelings listening to the organist play "Nearer my God to Thee" and took my seat on the stand next to Bell.

Father Brian spoke, and so did some of the family members. And then… Father Brian announced a musical number – Father John's favorite song "In The Shadow of The Cross."

The last stanza of the song struck me – it meant more to me than a thousand sermons I could have listened to:

"In the Shadow of The Cross we find our peace"

"In Jesus' love all burdens cease"

"Through every trial – with every loss"

"We find hope in the Cross"

For the third time I stood in front of the congregation. I placed the book he cherished on the podium, and looked down at the picture of Father John, and his childhood friend – hoping it would give me strength to do what he wanted me to do. It was almost as if I gripped that book – the same way I would grip Tina's leash, hoping I could hold on to him the same way I wanted to hold on to Tina.

"It has been a little more than a year since I stood here – it wasn't easy for me then, and it isn't easy for me now. I don't feel like I lost a friend, a mentor, a counselor – I feel like I gained an Angel in heaven – who could keep an eye out for me like he's coaching me from above."

I could feel my sadness, but then a sense of comfort, and I continued… "He taught me that keeping the good memories would mean I really didn't lose something, but would carry those moments with me always…"

I paused for a moment unsure of how to proceed, but I thought about the lesson he may have wanted me to share… "What Father John taught me was that I wasn't alone. He taught me that I wasn't walking the path of healing without help. He taught me that he truly understood as no other could… and he was right."

I opened his little black leather bound book to the passage and stared at it for a second. "I'd like to share a story that Father John didn't share with very many people…" and I went on.

I told the congregation about the night in Viet Nam Father John lived through – only because his childhood friend kept him alive. "It wasn't just a story - it was a glimpse into the depths of his faith, his struggle, and his humanity. Even now, its weight lingers, like a lesson I will carry with me forever. This story, his story is the message of true love – of an ultimate sacrifice.

His friend didn't just save my mentor… but saved me, he saved so many of us too - in many ways."

I looked at the many faces of people that have been helped by my friend, and choked back in my voice and said: "the man that saved Father John… saved every one of us that have been helped by him." I went on to explain that his story not only shaped the way I saw him, but changed the way I saw myself. "Father John once told me that someday – I too could be the light that would help someone else. I didn't fully realize this until today.

"Until today – I may not have realized that my partner – Tina – by saving me may have been the force that could save others as well."

**

After the service concluded – we all proceeded to the church cemetery where a Military Honor Guard performed the 21 gun salute, and the ceremonial folding of the Flag. His final resting place was next to a man who held our dear Father's life in his hands, and who sacrificed himself so others could come to know the love and service we have come to depend on.

Draped gently across the crafted stone of granite – the monument for 'his' friend, was a colored ribbon and medal now faded from the years of weather – a medal no one could bring themselves to touch… and at the base of the tribute stone was a simple inscription…

"Charles J. Hawkins Jr."

"Walk Softly – Resting here is a Hero who will forever hold in his hands… A Piece of My Heart"

**

I've lived a lifetime of facing the things too painful for most, even too painful for me, but I wasn't alone. My wife, my dogs, and friends that became family like Wade, Father John – and even Charlie… a growing group for support that has given me hope. My journey hasn't been easy, but like Father John said: "Tough times call for strong men" and I can only hope I would never let him down.

Our drive toward home was quiet, but not silent. Both Bell and I remembered the funny moments we'd spent with Father John, and it made us feel like he would have wanted us to remember him that way. He wouldn't have wanted us to remember how frail he'd become – or how his health had diminished recently…

Father John would want us to remember his crooked smile, his wisdom and wit. He would have wanted us to "drive-on" and not be sad. He would have wanted us to have the joy we all deserve.

I could tell by her smile – that Isabel had something on her mind. I looked at her and said "what ya thinking?" She said "a couple of months ago he called on one of the members of the congregation to open the service with prayer. I guess this guy felt honored – and he prayed, and prayed, and prayed and kept going on… when he finished Father John approached the pulpit and said '*our next speaker will be…*'" I burst out laughing and said "he really said that?" still chuckling "I guess I could really see him doing that." Bell said "I'll miss his humor…"

Bell and I stopped at our café where we met a large group of our friends. We all reminisced about the men who helped us all… who saved us all.

We all agreed that we should drink a toast in his honor, and knew he would want us to laugh.

So we did.

We enjoyed good memories, conversation, laughter, and maybe even a few tears. I sat in the café, nursing my second cup of coffee, and I noticed a young man in a crisp, newly issued police cadet uniform walk through the door. At first, I didn't recognize him, but when he smiled, it clicked.

We shook hands, and he pulled up a chair. "I wanted to thank you. What you said to me that day a while ago - it stayed with me. Got me through a lot."

He told me about his father's passing and how he'd found a purpose in the loss. "You and Father John… you both showed me what it means to be strong. I figured, maybe I could try to do the same for someone else someday."

I looked at him, trying to think of something profound to say, but all I could do was grin. "You're gonna do just fine, kid. Just don't forget - being strong doesn't mean you're invincible. It means you keep going, even when it's hard."

I had no idea at the time I went on a Sunday ride – feeling the grief, the loss, and the anger – that a young man facing his own struggles would find anything of value in those few words I said.

**

When Bell and I got home we were greeted by the familiar wet nose and cheerful eyes. I smiled and walked to the picture I was given a little more than a year ago… I stood there with Athena at my side and touched the image hanging on my wall…

Of my little girl who saved me.

For the first time… I could look deep into her eyes and not think of just the pain, but the sacrifice – the love, and the hope of a bright future she has given me. I stood for a moment with Bell looking on, and I smiled then whispered…

"I Love You Tina."

Chapter 41

Homeless

Life has a way of swinging between calm and chaos, often separated by nothing more than a single heartbeat. It's in that brief moment – that bridge…

Where Heroes Run.

I've spent decades learning to live in that space - the split second between peace and the storm - where instincts take over and everything else fades. It's a place where you learn to deal with the twists life throws at you…

The moon wasn't out – yet… but it wouldn't have mattered. When it showed – it was merely a sliver, only a thin slice of light that mocked the trials of those who needed to see… at night.

I knew it was going to be a cold night. I knew that springtime in the Rockies was only a glimpse of the things that could come… but took it's time in coming. I pulled the collar of my faded – old olive-green Army jacket up to my neck in hopes I could face another night… in the cold.

It had been quite some time since my last hair cut, and the same for my last shave, and what I thought I once knew… was nearly forgotten. Or so it seemed. I found parcels of forgotten food in dumpsters. I found the remains of trinkets and things that I thought would bring a sense of comfort… a piece of string? A little cloth – anything – everything I thought I could use to ease the harsh nights… Or just to blend in and do what the others were doing.

I found a little place under the overpass where Main Street crossed above the railroad tracks, and there, tucked into the shadows, was a decent enough spot to spend the night. But sleep… sleep never comes easy on the street.

I lay there, watching the others drift in one by one. The forgotten. The fallen. The wanderers who, like me, had nowhere else to go. At least for the night. They settled into the cracks of the city - each with their own ghosts, their own stories - but here, we were all just looking for the same thing: a moment of peace before the cold came creeping back in. Because rest, for the homeless, never comes freely. You borrow it. You steal it…

And sometimes, you never get it back. In the darkness, alone in my thoughts… I started to doubt why I was even here.

I must've dozed off here and there, but with the first light of dawn came that dog - soft, warm, and breathing. Nuzzling at my neck.

That dog.

She was beautiful in a ragged kind of way - sleek, alert, not quite a stray… not quite tame. She'd found me, though I couldn't imagine why. Maybe it was comfort. Maybe it was chance. But I gave her the last of the crust I'd saved from a half-eaten pizza I'd pulled from a dumpster the night before.

The others watched, silent. Like they knew something I didn't.

The dog stayed close.

Not clingy - just there. Watching. Like she was sizing me up. Smart eyes, dark and clear. A working dog, I could tell. Shepherd maybe, or part of one. Not like the mutts the shelters tossed out on bad luck and broken legs. No, this one had purpose written in the way she moved - silent, deliberate, and alert.

She lay beside me without asking. Like she knew this patch of dirt and gravel was ours now.

And I'll admit… it felt good. Even out there in the cold. A little warmth, a little company, and the kind of loyalty you don't earn - you inherit. She didn't beg. She didn't whine. She just… watched.

Then, just as the sun pulled itself over the skyline and lit the rusted rails in gold, she stood up.

Stretched.

Looked at me one last time.

And disappeared.

The mornings came cold, even when the sun was shining. Spring in the city was cruel like that. It promised warmth - but offered little more than a bitter breeze and the hard ground beneath my back.

The others stirred around me - some coughing, some cursing, one just sitting up and staring into nothing. No one said much. Words were a luxury. We all had our own demons to fight, and silence was safer than sharing the weight of them.

The dog came again. No sound. Just that sudden presence - like a shadow that never quite belonged to the light. She padded up slow, head low, eyes wary. I didn't have to ask her name. You don't name ghosts.

At least – not when the others could be listening.

She curled up next to me without a word - not that I'd have spoken if I could. There's something about the quiet that settles when a dog chooses you. Not out of need. Not out of fear. Just… trust. Maybe it reminded me of a time when I used to have that. A time when someone or something could count on me without flinching. Maybe that's why I let her stay. Or maybe, truth be told, I needed her more than she needed me. The warmth of her side was more comfort than I'd had in weeks, maybe… I lost track.

And then, like clockwork, came the cop car.

No sirens. No rush.

Just a slow crawl past the underpass, engine barely humming. I watched it, waiting to see which kind of cop we were getting today.

The passenger window rolled down. A face I'd seen before - too clean for this place, too calm.

He held out a paper bag.

"Hey, old-timer," he said, like I was some regular at a corner bar. "You eat yet?"

I grunted. Didn't answer.

He set the bag on the ground. No lecture. No push.

"McDonald's this time," he said. "It's a little cold, but hell… so's the air."

And then he was gone.

The dog didn't move. She watched him like she knew him. I didn't say a word. I waited a few minutes - always wait, in case someone decides they want your meal more than you do - and then opened the bag.

No note this time. Just food.

I split the sandwich. Half for her. Half for me.

She didn't rush. Took it slow. Like she was savoring more than the taste.

**

It was nice to have something in my stomach. Hunger is like the feeling of loneliness – something you can't escape. It's always there when you least expect it – or maybe you do? But it haunts you – it begins to command you, and it will never leave you… unless you feed into it. And then - evening and looming darkness sneaks back - reminding you… you're alone.

The wind rolled low along the concrete like a tired breath, scraping trash and last year's leaves down the gutter. I pulled the collar of my old field jacket tighter. The fabric, worn and fraying at the seams, still carried the weight of a hundred cold nights. Olive drab, Army-issue - it didn't raise eyebrows. Just made me look like someone forgotten.

Inside, tucked beneath layers of stitched wool and time, something heavy rested against my ribs. I never shifted it, never adjusted it. I slept with my arms crossed just right to keep it close. Not that anyone noticed - not out here. Out here, folks kept their eyes on the fire barrel, not each other.

The 'stray' lay still beside me, her head resting atop crossed paws. No leash, no commands. Just loyalty wrapped in fur and muscle. She hadn't moved in ten minutes, but her ears twitched once, just before I heard the footsteps.

Boots. Maybe not steel-toe, and not soft like sneakers. Work boots.

A man in a reflective vest and blue utility coveralls rounded the corner, pushing a squeaky-wheeled cart that looked like it came straight from a public works garage. He stopped five feet away and leaned down, setting a bag by the trash barrel without saying a word. The vest fluttered in the wind as he turned to go.

"Wade?" I said with my voice as low as I could.

The man paused, barely tilting his head. "Cold night," he said. "Bag's got food. Long-johns too." He 'nosed' toward the dog and said "Figured your girl could use a biscuit."

I nodded. "Appreciate it."

No handshake. No lingering look.

Wade disappeared like fog in headlights.

I opened the bag. Bacon cheeseburger, still warm. Fries, half-greasy. A biscuit wrapped in a napkin for 'the stray'. And beneath it all - a folded square of brown paper towel.

Unfolded, it read: Tip came in. Six blocks east. Third alley. Midnight.

I didn't smile. I never do these days. But my grip on the bag tightened just a little. The weight at my side shifted with me - like a whisper that hadn't yet spoken. The note crinkled in my palm. A time. A place. A man who claimed to know things the city pretended not to see. The dog stirred beside me. Her ears twitched - her nose lifted to the wind. I handed the biscuit to the stray. She took it gently, her tail thudding once against the concrete.

I leaned back against the wall, pulled the coat tighter. Sleep would come in fragments tonight - just like always. Someone was watching us. Or maybe hunting. Either way I had a date with a ghost... and not much time to find out if it was real.

I tried to get some rest... I closed my eyes. But not for long.

"Sometimes to catch a ghost, you've got to learn how to vanish first."

Chapter 42

No Ordinary Dog

The city's shadows bring a kind of silence most people never notice. It's lonely. It's raw. It's in these shadows that few feel safe in walking. It's quiet – too quiet. And if it weren't for the chimes ringing from the cathedral… it would be silent.

I counted eleven this time, and I knew it was almost time.

I started walking - staggering a little maybe. Trying to look the way I was expected. I paused on occasion - maybe to appear broken, or maybe to seem too tired to care. I leaned against a building close to the place I'd read in the note. I felt the calm of fur against my fingers as she lifted her head to let me know…

She was by my side.

The wind shifted. Cooler now, tinged with the scent of rain and something else - something metallic and sharp. I caught it just as the mutt lifted her head and stood, ears high and still.

I followed her line of sight.

Movement. Half a block down, someone slipping between the shadows of a boarded-up storefront. Same shape. Same coat. Maybe this was him.

I was walking, or more so shuffling my feet, on my way to where Wade's directions - still crumpled in my coat pocket, instructed me. My steps slow, I tried to watch everything in a way that wouldn't attract attention to what I was doing. The dog sniffed and wandered with me, nearly always at my side now. I made it look as though I was hoping I'd find my next meal…

There was a growing knot in my stomach. I hadn't even decided yet if I'd go all the way to the location, but I was moving. For now, that was enough.

And now... this.

I didn't speak. Didn't call out. Instead, I took one slow step forward.

The dog was already gone.

No bark. No hesitation. Just a flash of muscle and discipline, a ghost gliding over broken glass and wet concrete. She didn't lunge like a stray. She cut the angle - hard and low - head down, tail still, the way I had seen a hundred times before.

I should've been shocked. But my hand was already half-lifted, forming a signal I hadn't used for a while.

"Go," I whispered, almost to myself.

What happened next was fast and clean.

The guy pivoted - saw the blur - and tried to run. Too late. The dog hit him square in the legs, not biting, not thrashing. Just force. Precision. She dropped him like a bag of bricks, and then stood over him, her body low, growling just enough to keep him flat.

I approached slowly, boots echoing in the empty dark.

The guy cursed and tried to crawl. A deeper growl stopped him cold.

I knelt beside the dog and laid a hand on her back. She didn't move, didn't even look at me. Her job wasn't finished.

"Where'd you learn that?" the guy croaked, eyes wide.

I didn't answer. I was still looking at the dog - not with surprise, but with something more like recognition. She wasn't panting. No wild eyes. No trembling. Just calm focus. Trained.

No tags. No collar.

But no ordinary dog.

The guy froze beneath her - breath shallow, eyes twitching, every muscle trying to calculate a way out.

I crouched lower, brushing the dog's flank again. Still no tags. No collar. Just the faint tremble of her breath beneath my fingers. But she held him fast.

The guy's voice cracked. "I ain't who you think I am."

"Probably not," I said quietly, scanning the alley. "But you know something."

His gaze shifted left - too quick. Not fear. **Anticipation.**

"I don't know who the guy is - but I've seen what he does. I couldn't go to the cops. They'd think I'm crazy. But the nurse - the one who does the clinic - she said I could trust you. I doesn't know much. I only knows the guy uses patterns, and always leaves thems where no one looks – mostly in that big field with all the weeds. I thinks the guy killing us is like a Marine or sumptin, and I thinks he only kills people no one will miss."

I stared at him. Something in those words slid deep - lodged like a splinter behind the eyes. I remembered that at one time someone talked like that. And that last time we didn't listen.

I reached down to him, his fingers trembling in my hands as I slowly began lifting him up from the ground. "Alright. Let's get you outta -"

Crack.

A gunshot shattered the moment. Loud, high pitched and painful…

I turned my head – and another shot rang out.

The sharp, brutal *crack* that echoed off concrete and steel. I felt the percussion in my teeth.

The man jerked hard, his body arching once before collapsing into **dead weight.**

Athena whirled, a blur of teeth and fury, launching toward the direction of the shot.

I was already moving. Reaching for the familiar weight I'd kept close to my chest. Now - gun out, my back low, pivoting to cover.

Movement - ten yards away. A shadow peeling away from the darker edges of the alley. Fast. Precise.

Another shot barked - but missed. The shooter was running as I returned fire. But Athena was faster.

She tore through the gap like lightning, her paws hardly touching the ground. I saw her hit him - a clean, perfect strike - and then the growl, **feral and pure.** A cry followed - high-pitched, panicked - and then came the sound I recognized from a dozen take-downs:

Teeth on flesh. And then another shot rang out, and I saw the flash from the muzzle. It wasn't a memory anymore – I was reliving my worst nightmare; of another dark alley – another dark night when I was shot – my partner dragged me to safety in spite of her wounds. In mere seconds I relived it – the night I lost my Tina – and now my fear... of losing my Athena. I called her, but all I could see were the silhouettes of darkness in the shadows... I was so afraid of losing her. I called her again...

The man flailed, breaking free, but Athena held on long enough to do damage. When he finally slipped into the shadows, he was bleeding hard.

I called her back **again**, my breath ragged and panting. "**Athena** - *here! Come!*"

She hesitated - and all I could see in the shadows of the alley was that silhouette: like a punch to the gut the fear and horror from that night I got shot, and my memory of Tina; it all came back to me in an instant. But after I called out again - this time she came. Solid and strong she looked proud, still cautious – like a wolf still on the hunt for prey. And my heart could beat freely once again.

But Athena stopped, and then turned. She stared into the darkness one more time before she came back to my side.

And I dropped to one knee, pulling her close, hands trembling slightly as I checked her over. No holes. No blood. At least blood that wasn't someone else's.

"Good girl," I whispered, and this time, it cracked in my throat. "You did good."

I looked down at the informant. Too still. A pool forming beneath him.

He was gone.

And the only lead we had now... I held in my arms while the shooter was running somewhere through this city with **deep bite wounds** and one hell of a reason to stay hidden.

I stood slowly, my hand still on Athena's back. The informant's blood pooled in the cracks of the alley, catching the glint of a broken streetlight from the empty street.

I didn't want to say it. Not out loud. But the guy was right. This wasn't some junkie with a grudge. This was intentional. This was precise. And close enough to take the shot without even grazing Athena.

I touched her side, stroked her fur - making sure again - no blood. No wound. Just a deep, steady breath.

I could hear the rush of engines from cars, and then... Footsteps now. Fast ones.

As they approached the alley where we stood, a voice called out. "Sergeant Jack - Jack Duncan?"

A man rushed into the alley, badge out, service weapon still lowered but ready. He had an athletic build – yet a small frame. Civilian clothes, but the kind you wear when you know things might go sideways. His necktie loosened just enough to show his open collar – and he had a wadded sandwich wrapper showing past the edges of his coat pocket.

His eyes scanned the scene fast.

"Detective Sanchez, Major Crimes." he called out and looked down at the body. "Guess I'm in the right place."

I stood straighter, but didn't offer a hand recognizing a long known associate on the force... "Who called you Tony?"

"Wade - Wade Callahan from County. Said things were about to get interesting." He glanced at Athena. "He didn't mention the dog."

"I didn't think *she* needed an introduction," I muttered.

Detective Tony Sanchez gave me a long look, then crouched near the body - sharp, practiced, nothing wasted.

"Tell me what I'm looking at here, Sergeant."

"You're looking at a man who tried to give us some information on who's been killing all the homeless guys around here. And someone who wanted him dead bad enough to shoot clean in the dark and vanish without a sound."

He stood, brushing his hands off.

"So we've got a killer who seems to be trained, very careful, and killing ghosts. With no witnesses. No fingerprints. No apparent motive." He turned to me and said "Except you."

I didn't blink.

"Yeah. Me. But you're only witness… is her" as I leaned back down and stroked Athena's fur…

Sanchez studied me for a bit longer than necessary. Then he blew out a breath and stood up straighter. "We were a bit concerned – that you were done. After losing Tina – losing a partner like that and getting shot?" He paused and shook his head slightly "I realize it was tough, and you made it back, but you're in over your head here Sarge." His voice was neutral, but the edge was there. Not quite an accusation. Not quite sympathy.

I didn't answer. I didn't need to.

Sanchez gave a humorless chuckle, more air than sound. "Hell of a way to try something new… like going under-cover."

He stepped back, eyes sweeping the scene one last time before fixing on me again.

"You've got so many people who respect you in this department," he said. "And some who think you should stay doing what you're good at. But we've loved having you back." As he scanned the scene again – "I think I'm stuck with ya."

He hesitated.

"Look… Wade vouched for you. That's rare. You've never been involved that much with investigations – especially cases involving multiple agencies. And now we've got a body, a whisper of a name, and a suspect who slipped past us like smoke." He jerked his chin toward Athena. "And a dog who apparently doesn't miss."

I folded my arms, silent.

Sanchez reached into his pocket, pulled out a folded sheet of paper - crime scene photos, maybe. Or something from a case file. He didn't offer it yet.

"This is going to get worse before it gets better," he said. "And I don't have time to babysit some rogue Sergeant playing hero with a dog and a chip on his shoulder."

I raised an eyebrow. "You always this friendly?"

Sanchez ignored the jab. "But I also don't have the luxury of passing up help that knows what the hell its doing."

He finally held out the paper.

"You want in? Fine. But if you're in… you follow my lead."

I took the paper, unfolded it.

My eyes narrowed as I scanned it. Athena moved closer, like she knew the game was changing.

"Fine," I said. "But if I find him first… I don't wait for backup."

Sanchez looked at me. Didn't smile… Didn't argue either.

**

As more officers arrived – I took Athena back down the alley, into the dark, and she picked up on a trail of blood – leading out to the street north of the businesses that formed the ally.

We walked around long enough to see… the trail was now cold. Gone.

I knelt down again - searching the darkness for something - anything…

I feel the familiar nose under my chin as our eyes meet, and I know one thing for certain…

She really is no ordinary dog.

Chapter 43

In The Squad Room

I stood, and Athena stood with me - head high, tail calm, eyes watching me. I gave her a nod, just a tiny thing, and she responded like she always does: like she too always knew what I needed before I did. We walked together through the alley, stepping around the stained outline on the ground where the informant had bled out. Sanchez stood further up the street, his voice low and his hands mimicking the instructions he was quietly giving to the Medical Examiner and a few uniformed officers.

He caught sight of me, and his mouth twitched in what might've been a half-smile. "Jack," he said, "it looks like we're gonna keep your cover alive a little longer" as he glanced over toward the opening of the alley.

I understood right away. Two of the nearby homeless guys were ones who'd been hanging close since the action died down. They were watching us from the mouth of the alley. One was smoking something homemade, the other sipping from a paper-wrapped bottle. Sanchez gestured, and one of the uniforms stepped forward.

"Sorry, man," the cop muttered like he hated to do it, snapping cuffs on me in front of the bystanders. Athena growled once, low in her chest, but stayed put. I smiled…"It's Ok… Good girl."

We made a bit of a show of it - nothing too theatrical, just enough to sell the lie - and then I was led to the squad car.

It was my friend Stan who opened the door. He was another K9 cop, though younger than me, he was sharp as ever. We'd been on more than our share of chases together. He'd brought me food, and notes from home while I was out here. So he recognized me instantly, even under the beard and grime.

He gave me that crooked smile of his. "Damn, Jack. You look like ten miles of bad road."

"Thanks for the warm welcome," I whispered. "You gonna spring me from these cuffs, or just admire my new jewelry?"

Athena hopped into the back seat with me and Stan closed the door. Once inside he hopped in then turned around from sitting in the front seat. He grinned and clicked them off. "You guys comfy? He smiled – "I'll drive you back myself."

Halfway to the station, he handed me his cell. "You might wanna call Bell."

I didn't realize how tight my chest had gotten until I heard her voice. There was no "hello," just:

"Jack? Are you alright?"

"Yeah," I said, voice cracking more than I'd expected. "It's over. For now."

She was waiting for me by the time we pulled into the garage. Bell didn't run to me - she walked, fast and purposeful, like a woman with a mission - and wrapped her arms around me hard enough to make me wince.

She didn't cry. Bell's not the crying kind. But she held me like I'd just climbed out of a grave. And then she looked down at Athena.

"She okay?"

I nodded. "Vet's meeting us inside. Standard procedure."

Bell kissed my cheek and handed over a paper bag that smelled like heaven: the double burger's – the warm fries… our special we usually got at mine and Tina's – now Athena's and my special burger joint. It felt like I hadn't had real food in weeks.

Inside, a young vet tech in scrubs - and a woman with confident eyes and gray streaks in her braid - were already waiting. They gave Athena a calm once-over, checked her gums, and gently swabbed a few bloodstains clinging to her whiskers and jowls. She sat through it with the patience of a statue.

"Dog's a rock star," the vet said.

"You have no idea," I replied.

We sat in the break room after that. Me, Bell, and Athena - finally reunited and off the clock. I peeled off the grungy jacket but kept the rest of the undercover look intact. Sanchez had made it clear: don't shave, don't wash the clothes, not yet. The streets believed in the 'old man' persona now - and that kind of credibility was hard to earn.

While I ate, the murmurs of voices filtered in from the next room - the Squad Room. Bell poured coffee and tilted her head toward the noise. "Sounds like a war council."

"Close," I said.

She gave me a look. "You going in?"

"In a minute."

When we finally entered, the room was already half full. Sanchez stood at the whiteboard, flanked by Wade Callahan – my buddy and former Army Partner, now detective with the Sheriff's office. The county was already involved. Wade caught my eye and gave the smallest nod - like soldiers do when no one else understands.

"Morning," Sanchez said to the group. "Appreciate y'all being here at stupid o'clock. We've got something important."

He gave a summary - short, precise - of the alley incident. The near miss. The takedown. The blood.

Then he said, "What most of you don't know... is that we've had an officer embedded for the past few weeks, posing as one of the unhoused."

He paused, let it hang.

"That officer is our own – Sergeant Jack Duncan."

Every eye turned toward me. I felt Bell's hand tighten around mine, then release. Athena sat at my side, calm, proud, ready.

I stepped forward.

"I didn't do it alone," I said. "She kept me alive out there." I scratched Athena behind the ear, and a few of the officers smiled.

There was a long moment of silence - not awkward, just thick - and then someone started clapping. A few more joined in. Not a standing ovation, but the kind of thing that means something when it comes from other Cops.

Sanchez raised a hand to calm the chatter. "Sergeant Duncan's off the street for a few days. We'll probably think of a good cover story on why you're not out there – like you've been in jail or something, but for now… Rest, recharge. But keep the look - it's working." He turned back toward the others and continued: "Meanwhile, we'll be cross-agency now – both the County and Metro; we'll be in full coordination. This case just got bumped to priority.

"We've also got Sgt. Jack's wife - who just happens to be one of the supervising nurses at the hospital - and we'll ask her to put out an alert - let's say to all hospitals within a 500 mile radius - and have them report any injuries that might resemble a serious bite… from… her" as Sanchez nodded down toward Athena - smiling at my feet.

The room began to buzz with conversation, plans, and strategies. I leaned back against the wall, Bell at my side, Athena now curled into a tight spiral at my feet, already half asleep but ears still listening.

Outside, the first gray streaks of dawn crept in over the city. Bell and I walked Athena out into the back parking lot of the station, and as if it were right on cue - Athena and I stretched, yawned, and I was able to smoke a real cigarette - for the first time in a couple of weeks.

Chapter 44

Home

We pulled into the driveway just as the sun was breaking over the rooftops, a soft amber light reflecting from the front-room windows. The hum of the engine died out, and for a long second, I just sat there - still. Quiet. Breathing in the familiarity.

The front door slammed open.

"Grandpa!" Evelyn's voice cut through the morning air like a song, feet pattering down the steps, followed by Izzy and the rest of the grandkids piling out like a jailbreak.

I opened the car door, and as I got out I knelt just in time to catch my youngest granddaughter Evelyn's arms around my neck. She held tight for a second, and then pulled back, wrinkling her nose.

"Grandpa, you stink."

That one got a laugh from everyone, even me.

Athena hopped out and trotted up beside me, tail wagging, tongue out - filthy from days out in the alleys and underpasses. Izzy clipped her leash with a practiced hand.

"C'mon, warrior dog. Bath time."

Inside, it hit me - the smell of coffee, toast, a trace of cinnamon, and something warm I couldn't quite name. Even though Bell wasn't in the room yet, I could feel her presence in every quiet corner of the house.

Clichés started bubbling up in my head - *home is where the heart is, you never know what you've got 'til it's gone* - and I grumbled at myself. I never liked clichés. But damn if they weren't true sometimes.

The shower was a little piece of heaven. I let the water run longer than usual. No cold concrete. No rusty pipes. Just steam and the familiar tile under my feet. I caught my reflection in the fogged mirror - tired eyes, and maybe even a couple new lines.

Downstairs, the kitchen smelled like a diner at sunrise. Bell handed me a plate stacked with eggs, toast, and hash browns, and a mug of coffee so strong it could walk on its own. I kissed her cheek.

"I figured you'd still be hungry," she said, in that tone of hers that wasn't a question.

My son Jason was already corralling the kids toward the door. "Shoes! Backpacks! School! Let's go!"

The house emptied quickly after that. A blur of lunchboxes, shoelaces, and a final slam of the front door. Then - quiet.

The kind of quiet you can feel.

I leaned back in the chair, mug in hand, and watched the dust dance in the sunlight pouring through the curtains. I never meant to doze off, but I guess my body had other plans.

I woke up around noon to the sound of a truck door shutting. It was Wade.

He let himself in through the side gate like he always did, boots on the patio, a paper bag in one hand and a bottle of hot sauce in the other.

"Figured you'd be up by now, slacker," he said. "You got huge a burrito coming your way, but only if you pour the beer."

We settled in on the back patio - Athena curled at my feet, freshly scrubbed but still drying. Wade kicked back, chewing slowly, watching the wind roll across the trees.

"So," he said eventually, "you glad to be home?"

I nodded. "Yeah. For now."

We didn't have to say it out loud - we both knew I wasn't done. Not even close.

"It wasn't supposed to go this deep," Wade said. "You were just supposed to get a feel for the trafficking routes, blend in, and listen. A couple weeks, tops."

"Then the bodies started piling up," I said quietly.

Wade didn't respond right away. He just stared at the ground, like the answer was buried somewhere under the deck.

"Different methods," he said finally. "Same kind of victim. The broken. The invisible. Someone's keeping score."

I nodded. "Stabbings. Strangulation. A couple shootings. One looked like piano wire."

"I remember that one," he said, shaking his head. "No prints, no video, no witnesses. Just a guy with his last breath caught on the wind."

We sat there for a moment, letting that hang.

"I've been thinking," I said. "Back when I was prepping for this op - digging out that old Army jacket, finding 'scuffed-up' boots with soles already half worn out - I kept thinking how it felt like gearing up for Iraq again. You know? Just this time, the battlefield's got trash bags and alley cats instead of sand and mortars."

"You're not wrong," Wade muttered.

"It's not just the gear though. It's the mindset."

"Yeah?"

"You go in knowing it's gonna suck. Sleeping when and where you can. Stomach turning from whatever you can find to eat. People either ignoring you or looking at you like a problem. And yet... somehow you've got to stay sharp. Alert. Like a ghost with eyes."

Wade let out a low whistle. "And they wonder why we drink."

I chuckled and reached for the cooler.

As Wade left, that surreal feeling of having a day off - and still living behind the badge - didn't bring the kind of peace, that having time away from work gave to other people.

As he pulled away I gave him a wave, and he nodded his head in return.

But it wasn't before his car disappeared from around the block; I saw two police trucks pulling up to the house from the other direction.

Two of my closest friends, allies, and partners – Stan Parker, and Nick Hauser – showed up to my house for some friendly 'off-duty' dog time… I met them with a smile, and we walked around the side of the house so I could show them to the back yard. The sound of nails tapping across the wood floor echoed through the house as Athena charged out the back door. In a blur of fur and wagging tails, she greeted the two visitors waiting by the gate - Stan and Nick - both still in their uniforms, each with a K9 in tow.

"Thought we'd give the kids a little recess," Stan grinned as he let Aries, his thick-coated black Belgian Malinois, off the lead. "Figured Athena could use the company before things get too real."

Nick unclipped his large German Shepherd/Malinois mix, Thor, who wasted no time diving into the chase across my backyard. The three dogs bounded through the dry grass, barking and leaping, shedding the discipline of their training just long enough to remember they were still dogs.

I chuckled, standing beside them with a coffee mug in hand. "She's been edgy lately. I think she knows something's coming."

Stan nodded, watching the dogs with narrowed eyes. "She's a sharp one. She'll be ready - and so will we. We'll keep an eye on you, Jack. You're not going into this alone."

Nick leaned on the fencepost and gave me a look. "We've all worked too many years for this to end sideways. Whatever they've got you doing out there - undercover or not - we've got your six. You give a signal, and we're there."

I looked at both men. No speeches. Just a slight nod. That was enough.

The dogs tangled in a pile of fur and happy growls. For a moment, things felt normal.

It wasn't long after Stan and Nick left that Bell told me Detective Sanchez was at the door and wanted to see me. I told her I'd be right in, and that she should invite him in so we could talk… so much for getting a day off I thought.

He entered the front room holding a brown envelope and a lukewarm cup of convenient store coffee. "Got your packet, Sergeant," he said, tossing the folder on the table between us. "Alias details, cash, burner phone, a locker key at the bus depot for a drop site in case things get hairy."

I thumbed open the envelope and flipped through the IDs. Photos of me with a two-day beard, unkempt hair, and eyes that looked like they hadn't seen sleep in a month. Not far from the truth, really.

"Name's Jordan Ray this time," Sanchez muttered, sipping the bitter coffee with a grimace. "Mechanic, semi-transient, did some time for boosting cars and getting into it with a biker gang down south. You're a known ghost. Unreliable. Dangerous if pushed."

"Sounds like my kind of guy."

Sanchez grinned, but it didn't reach his eyes. "Just don't go getting *too* cozy in that role. Your wife already warned me what happens when 'Jack disappears' for too long." Tony looked over toward Bell: "it's a good thing your nurse friend at the mobile clinic was smart enough to contact you about the tip; who knows where it would have gone if you'd have never given Wade the information."

I smirked, and then glanced toward Bell. She was now sitting on the floor with Athena, gently rubbing behind the dog's ears as they both looked like they understood more than either of us wanted to admit.

As if she could hear my thoughts, Bell looked up and gave me a nod. The kind that wasn't just about trust - it was about permission. It was like she was saying "Go. Do what you have to. Just come back."

I looked over the packet – the ruse I was supposed to become. I looked up at Sanchez – shaking my head a little: "this is all fine, but in a world where names and Id's are just a blur for most of these guys – I'm not sure if all this is necessary."

Sanchez cleared his throat. "Let me remind you – this is still my case" he said while trying to swallow... "Look - you're not trying to 'be' a homeless guy – we just want you to blend in so it's not too obvious."

I told him I understood, but I looked long and hard at him "I really do know what you mean – sir – but try to remember, I've got a feel for what's going on out there. I'm not saying I don't appreciate what you're doing for me, and I'll try to use the profile you gave, but you need to realize – out on the streets, being invisible means survival. So when push comes to shove remember... I was there!"

Sanchez continued "We'll rotate your check-ins. One of the rookies will be your dead-drop runner if Nick or Stan aren't available. We'll do our best to keep you fed this time, and we'll make sure someone's close, but not too close. We'll keep fresh batteries for the phone in the bus locker." Tony paused for a second... "We'll make sure someone see's you every 72 hours unless there's contact. If you're dark for longer than four days..."

"Then you come looking," I finished.

He didn't respond. Didn't need to.

We both knew that if I went silent, it wouldn't be a rescue mission - it would be a body recovery. And even then, there wouldn't be much left.

I rubbed a hand down my jaw. "How long do I have before I go under?"

Sanchez checked his watch. "We haven't had any reports come in from medical yet – if this guy's getting patched up anywhere he's been pretty careful. So I'd say at least forty-eight hours. Long enough to get the look right, and take the edge off.

I looked over at Athena – then back at Sanchez "have you put the word out to any 'Vet's' – he could try to find one that would help him."

"I'll look into that – good call Jack" as he crumpled his empty coffee cup… "You'll hold up at that trailer on 63rd - the one behind the old feed store. No real utilities. But you can use the cold to get your mindset straight."

I nodded. "Yeah… the grind. Hard floor, no heat, crap food, and worse dreams."

"That's the one."

We stood there in silence for a long second.

Then Sanchez added, "And Jack? One more thing."

I turned back.

He motioned toward Athena. "I wasn't sure at first - but after seeing how she handles herself, and that she's really our best witness, well I guess I've got no complaints. She's been trained, you know. If she's with you, she's got your back."

I looked at Athena, already dozing again - not because she was lazy, but because she knew rest was part of the job.

"Yeah" I said quietly watching her breathe – "she really does."

Sanchez didn't press it. Just walked out, empty coffee cup in hand, the door swinging slowly closed behind him.

Bell just smiled at me… "You've had a busy day."

All I could do is shake my head and chuckle "Yeah" I said rubbing my neck. "might take a ride – clear my head."

Bell agreed, but…

I was halfway rolling up the garage door when she stepped into the garage – Athena wagging close behind her… "You're not really thinking of riding that thing without your helmet, are you?"

I grinned. "What? - afraid I'll mess up my hair?"

She didn't smile. "I'm serious, Jack. Not just for your head, but your face. Someone out there sees you, recognizes you? That whole identity you've built... gone."

I hesitated.

It wasn't just the safety lecture. She was right. Every time I stepped out that door, I was walking a line - the man I used to be, and the ghost I had to become.

Reluctantly, I reached up to the shelf and pulled the helmet down.

"I liked it better when I only wore this for the wind," I muttered.

She handed me a pair of gloves. "Yeah, well... I like it better when you come back in one piece."

I gave her a smile - nothing more - and threw my leg over the saddle. The engine rumbled to life, a familiar comfort that almost drowned out the noise in my head.

Then I dropped the visor, tucked my thoughts in behind it, and disappeared into the streets.

Chapter 45

Calm Before the Storm

The next few days passed in a blur of quiet routine. I cleaned my pistol, re-packed gear in a little canvas 'day-pack' I've had for years, but never thought I'd really ever use. I checked in with Stan and Nick about schedules, and made sure Bell had enough supplies to hold down the fort. Even though I know she's more than able to care for herself – it's just one more thing to ease my mind. Bell kept the house calm - or maybe I just clung to that illusion. The dogs played in the yard, coffee filled the kitchen air each morning - and for a moment, I almost believed it could all just go away.

Every night when either Sanchez, Wade – even Stan or Nick would stop by, we would re-read files – look over profiles, and even review the areas of the big field where 'the bodies' were discovered. I reviewed my notes over and over. Looking. Searching… for any kind of pattern. The break was nice, but wasn't really rest at all. I kept making mental notes - where not to sleep, who not to trust. But deep down, I already knew.

I watched Athena watch me. She could tell I was planning something. That I was thinking. And I wish she could tell me where she bit that guy…

There's a strange kind of peace that comes with dread. Not fear - that's different. Dread is slow. Heavy. It doesn't sprint - it lingers. You don't *prepare* for the streets. You just survive them. And hope you come back with most of your soul intact.

My family has always been used to the coming and goings of all the Officer friends I've had over the years, but even they could tell – something about this was different. I wish I could tell them. But somehow – they always seem to know. Kind of…

It was a late spring evening. It was pleasant. My kids, grandkids, and wife sat with me by the camp-fire we made in the fire pit in the back yard. They could tell something was on my mind… and all they knew was – I wouldn't be there with them when school let out.

"Where ya goin grandpa" they would ask... all I could tell them was – that I was going to do some police work.

I wish they could truly understand.

The light from the fire was fighting for its will to live. As the evening stars began to shine, the flames - once bright - danced into a soft, fading glow. And it was then I figured I should do the same.

Even though I knew what to expect, I also knew I'd be leaving the comfort of home for a while. I did my best to sleep, but it wasn't easy.

It was the same kind of restless slumber one feels before deploying into combat.

I woke up to a nose in my face - and the aroma of coffee brewing. My partner and I walked into the kitchen and shared a breakfast that somehow felt surreal, yet satisfying.

It was a quiet time - reflective, silent, and maybe even a little nostalgic. It reminded me of our mornings in the combat zone. Back then, Bell, my K9 Gunner and I would eat breakfast before Wade and I headed out to find - and disarm - IED's.

I heard a car door close out front. It was Wade.

Bell glanced at Athena and smiled. "Looks like your ride's here."

Athena perked up her ears and gave a subtle grin. It was like she knew she was the star of this show.

Bell walked us to the door. Athena sniffed at the large black garbage bag - my 'homeless' clothes - and Bell said gently, "I figured it'd be best if you changed at the station."

Her hug was the kind you want to last forever. I didn't say a word. She just whispered that she'd try to see me at the mobile clinic soon, and that it wouldn't be long.

I picked up the bag and stepped out to meet Wade.

But before I climbed in, I turned one more time to catch a final glimpse of the smile I didn't want to leave behind.

We got down to the station, and Wade drove through the double-gated entry - the sallyport, as we called it. Like a holding chamber for vehicles, sandwiched between two heavy security fences. Wade was doing everything he could to keep my identity a secret…

We didn't talk much; we'd known each other for so many years words weren't always necessary. He did tell me that once I got changed – we'd meet in the squad room for the final briefing.

I opened the bag. I wished I hadn't.

Athena tilted her head – looked at me like *"and you got mad at me when I smelled like that!"*

"Sorry girl – this is the part of the job I wasn't looking forward to either."

I bent down to undo her collar; she sat proud as if she knew we were going back to work. I didn't have to tell her to 'heel' – she simply knew… she always knows.

We walked into the large room where we held briefings, and amid a few jeers and some complementary applause – I was met with the confidence I knew I'd be ok.

I mean – if they would have been solemn and silent… I would know for sure – I was screwed.

We went over the general locations – where the bodies were found, and the logistics of keeping me under surveillance, and fed. Sanchez wanted to make sure the burner phone I could carry was kept silent – and only used for texting.

It was comforting in a way, knowing that the lead investigator – Sanchez – not only wanted to catch a killer, but also keep me alive and in good shape. Before the meeting ended, Nick suddenly jumped up and closed the door to the squad room.

I turned quick and Athena sprang to her feet. Sanchez snapped, "What's going on?"

Nick said "There's a real estate developer in the lobby… asking questions about the murders."

Sanchez frowned "Why the hell should *he* care?"

Nick paused, and then added, "Well… one of the victims was renting from him. And I think the city's looking to offload some abandoned property near where we'll be working - he's probably got his eye on it."

Sanchez didn't say anything for a long second. But I caught the look he gave me. Something wasn't adding up - and we both knew it.

"Let's go to work"

Four men walked side by side, Athena stepping quiet at first, our boots crunching against the gravel of the back lot behind the station. We'd gone over the plan already - more than once - but talking it through again wasn't about logistics. It was about steel. About resolve.

Nick broke the silence. "Uniformed units will roll out first. Flood the area, flash the lights, shake the trees a bit. Anyone with half a brain who's watching will think it's just another patrol surge."

"While we slip you in through the side streets," Stan added. "Low profile, no chatter. In and out."

Nick nodded. "You'll have food, communication, and line of sight in three directions. Wade and I'll set the trail cams." Nick paused, and even chuckled a little: "like the Chief likes to say - If a squirrel farts near you, we'll know it."

Wade let out a low chuckle too, but it faded fast. "We'll rotate check-ins every twelve hours. And if it hits the fan? We're not far. You know that."

I stopped walking. The others turned with me. I looked at each of them - Stan, Nick, and Wade. Each man had been with me through fire, loss, and blood. Some scars you could see. Others… lived deeper.

"If there were anyone else watching my six," my voice steady but low, "I'd be worried. But you guys? You've already stood with me in the worst of it. Iraq... Tina... that night I should've died."

I could only give a half-smile that didn't quite reach my eyes. "I'm only still breathing because of you."

There was no reply - none needed. Just four heads nodding, four hearts united, and four paws at the ready. They all understood exactly what I meant.

We walked on.

Our ride was quiet. Athena resting her head on my lap, and my pack at my feet. It didn't have much, but it was probably more than most I would be mingling with. Through the heavily tinted windows of the car I could still see how bright the sun was shining. I didn't say much – I didn't have to.

Sanchez was listening to the radio chatter on the patrol surge, and we kept at a distance until he was sure I wouldn't be seen getting out of an 'unmarked' police car. I mean – who doesn't know what an unmarked police car looks like?

"You ready?" he said with a half smile.

"No time like the present" I chuckled.

Athena perked her ears as Sanchez pulled his car off the pavement; gravel crackling under the tires and tall grass brushing against the side of the car.

"It's 'go' time Sarge."

Before the car came to a complete stop – I cracked open the door, Athena standing on the seat next to me. The strap of my pack in hand and my dog at my side – we got out as if we'd done this a hundred times. Steady and smooth.

I tapped the back of his car with my palm, and Sanchez pulled away quick - like he was never here. A hundred yards ahead, through sappy elm trees, tall grass, and a downtown forest, I could just make out the shape of the abandoned trailer. I was in for a treat.

We waded through the brush - burrs and sticker weeds clinging to my pants. Athena wasn't faring much better. When we finally got close enough to see the trailer without the grass in our faces, I looked over at her - covered in shards of grass and cockleburs.

I chuckled. "Looks like you're in camouflage too."

Truth was, that's exactly how I wanted her to look.

Out of habit, I pulled my pistol and cracked open the door to the trailer. A quick glance told me everything I needed to know - we were alone. And no wonder.

I probably should've given more thought to why no other homeless guys had claimed this spot. Even I didn't want to step inside.

Black widows, wasps, hornets - they had full occupancy.

Time for Plan B.

I scanned the area. Coast was clear. I thumbed out a quick message to Sanchez:

Observation Site A - no-go. Moving on. Will apprise.

I gave the trailer one last look. The roof was sagging, like it was exhaling its last breath. Part of me wanted to at least clear a space out - but the buzzing inside told me I'd be playing eviction games with too many eight-legged tenants. No thanks.

Athena shook off, and I crouched next to her, picking a few burrs from behind her ears. "You and me, girl. We'll find better." We carefully slipped away from the ruins and back into the weeds… I looked down at my little girl again "it's no wonder why they dumped the bodies here."

We slipped through the tree line again, moving toward the ridge line that flanked the old railway spur. Back in the day, this used to be a cattle loading area. Now it was just overgrowth and rust. I knew there were a couple of train cars left behind out here - tagged-up husks full of broken glass and graffiti. But there was one I remembered - an old steel-sided boxcar half-derailed, listing to its right in a shallow ditch.

Maybe.

We bushwhacked about a quarter mile, staying out of sight from the highway and anyone wandering through the camp zones. The trail was barely visible, but instinct kicked in. Old soldier tricks - step light, listen hard, and trust the dog.

There it was. Sunlight bouncing off a side panel, the red-orange paint flaking like sunburned skin. I approached from the high side, careful not to silhouette myself, and peeked through the open side door.

It wasn't pretty - but it wasn't full of spiders either.

Old crates, some busted-up furniture, and a pair of moldy boots someone left behind. It smelled like rust, mildew, and dust - but it was dry, it was off-grid, and nobody had claimed it in a while.

Athena jumped in first - tail wagging like she approved. Good enough for me.

I slung my pack inside, followed it in, and gave the place a once-over. I'd need to clear the back corner, rig something up for warmth, it was warm now, but when the sun goes down… I thought to myself - maybe use one of those crates to elevate a pad. But this… this could work.

I sat down on the edge of an old pallet, pulled out my burner phone, and typed:

Observation Site B: viable. Settling in old rail yard.

I sent it off. Then turned to Athena and smiled.

"Welcome home - such as it is."

Somewhere beyond the tracks, a freight horn moaned in the afternoon heat. I listened. Waited. Nothing. Just the wind through rusted steel. But still - something told me we weren't alone out here. It wouldn't be too long before night set in.

Chapter 46

Into the darkness

We sat at the edge of the old boxcar. Just the two of us. I ate a sandwich Bell packed for me, and Athena enjoyed a can of soft food… it wasn't much, but it was the perfect evening as we watched the sun set in the distance. A little moment of peace where so much is broken.

The sky lit up in shades of crimson and gold, shadows growing longer with each passing second. Somewhere out there, coyotes were starting to stir. Athena's ears twitched once - but she stayed calm.

"You smell 'em, don't you, girl?" I asked, brushing crumbs from my lap. "We'll let 'em be if they let us be."

The air was changing - cooler now. Crisper. Like the land was holding its breath.

The wind shifted, carrying with it the scent of sage and creosote from the dried edge of the riverbed. Athena looked west, eyes following a line of dusk as the city behind us began to flicker to life. The patrol surge had ended. You could feel it - like pressure easing off a wound. The heavy presence of law enforcement lifted just enough for the forgotten to resurface. Shadows began to move again. Slowly, carefully. Returning like shadows after the authorities retreat.

The night migration was beginning.

They came out of alleys, drainage tunnels, abandoned RVs. Some limped, others wheeled carts. Silent silhouettes crossing back toward the safety of the urban woods - home, for lack of a better word.

I checked the burner phone. 11:42.

Still time.

"Athena, stay," I whispered. "Watch our stuff."

She didn't move, but her ears turned slightly, tracking me as I dropped down from the edge of the car and crossed the yard. I blended in like smoke - faded jeans, torn jacket, a month's worth of stubble and dirt. Just another shadow in the dark.

I didn't go far. Just far enough to feel the pulse of the place. I nodded to a few familiar faces, offered nothing more than a glance. No one asked questions here. That was the code.

Then I saw them.

A car stopped on the old maintenance road a little past the old freight loading ramp. Lights go off. It waits. It's not long before another car pulls up – a little past the first. The lights turn on from the first car and two silhouettes stand in the light casting shadows. Not residents. Too clean. Too rigid. A handoff, maybe? No - this was bigger. One guy handed something off in a bag, another passed cash. But the third – simply watching the shadows. Watching for interruptions.

This could have been a petty drug trade. But this looked networked. Organized. Smooth.

This was what Wade was chasing. This was why we started all this in the first place.

I backed off slowly, slipping into the weeds behind the rail fence, then looped back toward the car from the north side. 11:59.

Athena met me with a glance but didn't move. Good girl.

I climbed back inside and ducked low. The burner buzzed once – silent, short, and soft. A code ring. I answered without speaking.

Sanchez's voice was low. "About that alley from the other night – you know – when the informant was shot? We combed that alley three times. No brass. Nothing. The forensics team looked everywhere."

I kept my voice just above a whisper. "That means revolver. Six-shot, probably .38 or .357. Small. Probably could fit into a pocket." I paused – took a breath "I'm leaning – thinking maybe that it was a magnum load – pitch was too high – too sharp."

"Clean shooter," he muttered, then continued "we've got lots of samples, but the crime lab hasn't made any matches – but that's about it."

"Yeah? He's probably smart. But this one wasn't like the rest. He didn't leave a shell casing. This wasn't random. He may not have planned this one." I paused, then "the way that informant talked – my guess is he saw something, and our shooter is the one leaving bodies in the field…"

There was a pause. "You got eyes tonight?"

"I saw a drop. Big one. Three guys. Two buyers, one watching. This Ain't local."

"You think it's our guy?"

"I think it's something bigger."

"Copy that," Sanchez said. "We can track your phone, but still - Keep your head down."

The call ended. I leaned back against the cool steel wall of the boxcar and exhaled. Athena pressed up beside me, quiet as a ghost.

The city outside carried on, unaware. But I could feel it.

We left the old boxcar behind as dusk settled deep into the bones of the yard. The smell of creosote – that heavy burnt oil mixed with dirt and urine hung thick in the air. Athena walked tight beside me, silent but alert - head low, ears twitching at every echo that bounced off the steel skeletons surrounding us. This was the hour when shadows started moving on their own.

We kept to the edges. Always the edges.

There was an all-night corner market a few blocks over - flickering neon in the window, and a little bell on the door that hadn't worked in years. I'd been there before. It was run by a guy who looked the other way, didn't ask questions, and didn't call the cops if you looked rough around the edges. My kind of place for now.

I told Athena to stay behind a half-toppled vending machine just outside, and she obeyed without protest. She knew the routine. I slipped inside.

The air smelled of expired jerky and pine disinfectant. A security mirror stared down at me like a swollen eye. The clerk barely looked up from his newspaper.

I made my way to the counter with a bottled soda and a pre-made sandwich – I asked for a pack of brand-less, off-label cheap cigarettes. Just enough to keep the act believable. I pulled out a few crumpled singles, mostly stained and worn, and dug the rest from my pocket in loose change - quarters, nickels, even a Canadian penny that somehow passed as legal tender in this part of town.

Never flash a twenty. Never even flash a ten. A guy with bills like that doesn't belong out here. You pay in what you could've found under a soda machine or between car seats in a fast food lot.

I mumbled a half-hearted "thanks," and left with my bag.

Athena was exactly where I left her - ever the good soldier. Her tail thumped once against the concrete when I returned, and we moved on without a word. No leash needed. She didn't run. She didn't wander. She was more disciplined than most men I'd worked with.

I thought it would be best if we cut back through the tall grass and trees before making our way to the freight yard. I told Athena to stay behind me so I could at least try to keep her from getting tangled in the weeds again.

I stepped off the sidewalk and tripped over something buried in the grass. At first I thought it was an old campaign sign. It wasn't.

It was a city notice. A proposition, half-warped from rain and sun, stapled to a chunk of plywood. Something about selling off the land we were standing on.

I might've dismissed it - except for one name.

Bane Kingman.

Proposition backed by the Chamber of Commerce. Promising jobs, revitalization, and "long-term economic growth." The wording was slick. Clean. Every lie wrapped in a bow.

Same guy we saw at the police station. Same stiff suit. Same smirk behind the handshakes.

Back at the yard, the quiet had shifted - not silence, but the kind of hush that comes before something breaks loose. A cluster of shadows slinked along the far edge of the treeline where the scrub met the freight lanes. Like me – they were doing their best to stay out of sight.

Athena caught their scent first. Her nose twitched. No growl. No warning. She knew the rules. Watch, don't engage. These weren't threats - not yet, anyway.

We stepped carefully back toward the boxcar. A loose rhythm of shuffling feet and low voices started to fill the edges of the yard, echoing between the boxcars and graffiti-tagged containers. The freight-yard was coming back to life; at least for a little while. It wouldn't be long until the shuffle in the shadows would fade into the silence, weary warriors of the forgotten would finally rest.

It was just enough for now – to just sit and watch. This time I was better prepared – more experience in this life. I broke the sandwich we bought in two, and we sat in the opening of the box-car and ate. As the shuffles turned to silence, I slipped back into the shadows to relax on some forgotten shipping blankets. I could feel the comfort of her fur against me, and the warmth of her loyalty. The only thing that broke the loneliness of the darkness was the quiet light of a cigarette, and the company of my partner.

Right at the moment I could almost feel myself sleep, I felt Athena tense…the only light that let me see the faint silhouette of her head allowed me to see her ears – sharp and focused. She looked around – springing to a sitting position, and then Athena's ears perked again, this time sharper. Her gaze locked toward the rail yard.

I followed it as we inched our way toward the opening of the box-car. I could see Athena's nose twitching wild – she was looking for something, but what?

Movement. Not the slow shuffle of some lost soul looking for a place to sleep. This was business. Quick, purposeful. Two men. One handed off a small package. The other slipped something into a pocket, and then checked over his shoulder.

They didn't see us. Not yet.

I knelt beside Athena and whispered, *"Easy, girl."*

She didn't move. But I could feel the tension in her shoulder - coiled like a spring. She wanted to track them, to herd the situation into something she could control. So did I.

But I'd learned my lesson a long time ago. You don't chase shadows in someone else's house. Not until you know the rules.

One of the men stepped into a floodlight that arced from a utility pole a few cars down. Briefly, just a glimpse - but enough to make out his build. Thin. Angular. Jacket too big for him. And his arm… stiff. Maybe even wrapped.

I stayed low, heart ticking up a notch.

It couldn't be. Or maybe it could. I looked at Athena – the fur on the back of her neck raised, and she started to crouch as if she was ready for action.

I couldn't be sure. Not from this distance. And even if it was - what the hell was he doing back here, already moving?

The two figures slipped away into the dark, swallowed by the sprawl of boxcars and silence.

I waited.

Then I stood, brushing dirt from my knees.

Athena looked up at me, waiting for the next move.

We stayed still for a moment longer. Just the sound of the wind threading through rusted metal and the soft press of Athena's breath beside me.

My hand slipped into my pocket, brushed the edge of my phone. I thought about letting Sanchez know.

But then I thought about the angle of that arm. The oversized coat. And I let the phone stay where it was.

"Not yet," I muttered. Athena nudged my hand.

"Yeah," I said softly. "Me too."

Chapter 47

Hunches and Suspicions

Call it a hunch – or is it simply the years of knowing the world we live in isn't always the way it appears…

Something wasn't adding up. Something was right in front of me, but what? It's like a whisper. A voice from somewhere in the depths of my mind. A voice small, still, and near silent - yet telling me - even calling to me… I learned to listen… There was a missing piece… find it.

The chill of the cool spring air started to warm – the light from the open door of the box-car began to bring another day on the streets to life. And with the light of a new day came hunger.

I pushed aside the freight blanket – Athena stretched as she stood. "Hungry girl?" I smiled – and Athena looked like she too could use some food.

But I couldn't wait any longer. Something was eating at me more than the hunger. I felt like I had to let Sanchez – Wade – someone… know about the drug deals going on around the freight yards. It wasn't time for a check-in, but I didn't want to wait. We stood at the door of the old train-car and looked for any movement – for any sign of life. I couldn't see anything.

I told Athena to seek – "find 'em girl" as she looked at me: "go – see if anyone is around…"

She hopped out into the greasy dirt and started to sniff – head turning – ears focused… her nose looking for an invisible trail; she was trying to find anyone who could be nearby.

I watched her from the open door – and lit a cigarette. For five minutes she walked the abandoned tracks – all around the empty steel containers. Nothing.

I called her back and she hopped back to where she could watch.

"Stay – watch" I told her – then I walked back to the shade and made the call.

I hit Sanchez's number. It rang twice.

"Jack?"

"Yeah," I said. "Look - I know it's early, but I didn't want to wait."

"You alright?"

"Yeah. I mean, I'm okay. But I saw something. Couple of guys out by the east side of the yards - looked like a drug deal going down. One of 'em... could've been the guy. The one from the murder scene."

Silence.

"You sure?" Sanchez asked, his voice suddenly sharper.

"No," I admitted. "Not completely. But it didn't feel right. I've been watching them for a few nights now. Around the same times. Same place. Thought you'd want to know."

"You were alone?"

"Me and Athena," I said. "She swept the area a minute ago. No one's there now."

"Alright," Sanchez said. I could hear him scribbling something down. "Listen. I'll get this to Wade and see if we can send someone out. But I want you to head over to the rescue mission - grab some food, get warm. I might have someone swing by to talk to you - low profile."

"You mean undercover."

He didn't answer directly. "Just someone you can talk to."

I lit another cigarette. "Copy that." My mind started in again on a hunch... "Tony – can you do something for me?"

"What's that – Jack?"

"Something's been bothering me. I keep thinking about that day at the station – seeing that real estate developer – then seeing his name on a public notice about the vacant land where you dropped me off… could you see where this Bane Kingman was on the days these murders took place? I just got this feeling something's up with all this."

Sanchez sounded puzzled: "Jack – Kingman – he's a pretty big guy here in the city – if we go poking around like this, we better have some pretty solid suspicions about it."

"Look" I said kind of sharp – "I just need to see if you can find anything about where this guy was when these murders happened – not a full scale investigation – just see if you can find out where he was."

I could almost hear Tony shaking his head on the other end of the call: "ok Sarge – I'll look into it, but if anyone finds out – we'll have to explain why we were looking into this guy."

"Oh - and Jack?" Sanchez added. "If Athena's in rough shape, call Nick or Stan - see if they can pick her up. Might be good for her to get cleaned up and fed. I bet your granddaughter's been missing her."

"Yeah" I smiled, "She'd like that. They both would."

"Keep your phone on. I'll be in touch."

Click.

I stood there for a long second, staring out past the boxcars toward the warming sky. The streets were already waking up - shopping carts squeaking, distant sirens, and a couple of gulls screaming overhead like they knew something the rest of us didn't.

Athena padded back over to me and sat, licking her paw.

I pulled out my phone again and texted Nick.

You up? Can you or Stan come grab Athena? Sanchez said it's ok - thought maybe Izzy could give her a brush and bath. She could use the love. I'll be at the mission for breakfast.

I hit send. Athena looked up at me, tail thumping once.

"Go see Izzy, girl. Get rid of those damn burrs."

She tilted her head. Probably didn't care about the burrs - but she'd never turn down a ride with Nick and a belly rub from Izzy.

Athena and I made our way down the familiar stretch, past burnt-out drums and old pallets, toward the back side of the rescue mission.

She walked ahead with purpose, tail swinging, nose up - maybe she smelled the bacon. Me? I was trying to figure out how I'd recognize the guy I was supposed to meet.

My phone buzzed. I ducked into the nearest alley - just in case. Out here, even a text can get you made. I looked at the text message, and it was Stan. He said Nick was on his way down, and that I should meet him on the north side of the church so he could pick up Athena. I simply responded with a smile emoji.

We kept walking.

By the time we got to the church it had warmed enough for me to fold my jacket, and stowed it in my day-pack. Now I had to be extra careful – so my pistol wouldn't show from under my shirt.

I sat down on the steps, and Athena walked around sniffing. "You're not going to find your ball out here girl" I said smiling, and then lit a smoke, and waited.

I was about half-way through my cigarette, and I could hear the familiar sound of Nick's Ford F-150 police truck. "Really?" I coughed as Nick was getting out. Thor was in the back kennel, and I could hear him give a little bark. Athena responded too, and I tried to hush them so no one would notice us.

"You know she's not going to want to ride in the back – she's a front-seat kind of dog." I said with a chuckle.

Nick had a few dollars and a fresh pack of 'good' smokes for me, and said Sanchez talked with Wade, and that there would be someone waiting for me at the mission cafeteria. "We've got a big guy from the State Investigations office – working Narcotics for now - that can talk to you, get a better read on it. But he's new to this type of undercover."

I coughed again "what?" I shrugged… "New?" I said, raising an eyebrow. "You sure you want to send him into the jungle without a map?"

"He's sharp. Just green on the homeless angle."

I just smiled "I'll try not to break his ego"

I thanked Nick for the care package – putting the good cigarettes in my pack, and told him I'd only smoke these ones when no one is looking.

"Take good care of my little girl" I said, and by the time my cigarette was burnt down to the filter – Nick, Thor, and Athena were out of sight. It felt lonely, but I knew she'd be back with me later this evening.

I turned and started walking - alone, for the moment. It was only a few minutes before I was around the corner and halfway down the block to the church's rescue mission. I couldn't help but chuckle at the sign posted next to the double doors: **"No Drugs – No Contraband – No Weapons."**

I could feel my sidearm pressing lightly against my ribs, the weight tucked under my shirt. For a moment, I thought about slipping my jacket back on, but I was already at the door.

The entryway had been freshly painted. The tile floor looked scrubbed clean, and the smell of varnish still lingered in the air. Maybe it was because my senses were on high alert - when you're in the zone, you notice *everything* - or maybe it was just that I knew who took care of this building. They did things right.

I don't come here as often as I used to - not since Father John, the good Reverend Forsythe, passed away. Not that I don't appreciate Father Brian. He's a good man, and everyone in my family seems to like him. Still, it's strange trying to open up to someone young enough to be one of my own kids.

I was still sorting through those thoughts when I stepped through the door and heard his voice: **"Welcome, brother... you look hungry. Come join us. All of God's children are welcome here."**

I hadn't expected to see Father Brian right off - not like this, smiling, warm, arms already outstretched in a hug. He greeted me like an old friend, and then gently guided me toward the dining hall.

Father Brian paused then turned to look away, looked around, and then looked back at me. He gave me the slightest wink - like he knew exactly why I was here.

Father Brian led me to a table, and he said they'd be serving the breakfast in a minute – well – serving at the cafeteria style kind of serving as it were...

I looked around. I wondered. I thought to myself "how am I going to recognize the 'narcotics officer' and then I saw him. He looked like he stepped right out of a dime-store detective novel - the kind where the detective is trying too hard to blend in. A faded army jacket, aviator shades *inside*, and a Dodgers cap pulled low like he was auditioning for a 'don't ask, don't tell' remake of *Miami Vice*.

The mustache wasn't fooling anybody - dyed too blonde for his hair color, too thick to be an accident. It sat on his lip like it was waiting for a stronger chin to come along.

He was leaning against the wall like it owed him money, arms crossed, trying to look casual - but his boots were too polished and his posture too squared. I've worked with these types before. Cops try not to stare. Narcs? They stare while *trying* not to.

I turned back to Father Brian, who was still smiling like he hadn't just escorted me into a trap with free coffee.

"Who's the guy by the wall?" I asked. Brian didn't even glance. "I'm sure I don't know," he said with a grin that said he knew exactly.

Volunteers began to serve the breakfast at the cafeteria style line. Some served while others directed the confusion into an organized chaos. Almost reminding me of boot-camp. But I kept my head down - hoping none of the volunteers would recognize me.

Looking down - a little at the tray on the service line, and even at the floor - I noticed the boots close to mine were a little too nice for this place. I turned my head just enough to confirm it was exactly who I thought it was. But I knew this wasn't the place to talk to him. And… this wasn't the place for him to blow my cover.

I slid my tray through the serving line - nodding my head in thanks to the volunteers the way most of the others did. I walked slow - as quick as I could to a table nearly full, and slipped into a seat just tight enough no one else could fit. And I watched.

Father Brian was making his way around to the crowd chatting, smiling, and inviting lost souls to sit with him - counsel with him, and while most simply want to enjoy a hot breakfast, I was looking for an opportunity. I couldn't see the Narc anywhere in the dining hall.

Father Brian finally made his way to the table where I was sitting, and in his 'fatherly' way conversed a little with each of the men sitting close by. When he approached me I was nearly finished with my meal, and he pat me on the back ***"Brother - I haven't seen you here before… could we have a few moments to talk?"***

I grunted a little, and nodded my head - then stood with my empty tray and followed him past the garbage barrel, and dirty tray rack. We walked down the hallway and out through the back door of the mission… and it wasn't long before we were back at the chapel… and in Father John's old office - now in use by Father Brian.

Sitting in the chair I used to sit when I counseled with Father John - was the Narc…

"You're in my seat" I half chuckled - with Father Brian smirking under his breath… but he got up and moved and grabbed a folding chair from nearby.

We all sat.

I looked at this guy - shook my head a little… "you know that a man's mustache will turn grey before his hair does - don't you?"

He reached his hand toward me - and we shook hands, but I had to tell him "if you're gonna play homeless - you might wanna ditch the Hollywood costume prop kit. Trust me - people on the street notice – while trying not to look like they notice."

He blinked, and then actually smiled. "Point taken"

Father Brian - still smiling said "Jack - this is detective Valenti from the State investigators office - Wade arranged for him to work with you on the exchange you saw."

Valenti said "You can call me Chris."

"Well Chris" I choked - "I'll try to keep you updated with what's going on with it, but right now - I'm reporting to Sanchez." I leaned back in the chair that still - somehow - felt like it belonged to Father John, even though he'd been gone for a while… "If you really want to be a part of this - I suggest you roll around in the mud for a while before coming back out here."

Chris listened - raised his brow and before he could speak I continued: "cause out here - people really notice the little details, especially the things that don't belong."

Valenti struggled with a smile; I could tell he got the message.

The three of us sat in silence that held more weight than words, Father Brian smiling with his quiet calm - leaning back now in Father John's old swivel chair. Valenti was trying to look like he wasn't second guessing the whole assignment, and me?

I was just wondering how close we really were to finding the man who started all of this… And whether Athena would recognize him again - if we ever saw him. I wasn't sure – what scared me more.

Chapter 48

A fox in the Hen House

We talked in the office for a while and decided it would be best if we weren't seen leaving together. Valenti left first, and I remained behind, sitting in the familiar chair - itself feeling like an old friend.

Father Brian - now sitting where Father John used to - turned to me and asked how I was holding up.

"This isn't easy," I said. "But someone has to do it. Wade and I talked about it for a while before I said yes - then everything went to sh… Crap." I still wanted to show some respect for where I was.

The office still held onto the memories - so many moments I'd spent here with Father John. It almost felt like he was still here. I could swear I caught a hint of his Old Spice aftershave lingering in the air, like he was sending me a message.

Now nearly noon I had to shield my eyes before they adjusted to the sunlight. I turned once more – Father Brian standing in the doorway leading out to the back parking lot of the church. He raised his hand in a gentle wave – I waved back as I reached for my phone… it was almost time for my noon check-in.

Sanchez said Wade and his people were going to try and set up surveillance for the next drug buy – maybe even try to catch some identities. I told him I could try and watch from the box-car where I was staying, but I could only make out dark shadows and vague descriptions of vehicles. I told him that if I were to get much closer I'd probably scare 'em off to another location.

Sanchez said he left some dollar bills in the bus-depot locker knowing I didn't want to 'flash' any bills larger than that. I thanked him, and hung up… then continued to walk.

I made my way past the hundred acres of weeds and elm trees, but didn't feel like wading through all that tall grass, so I took the long way that wandered me past the warehouse district…

All around me were the ghosts of society. Kicking around the trash and refuse discarded like hens scratching for feed.

I kept walking.

I picked up an old empty bottle of 'Mad-Dog 20/20' the kind of 'rot-gut' that told a story on its own. It's just the right prop I needed to keep up the appearance.

Like the rest – I wandered – blending in, and silently looking for patterns, clues, or any kind of sign someone may be watching. I follow the crowd because the crowd of the destitute knows where to find what little that can bring comfort. I watch while I walk, near aimless in my path, but like I did the time I was out here before - I watch what the others do, and I do it.

I should have known, but lost in my thoughts and my focus to what others were doing… I was there.

It felt like I was hit in the gut. The pain hit first. Then the loss. Standing in the spot where I was shot several years ago – the same alley - the same dumpster – the same place where Tina dragged me. And where I held her for the last time. I knelt as if in prayer. I felt the ground and brushed away the papers and leaves… and I could almost smell her blood again – and feel her fur in my hand… it was more than I could bear.

I wiped away a hint of moisture with the back of my hand. I wanted to cry… but couldn't. I wanted nothing more than to be home - with Bell… with Father John… with Athena. In that moment, I wanted to give up on all of this. But… Duty. Strength. Resolve…

I had to finish what I started.

I looked around. The alley was empty.

I was alone - with my thoughts. I reached for the phone. Bell.

"Are you all right?" she asked, barely above a whisper. I told her where I was.

I told her what I was feeling. I told her I wanted to come home. But my wife - my rock - talked me through this… one more time.

The phone call ended, and I just stood there… for how long, I couldn't say. The sun had shifted - shadows now stretched longer down the alley, and the concrete had lost its warmth. I hadn't even noticed the time slipping past me.

But something shifted inside me. Not strength exactly… maybe it was grit. Maybe it was Bell's voice, reminding me who I was. Maybe it was Athena, still out there, waiting.

I straightened up and started walking.

The city was beginning to change its tone - the golden afternoon giving way to that murky shade between daylight and dark. Neon flickers replaced storefront reflections, and somewhere in the distance, a siren wailed. Another thread unraveling in this tattered place.

Stan had sent a location. A small parking lot tucked behind a shuttered warehouse - where the pavement buckled and weeds fought their way up through old cracks. That's where he said they'd bring Athena. And maybe, just maybe, this was my way back in. To get my mind - back into the circle, back into the case… maybe even back to myself.

The plan was simple: show up, act natural, and blend in just long enough to get eyes on whoever was running things tonight. Wade and the others were moving in, too - circling like wolves, staying just out of sight. Unmarked cars and plain clothes; it wasn't a sting… not yet. Just recon.

But something was already off. I could feel it in the air - too still. Like the city was holding its breath.

And before the night was over… another body would be found. Just inside the edge of the urban forest - where the shadows thickened and the trees swallowed screams.

But that was still to come.

For now… I had to move.

I make my way through the maze of metal and concrete. The neighborhood is a sprawl of old garages, machine shops, and nameless cinderblock buildings. A graveyard of rust and rebar. I'd been in enough of these to know - deals went down here that never made the news.

These are the industrial buildings - places with faded signs and rusted fences, where body shops bleed oil into the gutters and old carpet-cleaning vans sit baking in the sun. Welding sparks flicker behind dark windows and somewhere nearby, a compressor kicks on with a rattle. It is the kind of forgotten corner of the city where every door leads to a different shade of trouble. It is a forgotten industrial strip where fabrication yards, and half-shuttered businesses blur together in the fading light.

I wasn't sure what I was walking into… only that I'd seen enough to know the night wasn't done with me yet.

It's where I found Athena.

Stan was driving his personal truck. He wanted to keep a low profile ensuring our cover. But it was good to see him.

He kept his voice low, but still tried to lighten the mood with his wit. "Enjoying your vacation?"

I did my best to appreciate what he was doing. My mind was still reeling from that moment in the alley. I told him where I'd been just hours before, and his mood shifted…

"Sorry man" he stammered… "I didn't know"

"I'll be all right – it's just that… every alley – every dark corner out here - reminds me of it all over again…"

Stan nods, giving me a quiet pat on the shoulder. "I'll check in with Wade and the crew. They're already moving." I watch him disappear into the shadows, slipping between rows of silent, buildings. I turn back toward Athena ears perked, eyes scanning the street. Always alert. Always my shadow.

"We've got some time to kill girl. Enough for a bite, and maybe clear my head before it all kicks off again."

I reach into my pocket, and feel the fresh battery and folded bills Sanchez had left me from the depot locker.

"Come on, girl," I murmur. "Let's go find a sandwich. Maybe even a cold Coke."

She tilts her head, tail wagging - I sat down on the ground and just held her. I paused - caught in the feeling of comfort just a moment longer. I rest my hand gently on Athena's head. Her warm breath, steady and loyal, grounded me. She didn't know what was about to unfold - but she'd been in enough tense moments to feel it in my body.

I gave her one last pat and a nod she somehow always understood. "Stay close girl," I whispered. Then I straightened, and I could feel the softness shed from my face, and walked out into the night – I was a man with a mission again.

Night had fallen hard now. We make our way back to the box-car, and sit in the quiet for a few moments watching the movement of shadows in the dark. I shared my sandwich, and I poured her some bottled water into plastic cup I'd found.

We could see the occasional passing of cars on the road as workers would come and go… and then it gets quiet. Too quiet. I can feel the buzzing of my phone so I step back into the shadows and look. I missed my midnight check-in.

Sanchez asked, and I responded… "Nothing yet."

We wait a little longer – shadows still moving through the field close to the usual spot the deals would happen. It had never stopped them before; I could see no reason why it wouldn't 'go down' the same way tonight. And I was right.

The mid-sized car stops first. It waits. Silent and quiet. The field between our box-car and the dealer is now empty. Maybe even the ghosts know when it's time to hide. Five minutes go by.

It looked like an older Chevy truck this time. It passes the car, and then it stops twenty feet in front. The lights come on from the car, and two men step out of the truck and stand where the individual in the car can see them. And they wait. But not for long. I tell Athena to stay, and I crouch low and try to get close enough to see – or maybe even close enough to hear something – anything.

Just like the other times – the man from the car steps carefully into the light and pauses. I can hear him say something, and one of the men from the truck answers – but I can't quite hear. It sounds rehearsed.

I'm trying to freeze whenever I see them looking toward the field, but my foot slips. All three look and the man from the car says in a nasal voice "it's just one of those drunken junkies – nothing to worry about." As he points with his left hand as if it is a pistol, and motions it in a way mimicking the firing of a handgun…

I let out a breath – silent but relieved.

I back my way out – back to the shadows of the box car, and Athena is nearly in attack-mode. "What's a matter girl?" I ask, but she's nearly ready to leap. "Calm down girl – whatta you see?"

I hold her back – I'm trying to keep her silent. We watch together – and I can't help but think – somehow – she really doesn't like this guy – the guy who drives the car.

He passes off some packages – favoring his right arm. My mind begins to stir.

I watch the exchange – the packages – the envelope, and from this distance I can't tell what's in them – but we all know. In the distance I can hear sirens, but not heading towards me. I'm holding Athena tight and as the truck pulls away the man from the first car gets in, and drives away. Faster this time. As soon as the lights from the exchange fade away into the dark, I get a text from Wade. He wants to know if I could see or hear anything… I couldn't. I get another text from Sanchez: "another one – found in the forest – call!"

I hid back in the shadows of the boxcar – pressed Sanchez' number. Another body was found in that field where the abandoned trailer is. "Homeless?" I asked… he was silent for a moment – I could hear him breathe heavy… "Yeah – it was."

"When? You need me to come in? – what you want me to do?" I was anxious – I wanted to help! Sanchez simply told me to hold tight – there's nothing I can do at the moment – he didn't want me hanging around another crime scene… he said we'd talk soon, but for me – it wouldn't be soon enough.

For several days I repeat the wandering, the watching – the blending in. for several nights it's all the same – but different vehicles except… that one mid-sized car.

Each time I try – I can't get close enough to see or hear anything. Sanchez sent a text: "meet Wade at Fr. B tmrw @ noon." I simply replied "k – will need food."

Athena lay quiet, but I could tell she knew something – wanted to say something. I wrapped myself in the freight blanket, and she rested next to me. I knew the only way I could get any sleep was… Athena was next to me.

When the faint hints of light rested within the walls of the boxcar, and I could feel Athena stirring, I knew it was time to start wandering. I could use some chow - Athena could too.

We wandered the streets – again – even found some food at a different convenience store. We ate, and then wandered again.

We made our way back into town – toward the chapel. I wondered what the kids at the church school would think if I walked into Father Brian's office with Athena… but the school yard was silent. No kids playing – no teachers cars in the parking lot. I was hoping that nothing was wrong, but then thought – schools out for the summer. I missed my grandkids.

By the time I climbed the stairs to Father John's – I mean Father Brian's office – Wade, Sanchez, and even Valenti were waiting for me. Wade had a big bag of 'our burgers' waiting for me. Father Brian had a big can of soft food for Athena… but she ate burgers: "I'll save this can for later" I laughed with a mouth full of 'double-burger.'

We all started brain-storming – even Father Brian wanted to be a part of things – and he is. "Why didn't anyone just jump in and arrest those guys?" he blurted out… Wade chuckled, and Tony smiled at him: "Father – we need probable cause to make an arrest – we need a reliable fact that's based on a reasonable suspicion. Just because someone's handing off packages doesn't mean we can just go and arrest them – some of these exchanges could be decoys, and if we tried to arrest someone handing off packages of let's say – comic books – or candy – we'd blow any chance of getting these guys."

Father Brian seemed to understand, but looked disappointed. I could tell he just wanted to help. We kept talking…

I asked Sanchez what he found out about that real estate developer - Kingman - and he said I wouldn't like what he had to say.

"Kingman was out of town - every time one of the murders went down. And..." he continued - "he's at a conference in Denver now."

"Right when that last one happened as well." I couldn't help but think out loud "once or twice would be a coincidence, but every time? Something's not adding up..."

So I suggested we have a marked unit drive past the next time we were watching the exchange. Father Brian looked puzzled.

Wade nodded, "Sometimes the simplest moves get you the best intel. A plain marked car cruising by, a casual chat with whoever's out front; like we're checking to see if 'they're' all right – hopefully we can identify drivers, lookouts, anyone. That might tell us who's running the show. Might blow that operation, sure. But better to get a name and a plate than nothing at all."

Sanchez leaned forward. "I agree. We can't risk a bust without solid evidence, but tracking who's making the calls or driving the vehicles? That's a start. It's the kind of info that can lead to warrants, surveillance, and maybe a bigger break."

Father Brian's brow furrowed. "So you're saying sometimes you have to lose a little ground to gain more?"

"Exactly," Tony said. "It's a slow game. Patience is our best weapon."

I looked at the faces around me - all determined, but knowing how fragile the balance really was. Wade's quiet voice cut through, "And every time we get close, Kingman's out of town. That can't be a coincidence."

I shook my head – almost wondering out loud – "and here I thought Kingman was going to be the Fox in this henhouse."

Chapter 49

Behind the Lights

The air in Father Brian's office still held the hint of burnt coffee. Papers lay scattered across the desk, his notes from the last homeless outreach, but nobody was reading them. WE sat in a loose half-circle, shoulders heavy, as though the weight of the city itself pressed down through the stained-glass windows.

I shuffled in my chair – Athena resting at my feet. "I want Nick to do the drive-by" – my eyes looking at the dust dancing in the colored light from the window above. "But I think he'd better use a patrol cruiser – not his K9 truck… I think it would look better this way."

Sanchez and Valenti agreed, and Father Brian looked puzzled. Although he agreed to be a part of our plan – he still wasn't used to the way we think – of how we have to make things look like we don't know what we're doing… all the while – we really do. At least hope we did.

"Nick has that kind of presence – like – well - he's huge, and he can appear quite intimidating. I've seen men twice as mean back down from him" I scanned the eyes of the men in the room and continued…

"Just his size and tone of voice can command respect – especially for those shadows in the dark. He's friendly – yet knows how to play that edge, and he knows how to play the part we'd be asking of him."

The conversations continued – amid the hum of our voices chattering Sanchez answered his phone – held up his hand as if to try and silence us for a minute. We watched as he sat listening quietly, and Tony simply acknowledged with an "alright then…" and then put his phone away.

"That was the Medical Examiner's office. The toxicology report came back on the body we found in the big field – Fentanyl overdose."

"It wasn't an accident," Father Brian said finally, his voice flat. "Nobody takes fentanyl by mistake. Not like that."

I rubbed at my jaw, thinking about the crime scene photos Chris had slid across the desk earlier. The puncture marks, the way the syringe had been left out almost too neatly. It wasn't a junkie's chaos. It was an obvious placement.

"Somebody wanted it quiet, but still wanted to send us a message," Valenti added "And wanted us to see it."

Athena shifted at my feet, her head rising at the edge in Chris's voice. Her ears caught the unspoken danger before I did. I reached down and rested a hand on her neck, more for my own steadying than hers.

Father Brian leaned back, eyes fixed on the crucifix above the door. "If they're targeting the homeless," he said, "wouldn't that mean they're targeting us too?"

"Not if we can keep all this a secret" Tony said softly: "obviously we need to keep Jack's identity on the down-low, and make these meetings look like nothing out of the ordinary. We know someone's watching, and that's what we're trying to find out."

I hadn't realized how long we'd been talking in Father Brian's office. The late afternoon sun was setting as Father Brian walked me back over to the rescue mission with Athena trotting quietly by my side.

I could tell he wanted to talk, but knew talking could give away my identity. So we walked in silence. He opened the door to the cafeteria and invited me to have some vegetable soup they were serving. Some of the men were taking turns in the showers while others sat quietly eating.

I thought this would be a good time for me to get cleaned up as well, but wasn't sure how to deal with Athena. I looked down at her – I smiled. "We'll wait a little longer girl" I whispered. She shook her head sharply flopping her ears – like she was trying to 'clear' her nose of something unpleasant… me.

I watched as Father Brian made his way around the diminishing crowd seated at the tables. I finished my soup, stood to leave, then before I walked out the doors to the street – gave Father Brian a little nod.

I found an alley a couple of blocks away from the mission, and I fed Athena the canned food Father Brian gave earlier, scraping it onto a piece of cardboard laid across my knee.

She wolfed it down, and then licked my fingers, eyes bright as if she hadn't a care in the world. "Yeah, girl," I muttered, tugging my jacket tighter. "You've got the better deal. At least you don't have to think about keeping Nick safe."

We cut across an empty block, past a chain-link fence under a humming streetlight. The city smelled different at night - stale fry grease, exhaust, and something metallic that reminded me of the rail yard.

I paused when Athena's ears twitched. A dark sedan rolled slowly at the end of the block, its engine low and steady. For a moment it matched our pace, and then slipped away into the next street.

My hand brushed against my pocket, where a badge used to sit, and then felt the hollow space it left. I wasn't wearing one right now, but habits die hard. Athena leaned against my leg, eyes fixed on the fading taillights.

I lowered my hand just a little – enough to feel the comfort of my pistol… then even more to sense Athena's fur through my fingers, and reassurance of her presence.

"Yeah, I saw it too," I whispered. "We're not invisible anymore."

We continued down the street passing alley-ways and store fronts as we approached closer to the industrial district. I saw a police cruiser patrolling slow and I turned my head to look in all directions to see if anyone was looking.

The cruiser crossed the street and pulled up to the sidewalk where we stood. It was Nick. He smiled and said loudly enough in case anyone was listening "hey ole timer – doin ok?"

We talked quietly for a few moments – I told him I'd send him a text message as soon as the 'deal' was beginning.

That way he wouldn't be driving up and down the road – possibly deterring any action from the suspects. Nick didn't say a word when he slid out into the street, but I knew where his mind was headed.

Midnight in this part of town wasn't coffee-and-donuts time - it was when the shadows came alive.

Athena and I made our way through the district and headed toward the train yard. I climbed up into the boxcar – Athena jumped in behind me. And we waited.

I kept checking the time. I knew Nick was waiting in the shadows – I knew the rest of our team wasn't too far off either.

I slipped a chain slip-collar over Athena's head "sorry girl, I need you to stay right here and watch our stuff for a minute."

I knew she'd be ready to attack the guy who always showed up first - the one with an irritating nasal voice – as if she knew something I didn't.

I attached her leash to a freight hook on the side of the boxcar then I slipped off the edge of the boxcar door, and crouched low into the tall weeds and dry grass.

It reminded me of basic training all over. I got down onto my belly – into a low crawl position and made my way through the thickets until I was a good hundred feet or so from where the last 'deal' went down.

I couldn't tell exactly how long, but it couldn't have been more than 15 minutes when I saw the mid-sized sedan pull to the side of the road and stop. Lights go off, and it waits.

And again – moments later another car drives past and pulls in front of the first car – headlights come back on.

Figures stood between them, one tall and jittery, the other hunched like he'd folded himself small on purpose. I knew this would be my only chance to send Nick the message – since the lights from the first car could hide me in the shadows.

We called it a 'wall of light' knowing that it is hard to see what's in the darkness when the brightness washes out your night vision and conceals everything past the light source.

I sent the message: "ready."

Nick rolled his cruiser up slow, no siren, just the growl of the engine echoing off the abandoned train cars.

When he stopped, the wash of his lights spilled across the buyer's car, painting the whole picture in stark white.

For a breath, nothing moved. Then one of the shadows flicked a lighter, seeing Nick's size as he got out of his cruiser - a brief spark that told me nerves were running thin.

From where I sat, I couldn't catch all the words, mainly the rhythm of Nick's voice - steady, low, carrying authority like a brick. The kind of tone that said cooperate, and this won't get messy.

I caught the faint outline of his hand moving, jotting something in his pad. A license plate number, maybe.

I slowly moved my hand down to my side to retrieve my pistol. Nick was there in the alley with me the night I got shot – the night I lost Tina… and I knew that Nick knew – I would be there for him too.

As my hand got close to my side I felt a wet nose next to my hand. I turned my head slow – and looked Athena in the eyes. "Really" I whispered as low as I could. She must have slipped from her collar. From the lights a hundred feet away… I could see her smile as if she was telling me – "*you're not out here alone.*"

Athena's ears perked at a laugh – sharp, too loud for the hour. My gut told me it wasn't amusement but nerves breaking at the edges.

Nick didn't rise to it. He just leaned a shoulder against the cruiser, flashlight beam cutting across the inside of the suspects car like a scalpel. Athena's body tense – ready to spring.

After a minute, the buyer's engine turned over, tires crunching on gravel as the car eased back and slipped into the street.

The other one followed slow, headlights off, swallowed by the dark. Nick stood there for a moment, watching, before climbing back behind the wheel.

I let out the breath I'd been holding. Whatever game was being played here, Nick had just gotten the first move on the board.

We sat in the darkness for a few minutes. Just the two of us. Quiet and dirty.

I sat up and holstered my pistol. Athena stood and shook off some weeds. We were alone for the moment – which is usual after the sighting of a police car. Something like that chases the ghosts of society back into the shadows.

Athena and I slowly back out of the field between the boxcar and the road where the alleged drug deals were taking place.

I felt my phone buzz in my pocket. I waited until we were back at the boxcar before I could see that Nick sent me a text message. It read *'meeting with Sanchez – I think I got what we need.'*

I called Sanchez from my would-be sanctuary. He told me that Valenti was working on the one suspect vehicle that appeared to be the 'buyer,' and that the guy in the sedan with the 'gimpy' arm?

Julian Welch. Name didn't mean much yet, but the way Sanchez said it told me it would. Tony said his address was near the river in an apartment complex.

I asked him if we should start heading that way to see if we could spot anything. Part of me already knew the answer.

I scratched down what Tony gave me, and I stared at the numbers for a second before it clicked. "Wait a minute… that place? I thought it was abandoned. Nobody's lived there for years." Still, it was worth a look.

Sanchez told me I sounded tired: "you've been out for a while – up for a break?"

"Yeah – I think both of us could use a break, and a soft place to sleep for a bit."

Sanchez said they'd put eyes on the apartment building, and that they'd let me know if they saw anything. "Wade isn't far from you – got a place he could pick you up? We can track you – just say the word."

I grabbed my little pack, and Athena seemed to know… we're going home. I sent Isabel a message letting her know.

The 'light-rail' station wasn't too far from the old freight cars and abandoned tracks, and so Wade met me there and drove me home. It was once again the comfort I'd missed, and the grooming I'd neglected for some time now. It was the familiar face, and warm embrace of my wife I'd missed the most.

Nights later, I waited down the street, Athena breathing steady at my side. No lights, no voices, no traffic. We sat in an unmarked car watching the streets I'd walked – this time I didn't feel quite so alone. This time I wasn't quite the ghost, but I still walked in the shadows.

We watched the two-story apartment building. We waited for any kind of a sign that someone lived there. Nothing... no one. Just one man slipping in and out of that brick husk like he owned it.

Welch. Nobody else. That silence told me more than a crowd ever could. I sat and watched, thinking how sometimes silence is louder than noise. If anyone else lived there, they were doing a good job of hiding.

Welch slipped in and out like a ghost with a key.

The next day the group debated our next step. Too soon to push, but too important to ignore. My suggestion - I could keep a foot in both worlds. Home by day, ghost by night. A cover identity was floated, nothing nailed down.

We discussed putting marked patrols on the road where the exchanges were being made.

This would obviously keep the dealer out of that area. We tried to get a warrant for a tracking device, but we were told we didn't have enough on the guy yet.

Valenti suggested posting marked units around the most likely areas where drug deals would take place – except for an area where we'd watch with unmarked vehicles, and post officers who could try and get the evidence we'd need for a warrant.

He also suggested he could try and have one of his men try to make a 'buy' so we would know for sure we had the evidence we'd need.

It wasn't airtight, but airtight plans don't exist in the real world. What we had was enough to keep moving forward - and forward was all we had.

Chapter 50

Oops – Not Really

Night after night we all took turns watching the apartment building like we were playing tag-team waiting for something we could use. Suspicion isn't enough. We needed something solid.

I could count at least 20 units at the apartment building. And the only one with lights on – was the second story window overlooking the parking lot nearest the street. It didn't add up. One man living in an empty apartment building?

It's obvious to most Cops what the reality is when you suspect someone. But suspicion doesn't win in court. We needed something real – we needed to find something – anything that could confirm what we were thinking.

My partner and I sat again watching – waiting.

This evening we watched the lanky figure walk out of the apartment building, stop and look this way and that – then get into his car. Athena's ears perked straight – and a low growl rumbled from her chest. She tightened tense just as she had when we would watch him from the rail yard. "I know little girl" I said low and steady – "I know that you know too."

We watched him drive down the street and I radioed that he was on the move. It was time for someone else to watch for a while.

We stopped at the station to drop off the unmarked police car so I could drive my own truck home. At least something in my life seemed normal again. My wife – Bell – welcomed us with a nice dinner, and we settled in for the night… at home.

**

The next morning we all met at the police station. Sanchez asked that we meet in the investigator's - or Detectives squad room. Every one of us has little pieces of the puzzle and when we put them together the picture began to take shape. But what was the connection?

We weren't even an hour into our discussion when Stan looked up at the security display screen. "Well I'll be..." as Athena's ears perked up again, "isn't that Kingman in the lobby?"

Sanchez looked up – puzzled at first – then a little disturbed. He shook his head, and called down to the front desk... "Don't tell him you're on the phone with me – just ask him what he's doing here, and I'll listen."

Sanchez put the phone on speaker mode so we could all listen: and Kingman was inquiring about our investigation into the murders.

We all looked at each other wondering again – why he kept coming down to the station – instead of having his lawyers – or even him making a phone call to a Council member to answer his questions.

For me – and I'm sure for the rest of us – this is just another part of the picture giving us a broader suspicion. And then again – how do we prove – how do we connect...?

Valenti said "maybe we should find a more secretive place to plan this investigation – you never know if someone with his wealth and resources is watching us – as much as we should be watching him."

Wade nodded in agreement "exactly – we need warrants and probable cause – he doesn't."

Stan suggested "you think Father Brian would mind if we met in his office?"

Nick raised his hand, and offered to contact him, but Sanchez said it was his responsibility.

We were all about to leave when Wade turned and asked – "who owns the apartment building where this Julian Welch guy lives?" We shook our heads – not knowing – when Sanchez said – I'll look into that - also.

**

Call it instinct – or more than thirty years of not trusting, but I just had to do something while we were waiting. I stopped at a familiar burger joint on our way home... Athena knew it well... it is our little place. It was Tina's favorite place.

Bell asked me if I wanted some lunch. I told her we stopped at our little burger joint – she smiled "where's mine?"

"Sorry babe… I wasn't thinking."

I asked her if she wouldn't mind taking care of our little girl for a little while – she said she'd love to. "Where ya going?" she asked pleasantly.

"I'm thinking… I'd like to take the bike out for a little while. Maybe a ride would do me some good."

I went to the closet – found my heavy leather jacket, chaps and gloves – and my 'girls' walked me out to the garage.

Bell smiled as I turned to Athena "sorry girl – I'm ridin' alone for a minute." Bell leaned in to give me a kiss and chuckled "you need a shave – and a haircut wouldn't hurt either…"

"Maybe when this is over hon – right now this look will really help me."

I swung my leg over and rested onto the seat. I could feel my Colt .45 through my jacket and thought out loud… "I'd rather have Athena with me." And as if Bell could read my thoughts – when she saw me nudge my pistol with my elbow she chuckled "a dog doesn't need re-loading."

Bell looked up toward the shelf at my helmet. I just smiled at her and said "not this time – I'll tell ya later."

I fired up the big "V-twin" and it echoed through the garage. I backed out into the driveway, and headed down the street. It felt good. And before I realized where I was… I was pulling into the parking lot of the apartment building where Julian Welch was living.

Weeds found a way to show through the asphalt. Paint seemed to forget its place on the building's exterior. Tape held some of the ground floor window in place. In short – it was a dump. I shut the engine off, and stood, I walked toward the front door. It was locked.

I rattled the handle a little and shook the door. I wandered around the front – looked around, but couldn't see anything. I saw my reflection in one of the broken windows and I really did look like a 'biker.'

I don't know what I was thinking – why I drove here. I just felt like I had to see something – find something. I stood for a moment – smoked a cigarette, and when I was about to climb back onto the bike – the door opened.

There he stood.

Not tall – not short, but looked like a proverbial picture of Ichabod Crane. Lanky – thin face with a large nose, and his voice. That nasal tone that could make cats run.

"What do ya want?" he said with a cold stare.

"I wanted to know if you had apartments for rent."

"We're full – no room for anyone else" he blurted back.

I thanked him for his time, but the way he looked at me. As if he knew me. As if he'd been watching… but I could tell – he hadn't put his puzzle pieces together…

Yet.

I pulled away slow. That empty hollow feeling gnawed at me. Why did I come down here? What was I thinking?

I picked up speed – shifted gears, and then saw the 'red and blue' lights in my mirror. I pulled over.

Sanchez got out of his unmarked police car and walked up to me.

"What the hell were you thinking? What did you go there for? His voice rough, his words shot out at me… "Are you trying to blow this for us?"

"Sorry sir – I was actually just questioning that myself."

"I was already tracking you with your burner phone – and – the unmarked unit called it in when he saw you pull up."

"Well – I guess I would have had back up…"

"Look – when we started all this – you agreed I'd be in charge – so look Jack – no more rouge – no more secret stupidities…" and then his scowl softened and he asked… "so – what'd you find out."

I couldn't help but smile about this time. "I asked if there were any vacancies – if I could rent an apartment…"

"You get in?" Sanchez interrupted.

"No – he said the building was full – that he didn't have any vacancies." I continued: "He was favoring his right arm – and had a long coat covering it… interesting – huh?"

"Yeah – that is. But let's get off this street – meet tomorrow let's say 9am at Father Brian's place."

I smiled "I knew he'd want to be a part of this."

**

I got home and I could tell Bell wasn't happy. "I got a call from Sanchez right after you left – told me about the meeting tomorrow. I told him I didn't know where you were going – so he told me he'd track the phone you have." Bell now shaking her head – her hands on her hips… "Sanchez didn't sound too happy you'd left… what did you do?"

I filled her in, and I could tell she felt the same way Tony did. But she also knew – I'd been in a lot tighter situations. And maybe that's what worried her the most.

I went back out to the patio to play with Athena, but my granddaughter Izzy was already out back brushing her. I watched and we chatted with Izzy stopping only for the occasional hug and tummy scratch for Athena.

Then Wade called and said he was on his way over. Great… another lecture.

Wade showed up with a six-pack and a look that said it all. He knew that I knew – exactly what he was thinking.

"Come on man – you know better than anyone – you don't go into combat alone" as he cracked open the first can, and handed it to me.

"I know but…"

"There are no 'butts'" he interrupted popping open a can for himself. "Look Jack – I've known you for over 40 years – we breathed the same desert sand – your dog Gunner saved me – tackled me to push me away from that bomb we didn't see. And even Athena – she found my grandson when he was lost – look – we've gone through too much for me to lose you over a 'hunch' – combat – PTSD – we've gone through it all – together."

I could tell he truly meant it – I took a sip of beer and smiled "I love you too man" with a 'kissy-face' sort of mocking his real feelings...

He just shook his head and smiled back with a chuckle "Jack – you pulled me through some pretty tough times – hell – we all pulled each other through it all – you getting shot – heavy stuff – everything."

We sat silent for a few minutes watching my granddaughter – she'd heard it all before as well. Those minutes turned into a few hours. And as the afternoon drew on – and we were now alone, all Wade could say was... "I'll see ya in the morning bud" as we did the soldier shoulder bump since 'hugging' wasn't the norm in our world.

**

I could smell the coffee brewing before I could finish climbing the stairs to Father Brian's office. Something that makes me miss Father John even more. It appears that I was the last to arrive. And I couldn't help myself...

"I suppose by now we've all discussed the successful Intel I gathered from my 'lone-wolf' expedition yesterday?" I said with a slight chuckle.

Sanchez – standing beside the large desk Father John used to occupy, simply said "Jack, you may be more right than you know."

"What?" maybe I wasn't going to get yelled at again?

Sanchez continued: "Kingman's visits to the City offices – mainly the police station, his 'convenient' absence out of town only at the times the murders occurred, and the fact public records show he's the owner of the building this Julian Welch guy lives – all puts us in a position a little closer for getting a warrant. It's all circumstantial right now, but we're getting closer."

We all sat silent. Sanchez went on: "if you guys think this is fishy, well then – how about this Kingman owning a number of the vacant apartment complexes around town, and the only one connected to the city utilities is – the one Julian Welch is living in."

Tony now looking proud "so gentlemen – let's ask ourselves why Kingman owns so many 'abandoned' buildings paying premium property taxes, and nobody seems to be living in them?" he chuckles "and it gets even better."

Stan pipes up "ok Sarge – spill it."

Sanchez takes a sip of coffee Father Brian handed him "if any of you don't believe in coincidence – well here's one. I was doing an internet search on this guy, and found Kingman was mentioned in an obituary – where he is listed as being married to one of the decedents survivors. A Marion Welch – who also had a nephew… wait for it… Julian Welch."

Nick coughed "does this mean we can now get a warrant?"

Valenti reminded us that this is still - all circumstantial, and according to the Tax Return Privacy Act (26 U.S.C. § 6103) – we'd need a Federal Judge to issue a warrant for the federal taxes…

Sanchez interrupted Chris: "let's not get too far ahead of ourselves. I don't want to piss-off a federal judge with circumstantial evidence" he pauses a moment looking around the room, and then looks back at Valenti "you get several of your narcs together – and start pestering this Welch for whatever drugs they can get from him. He's going to recognize some of them as 'heat' – maybe, but after several of your guys – or even girls, can bother him enough – one of them will get a score from him."

And then Father Brian raised his hand with excitement "and then you guys can give him the interrogation room treatment like the movies?"

We all laughed a little… Wade smiled at him "it's kind of like that Father, but – we only want enough information from him that will get us a warrant from the Federal Judge."

"In the meantime - we're going to watch these guys as close as we legally can. We don't want any more 'oops' moments" as Sanchez looked directly at me with a half smirk.

Valenti said he'd get some of his guys from the State investigations section to start 'tails' on Kingman – since he's hung around the station here enough to recognize some of the city cops.

Sanchez said he'd start digging everywhere he could so we could find out as much as we can about both of these guys. "And Jack... no more solo adventures." He grinned - "unless I know what you're doing."

Chapter 51

Cat and Mouse

I wasn't really compromised, but I'd been seen. The way he looked at me bothered me. Not in the way that made me afraid – I'd faced these kinds before... to many times.

I guess I was struggling with the thought he might cool things down, and that we might not get the evidence we'd need to connect him with our suspicions. Yes – I've been rethinking what I did, and not sure I really regret it.

Before we left our meeting in Father Brian's office – Sanchez did a county records property search, and gave me a list of Kingman's holdings.

"Here... I want you to check these out – see what you can find, but no contact – no – nothing... just see – poke around... take an unmarked car and just see what you can see."

"Tony – I've got something better..."

"Your bike?"

"Yeah – I think I can blend in better that way."

We all had our assignments – and we all started looking into the little details that would hopefully catch the ghosts that were haunting our streets.

**

I didn't like going out on assignments without my partner. I'd spent this lifetime learning to trust her instincts. Actually – all of my partner's instincts. Dogs just have a way of making you feel safe.

I had my list, and I already knew what I needed to know about the apartment building I'd already been to, and one by one I looked – I searched for anything that would confirm our suspicions. Most of the properties I started looking at seemed pretty legitimate – commercial buildings, stores, and even some 'high-end' apartment high-rises. Then I got closer to the bottom of the page.

I pulled into the parking lot of another apartment complex – much like the one I found Welch in. It looked abandoned – it looked empty… it also looked like – a dump.

I got off my bike, and started walking around – much like I did before – but I couldn't see any cars – I couldn't see any signs of life. Dead. I walked closer to the main entry doors, and looked down. I knelt a moment and felt an oil spot… "Fresh oil." I rubbed the residue in my fingers a moment longer and then wiped it off on the side of my leather chaps. I couldn't see anything of use through the windows, but what I didn't see said more. At least it did in this case…

It wasn't about what was there – it's about what isn't there. "Basic investigation 101" I chuckled. I couldn't see through the upper story windows – what I'd found was enough.

Six more times I found the same thing… abandoned, deserted, and run-down wrecks of empty shells that reeked of mold and rot.

Before I left the last forsaken building – I pushed my bike over to the shade of a large elm tree. I can't say why, but I just sat there and watched for a minute while I lit a cigarette… and I thought…

"Why would someone let buildings like this sit empty when they could be making him so much money?"

My phone buzzed again, and I saw it was Stan:

"Has anyone gotten a hold of you?" Stan sounded urgent.

"No – I've been out here checking on these properties."

Stan continued: "Um – Jack – one of the 'State' guys is following Kingman toward the airport – they think he's heading out of town!"

"Does Sanchez know?" I asked…

"Yes – and he's got Valenti moving quick on the drug buys – to see if we can keep anyone else from getting…"

I interrupted "Because every time Kingman leaves town – we find another body…"

"Exactly" Stan blurted – "I think you better come with me!"

**

I drove my bike to the parking lot behind Father Brian's office, and Stan was already waiting. I shut down the engine, and climbed into Stan's K9 truck. The sun was close to the horizon and the shadows were growing long. Valenti reported over the radio that his narcotics informants weren't able to make a successful buy from Welch…

Valenti also reported the State investigators confirmed Kingman boarded a plane for San Diego.

We pulled onto the street - I told Stan to head toward the old field we sort of named 'the urban forest' – where all the bodies were found…

Sanchez called over the radio – said Welch could be driving a 2024 Mercedes AMG GT…

I looked at Stan "that car's got to be over a hundred grand!"

He responded – "wait - I thought you said he drove a '92 Camry?"

"That's the car he usually drives when I'd seen him at least."

Stan got on the radio and broadcast that Welch could be driving either car – then turned to me "how does someone living in such a dump afford such a nice car?"

We both looked at each other – and almost in unison said "Drugs!"

An officer in a marked unit called out "24-J-2 – I just spotted a 92 Camry matching the description and plates of the suspect! – heading south on 3rd toward the tracks!"

Sanchez responded – and directed units to head toward the area where the exchanges were being made – and others to surround the urban forest area.

Stan asked where we should head with his dog Aries – Nick asked where he and Thor should go… and before he could respond Stan called out again that "we've got him" as Stan whipped his truck around to the opposite direction nearly throwing Aries to the side… while I called out our location on the radio.

I flipped the switch to Stan's overhead lights on the truck – and we began to make the traffic stop.

Nick said he was on his way with Thor – and the rookie who first saw Welch said he was right behind us.

The Camry stopped, and Stan hopped out of the truck. At first it appeared it was a typical traffic stop. I rolled down my window so I could hear… the typical 'driver license, registration, and proof of insurance' – anything in the vehicle like weapon, drugs, alcohol – contraband of any kind? And the typical answer – with that nasal irritating voice – "no."

Welch handed over the appropriate information Stan asked for – the rookie standing in the typical 'back-up' position about three feet from the back right corner of the car – where the rear roof support would help conceal him from the sight of the driver – and me – I was sitting in my biker leathers… just waiting.

Stan walked back toward our truck – backing slow at first, never turning his back from any suspect – giving a slight nod of recognition toward the rookie. We already knew there wouldn't be any 'wants – warrants, or any other violations' than the expired registration that dispatch would indicate – we already checked… but Stan had an idea.

He handed me the license, registration, and insurance info, and stepped toward the back of the truck opening Aries kennel. I could hear the familiar 'click' of Aries leash onto his collar, and the gentle prancing of paws on asphalt. Stan walked him up toward the Camry, and told Welch to place the keys on top of the car with his left hand, and step out of the vehicle. He did.

I could see the driver side door opening slowly and Welch ease out of the car. Stan was standing slightly toward the rear of the car by now – and as soon as Welch saw Aries – he nearly 'freaked-out.'

"What's that DOG doing?" Welch nearly shouting in a panic.

Stan ordered Julian to simply stand where he could watch him, and walked Aries around the vehicle. The rookie stood there and watched.

I could see in the side mirror of the passenger side door – Nick's truck pulling up behind the rookie's cop car. I could hear Thor's heavy paws trotting along the sidewalk. Julian Welch stood nearly frozen with fear.

I wonder why?

Still wearing a long heavy overcoat and appearing to favor his right arm Welch could only watch as Aries sniffed around the car. Stan casually asked why Welch was wearing such a heavy coat on such a warm evening.

When Aries passed by the trunk of the car – Julian looked even more nervous. He started to move as if he would walk toward Stan and Aries, but Nick – in his deep voice mirrored Thor's bark when he told Welch to STOP!

Welch nearly fainted in fear.

Aries was really interested in the trunk area of the Camry. Back and forth until… he simply sat.

"Well Mr. Welch – Sir – is there anything in this trunk that we need to know about – why the dog would indicate the presence of narcotics?"

"Well NO officer" Welch choked with nasally voice.

Stan gave the 'nod' to Nick – who grabbed the keys off the roof of the car, and proceeded to open the trunk. Aries couldn't wait. He jumped into the trunk and indicated on an envelope.

I got on the radio – watching a procedure I've done a thousand times – and asked Valenti if he had a field drug test kit…

"I'm two minutes away Jack" Valenti said eagerly "I'm one step ahead of ya."

Before Valenti arrived Stan already had enough with what Aries already indicated on – and from 20 feet away – I could still hear the comforting familiar sound when the ratchet of the handcuffs clicked around Welch's wrists.

Julian jerked in pain when Stan touched his arm to cuff him.

Stan didn't even have to ask – Valenti showed up and approached the Camry – drug testing kit in hand. I'd seen it so many times – it was routine, but Welch? He watched intently, his face washed in dread. Maybe in part from the spotlight from Stan's truck, and maybe because of the smiles from Stan and Chris knowing the test… is positive.

Fentanyl.

Valenti turns to Welch "I'm guessing you have a prescription for this?"

Welch remained silent. Stan motioned his head to the rookie to come over and had the new guy read Welch his Miranda rights – then put Julian into his police cruiser.

I called Sanchez updating him, and he told me to have some other officers do the vehicle impound, which would include an inventory and the search incident to arrest… but they wouldn't find anything else.

Sanchez said he'd meet us at the station.

After the rookie escorted Welch into the interview room – I watched from behind the 'mirror' that everyone knows is an observation room…

Welch was cuffed to the table – Sanchez chuckled as he told the 'greenhorn' officer "turn up the thermostat – let's make him sweat a little…"

After hearing us discuss the possibility of Welch being a person of interest in the 'homeless' murders - the rookie seemed excited that we could now get some DNA evidence to tie Julian to the crimes.

"We still don't have enough to get that" Sanchez said disappointed. But that doesn't mean we're out of luck… his face turning to a smile.

As soon as Valenti showed up to the station, and reported to the 'secret' observation room that everyone knows about – Sanchez said "ready?" and they went to have a little 'chat' with Mr. Welch.

I could tell that this little weasel was getting nervous – squirming in the chair – fidgeting with his hands and shrugging with his shoulders, and even more so when Sanchez and Valenti walked into the interview room.

Even I could tell the little room was getting warm – Tony and Chris were both showing signs – loosening their ties – opening their collars… and Welch? With that long coat on – he was even more uncomfortable. They suggested he could take the coat off, but he just shook his head.

The questions – routine – Welch silent… he was offered a glass of water, and Julian never touched it. It was almost like he didn't want to leave his prints on anything – anywhere, but we knew that would be impossible – especially if he spent the weekend in the lock-up waiting for a bail hearing.

Even in a nervous way – he was as cool as he could be – a paradox that we had to break. His silence spoke more than the phone we now had in our custody… sitting in the plastic possession bag with his Panerai Italian dive watch, and his John-Hardy ring and necklace… and the phone kept buzzing… over and over came the same ID on the display…

'Uncle Bane'

Tony and Chris left Welch in the room alone for a minute while I showed them the phone – through the protection of the personal property bag of course… they thought that was pretty interesting:

"Maybe dear little uncle is waiting for confirmation that it's safe for him to come home from his little alibi trip" Sanchez chuckled. "I wonder how well this can 'play-out' for him."

Valenti posed the idea that when his nephew isn't responding to the calls, that Kingman is going to know something went wrong – and come home anyway – but that he'd make sure he'd be seen in front of cameras every step of the way – this "Kingman" guy seems like the "king" of alibis…

We talked for a few more minutes – came up with a plan that we'd put little nephew Julian in the lockup for the weekend – and no matter how hard dear uncle would try – there wouldn't be anything he could do until Monday morning's bail hearing. That might give us the time for Welch to break his pattern of silence.

Wade called the jail and had some Deputies pick Welch up in the transport van so they could book him into jail. He knew they'd at least be able to get his prints – and hopefully something a little more.

Sanchez asked Wade if he could keep an eye on things while Welch was at the Jail – knowing Wade still worked for the County. Wade said he'd be quite happy to spend the weekend in his old 'stomping' grounds at the Sheriff's office complex.

Valenti said he'd have his guys from the State investigations office try to keep tabs on dear uncle Bane – maybe see when he gets back into town, and hopefully see how well we spoiled his weekend plans for the perfect alibi.

**

I called my wife – I told her briefly what was going on, and that she might want to head down to the jail since there might be an intake from our arrest – that could have an injury. I told Wade… "I've gotta watch this."

Wade agreed and said their medical staff would probably be off for the weekend, and it wouldn't be that far out of the norm to have a hospital nurse – especially one from the ER to come and do an intake medical evaluation.

Still in all my leather gear – I went with wade down to the Jail, and we watched as the intake Deputies began the process. Clothing change into the drab prisoner outfit – so cute… and Wade told me to wait behind this observation mirror so he could ask some 'routine' questions through this process.

"So – I see your arm is in a hard cast - how did you hurt your arm Mr. Welch?"

Silence.

"Come on – these are just routine – we want to make sure you're safe in here…"

"I live on the second floor – I broke it when I fell down the stairs carrying my video game console."

"Yeah – I get it… that 'right to remain silent' thing?" Wade motioned for some Deputies to escort Welch to the medical exam room. And Wade let me watch as 'Nurse Duncan' from the hospital – all in uniform, conducted her intake exam…

But true to his nature – Welch said nothing…

And when we were done with him… we watched as the Deputies led him away doing his prisoner shuffle as Julian was trying to get used to his legs being shackled.

Chapter 52

Jailhouse Rock

There comes a time in every investigation – a cop just knows, but hasn't proven beyond a reasonable doubt…

I knew it was Julian Welch in the alley that night. I knew he was dealing drugs… and dammit - I knew he was a killer. But why?

A typical drug dealer wouldn't risk dropping bodies into a vacant field with repeated and daring boldness. There had to be something more, and I couldn't put my finger on it – none of us could. Yet.

I was home for the weekend, and I was beginning to feel a slight sense of being normal myself. We had the kids over – the grandkids, and this time… I didn't stink. I was showered, shaved, and Bell even took me in for a haircut.

Like I said – it felt normal, but I still felt like I couldn't trust it – completely. And I only had a comfort no one was going to die because deep in my instinct – I knew the killer was behind bars.

Wade was calling me from the Jail – trying to keep me posted on everything Welch was doing – or in this case – wasn't doing. He wasn't using the utensils – he would eat with his hands. He wouldn't use cups, and kept anything he thought would transfer DNA – to himself. Smart.

He might have been an ugly man, but he wasn't being dumb.

Stan and Nick came over – we enjoyed some drinks while we watched our dogs play together. My granddaughter Izzy had a blast with the three K9's – we watched them play for hours. As they were getting ready to leave… Sanchez called.

"Do you remember what Kingman's wife's name was?" he asked as if he already knew the answer…

I didn't – neither did Stan, nor Nick.

He went on – reminding me of that obituary he read mentioning Kingman, and then said… "The woman he was married to… isn't his current wife!"

"You mean?"

I could hear Sanchez smiling through the phone… "yes – divorce papers."

Being the weekend – we wouldn't have access to the records office, but it was a glimmer of hope we could find something we could use. "Come Monday" Tony continued: "we're gonna make you a real investigator."

I'd spent a lifetime in uniform – in the field… it's what I loved. I have a hint of what these guys do, and wasn't sure I'd like it. Tony went on to tell me to have a good weekend – that Valenti is using his team to not only track Kingman, but found a similar looking Camry to try and find buyers since Welch is out of commission for the moment.

I asked if they thought of staking out the seven abandoned apartment buildings – or even some of the warehouses Kingman owns – maybe some of Julian's suppliers are making drops – not knowing he's 'in the jailhouse now' as I hummed the "Oh Brother Where Art Thou" tune under my breath. I asked Sanchez if Valenti thought of asking the DEA for resources – I mean, any kind of help… would help.

**

The house seemed quiet, but it was nice. I asked my wife if she wanted to go grab a burger… and when I said that… ears perked. Bell just smiled. Athena knew what that word meant. Before I could even grab my keys she was waiting at the door.

Other than the messages Wade was sending me – I could leave that world behind – even if it was for just a little while.

**

I wasn't dreading the Monday morning "get back in the game" – but I didn't want my weekend to end. Callahan – Wade, made arrangements with Sanchez for us to drive down to the County records office together. I told them I could ride my bike down to meet them, but they thought this ride could be a good chance for us to chat in private.

I gave my girls a hug, and walked out to meet Tony and Wade. Sanchez pulled out into the street – and gave Wade the look that said 'go ahead.'

Wade started explaining some of what he'd already been telling me, but I could tell Sanchez wanted us to hear it all again. How Welch did his best not to leave any hint of evidence he's been in jail. "Even when he used a carton of milk – he crushed and tore it before dropping it into the garbage can – even then – he shook the can so the pieces of the carton would mix with all the other garbage."

We pulled into the parking lot of the county office – proceeded to check in, and found our way to the basement file storage room. The clerk showed us where we could find the boxes of the records we needed. And we started digging.

We kept digging until we found an exhibit clipped to the back of a motion - copies of old tax returns. A highlight marker from years ago still bled neon yellow across the lines: *Schedule E - Rental Income.*

"Check this out," Callahan said, spreading the pages. "Kingman's got quite an inventory of income listed for his properties, but seven of these properties, all show income from being 'rented'... but these addresses match the vacant apartment buildings out by the old part of town. Same ones Jack tagged as abandoned."

Sanchez leaned over his shoulder "The same place Julian lives." The numbers stacked neatly year after year. "He was paying himself. Fake tenants, fake rent. Maybe this is… Long-term laundering, hiding in plain sight?"

Callahan closed the file with a sharp snap. "And the best part? This isn't IRS confidential. It's all sitting here in public record."

I couldn't help but interject: "now the trick is - to prove the income he's paying taxes on – is coming from somewhere it shouldn't be."

Sanchez had the kind of grin that a detective only gets when a ghost suddenly bleeds back into daylight. "This just may get us that warrant."

Sanchez slid the box back into the pile. "Kingman thought he buried it in a courthouse graveyard. Guess we just dug up the body."

Callahan stacked the pages, neat as cards in a dealer's hand. "We've got smoke," he said, "but now we need fire."

He wasn't wrong. Kingman's phony tenants proved he was hiding something, but it didn't tell us what money was filling his pot.

That's where Julian came in. The kid never touched a paycheck, never filed a W-2, but he drove a hundred-grand Mercedes and wore watches worth more than my first house. Drug money comes in cash, dirty and fast. Bank records would show the rest - those deposits, neat and regular, feeding accounts that wrote the checks for Kingman's 'rentals.'

And Julian's phone was sitting in evidence lockup. If we were lucky, the same idiot who shredded his milk cartons forgot to clear out his banking apps or his text messages about "drops" and "deliveries."

It was enough to push the judge. Enough to make the paper trail Kingman thought he buried… start to bleed.

Sanchez pushed the box back into place like a coffin lid. "We've got his ghosts," he said. "Now let's see if we can drag 'em into daylight."

As we were walking back out to Tony's car Callahan got a call from the Jail. They told him Kingman was there – getting his nephew out.

We knew we didn't have enough time to get this information to a Judge so we could get the warrant – at least before we could stop Welch from leaving his party at the County Jail.

We decided we'd have to work fast – almost like a dragnet – we had to keep tabs on all the players while we worked to make the connection, and answer that one nagging question… Why?

It didn't make sense to me – why someone would want to kill homeless guys and dump their bodies in the hundred acre forest.

Why would Bane Kingman wanted an air-tight alibi every time there's a murder? Why the forest of weeds, trash, and elm trees? Why would this worthless property have any kind of connection?

We kept trying to make these pieces fit and Tony said he'd start digging some more – "there's got to be a connection in all of this."

On the way back to the station Sanchez said he'd get the warrant application put together while Wade and the Deputies started working with Valenti on surveillance. I got dropped off, and now it was time for me to get my police truck – and go to work.

I dusted off my dash, wiped off the windows and if felt like I was back home. I was back in the game.

I called Bell – told her I was on my way home to pick up my partner. I knew she'd have Athena's gear waiting and ready. By the time I got my little girl's gear fastened – she was ready. She loved our undercover work – but this is where she really shined.

Back in the truck – the calls – the radio traffic was heavy. Every time my phone rang Athena's ears perked, and her eyes told me she wanted to find something. I knew Welch's Camry would be locked in evidence at the impound yard for a while so I'd have to keep an eye out for his hundred-grand Mercedes. I have to hand it to the guy – he wasn't stupid. He kept his DNA knowing we didn't have any previous samples to compare the blood from the crime scene to, and I had to figure by now he'd suspect we'd be watching him.

I had a list, but couldn't move until I got the word. In my world there's nothing worse than waiting at the start line – when you're running a marathon. Seven 'abandoned' apartment buildings – three empty warehouses, and who knows where else they're hiding the evidence. I mean… A paper trail can tell you what's hidden. My girl's nose tells you where it is.

The phone buzzed. Sanchez didn't waste words "Warrant's in hand."

I didn't even realize I'd been grinding my teeth until I felt the ache in my jaw. That was the gunshot at the start line. No more waiting. The leash was off.

Athena's ears perked before I even moved. She knew. We were rolling.

I didn't know where Welch was, and I didn't know where Kingman had gone, but Valenti's team was on it. I caught snippets of chatter over the scanner - one of his men spotted a black Mercedes parked at a law office downtown. Something about the way it gleamed that told me Kingman didn't like to be seen without reason. I made a mental note: keep an eye on that. I thought "What the hell's he doing there?" as if I didn't know. "Lawyer's office. He's either scared, protecting his nephew, or he's moving something."

Meanwhile, Athena and I were walking the grounds of Kingman's holdings. Seven abandoned apartments, three warehouses, and more weeds than I cared to count. Athena froze suddenly, nose to the ground, hair standing up. She clawed at the dirt near a loading dock and gave that sharp bark then sat when she caught a scent.

I knelt down, sniffed the soil. Nothing obvious - no stash, no bag, no box. Whatever had been here, it was gone. But Athena wasn't wrong; she *knew* it had been here. I could feel it in the air, in the residue of what she'd hit. Whoever moved it had done so fast - and clean.

I straightened, scanning the yard, the wind teasing the tops of the elm trees. Two steps behind, I thought, and we'd have to close that gap before Kingman or Welch could cover it all up.

I listened to the radio. Valenti's men were tailing Kingman's Mercedes, noting every stop until they finally reached Kingman's mansion. And Welch now pulling away in his 'not so anonymous' Mercedes coupe. I could picture Welch behind the wheel now, his shiny Benz, pretending nothing had changed. But I knew he'd have to start using it. And Athena and I? We'd walk, sniff, and watch. Eventually, something would lead us to the rest.

Athena's nose led us, and from building to building I could feel her excitement. It was subtle, but I knew it meant something had been here. I kept my head low, eyes scanning windows, doors, even the weeds, while the radio kept Valenti's updates coming in bursts.

"Mercedes spotted at a storage facility," one of his guys said over the comm. I scribbled it in my mind, storing it for later. Welch was out there, cruising in his new toy, unaware - or maybe pretending - not to notice the surveillance. But Athena? She didn't miss a thing.

After we hit the first abandoned apartment and found nothing but trash, mold, and that familiar stench of neglect. Nothing now, but we knew it was there. I called it in to let Sanchez know. At the next building Athena circled, paws scraping the concrete, ears up. She would stop suddenly, low growl in her throat. I would lean down again and again. Nothing visible. But she had a "hit" on something… something invisible to me. My gut told me these weren't just a random sniffs.

We moved to the next building. Same thing - abandoned, silent, nothing that told a story. But Athena paused at the dumpster. Again. Sniffed, pawed at the ground. Nothing left behind but residue, a trace of the invisible past. Whoever had been here knew what they were doing. Whoever had moved it left no prints for me to follow, only the ghost of what had been.

By the fourth building, I was thinking like Kingman. If I were moving product or covering up a crime, I'd spread it thin, clean up fast, and make sure no one could trace the pattern. And that's exactly what Welch had done.

Sanchez called – "Jack – interesting thought… I just read the city council approved a huge development for that abandoned patch of weeds – you know – that urban forest as you like to call it…" he sighed – "only thing Kingman needs now is for the city to approve the sale of the land – and word has it – the value has dropped considerably since all the murders started happening around there…"

"Uh… that's a little more than interesting Tony – that's pretty much the smoking gun – that he's been trying to hide…"

Athena gave a low whine, nudging me toward the fifth building. I followed, my heart picking up speed. Each step was methodical, each corner scanned. I had to trust her instinct as much as my own. She hit again - back near the loading dock. I knelt, eyes on the ground. Nothing. But I knew she was right. Something had been here.

And then it clicked. The hundred-acre forest. The weeds. The elm trees. The trash. Kingman wanted isolation. He wanted control. Whatever was hidden, whoever had been dropped in that hundred-acre stretch, this was all connected. Athena had just given me a breadcrumb. I had to find the trail.

We paused, Athena sitting at my side, ears twitching, eyes bright, and my mind in a whirl – deep in thought. The Mercedes sightings, the buildings… the forest… all of it was coming together. I could feel the dragnet tightening, Valenti's team circling, and the warrant in hand - but we still didn't know exactly what Welch or Kingman would do next.

Athena nudged my hand, insistently. I glanced at her, and knew what she was saying: follow the trail, and don't let it slip away.

Chapter 53

Lucky 13

One of Valenti's men following Welch sees him pull into one of Bane's upscale apartment complexes - the kind with valet parking and cameras in every corner - and disappears. The Mercedes gleams under the sunset lights, but there's no sign of the driver. I know him well enough to suspect he's not gone far, just hiding in plain sight.

Meanwhile, Sanchez is back at the courthouse basement, and he said he'd be searching through the financial records with a fine-tooth comb. He reported that the deposits are there - cash, clean or slightly scrubbed, all landing in accounts that feed Welch's trust fund. It's the same pattern he's been using for years, and the paper trail is starting to look like a roadmap. The money was coming from Kingman's holdings, running through "fake rents," right into his nephew's hands.

I can't shake the other detail. The pistol. It's got to be a .357 Magnum. A more distinct sound – sharp. I know it has to be, and I know it's out there somewhere - the same one Julian used on that informant months ago. But where? It could be tucked in a storage locker, a glove box, hidden in plain sight inside one of these buildings. That thought keeps me uneasy, because I know the kid well enough: he's comfortable with deadly things just out of reach, waiting for a trigger.

Athena senses it too. Her ears twitch, her nose quivers, but even she can't sniff out a gun hidden by someone as careful as Welch. I think about the Mercedes one more time, then about the forested hundred acres in the distance. Whoever moves next, it's going to be a game of chess - and right now, I'm staring at the board with half the pieces missing.

Sanchez called back "he's got those seven empty apartments, three warehouse... and it looks like there's three storage unit facilities he owns."

I chuckled "lucky 13?"

Sanchez sighed "yeah – it looks like your night isn't over yet Sarge."

I told him we had some hits on the outsides of the buildings, but we haven't had time yet to do walk-troughs inside. I told him Stan and Nick should be coming on duty soon – maybe we can get some more paws on the ground to go through them more thoroughly. Tony thought that would be a good idea. "The puzzle? Well maybe we can find some of the pieces inside."

I thought so too, and I couldn't think of a better place to start. We stopped for some chow at a drive through waiting for the call that Stan and Nick were on duty.

Valenti reported his guys still had confirmation that Kingman was still sitting quietly at his home, and they couldn't tell if anyone else other than his wife was there with him… so I thought – where did Welch go?

As soon as I heard Stan report his 'on-duty' call – I asked him if we could meet – and soon – Nick would join us. We got together at a park on the southwest side of town, and we let our dogs play a little while we came up with a plan. We didn't want to be too far from each other – so we decided to hit each apartment building together – each of us searching for something – anything that would lead us to who killed the homeless guys, and where were the drugs stashed.

We started at the most obvious place. The 'vacant' apartment where I met Julian Welch.

The main door was locked, but not for long. With a little 'tap' from a ten-pound sledge hammer it opened right up. I let loose of Athena's leash as she pranced proud into the main lobby and she started looking around. Nose twitching – ears straight – I knew if anything was here – she'd find it. I snapped my fingers, and she turned to look at me. I pointed toward the stairs, and she knew where I wanted her to go… I wanted to see what was in that second story apartment with the window that overlooked the parking lot.

Stan called for a patrol officer to watch the front of the building. Nick began to search the ground floor, and Stan wasn't far behind me. Nick hollered out he was getting all sorts of hits – Thor was indicating everywhere, but they weren't finding anything. I called back down to him that – that's what we were finding on the exteriors of the buildings.

Once I found the apartment I believed was Julian's – I knocked quietly with the sledge – Aries and Athena sprang in eagerly. And wow!

I thought we'd find a run-down mess littered with trash and filth. The outer shell of the building had hidden well – a lavish life with a nicely decorated home. Top-notch furniture, first-rate appliances, high-end computers, and an entertainment system that would rival a well-stocked electronics store. I couldn't have been more surprised. We all just stood for a moment.

"Go – go find it little girl" I told her, and she started her search while I called Sanchez and told him about all the electronics: "You might want our tech experts to see what's on them" as I was staring at the computers. I walked over to the console where the electronics were. The best products money can buy – unmatched… and the games?

I put my gloves on so I could thumb through the many game cartridges, and every combat, every violent, and every killing game you could imagine… were right in front of me. Each game placed carefully in alphabetical order – the remotes placed all in a line parallel with each other.

Athena padded around the apartment, nose to the ground, ears swiveling. She paused near the corner of the living room and gave a soft growl, tail stiff. I crouched down, sniffing the air - nothing obvious, no stash, no bag, and no weapon. But her body told me otherwise. She'd hit on something.

I stepped over to the sofa and checked behind the cushions, the cabinets, under the rugs. Still nothing. Whoever had been here was careful. Too careful. Bed was made, no dishes in the sink, even the picture frames were level with each other – something told me this guy was more than methodical – he was meticulous – almost compulsive. I glanced at the stairs leading to the balcony - that view over the parking lot. Whoever's here could watch every approach, every visitor, and still remain unseen. Julian knew what he was doing.

Nick called out that Thor was still pulling multiple hits on the first floor, near the closets under the stairwell. Stan's dog sniffed near the window ledge. I signaled for them to hold. Athena tugged toward the entertainment system, giving a short, excited bark. I knelt, checking behind the consoles, the wiring… nothing. But I could feel the tension in her body.

My gut told me the gun - the .357 Magnum - was somewhere here. Not visible, but nearby, hidden in plain sight. Julian wanted it ready, but he didn't want anyone finding it. That's how killers think. And now I had to figure out which ghost she was tracking.

I glanced at the rest of the team, the dogs scanning, moving from room to room. Each hit, each sniff, was a breadcrumb, a ghost of the past. Whoever had moved the stash - drugs, money, or weapons - was methodical. And Athena, as always, was ready to follow the invisible trail.

Nick entered Welch's apartment – stunned as much as Stan and I were. "Nothing Sarge – we have plenty of hits… but nothing."

I nodded my head – then shook it a little… "We're still looking for that .357 I know he's got to have."

"How do ya know it a 357 mag Sarge? From the crime scene? Nick replied.

"Well – it's just experience. The slug from the body could have been either a .38 – 9mm or a .357 – it was pretty mangled, but the 'crack' was too high pitched to be a.38, and there weren't any shell casings – so we know it has to be a revolver… so – it's just the years and experience – that's what my gut's telling me."

Stan wiped sweat from his forehead, looking around the pristine apartment. "So we're chasing ghosts then? All these hits but nothing to show for it?"

I studied Athena's body language as she continued working the room. Her tail was still rigid, ears forward - she was locked onto something specific. "Not ghosts, Stan. Echoes. This place has been scrubbed, but you can't erase everything."

Thor suddenly gave a sharp bark from the kitchen area. Nick rushed over as his partner pawed at the base of a cabinet. "Got something here, Sarge!"

We all converged on the spot. The cabinet looked normal - expensive granite countertop, sleek modern design. But Thor was insistent, whining and pawing at a seam in the wood that I wouldn't have noticed otherwise.

I ran my fingers along the edge and felt it give slightly. "Well, I'll be damned." The panel wasn't secured - it was a false front. Behind it was a hollow space, just big enough for...

"Empty," Nick said, shining his flashlight into the cavity. "But look at this." He pointed to scuff marks on the wood inside, and what looked like oil residue.

I nodded grimly. "Gun oil. Something heavy was stored here recently. Something that left marks when it was moved."

Athena suddenly perked up again, trotting toward the balcony door with renewed purpose. Through the glass, I could see the parking lot below - and beyond that, the forest where we'd found the bodies.

"He had a perfect view," I muttered. "Could watch us coming and going during the investigation. Probably moved everything the minute he knew we were getting close."

It really was going to be a long night.

Site after site – with flashlights searching, and the dogs frustrated with each empty hit – we needed to find something – for them… for us. We'd gone through twelve places already. Twelve empty shells, each one leaving Athena twitching and me thinking we were chasing ghosts. Trash, dust, faint residues, and echoes of what had been - nothing but concrete, junk, and filth. My gut throbbed like a warning bell: the .357 wasn't going to show up easy. That kid hides things like a fox.

We pulled up to the thirteenth unit, the last one on our list. Athena's ears went stiff before I even cut the engine. She was already dancing, tail high, nose twitching like she could smell the tension in the air. I gave her leash a gentle tug, and she practically yanked me toward the unit door. Aries and Thor not far behind.

Stan and Nick fell in step behind us. I could hear the subtle hiss of their dogs picking up the same signals Athena had been following all night. I muttered under my breath, "Lucky 13, huh?" but there was no humor in it. Tonight, luck had a different meaning.

The lock clicked under my sledgehammer. Athena bolted inside, nose to the ground, ears swiveling like radar dishes. The smell hit me - faint, metallic, unmistakable. Gun oil.

"Here she goes," I muttered, following her inside.

The storage unit was small, cramped. Cardboard boxes stacked haphazardly, a discarded mattress leaning in the corner. Athena paused mid-step, low growl vibrating through her chest, pawing at a plastic bin near the wall. I crouched down beside her, scanning the floor. Nothing obvious. But…

Then I noticed it: the bin was slightly off-center, the floor beneath it scuffed. My fingers traced the edges. A false bottom. My heart kicked.

Stan and Nick circled, watching as I lifted the top layer of cardboard. My breath caught. There it was - nestled in a carved-out cavity, wrapped in a worn cloth, gleaming faintly under the flashlight: the .357 Magnum.

I held it in my hands, reverently. The weight, the cold metal, and the barrel that had fired once before and left a trail we'd been following for months. Athena nudged my leg, tail wagging lightly. She'd led me right to it.

Nick whistled softly. "You knew it was here, Sarge?"

I shook my head slowly, smirk tugging at the corner of my mouth. "I didn't know exactly where… but I trusted the ghosts." I patted Athena's head. "Good girl, good girl."

The unit suddenly felt smaller, tighter, as if the walls themselves were holding their breath. I tucked the revolver into my vest, careful, precise. One piece of the puzzle finally in hand. And for the first time tonight, the shadows started making sense.

Athena nudged me toward the back of the unit, still alert, still reading the invisible trail Julian had left. I glanced at Stan and Nick. "This is far from over. But we just turned the corner."

The dogs perked again – then unit after unit – we found what we'd been looking for. Cocaine, black tar heroin, and stashes of fentanyl. We called it out – and it wouldn't be long until Wade, Sanchez, and Valenti would show up. My little girl did it.

Outside, the wind shifted through the trees, carrying a faint scent of the forest where the bodies had been found. I glanced at Athena, and saw the gleam in her eyes. She knew it too: the next move was coming, and we had to be ready.

Lucky 13, indeed.

Chapter 54

The Fox and The Hound

The long night paid off. I was on my way home to catch some sleep when I heard one of Valenti's men over the radio report that Kingman was at the City offices. I called Sanchez – he said he heard it too. He told me once they finished up at the storage facility – he'd try and find out what he was doing there. I knew he was tired too.

I was uneasy. A ghost – Welch was a fox was on the loose. Someone who knew the back streets of the city… but so did I. So did… we. I knew if anyone could catch a fox… my little girl could. I'd looked into his eyes – up close, and only hoped he hadn't found out I was a cop.

I got home as Bell was heading off to work. I asked her if she was 'carrying' and she said yes. We'd lived this life for so long these precautions seemed normal now, but something was bothering me.

"Keep it close babe" as I leaned in to kiss her good-bye… "It's just one of those feelings – you know – like how you always remind me to wear a helmet."

I knew this guy had some real mental problems. But he wasn't dumb about it. From the way he was killing, the way he kept his apartment… a relatively 'ugly' person who had a flare for the nicer things, and resources that could keep him hidden. My mind kept turning – thinking… would he try to leave town? If not – what was keeping him here?

He had to know by now – we were on to him.

I wasn't sleeping well. Every time Athena heard something she would jump to attention and wake me. That didn't bother me… my suspicions did.

When I did get up – I had some text messages. I needed to call Sanchez. He told me he interviewed the clerk down at the city offices. She mentioned Kingman wanted to expedite his plans to develop the 'hundred acre' wasteland – where the bodies were being dumped. But the approval to sell the land was still held up by the Council.

"Well isn't that convenient" as I sipped on some coffee.

"Yeah – it's a bit curious – isn't it?"

I agreed – and we thought it best for the team to meet at Father Brian's office. And I asked him if that was a good idea – since we don't know where Julian is hiding… he paused for a minute… "let me think on this, and I'll get back to you in a minute – don't go anywhere."

I waited.

When Sanchez called back he told me that Valenti and the State investigators want to have a little chat with Kingman. They were going to get him in an interview room, and start asking some pretty deep questions… he also told me that the last place Welch might want to be right now is… down at the Jail. He already talked to Wade.

We decided to meet down at the County Sheriff's office.

I thought about taking the bike – it looked like a good day for a ride, but I wasn't about to leave Athena behind. I was getting ready to go, and while I was changing Athena ran out to the back yard. I've spent enough time with her to know which bark meant trouble. I grabbed my pistol, and ran out to see.

I charged out the back door leading to the large patio – gun in hand. Athena was already in an alert position at the back fence. I scanned the foothills behind my house – I couldn't see anything, but that didn't mean something wasn't there. Athena turned – looked at me… I asked her "what ya got girl?" and she began to patrol the fence line that looked out over the hills behind my house. It was nice over the years not having neighbors in back of us, right now I kind of wish I had.

I called Sanchez and told him I'd be a few minutes. I told him what Athena did. "You all right" he asked… "Yeah – I'm all right… I've got to do something before I come down…"

It had been years since I'd used 'em, and I had to dig through some old boxes in the basement to find 'em… "Got 'em" - "Finally!"

After replacing some batteries, and finding some straps – I secured some hunting trail cameras to the back of my house. If someone was going to sneak around – maybe I could at least see who it was.

Athena and I walk out the front door. I stop one more time and scan. I know this neighborhood – the people – the cars… all the usual. I stared a moment longer making sure everything that was supposed to be there – was, and if there was anything that was there that shouldn't be.

We got into the truck. I had the passenger side window down – Athena's head in the breeze as I drove slowly. If there was something here… She'd know.

I took the long way out of town to the Sheriff's office. It's just what I do when I want to see what's out of the norm. Athena's alert in the back yard really bothered me. I'd soon find out why.

I was the last to show up. As soon as Athena and I walk into their prep room – Sanchez slapped a file folder down onto the table. "You'll love this Jack" – the look on Tony's face told me he wasn't pleased.

"I do something again" I said with a chuckle…

"No" Sanchez barked… "open this" as he pointed to the folder.

I opened it, and took a breath that sunk to my boots. It was a roster of our Police department's personnel. Highlighted in that bold fluorescent yellow… were the K9 officers. I slid the file back across the table while Athena's name burned through me like acid. My little girl was on his list.

Sanchez said they tore through the computers Welch had… "He's been watching us for a while now… keeping one step ahead of us the whole way. He's not just a killer and a dealer – he's working us, and… working for his uncle. What we found is going to put his uncle away for quite a while…" Tony continued… "Jack – you're just lucky this whole thing that Wade started – didn't start through **our** department - or he'd have known it was you out there posing as a homeless guy."

I was stunned for a minute – the pieces were really adding up now. But Welch hadn't hacked into the County computers… yet. And we didn't know where he was.

I called Bell. "Whatever you do… don't go home." She knew she had to keep her game face on – she also knew – she could be watched at any time. She agreed, and knew she didn't have to ask why.

We were all talking – the moment wasn't complete chaos – but we were scrambling our thoughts. Everyone turning to each other with ideas – coffee spilling, and then silence when the phone rang. Sanchez answered. And was silent. I didn't like the look on his face.

"What?" Sanchez looked stunned…

"Dead?" Tony looked worried now.

My heart sunk – I could only think the worst – Bell? My grandkids? Panic raced through me… I reached down and stroked Athena's fur – I held onto her collar with one hand – the other squeezing my cup of coffee… and before any of us could ask – Sanchez hung up the phone… and for a breath held too long…

"Kingman's dead."

All Sanchez could do is shake his head in disbelief. "They were on their way to bring him down to the station – they found him in his driveway."

We began to gather our notes – files, pictures, and papers - Tony shook his head again "Leave it – we'll be back with more pretty soon.

**

We pulled up behind the row of patrol cars. Red and blue lights splashed across Kingman's house like some sick carnival. I saw the officers grouped near the driveway, heads bent low, voices hushed. Athena pressed her nose against the window.

Sanchez said nothing - just nodded at me. I got out, and the summer air cut sharp against my face. The smell hit before I saw him. Burnt powder – the copper metallic tang of blood - and something else I couldn't quite place.

Kingman's car sat crooked in the drive, engine still running, headlights boring into the garage door. He was slumped behind the wheel, head tilted back, mouth half open like he'd been caught mid-yawn. But the bloom spreading across his shirt told the rest.

A shell casing glittered near the tire. Another by the curb. Glock, by the looks of 'em. Welch used to be careful. Now he didn't seem to care.

Tony whispered, "Holy Mother of…" then paused.

I just stared. All I could think was - if Kingman was expendable, then no one was safe. Not me. Not Tony. And sure as hell not my family.

Wade whispered "why would he want his uncle dead? Wasn't Kingman his meal ticket?"

Tony – still looking around at all the mess "I don't know Wade, right now I'm not sure who was feeding who." Then Tony turned to me, Nick and Stan: " how about you guys start checking the perimeter – see if ya can pick anything up… I'll go have a chat with the wife."

"I thought he was divorced?" Nick questioned.

"He was – but" Tony said after another slight pause… "I guess he's got a new one."

Tony turned to walk toward the house. More of his investigators arrived to start processing the scene. We walked the perimeter several times – so I went to talk to Sanchez. I left Athena with Nick and Stan while I went into the Kingman residence.

I eased my way past the officer at the door – who had his notepad in hand documenting everyone who entered the large residence. I stepped into an entry way larger than my entire home. Ornate, elaborate, and almost gaudy in an extravagant way you'd expect from a museum. A tall grandfather clock ticked, and the ping of a chime echoed against the marble floor. The officer nosed toward the hall telling me where I'd find Tony.

He was sitting in a chair across from a 'Barbie' wanna-be kind of trophy wife holding some kind of designer dog. I didn't know what to make of it – it was just a lot of long hair, short nose, and a lot of bows and ribbons. So did the dog.

She sat nestled in a large pillowed chair – not relaxed, but back straight with both feet planted secure on the designer rug. It didn't fit.

I motioned for Tony and he excused himself from the 'wife' and stepped closer to me so she couldn't hear.

"Our dogs never picked up on anything around the house… someone must have approached from the street – clean and fast."

Tony and I walked back toward 'Mrs. Kingman' and the little fluff-ball gave a slight 'woof' – must have sensed Athena's smell on me.

Sanchez continued talking to the poor widow – asking her if she'd seen, heard – even sensed anything that could help us. But she was near inconsolable. Her eyes red, skin washed with grief, she looked the part as if I could ever trust someone in a circumstance like this. Maybe it was too many years of not knowing – if rich people - if people like this – really could be real.

As Tony continued – I watched. She would add an occasional sob when she spoke. I've seen too many times when the person closest to the scene – is the one who did it.

I heard a couple more men from Tony's office enter the room. They stood silent. Tony told the grieving widow that it is normal procedure to take some prints – so we could match the prints we found on a couple of shell casings. I knew they'd also check for gun powder residue. For a moment – she looked nervous.

The test came back negative. She took a sigh of relief.

Maybe I'm just too skeptical – maybe I'm a bit of a cynic. But I guess my suspicions could have been wrong…

I stepped back outside, Athena came to my heel. The summer air had turned heavy, oppressive, like the city itself was holding its breath. Kingman was dead, the fox was loose, and the one person who should've been watching was swallowed into her grief. I pocketed my notepad and glanced down at the driveway. A shell casing still glittered in the afternoon sunlight. Just one of many. And somewhere out there, the fox was watching, waiting. And I had a feeling this was only the beginning.

Chapter 55

Nuts and Bolts...

What we thought was a ghost on the run was really a fox circling the henhouse. And that made him twice as dangerous. He wasn't hiding in the dark; he was laying claim to it. Kingman no longer had a stake in the game – he's dead. All he left behind was a killer on the loose, and a grieving wife.

We were left almost second-guessing our every move. Sanchez organized our technical support teams at both the city police department, and the County Sheriff's department – to scan and clean any previous or even possible breaches in our computer systems... as for me?

After leaving the Kingman crime scene I went to pick up my wife at the hospital. I waited outside the entrance doors, and she hugged Athena... then me. "Good girl princess" she whispered.

For the time being we weren't sure where my family would be safe.

But we went home anyway. I knew Stan and Nick would be checking every possible nook and cranny for signs of danger – *why*? Because that's what I was doing. That's what we were all trained to do.

I scanned our street for anything – vehicles – people – anything out of the norm we'd known for years... nothing. We pulled into the driveway and I told Bell to wait in the truck. She held her little pistol tight.

I opened the front door and waited to see what Athena would do. I let her walk in first – not that her life was any less valuable than mine... it's just that her senses can detect anything – everything... that I couldn't.

She walked through the house without sensing any threats. I motioned for Bell she was safe to enter. Athena walked the back yard, but found nothing. I checked the trail-cams and couldn't see anything there either. But I still couldn't shake that feeling of unease.

"Keep that with you at all times" I told my wife, and Isabel nodded in agreement – holding her Smith & Wesson compact pistol tight in her hand.

I stepped into the garage – walked around looked at my bike. I wanted to wipe off the dust, but froze. I called Sanchez.

"What ya got Jack" he mumbled…

"My bike… I got home – did a quick check – couldn't see anything. When I got to the garage… I found what appears to be an 'eye-ball' drawn in the dust on the tank of my bike."

Silence…

I sent him a picture from my phone and then quickly wiped away all the dust. I had to think fast – I didn't want Bell to panic.

I walked back into the house – Bell still holding her gun. Before I could speak – she gave me the look. I don't know how, but she knew. How could I ever keep a secret from her? A combat nurse – years of working in the ER – 40 years married to her… somehow – she always knew.

I didn't have to say anything. "Feel like a vacation?" I tried to smile.

"The kids? Would he know about the kids?" her face nonetheless concerned.

"Pack a bag – we'll find someplace safe – I promise." While I muscled through my mind on where we all could go – and whether there'd have been anything on our roster – anything in my file that would indicate anything about my kids or grandkids.

I stood silent while Bell went into the other room to pack a few things. My mind picking through all the nuts and bolts of what we knew about Julian Welch. Did he have a safe place? Was he still using computers to hack into other hotels – or any place else? I felt myself sinking back into the feelings of loss – that same feeling knowing I'd never see my old partner Tina – ever again. In a fleeting moment I could feel Father John's pull on me – bringing me back to the reality – back to the fortitude I had to have in the moment. The strength I thought I lost, that he helped me find. I had to keep my mind in the game.

I took a deep breath – Athena turned to see… "It's ok little girl – it's going to be ok."

I went to my little secret place in the basement and opened my safe. Nothing seemed to be disturbed. I grabbed two Glock model 21 .45 caliber pistols. I could feel Bell behind me. I didn't even look back at her but only mumbled "just some extra back-up babe."

I don't know – again – how she knew what I was thinking. She draped my black leather vest across my back. I turned my head just enough to see her comforting smile.

"I thought you'd be wanting this" as she straightened the back of the vest around my shoulders. The custom vest felt familiar across my shoulders - black leather worn smooth from years of use. A place for two sidearms, extra ammunition, everything balanced and secure. Bell glanced at me as I checked the draws. She knew what it meant when I wore the serious gear.

"Call the kids Bell – ask them if they all remember that secret word we told them years ago – to go to a meeting place without question… the grandkids are out of school – so there shouldn't be any problems…"

Bell knew I was serious – something our family had to deal with our whole lives… and now – they would find out why.

We both dialed feverously – we got a hold of all four kids. We were out the door.

A meeting place with no cameras – no electronics – and no ties to a computer. It was quiet as Bell, Athena, and I sat in the truck. I stepped out for a cigarette, and I heard the slow hum of familiar cars approaching. My oldest son arrived first – alone and curious. "It's been quite a while since I'd thought about this place." It is a quiet little park out of the way – near our first home where the kids were raised in their younger years. And one by one the rest arrived. The last – my youngest son…

"Where's Izzy?" I asked… Jason simply thought she was with us. My heart stopped. He thought she'd come over to grandma and grandpa's place to play with Athena. Jason's hands shook as he dialed, texted, redialed. No answer. No response.

I called Sanchez… I called Wade… now I know how Wade felt when his grandson went missing. I remember how relieved he felt when Athena found him.

I told the family we wouldn't be safe here for too long – giving a brief update on what was going on. But I had an idea. "Remember my uncle who was something like a second cousin's dad's brother twice removed on the thirty-second of Juvember or something?" as I tried to chuckle in a panicked manner… "Well he had a cabin I'd been to years ago – I bet we can hang there for a bit."

Meanwhile – while driving I kept trying to call Izzy.

Nothing!

My phone buzzed – I had Bell answer it while I was driving. She said it was Sanchez… "ask him what he wants" as I was trying to hide my concern… she said "He's got Valenti shutting down the traffic cams so we can't be tracked – so you, Stan, and Nick can get somewhere safe."

I caught my breath for only a moment "Tell him thanks, and tell him where we're going, and that I'll be back down from the cabin shortly…"

Our small caravan wound its way up through the canyon – I struggled to remember exactly where we were going… Found it.

I got to the door – Athena anxious while I ran my fingers along the rough doorframe, pressing into the cracks where old wood had splintered and pulled away from the cabin wall to find the key. I hesitated, listening. Nothing but wind in the pines. I slid it in the lock. Athena pushed past me, low and ready – her training and instinct to protect me greater than any threat… and we could relax for a while in the tranquility of the mountains… but not really… one of us is still missing.

I motioned from the open doorway it was safe to enter.

I gathered my three sons and son-in-law – made sure they knew what we were up against. I made sure they all had the weapons I knew they would have had.

But no time to relax. I asked Jason what Izzy was wearing when he last saw her – but he didn't know – neither did the rest of his kids. All they knew was she wanted to be with her friends. And how many of us really know who, and how many friends a teen-aged girl has.

We had walls around us, guns in our hands, and mountains at our back. But Izzy was still gone. And none of us could rest until we found her.

I stood at the open door – a breeze brushed my hair. I could hear a bird. Seconds seemed like hours while the beauty of this picture – an irony of peace and terror... I could feel the heat rising in me in spite of the cool of the forest. My thoughts – my fears were interrupted by fur nudging my hand. I looked down into the caramel eyes that said *"come on dad... we've got work to do."*

Where do I go? Where do I start looking?

Nothing seemed to fit at the moment. "Combat breathing Jack" I thought to myself... "Breathe" I told myself... in slow – out slow – over and over... something here had to make sense. Nuts fit on bolts – threads loosen and tighten. Pieces that didn't make sense – had to make sense somehow – but how?

I turned – looked at my family. Without a word and a dog at my side they all knew I was about to do – what I had to do. And it wasn't going to be pretty.

I was mad.

**

I looked Sanchez square in the eyes. He tried to calm me, but knew he couldn't. Wade walked in – gave a slight nod. The bright fluorescent lights of the squad room seemed to mock my darkness – my anger.

"Look – I've given everything to this department for more than thirty years... my blood – God only knows how much sweat..." and my throat tightened as I wiped the moisture from my eyes with the back of my hand – "and tears."

Sanchez – always by the book – with a broken calm tried to hide his fear. "We're walking a fine line here Jack – the warrants only give us so much we can do – and now that Kingman's dead – and Welch is gone dark – we can't just go kicking every door and break through every rule..."

"That's not what I'm asking" my hand shaking – my elbows feeling the double Glock .45's under my leather vest.

"What are you saying then?" Tony's brow lifting slightly.

The squad room door creaked open interrupting Sanchez – the Chief's voice flat, final, and hammered like a gavel – and without any hesitation simply said "A Dragnet."

He continued "Jack's only the first on this list – if we don't pull out all the stops – who knows what else this guy's going to do." As he walked over to the counter and poured a cup of coffee… "I'm here for the long haul boys – every resource we've got – we've mobilized. Ain't a squirrel in this city going to fart without us knowing about it. Valenti's got the traffic cams up – and every road in and out are covered – every major intersection – we've got eyes on… wherever he's hiding – we'll find him."

I turned to walk out Athena at my side. Wade's eyes followed for a second "where ya headed bud?"

"I'm not going to sit here and do nothing – I'm doing what I've always done – what she's always done… Track!"

Wade stretched from his chair "not without me you're not – blood to the end bro – we've sucked sand in Iraq together – we've gone through the academy together – you're not going out there alone!"

I knew if anyone could track an electronic ghost - Sanchez and his guys could… but no one could track a wolf like my little girl…

And my little lamb was out there… somewhere…

Chapter 56

... The Wrench That Tightens

"Izzy's phone went dead three hours ago near the water park." Three hours that felt like three lifetimes, each second heavier than the last. I thanked Sanchez for getting that for us... we were on our way.

I turned to Wade while I was driving "Wade – if you had unlimited funds and infinite resources... where would you go?" as I scratched my jaw... "Why would Welch live in such a dump – redecorate it into a lavish apartment, and not use one of 'Uncle Bane's' upper-end high-rises?" Wade silently shook his head. "Seriously" I cracked "where would a man who's smarter, richer, and more ruthless than anyone you've ever met... hide?"

We pulled up to the water park – Athena jumped out, stopped and looked at me like "ya coming?"

"You really think we should park here Jack?" Wade looking at the lot – full of parents picking up their kids... where I'd pulled up to a marked drop-off zone.

"You really think anyone's going to tag our truck Wade?" my face stern but – trying to remember what we'd been through together... "We're in a marked K9 truck – you in uniform – I think we'll be all right."

"Yeah – but you look like a 'Hell's Angel' in all your leather."

I pulled my badge and hung it around my neck – "Better?"

Wade smirked and nodded his head.

We stood by the exit gate, and through all the foot traffic leaving the park Athena caught a scent when three teen-aged girls walked past. Athena's ears pricked, her head tilting the way she always did when Izzy's scent came around – I knew she had her scent. I stopped them politely (as politely as I could at the moment) and asked if they knew "Izzy Duncan."

They did – and they said they all arrived together, but she got a message from her dad telling her to come home – then dropped her phone in the pool. They said she went to a concession stand to call an Uber – then she left. That was the last they saw of her.

Wade took their names and information in case we needed to contact them later – sure enough – all three girls gave addresses near my son Jason's house.

If anyone could understand how I felt – Wade could.

Sanchez had scoured the digital trails - pinged cell towers, tracked Ubers, combed through traffic cams - all dead ends. The tech said nothing, but Athena's nose said everything. And I had learned long ago: when she spoke, I listened.

But she wasn't speaking at the moment Sanchez called. I put it on speaker so Wade could hear - "guys – why would dear widow Kingman be pushing for the commercial project – again?"

Wade and I looked at each other – Wade responded "interesting – but we don't know."

Sanchez: "you guys find anything at the water park?"

Wade replied "This Julian Welch. If he had access to any of the apps or ride services, he could intercept, redirect, or track anyone at will. That meant Izzy was walking right into his world - or worse, he was already there waiting."

Tony came back with "Welch's only relative is his aunt – the dead Kingman's ex – but she's a nurse living somewhere in Denver."

I scratched my head – "yeah – she'd be no help, but we'll keep looking – maybe start back at some of the places little Julian liked to hang-out… Izzy's got to be here close – but where?"

I motioned to Athena, and we stepped lightly across the parking lot. My mind ran through the map Sanchez had sent: cell tower pings, Uber route estimates, and nearby traffic cams. One mid-sized, charcoal-colored sedan had appeared in a couple of feeds. Vague. Unclear. But that was all we needed - a lead.

Before we hung-up from Tony – I asked "you play any video games Tony?" He said no…

"You know guys – I don't know much about these games either – but if we want to catch a gamer, we've got to start thinking like one. Patterns, strategy, risk versus reward… it's all a game to him. And right now? We're the pieces on his board – or the characters on his screen."

He had to know we were looking for everything – for any trace of what he'd done. The "Uber" car – probably ditched. The electronic trail he used – probably erased. But he may not have realized he had made some mistakes. The 'uncle Bane' killing – sloppy – hurried… and the apartment – the storage unit where we found what we do know about him… again – sloppy, but he had to know – that we knew – he wouldn't do that again. But now – this didn't seem sloppy… it seemed staged.

My gut instinct told me to go back to where we found what we did. Maybe – just maybe he slipped up again.

The abandoned apartment complex rose like a ghost, darkened windows staring down at us. Athena paused at the edge of the lot, nose to the wind, tail stiff. Every hair on her back stood on end. I knew she had a trail. I had to trust it - had to trust her.

I moved through the cracked lobby first, listening, smelling, and alert for anything Welch might have left behind. Athena's paws whispered across the floor, ears swiveling, nose quivering. Then she stopped at a stairwell, nose down, a low whine vibrating through her throat.

"She's here," I whispered.

I climbed the stairs slowly, Wade behind me - silent as the shadows, and we followed Athena's lead. Every instinct screamed caution - Welch… still out there, still clever, still dangerous. But Athena had found a thread, and we would follow it wherever it led.

Outside, the wind carried a faint smell of city streets mixing with something else - metal, sweat, fear. Somewhere nearby is my little Izzy. Somewhere nearby, Welch was still moving. And somewhere in the silence of this building, the first threads of a trail were waiting for us to follow.

Athena's tail stiffened, body low to the ground. We followed her carefully through the hallways, each step echoing against the peeling paint and broken floor tiles. The building groaned under its own weight, the sound masking any small noises Welch might make. My hand never left the grip on my Glock.

She paused at the cracked door to Julian's apartment, tilting her head and letting out a soft whine. I crouched beside her, sniffing the air. Yes - Izzy had been here. Recently. Athena could tell the faint trace of her scent mixed with the metallic tang of Welch's presence, a reminder that he was somewhere close. Too close.

I pulled out my phone, sending a quick ping to Sanchez. "May have a hit."

Athena had been here before – Wade hadn't. He was as surprised as we were when Stan, Nick, and I saw it. "Woa – he lived here?" his eyes reflecting the beam of his flashlight.

"Yeah – quite the place considering what it looks like from the outside."

Athena searched everywhere – she could see the invisible trail we couldn't. The look in her eyes said it all – disappointment. We knew if Welch was here with Izzy – what was he looking for? Why risk it all to make his way through town – past all the cameras… past… all of us. We kept looking.

I turned over the sofa – and the bottom had been ripped out. It looked like someone removed a package that was taped to the frame. Something we missed before. And he knew it. I don't know how, but he knew it.

I froze… "Wade… you think he could be watching us right now?"

We backed out of the apartment – out into the parking lot. I motioned to Wade and whispered "give me some light over here for a sec."

I got down onto my knees and felt the asphalt – weeds and all – and once again felt the fresh drippings of oil.

Sanchez answered my call – I told him what we found – what my hunch was… he said he'd have some tech guys make a visit there in the morning and sweep the place for any active signals – if he was watching, he had to know we'd have thought of that too.

I didn't know what else to do – other than keep an eye on the place for the night. We pulled the truck into the moon shadows – away from sight of the road. I stepped out to have a smoke, and call my wife to see how the family was holding up.

". . . and make sure if you do go into town – let me know – and don't use any cards – cash only… I don't know how deep this guy's gotten into our lives… Love Ya Babe."

We all got back into the truck to watch the place for the night. I thought I could catch a couple of "Z's" while we waited… Wade looked at me and said "how can you sleep sitting up in a truck with an 80 pound dog on your lap?'

"It's better than a freight blanket in a rail boxcar – or under freeway overpass."

"Sorry man… I had no idea what we started – would lead to all this."

**

I must have dozed longer than I wanted. I jerked to the buzzing of my phone. It was Tony.

"You guys ready for the blue wave?" His voice a bit perky now… we all had a long night, but now it was 'go' time.

Several patrol cars pulled into the parking lot – followed by our tech van. Uniformed officers set up a perimeter. It was like watching a perfectly executed football play unfold - every block in place, every man knowing his assignment. They sung like an orchestrated chorus in tune – everyone knew what to do. These guys were on their game and it showed. It was 8am, and they apologized for being late.

"Sorry Sarge – but we had something to do before we got here. We did your house first."

Sanchez made sure Stan and Nick's families were taken care of – so all of our K9 crew could be ready for action. The Chief made arrangements for my family to use one of the K9's that Izzy had been training at our facility she volunteered at… one of the dogs she'd been working with – Kip.

I still couldn't relax. Wade and I watched as the organized chaos of the tech team scoured the 'abandoned apartment complex.

I hate waiting.

We watched from the shade... I bet I smoked a pack of cigarettes... you bet I was anxious – Wade knew my blood was boiling.

Sanchez arrived in his unmarked car – disheveled and tired, but with a look of hope in his eyes.

"So fellers... I don't even know where to begin. I've been searching online, records, anywhere – anything that can get inside this 'gamers' head... what we know is Welch's only real relative is his aunt – the nurse in Denver – that his uncles widow has been trying to push through Kingman's land deal through the city Council – and... we've been focused on all the Kingman holdings that were abandoned – isolated, and even the lower valued properties where Julian has been conducting 'his' business, so..." as Tony fumbled with a notepad...

"We can assume that Welch has either held-up with friends, or maybe using one of the higher-end apartments his uncle owned, but – I've been searching all night with the nicer places – comparing all the known occupants against anyone who could be associated with little Julian – and then – it hit me. Welch's aunt – living in Denver is registered as one of the owners of an apartment in the deluxe condo building over on Main... I compared any possible utility usage – and it's so minimal I can't imagine anyone living there..."

Wade interrupted "but with the warrant we've got – we can still check it out?"

"Exactly" Sanchez said with a smile.

I called Stan and Nick on the radio – they were more than happy to head toward the fancy apartment condos.

Athena seemed to know what we were saying, but I motioned toward the door of the truck "let's go find Izzy" and Athena was already nosing at the door.

I didn't mean for the truck tires to 'screech' a little when Wade, Athena, and I pulled out onto the street. But I was in a hurry. My heart pounding hard enough for me to hear it in my ears.

Radio traffic was congested – officers all over the city were checking out the other properties now owned by the 'dear mourning widow' of the late Bane Kingman. Sanchez rolling – calling out orders – like he's directing an orchestra.

Valenti reported that his guys hadn't detected any movement from the Kingman mansion they were watching.

Nearly every Officer in the City – and many from the County Sheriff's Office were converging on every possession in the Kingman portfolio. Our Chief donned his tactical uniform – and was in the field right there with us. Every road had eyes – every officer retired or not was on the hunt volunteering time and resources to protect… when one of our own is in trouble – when one of our families is in danger… the rules of the game change, and the players stack the pieces…

In our favor.

Chapter 57

Good Wolf – Bad Wolf

A predator had my Izzy. A lone wolf who took my lamb was going to face the force of a real **Wolf Pack**.

"Breathe Jack" Wade trying to keep me calm "you're no good if you're not in control…" he continued "remember Jack – this is still a 'we're not sure' at the moment… we've got every wolf in our pack trying to find her, and we will – Jack – we have survived through the thickest – and thin – so just remember – in this game… we're going to win!"

I could feel the sweat creep from every pore. But Wade's right… I had to breathe – I had to be steady. I had to be on "my game."

We pulled up to the front doors – I didn't care where I was parked. I didn't even care about having Athena on a leash. In this match – the gloves are off. The door-man looked petrified when Athena approached – he looked stunned. Frozen. She ran up to him sniffing, but nothing. Wade Yelled "OPEN IT!"

The door-man in the 'monkey-suit' fumbled his steps to turn and open the door as Wade and I rushed in after Athena. Residents and patrons of the boutique businesses throughout the lobby were shocked as my little girl – searched for 'her' little girl.

Sanchez called on the radio pleading with me to wait for more units – more boots on the ground… but I reminded him what I said when we first turned Wade's narcotics investigation into a serial murder investigation… "Tony – I told you then – I wouldn't wait for backup!"

Athena bolted toward elevators – stairwells – she was everywhere like she wasn't getting any hits – or was she. Athena nearly frantic was onto something… we just didn't know it… yet.

I told Wade to run back out to the truck and get our 'little 10 pound door knocker' – he immediately knew I wasn't going to wait for a warrant if Athena got a hit on any door – on anything.

All through the lobby – past the fancy little stores, Athena scared the dandy's unfamiliar with rouge police procedures. Into a hallway she sniffed every crack – every door frame – every knob. She could sense something. It was all I could do to keep up with her. At the end of the freight hallway she stopped sudden – my boots screeched like the tires on my truck.

Athena bolted back out toward the hallway opening, and into the lobby. Again back and forth – Athena turned again racing to a corridor leading to a storage area. She was now beyond determination – far beyond loyalty. Athena is now – out for revenge. She's no longer tracking – she's hunting with a personal investment.

Athena stopped at the freight elevator again - barking uncontrollably. I tried to keep her calm as we waited for the car to arrive. She hated waiting even more than me. The elevator car door opened and she bolted in ferociously. She was sniffing every corner – every inch of the padded walls, nearly every button on the controls. If this wasn't a positive indication, I don't know what else would be. I pressed the button to the floor Sanchez said the 'aunts' flat was on.

Athena wasn't holding still. She continued to circle. She no longer held her mouth closed while she was on the trail – she was ready for business. We felt the car come to a stop with that familiar jolt. Athena was pawing at the doors before they could completely finish opening. I reached for my notepad to see which apartment number we needed, but I didn't need it. Athena was already on the move.

"Wade – where are you!" I called on my radio. But all I could hear at the moment was static – I tried to call out again "14th floor" hoping he could hear me – even though he had the same information I had.

Athena's paws were flying – I was panting with exhaustion. She was like pure energy on steroids. I passed a hallway window overlooking the city – and heard Sanchez telling Wade that Welch may have the place wired with cameras – that Julian may know we were there. I could only hear Wade's voice crackle into a hush as we ran deeper into the chasm of radio silence.

Yards ahead of me – Athena led me through the maze of doors and hallways. Then stopped. Scratching at an apartment entrance she was nearly frothing and her deep Shepherd voice kept nothing secret. I didn't care. I tried to open it – it wouldn't budge.

I backed to the opposite side of the hallway then lunged forward raising my leg high enough to give the door as hard of kick I could. And still – nothing, but I had to try again. I back up to get another run at the door, and my elbow hit the side of the fire extinguisher box mounted to the wall.

I crushed the emergency glass with my elbow, and pulled out the extinguisher; held it tight and swung it down onto the knob. It broke free, and I kicked the door again. It slammed open. Athena charging in with a purpose. Gun in hand – I followed.

Athena was leaping over furniture – she was scratching at every cabinet, closet, and corner. She nosed, and padded at a bathroom door – I kicked again to find the room empty other than Athena barking at Izzy's flip-flop sandals in the middle of the floor.

My heart sunk – I felt the tingle of pain behind my eyes the way you'd feel about to faint. But I couldn't. I reached down and picked up Izzy's beach-shoes and we walked back out into the main living area.

"Wade – **Where Are You!**"

I called again on the radio, and I didn't wait for an answer. I dropped the shoes – Athena stared at me with disappointment. I grabbed her behind the ears – held her face close to mine "find her baby girl – find our Izzy – Please baby girl – you gotta find her" pleading with Athena.

There was a look in her eye at that moment I could tell would bring the demons of Hell to their knees – she was about to face the fury and fire of the Devil himself, and take him to a place he would soon regret.

Athena once again searching – knowing each invisible trail could – at least should take us to our little Princess. And even the most microscopic trail now – was Izzy's only hope – and Welch's highway to Hell.

Head weaving – tail cut straight – eyes focused, and a nose even Judges trusted as evidence… Athena led me to a nearby stairwell. She scratched at the door – it opened, and she stood at the landing for only a second. And we headed down.

Each stair meticulously scanned – each landing cleared. She left nothing to chance – I could tell Athena wasn't going to make any mistakes. Each floor a switchback of stairs leading to a landing, and fourteen times I counted the sign indicating which floor we were on.

It was 28 sets of stairs ran in record time – each level trying – even crying for help on my hand-held radio "**Wade – Where Are You!**"

The display showing the main level showed me no relief. My knees were flaming in pain from the stairs, but Athena wasn't through. Neither was I. She found a door – sign said maintenance. It opened and… more stairs. Before I could catch my breath – her head turned her eyes pierced mine saying "*come on – this way.*" She was in full charge as I limped as best I could to follow. She stopped at a crossroad of doors.

Behind them I could hear the buzzing and whirring of mechanical systems. I listened close as Athena searched for the right trail. I cleared my head – even shook it a little – then noticed the placard on one that said "Telecommunications." I pat the door gently to see if it had been opened recently – it was tight, but call it a hunch and Athena's nose I gave her a nod "I bet she's this way girl."

I looked deep into her eyes for the slightest of moments – tears in mine: "girl – we really gotta be careful right now – we really need to go slow – please – for Izzy's sake." I forced a pretend smile "heel." And she did.

Ten thousand years of evolution and generations of breeding led to this moment. She was the Good Wolf – now facing the bad.

Is there a way to describe how many thoughts can run through a man's head in the fraction of a heart-beat? Is there a way to calculate how fast a grandfather can think amid pain, fear, and absolute terror?

We stood frozen… all **four** of us.

Looking back – I really couldn't tell you whether it was the sweat, tears, or sheer determination. I stood there dressed in black leather as I was when I was face to face with Welch at his apartment. And Athena crouched bearing teeth with a resolve I'd never experienced in any of my previous partners.

This wasn't just another moment in a career – for me it was a defining moment for a lifetime. The myriad of thoughts in my mind was an analysis of tactics, of life… of love.

Four sets of eyes now in a show-down stare where each heartbeat marked a moment of eternity. Five yards – 15 feet separated me from my worst nightmare and Izzy's salvation. I could feel the neurons in my brain firing faster than ever before… "Think Jack – Think!"

In the millions of thoughts I had to process in half a heartbeat – the first was for Izzy's safety… "Think Jack." I remember he was right handed but still saw that arm in a cast. His left hand holding a knife to my granddaughter's throat. "Think Jack Think!"

I felt my feet slide against the concrete Athena matching my every move; Welch shaking his head confidently. "I knew I recognized you from somewhere" his nasal voice scraping like nails on a chalkboard.

Athena's low rumble said more than I could and Welch turned his attention between me and Athena. My reflexes had to be spot on and my delivery had to be precise. While Julian would glance at Athena I had to communicate with Izzy using only glances. A squint of an eye – a twitch of her head. I was trying to get the message, and now wasn't a time for second guesses when seconds could turn into forever.

I could feel Athena watching Izzy – I could hear myself talking. My conversation with Welch was a distraction – a distant blur - while I watched Izzy blink three times – then look down toward the ground. Blink three times – look down… blink three times and look down – then she extended her fingers from her palm and quickly made a fist. She held her fist for a moment and I could see her shift her weight slightly… then held her fist again…

I'd seen her use these commands a thousand times at the K9 training course. Hand signals – obedience, and now she was signaling me. Blink three times and look down. This time she was training me. I got the message.

I felt my breathing go into combat mode – in slow – out slow… I felt the grip of my pistols with my elbows. "Check – double-check – and re-check" I thought – something every Soldier lived by, and something every Cop survived by…

Every moment and every movement now calculated – there would be no second chances. Athena's head dropped only enough for me to sense she could see something.

Blink three times and look down… got it. I gave the slightest nod and waited…

I hate waiting.

The distorted sounds in my head could only feel the conversation and now - even the painfully nasal tone of Welch's voice turned to a haze. Izzy shifted again – matching the movements of Julian's breathing. Her palms relaxing and her fingers beginning to reach out gently… my intent look piercing and hers fixed on mine. Izzy closed her eyes for a moment; Athena hunched her shoulders; I dropped my right foot a little more to the rear. Izzy opened her eyes.

It was the first blink – her fingers edged a little. Then the second blink – palms closing. The third blink felt like it took forever, and that… is how long eternity is.

Izzy clenched her fist – it snapped closed. She buckled her legs and dropped dead weight to the ground. With one flash - teeth met flesh while the chrome blade of the knife tried to fly. And amid the scream – echoing in the chamber of concrete came the sound of thunder.

It was one in a million. The shot placed perfect. Past Athena – above Izzy – the single shot from a .45 landing inside the lanky shoulder. The door to the communications room burst open and all I could hear was Wade shout:

"I'm here!"

Chapter 58

Marionette

Whoever said Big Boys Don't Cry… never came close to losing a granddaughter.

Wade busted through the door – gun raised and ready, but it was over for the moment. He scanned – assessed, and then took action. I was holding my granddaughter Izzy in my arms – both of us in tears. Athena locked tight holding the screaming Welch fixed in her teeth. Wade jumped in and locked the bleeding suspect in cuffs – only adding to the pain.

I grabbed Athena – held Izzy, and the three of us embraced.

Sanchez – the conductor in this orchestra – listening to our radio calls had the wave of blue – the uniforms from all agencies converging on the once envied high-rise affluent complex that now became a crime scene.

Officers, investigators, and crime scene experts come together while I took my little Izzy… and we walked out into the sunlight.

For a moment I could relax… and in the warmth of peace I could think this nightmare was over. I walked Izzy to the truck – still parked in front of the building – Sanchez standing by his car with a 'first time I ever saw him smile.' I pulled my phone from my vest, called Bell… "I've got her… she's safe."

I could almost feel her relief through the phone.

I've always known Sanchez was 'totally by the book' but Tony also had a human side to him. Even though he rarely showed it. Izzy sat in comfort with Athena, and I knew what Tony had to say…

"You know what procedure is Jack – she needs to get checked out by medical."

"I know – and we'll get her there in a minute."

"First" Tony interjected "I need the sidearm you used, and… sorry, but now you're on administrative leave until the review is complete."

"I know" I hummed… "Both?" I questioned…

Tony knew I was carrying two .45's – but knew he never wanted me vulnerable. "Naw – just the one you got 'em with."

More officers arrived – units from all over and every local agency. Several ambulances showed up – "standard for something like this I thought" – and I knew Izzy wouldn't want to ride in one, so I told one of the EMT's that grandma's a nurse – that I'd probably be taking her to get checked out.

While Izzy and Athena relaxed for a minute – I stood by and smoked a cigarette… I deserved this one… and I stood watching as Wade walked Welch – still screaming in pain… out to one of the waiting ambulances. I had to call Bell…

I updated her on what was going on – what the EMT said, and that Julian would probably be at the hospital soon. She said she'd call their dispatch, so I could bring Izzy to the hospital. She'd meet us there.

Athena wouldn't leave Izzy – not for anything. It was like they clung to each other – like the comfort of a warm blanket. The ride to the Hospital was quiet where our glances met and her smile – knowing that silence and understanding… sometimes that was all you need. She blinked three more times… and laughed. I knew this would be something we'd never forget… something we'd share… forever.

By the time we arrived at the hospital – the ambulance #451 with Welch was still in the ER drive approach. Bell – and the rest of the family standing with Father Brian met us at the main entrance front doors. Wade, Stan, Nick – even Sanchez wouldn't be far behind, and… The Chief of Police – standing with my family and a huge smile – still in his tactical gear – just had to have a hug too. This is a life of love – where family goes far beyond tradition… it's solidified by bond, and sanctified by blood.

My youngest son – Jason – still showed the distress mixed with relief a dad would go through when a child is traumatized. He followed his mom and daughter, but waited outside the exam room intently. Athena however… wouldn't leave Izzy for one second. And no one was going to stop her.

I sat surrounded by the flood of family, friends, and associates – my relatives in Blue who dropped everything - doing what they could to help. The Chief pat me on the back – motioned for a private moment so we could discuss a few things.

Sanchez – Tony – said "Jack – a lot has been going on – we've extended the warrants based on what we've found, and what's been happening, and it appears the widow Kingman… Ummm Annette Kingman has been meeting with lawyers, accountants, and transferring most of the Kingman estate to a corporation off-shore." Tony shuffled through some papers – looked at his note-pad "looks like the money and holdings are going to the Cayman Islands."

I scratched my brow "interesting…"

Sanchez continued: "she's keeping some into her personal accounts – but according to how much Kingman had? It's a drop in the bucket."

"Anything getting deposited into the Julian Welch trust" - I couldn't help but wonder…

"That's the interesting part Jack" Tony shaking his head… "She's hired lawyers trying to find the loophole Kingman was notorious for – he wouldn't do anything without a sure way out, and at the rate she's going especially – using the same lawyers who initiated the trust in the first place." His brow perked… "It won't be long until they do!"

The Chief – really interested in what Tony was saying: "So no high price lawyers on their way down to talk to poor little Julian?"

"Not at this time – I don't know sir… but Valenti's men – they haven't seen any action from any of the lawyers parked at the Kingman mansion, or the offices – I mean – we're really trying to understand what's going on here. We know that 'uncle Bane' was pulling the strings to this puppet…" Tony paused for a second… "Or do we?"

"Where ya going with this Tony?" the Chief looking puzzled…

"Not sure yet, but… something doesn't smell right… something's bothering me… can't put my finger on it." Tony paused "It feels like she's giving her pieces away, but not losing the game."

"Well – how about we go have a little chat with Welch" the Chief suggested. Sanchez and Wade agreed – they looked at me, and Wade asked "you up for this Jack – or – you want to listen just outside the door?"

"I don't want to look at the guy for now – besides" as I smiled at the Chief "I'm on administrative leave for now. Right now – I'm playing grandpa – I'll leave work to you guys, but…" as I coughed a little clearing my throat "I wouldn't mind listening just outside the door."

A Patrol Officer stood outside Welch's Emergency exam room – a brief peek – I could see Julian chained to the bed – leg shackles on both ankles, and the cast for his previously injured arm zip-tied and chained also. A doctor and nurse trying to examine his left arm, and Sanchez excusing himself politely "we just need to get some pictures of the injuries folks – any problems?"

Knowing the situation – knowing Bell – Nurse Isabel Duncan so well, they turned to Welch while holding out his left arm - Tony started to position the camera – the Doctor smiled "This is going to hurt just a little" as he repositioned Julian's arm for the pictures. I could hear the pain – I could hear everything, and while it wouldn't be funny normally… today… this was funny.

"Is he ok for now so we can ask a few questions?" The Chief asked with respect…

The doctor said he'd be just 'fine' to talk as long as we needed.

Sanchez started "Mr. Welch – we have a murder weapon with your prints, we – well our forensics lab has – matched fentanyl from your drug stash to one of the homeless murders, a piano wire from another, and…"

Tony chuckled "the knife you had, well it matches one used in a murder, and I'm sure we'll be able to prove it."

Welch interrupted "I ain't talking. My lawyers are going to be here any minute – my uncle's going to make sure of that!"

The Chief – stoic and yet humored in a way said "your uncle isn't going to send any high-priced lawyers…"

"Sure he will…" Welch blurted.

Sanchez chuckled "unless he made arrangements before you killed him – I'm pretty sure he's not talking to anyone about getting you out of here."

"WHAT!" Welch shouted… "My uncle is dead?" his voice panicked.

Wade interjected "look - we have your prints on the shells from the crime scene, and – well – everything points – to you."

From the hallway – I could only peek to see the terror in his face… him not knowing that – he loaded the gun that killed his only hope for escape.

"I want a lawyer" Welch commanded.

The Chief said "We'll make sure you get representation – and we'll stop asking questions for now – what lawyer do you want to call – we'll let you make that call."

Julian was silent – Sanchez handed him a phone. He dialed, and spoke quietly – I couldn't quite hear, until Welch said – "WHAT?" in that nasal voice "what do you mean you don't represent me anymore!"

Wade calmly noted "does this mean you'll be asking the Judge for the public defender's office to represent you?"

"Well – yeah…"

Sanchez piped in "well Julian – as soon as you're back on your feet so you can stand before the Judge and ask – I'm sure he'll let you have legal representation." The look on Tony's face looked almost painful as he was trying hard not to crack a smile.

Welch sat in silence. The Chief nodded to the waiting medical staff, and they began to bandage the chewed arm Athena crafted precisely.

When the procedure was done – Sanchez motioned for the uniformed officer to secure Julian's treated arm to the waiting chain attached to an approved 'medical restraint.'

I leaned back against the wall as Wade, Sanchez, and the Chief stepped back into the hallway. Sanchez said he got a text from Valenti to call. We all walked down the hallway to the waiting area, and we waited while Tony spoke to Chris.

Tony listened intently – although the conversation didn't appear tense. We watched him nod his head a few times – shake it a few times… write some notes, and then said "Ok then…" and hung up.

"What's he got?" the Chief softly commanded.

"Well…" Tony still looking puzzled… "She – um… Annette Kingman, well – Valenti's phone tap picked up something interesting. After all the lawyers, accountants, and all her Cavalry left – she's been on calls to a burner phone registered to a cell phone company out of Denver." He paused for a moment, and cleared his throat – "this gets interesting. She spoke kind of cryptic – like she knew someone would be listening. She spoke like saying candy jars – marshmallows and crispy treats – and that it would all be filled soon."

Chief whistled low then "What in the hell is all that supposed to mean?"

Sanchez – still puzzled more than ever said – "the most curious part of the conversation Valenti told me was the voice on the other end said something like 'I knew the plan would come together when Kingman would **Marry Annette'** – and I'm going to have to listen to Chris' recording to see if I can make any heads or tails or this."

The Chief pat Tony's back – excused himself and said "I see a brave little girl I need to congratulate again…" and we all walked over to where Bell was bringing Izzy out. Jason met them first at the door – I wasn't far behind. Athena – glued to Izzy like she stole something. It was emotional while joyous – the family all together – including the myriad of Badges and Blue who felt the draw to a girl they saw as more than a victim, but one of their own.

The Chief left Tony to start piecing together the puzzle, and the uniformed crews to watch Welch. Wade looked at me as if to say "Beer-30 yet?"

I knew I could sure use one. Izzy overhearing this looked as if 'me too?' with a mock smile knowing what my answer would be.

Chapter 59

The Queen's Gambit

It was another long day for us, but we were home watching Izzy play with Kip and Athena. Wade – even Stan and Nick came by with the evening's supplies that could, and eventually would quench our summer thirst, and ease our tensions.

Valenti even called and congratulated us on our homecoming. He did apologize for not being there, but he was watching everything from a shaded office – keeping his guys sharp as we tried to see who was helping dear little Julian Welch all this time.

After several crushed cans and a few moments to let the calls – the interviews, and all the stress from my granddaughter – I thought about Tony, and what he was saying. I sent him a text inviting him to join us. I told the guys – Tony has been the real hero in all of this.

Father Brian arrived – and you know… hugs for everyone. I tossed him a beer, and Wade joked – "Father Brian – You? Drinking a beer?"

He just smiled – cracked it open, and said "it isn't against my religion."

We were all having a good time – Bell even pinning on a paper badge to my black 'T' shirt that said 'admin' across the top – and 'leave' across the bottom. Truly a Cop's wife humor. Sanchez came through the gate into my back yard…

"So this is where the party is?" His smile – once again surprising all of us.

Stan – the quarterback and track star – handed him a cold sweaty can out of the tub of ice… and the evening was pleasant. Tony smiled "Thanks, but this has to wait a minute"… and asked me if I could call my son - Jason over…

Tony said he talked with the DA's office "they said all the justifiable factors are there – it's only a matter of the paperwork." I knew it, but it was always good to hear. My son walked over, and Tony asked if he could have a few minutes with Izzy. "Of course - anything how we - well how she could help."

Izzy had the garden hose – Kip and Athena chasing the stream of water. I don't know if it was the three cans of beer, or a lifetime of skepticism, but I turned to Tony while we waited for Izzy and asked "has anyone tried to notify Welch's next of kin? You know – any relatives that might want to know he's in the hospital?"

Tony thought… "according to all we know – he's got an aunt in Denver – I think she's a nurse… and no – I don't think anyone has even thought to try and contact her – maybe I'll do that tomorrow."

We called Izzy over, and her dad explained that Tony was the lead investigator, and that he had some questions.

"Do you know why I need to talk to you Izzy?" Sanchez said politely - yet in no way condescending.

"I think so" Izzy said with some question.

With Jason and me quietly listening on - Tony wanted to know if Welch said or did - or talked with anyone on the phone while she was with him.

It wasn't a real long conversation, and Izzy was able to get Tony up to speed on everything that happened, and… let us know that Julian did talk with someone on the phone several times - heard mention of an island - money - some kind of holdings - he mentioned something about property ownership, and his 'cut' - even something about a plan? Izzy tried to let us know about everything - she was brave, calm, and unusually 'together' as compared to most teen-aged girls.

We all started to get real happy – you know – the kind of happy where you haven't lost your inhibitions, but relaxed enough to joke about the things you normally wouldn't have.

Sanchez didn't drink a beer, but he started chuckling – about the conversation he had with Valenti when we were at the hospital. Laughing – he joked about what Valenti said – "that mystery voice" still chuckling "said Kingman's plan would come together when he would Marry Annette – get it – the puppet - a Marionette… how Welch was only a puppet…"

We all froze…

As if the connection was suddenly shined on the picture we were trying to see through the missing pieces of the puzzle… Annette Kingman.

Tony was on his phone…

All I could see was Tony fumbling with the dial pad – I could tell he was excited. Finally. "Hey – Chris… um – any updates from your guys on the widow – um – Annette Kingman?" Sanchez listened… he paused, face scrunched a little…

Wade finally – in his three beer voice "What? Tony – tell us."

Tony kept listening – holding his hand up – kind of motioning for us to let him listen… he broke his conversation with Valenti for a moment and looked at us – with my family now trying not to listen in a very curious manner "They're – I mean… Valenti has his guys checking… hold on…"

It was confusion for a moment with our curiosity and Tony's back and forth… but "hold on – they're listening to a conversation she's on a call with… hold on!" Tony was silent – listening intently. "Something about… hold on…" he waited… then he was trying to talk to us as he was listening to Valenti – who was trying to listen to his guys… "It… is… What? Done?… what's done?"

We questioned Tony also – done what does he mean 'it's done' we all pretty much said at the same time. Tony hung up – and said – "Valenti doesn't know what it means – he was telling us what his guys were telling him in real time – so – whatever it means? I don't know."

"Can they get a trace on the phone Annette was talking with?" Nick asked, and Sanchez said it was the same 'burner' phone out of Denver… Valenti was trying to get a fix on where the signal was coming from, but that wouldn't be easy.

"I mean – just because a 'burner' phone was bought in Denver – doesn't mean someone couldn't use it anywhere." Tony said with a question in his voice.

"Guys" Sanchez smiled – "Valenti's got this – whatever happens – I know he's on top of it. I'm sure we can put this down for the night – we've got a special girl we're trying to celebrate." As he raised his soda imitating a 'toast' – but I could tell something troubled him – why? Because the same thing was troubling all of us.

And trouble it was,

We sat on the patio – laughing – cheering the kids as they'd throw sticks and rubber balls for the dogs, but Sanchez' phone rang – again.

"What?" Sanchez looked stunned. We all stopped what we were doing, and watched for Tony's next response. "What do you mean… **he's dead!**"

Things weren't making sense – and maybe it was because the long day was both emotional – and terrifying – what I thought was going to be an end – a pleasant evening, seemed to be getting more involved and confusing. Tony simply said "we gotta go!"

He motioned for us to get into his car – "I'll drive – I've only had a Coke, and you guys? – well – I'll drive!"

We got into Tony's unmarked car – headed toward the hospital. Sanchez didn't say much – we were already thinking the things he didn't want to say.

We rushed up to the room Welch was transferred to – and lots of medical staff were mulling around – looking stunned, puzzled, and worried…

The Officer watching the room too – was confused and not sure what to do.

Sanchez simply asked the Officer for a quick update, and he was hard pressed for words. "I don't know" he stammered – "it's just – a Nurse went in for a routine vital check – or something and came out in a panic."

Sanchez started questioning the staff – asking lots of questions – we just stood confused as everyone else. "How could this happen?" he asked – "his injuries weren't life-threatening – how could he die from a bite, and a gunshot wound to the shoulder?"

More officers started to arrive – crime scene tape was posted around the area, and Tony? I could tell his night was long from being over.

Sanchez – on the phone again with Valenti. "Your guys still got a visual on widow Kingman?" his voice stern – inquisitive and pressing… and he waited for a response. And he waited…

"Are you sure?" Sanchez questioned… he lowered the phone and told us Valenti's guys were checking – knocking on the Kingman's door… he raised the phone back to his ear… and waited.

"They're not getting any response from the Kingman house" he whispered... and asked Valenti if they'd seen her leave – or anything. Sanchez paused again – waiting. He lowered the phone slightly again and said Valenti's guys didn't see any movement from the house – the only thing they know is Annette Kingman is still in the house. He waited some more. Valenti told Tony "maybe she's in the shower – or something... give it a minute – they'll check again." Tony hung up, and I could tell – he didn't like waiting either.

The medical examiner's office arrived, and before they transported Welch's body – Sanchez asked them if they could do a 'draw' and rush the toxicology report – and he meant – a real RUSH! Tony called the Chief – at home, and briefed him on the sudden update.

Minutes seemed like hours, but I had to call Bell – I mean – in this case Nurse Isabel Duncan... she couldn't think of any reason Julian's injuries would have caused him to die – either. She said she'd make some calls.

"And now – I have to call his only living relative, and – not only tell her..." as he fumbled through his notepad "Aunt Marion – that her nephew was injured and arrested for murder – but he's dead."

"Um..." I paused... isn't dear Aunt Marion – Bane Kingman's ex-wife?" Sanchez looked like someone punched him in the gut.

"Holy Mother of..." he thought for a second. "And she's been living in... Denver?"

He called Valenti – and had the look on his face was like "can't this phone work any faster?" and he waited... and when Chris answered:

Tony's rush of words sounded like an auctioneer – nearly stuttering trying to get the words out – but what I remember the most was his "get someone in there right now! Find her and make sure she doesn't leave town!"

The silence was nearly deafening. The look on Tony's face said more than any of us could have imagined. "Chris – could you repeat that – let me make sure I heard you correctly..." Tony pausing once again... Kingman's wife – Annette? Are you sure? They broke down the door and found her... dead?"

As fast as things were happening - none of us knew how to make sense of what was going on. Tony was on the phone with Valenti still "Chris - we need to pull out all the stops - get a warrant for any and all transactions Annette Kingman's been doing - connect it to the husband's tie to Welch's drug activity, and say something like we're trying to see if tax fraud is involved... but - get the warrant..."

The summer sun was now once again finding its lazy way toward the horizon, and Tony had to make another call. Our dispatchers had located a number for Julian's aunt, and so he dialed again... but no answer.

Sanchez called back to the detective's squad room, and asked if anyone there could track down which hospital the 'aunt' worked at: "call all of them then – I don't care – I'm not getting answer from the number we got from dispatch."

I called Bell, and asked her if she knew any of the hospitals in Denver, and she didn't. I told her what was going on, and she couldn't believe it either. I asked how everyone was doing at home – she said it was going well – all Izzy could say was how bad she wanted to get back to the K9 training center... something she truly loved doing.

"Ok – got it... Thanks." Tony finally got confirmation on State employment records – so we could make an official Death notification for the aunt – and he started calling the aunt's employer. Tony dialing... again... and talking quietly. I couldn't catch everything Tony was saying, but before he hung up his phone, all I could hear was... "well thank you for your help – we'll see what we can do then... Thank you."

"So how'd she take it?" I asked calmly.

"She didn't" his voice even more puzzled... "They told me she went on some kind of sabbatical trip for a while... they didn't know exactly when she was coming back."

"You know Tony" I said scratching my head again... "My wife has been a nurse for over 30+ years... and I've never heard of one going on a 'sabbatical' leave... something's a little ripe in Denmark if you ask me."

"Yeah – I know..."

Chapter 60

Organized Chaos

At the moment there wasn't much more we could do at the hospital. Tony drove us home. The ride was mostly quiet.

"I sure wish there was a way to get a look at whose name is on all the accounts and property deeds down there in the Cayman Islands…" I could tell Wade's mind - like the rest of us, was going a million miles per hour.

"I've got some ideas, and all we can do now is - find how the pieces of this game are playing out." Sanchez mulling… either of you play chess?" he asked tilting his head toward us slightly.

Wade said he did - a little, and me… no. But I could tell Tony was thinking. "In the game of chess there's a strategy called a 'fool's mate' where you lure your opponent into a trap - even sacrificing pieces to do this." Wade nodded - I just looked more puzzled.

"A Gambit - like a Queen's Gambit is one of these plays - and somewhere on our Chess board - someone's been sacrificing pieces to try and keep us from looking - where they don't want us to look." Tony stopped at my house, but before he left… "have a good night guys - I'm going to have my 'diggers' polish off their shovels - cause we've got to find the play we've been missing."

I stood outside the car – still looking at Tony: "this game's getting – I don't even know what to say… the "King's" dead – and the Queen seems to – well… still be in play?"

Tony just shook his head and smiled as he pulled away…

Wade chuckled a little… "Jack… you up for a game of Chess?"

**

The rest of my evening with the family was pleasant. Even though somewhere deep - my thoughts were far from the fun I was supposed to be having. And no… I didn't play Chess with Wade.

My thoughts were on the game Big Boys play – where the stakes are real.

The family seemed tired, and mostly relieved that Welch no longer posed a threat. I could tell they wanted to go to their homes, and put all this behind them. But something still bothered me. My phone rang again.

"Hey Tony – what ya got?"

"Things are getting real weird Jack – Kingman's old lawyers – well they're still working on that land deal - for the land Kingman wanted to develop. They've been in contact with Council members – at all odd hours – pulling out all the stops, but we – I mean me and the Chief – well we convinced them to put a stop to it all – considering all of what's been going on surrounding this whole thing."

"So – we can't ask the attorneys who's behind this… because it's all client confidential…" I mused…

"Right, and from what some of the Council members said – the lawyers didn't seem too pleased about the hold we put on it."

"You think they're behind all this – the lawyers I mean?"

"Gut feeling Jack – no – they're all pretty straightforward kind of guys – great reputations and all… something's telling me there's something pretty fishy about the aunt."

"I agree – I mean this isn't adding up…" I couldn't finish my thought when Sanchez said "hold on – one of my guys is getting a call from… he says it's Valenti – that Chris has some… interesting updates… I'll call you right back."

"What's going on?" was on everyone's faces. I was trying to explain the web – the evidence – the proverbial game board and how the pieces were being set… my family as curious as ever – and maybe even a bit concerned considering the past few days…

Athena nudging up against my leg – as if waiting patient for our family good-bye's looked up – waiting for my response from the last call… everyone looking at me – wondering what it all meant. Almost paused – waiting with me… for Tony's next call.

No one had anywhere to go the next day, and so our small-talk conversation seemed almost empty as if we all knew what we were waiting around for... every time I tried to say anything Athena would nudge me again and look up as if she wanted to know what was going on – even more.

My phone – again... and yes... it was Tony. I picked up the call, I cleared my throat to answer, and before I could choke out the words...

"Jack – Tony – I just got off the phone with Chris – he's got nearly every investigator at his disposal, and – well Jack – they've been going through every screen – every camera – every angle... and Jack – your family leave yet?"

"No – just about to go – we're still by the door..."

"Hold 'em there a minute – they might want to know this too..."

"I think they can hear you a little Tony – they're here."

"Ok then, well Jack – remember the day you dusted the tank on your bike – the 'message' you saw?"

"Yeah... I remember..."

"Valenti's guys have been tracking back the video feeds – there's no way Welch could have been at your house."

Silence. All eyes on me... Tony continued...

"We have several confirmed pictures of him nowhere near your place any kind of time that would have happened, and... The 'ME's' office reported both Welch, and Barbie-Doll Kingman – Annette , they both were overdosed with Fentanyl, and the story gets better..."

We were all silent – standing, but I felt like I needed to sit...

"Valenti's team – even ours has been pulling out all the stops. We've been working together, and that mystery call from the burner phone? We tracked several of the calls – all coming from different towers... here in town... Your wife – Isabel – she's there with you too?"

I glanced at my wife – tried to force a smile wondering what Tony was going to say next... I told him "Yeah – she's right here."

"My guys went through all the security cameras at the hospital. They traced clear back to when Welch was transferred to his room, and we saw the normal comings and goings of the staff we **do** know, and one… one stood out close to the time Welch 'kicked' it."

"Got an ID on who that is?"

"No" Tony sounded concerned – "what we do think is – it's someone who either carried in a bunch of towels to his room, hiding the face, and hiding what we think is a 'her' face by keeping her back to the cameras. Whoever it is didn't want to be seen… and knew where the cameras were so she wouldn't be."

Bell had been motioning Izzy and her sister to take the younger grandkids out of the room, and then she moved closer to the phone – motioning her hand to her ear wanting me to put the phone on speaker. I did. She asked Tony why she was important…

"Well – as if any of this couldn't get any better folks – call it experience, but I think this nurse from Denver has been behind it all – this whole time."

"Keep going man" I nearly shouted…

"So – I started digging through the County records – again – and this Marion Kingman – or Welch as it was changed to – well, she was no match for Kingman's high-priced lawyers, and got hit pretty hard in their divorce – and apparently said some pretty mean things. The records didn't say exactly what she said, other than she'd get even with him – no matter what."

"And…???" Bell said impatiently. Tony continued:

"Like I said – we've been digging – anywhere – everywhere we can, and it appears the dear widow 'Barbie-doll' Kingman – used to be a student nurse in Denver… one of Nurse Welch's students while at the hospital there. And it looks like one of the addresses Annette Kingman had listed, was Marion Welch's home.

"Not too long after that – Annette came to live here, and somehow… attracted Bane Kingman's attention… which shouldn't have been too hard knowing his reputation…

"Now – I've got an old buddy on Denver Metro, and he's working with our DA on a warrant – and they want to do a search there at her place. They've already got eyes on it just in case she shows – but I'm thinking she's done there, but who knows… we'll see…

"We're trying to get an ID – we don't even know what she looks like – all the pictures at the Kingman crime scene – they've got nothing on the 'ex' and we only have old descriptions and the old driver license photo from when she lived here. We do know her height – approximate weight…"

Bell interrupted "but hair and such? All that could be changed or covered, and even if she was seen at the hospital – I bet she'd have had a mask on…"

"Exactly" Tony coughed… "This whole mess just got a lot deeper than any of us would have thought – we're looking for some kind of intellect that's been fueled by some kind of 'woman scorned' thing… but Jack – Isabel – what's got me a bit concerned at the moment is… she may think YOU have something to do with her losing the land deal – as if she wasn't already sitting pretty – if in fact we can prove she has something to do with the holdings and accounts – now in the Cayman Islands."

"Yeah – the game pieces look like it's leaning enough to the ex, but proving it? Tony – that's another story – that's what you're saying?"

"Kind of – Jack, but not really. What I'm saying is… I'm a bit concerned for your safety… if she's already done what we're pretty sure she's done – well Jack – keep your family close, and your dogs closer."

Tony said "with everything we've got so far – although circumstantial – I think we can get a Judge to sign a warrant for her place in Denver. Jack I'll keep you posted, but if I were you… I'd have your family over for a sleep-over."

**

The grandkids thought it was an adventure. The kids still looked a bit uneasy. Bell looked stressed.

We found sleeping bags, blankets, and pillows. We made hot chocolate and turned on funny movies.

Our basement family room looked like a party in full swing. My daughter helped Bell, Izzy, and her sister – Ayla as they fussed over the younger kids. They took charge and helped ease the tension they could tell the rest of us grownups were trying not to show.

My son-in-law and my sons helped me do a quick inventory on the weapons we had, and then we walked out to the patio and watched Kip follow Athena as they patrolled the yard. It was dark now. I had my guys help me reposition the patio lights to shine outward more toward the fence line. I stood watching – thinking if I could see any glimmer – any reflection of light reflecting off of eyes – off of anything. It's just what I do. The sky – only lit by the faint stars, was otherwise black. No moon. Little light coming from the streetlamps. Just darkness.

We stood in silence listening… nothing. The dogs weren't picking up on anything. At least that was a comfort.

I felt my phone. I answered. It was Stan.

"Just checking in – I've been thinking 'bout ya… hell – we all have."

We talked for only a minute – me – still waiting to hear from Tony. Sanchez had a way of keeping the fire heated. We'd never been friends, but now – I was learning how important he was to me… to my family. And when he finally called back… I felt a little more at ease.

"Got it" he seemed excited. "It was a stretch for a minute, but the Chief talked to their Chief, and well – squeaky wheels got greased. Our DA, their DA – everyone convinced the Judge – I've got my buddy in Denver on the other line… he's asking what you need from the house. Apparently Nurse Welch left a lot behind. She's either planned on returning at some point – or didn't think we'd check – something – I don't know – hold on…"

I could hear Tony talking on the other line… and when he came back to me – "so they're asking if there's anything you can think of like…?" he finished questioning…

"Clothing" I exclaimed… "Tony – if you can, have them get dirty laundry. That could give us something solid to work with…" I held on the line while he continued to talk to Denver PD…

"Jack?"

"Yeah – I'm here…"

I've got the Chief here – and I think they've got something out there."

"What's that?" I asked.

"Well – they got a lot of stinky laundry…" Tony chuckled, and "they said they got a lot of notes, papers, and some corporation papers… from the Cayman Islands.

"Enough for the 'smokin-gun?" I asked.

"Not sure – they're still looking."

Tony sounded more upbeat now… "Jack – I think they may just have found what could put her away for a while."

"Great!" my boys listening more close now… "How fast can we get the dirty laundry here – so maybe… maybe we can get a track on this Nurse Marion?"

"Chief heard ya Jack" tony nearly laughing… "He said he'd pay to have a plane get it here in a few hours. Denver PD said they'd be happy to get it all here – even send one of their guys with it."

I finished my 'talk-to-Tony' cigarette and finished with Sanchez. My boys told me to get some rest – they'd all take turns watching. I knew they would. I turned to walk in the house to see Bell standing at the doorway. Her half-smile – half-worried look said it all…

"You really think she would try something with all of us here?"

"Don't know babe, I don't know, but we're not taking any chances… anywhere."

"I have a shift at the hospital tomorrow" she said with some concern.

"I know… and I know you're concerned, but I'm looking out for you." I was trying to smile… but I wasn't sure if the smile… made it to my eyes.

Chapter 61

A Righteous Shoot

Sleep didn't come easy. If I got any sleep at all. But I guess I did…

I would see things in the night – pictures – memories… nightmares. I would see the face of my little Izzy – terrified with a knife to her throat. I would see the look in a man's eyes as I pulled the trigger. I would hear the screams of that man as the ferocity of love held the forces of hell…

At bay.

We would call it – a 'righteous shoot' when an officer was justified in using the force that could – and possibly would cause 'death or serious bodily injury' and in this case… that man survived.

Righteous – what does that mean? Morally right? Justifiable? That's what the dictionary would say… but what does that really mean?

I've sat on 'use of force' reviews before – I know what the law says, but when it's you in the 'hot-seat' – that's when it all changes.

Every time I closed my eyes I'd see the look in my granddaughter's eyes… I remember the terror I felt. Yeah – sleep didn't come easy, and when it did… the pictures would return over and over.

I sat in my bed looking at the love of my life. Awake knowing my sons were watching the outside of the house. But safe inside – the only demons were still striking at the gnawing question of choice.

Was it a choice? Not for me it wasn't – there was no choice between right and wrong. It was either him – or my granddaughter. So no – there wasn't a choice… I simply did what had to be done.

Thoughts – all through the night gnawed at me to know someone was watching. Someone was inside my house – my private place. No amount of protection can dissolve the thought – the terror… of losing someone I love.

I guess this is the difference between what has happened, and what could happen... and my phone rang.

I wasn't imagining Tony's voice – although I wanted it to still be a dream, but he asked if I'd got any sleep... I paused, and that silence told him what he needed to know.

"The Chief needs you at the station – report time's 08:00 – you ok?"

"Yeah..." I mumbled... "I'm ok."

Bell stirred – turned... and looked at me. "Everything ok?"

"I think so – not sure... I'll try to let you know when I wake up" as I scratched the 'sleep-crunchies' out of my eyes...

I relaxed in the shower for a few minutes – did the whole morning routine... I could smell the coffee as I was dressing... in my uniform this time.

My family fixed breakfast, but I didn't feel hungry. I watched the dogs through the window. Playful – yet patrolling. Always searching.

My mind was at ease for a moment – seeing Kip and Athena weren't picking up on any threats. I tried to eat, but couldn't. The clatter of dishes and chattering of my kids and grandkids seemed like a faded blur in the background of my mind. Bell could tell today wouldn't be easy for me. She could only think to herself that I'd be going through a use of force review, and knew that wouldn't be easy.

Bell and I both finished getting ready for our day – while Izzy was getting Athena ready. My wife Isabel in her duty scrubs for the hospital, and me – I decided to wear my 'class-A' uniform to work. Izzy met us at the door with Athena polished and prepped – in her nicest gear... without words – even my granddaughter knew today was going to be something important.

It wasn't unusual for me to drop my wife off at her work as we left for the station, and I made sure she had a little something extra for her 'fanny pack' so she could be protected. Bell looked at me and questioned "most Nurses don't wear these while we're at work." But she knew I didn't want her to be anywhere without her pistol.

She hugged Athena, and kissed me, and my drive to the Police station was quiet.

Before I could make it to the squad room – I was met by the Chief, and Detective Tony Sanchez. No words – just a pat on the back from the Chief, as we walked through the door – me – expecting to see a panel of my peers to evaluate my use of force.

But there wasn't one. I looked into the faces of the Officers – everyone silent – waiting… and the Chief – his voice stoic, stern, and low… said "Jack – the bad news is the DA said they didn't need a shooting review board… and the good news is – they determined your use of force was a 'righteous shoot.'

He turned me toward him – showing the smile he was trying so hard to hide, and pinned my real badge onto my uniform. Tony – smiled in a way that actually showed he was human. From the back of the seats in the squad room – I could now see Wade – Sgt. Callahan from 'County' walking up to congratulate me too. The Chief handed me my weapon, and told me "let's get to work – we've got a lot to do."

I had to call and tell Bell. Athena sat at my feet… smiling.

Sanchez chuckled: "you're not going to get any work done wearing that monkey suit – you might want to lose the tie and roll up your sleeves."

We walked down the hall to the Detectives squad room. Nick and Stan were already there with some of Tony's guys – looking at a bunch of files spread across a large table.

One of Tony's guys said "The guy from Denver PD said they didn't know what to make of some of these files – but they did notice some of this is pretty interesting."

"How's that?" Tony replied – his smile now turning back to his usual Detective face.

"Some of this just confirms what our computer tech guys picked up on – Welch wasn't just hacking into our files, but hotels, Ubers, the City's main computer… and… the hospital."

I felt that 'hit in the gut' feeling again – and Tony could see the look on my face.

"Jack – we've already been in contact with your wife's work – we talked with their administration – their tech guys – and they are doing what they can to clean their system too, and Jack – we've posted her description – as best we can – in all the Nursing stations throughout the hospital – and their security people are supposed to be aware of this."

I was obviously concerned – knowing this Marion lady had already been in the hospital – pretty much undetected, and killed her nephew right under the nose of an Officer.

I looked at tony "if she's had the information from the city's computer, and the hospital – you think she could put the pieces…" I paused, took a breath… "maybe she thinks I had something to do with her big real estate deal her ex-husband was working on – going south – that maybe she's blaming me?"

Tony hum-hawed for a sec – looking down at some of the files on the table – turned again toward me "Jack – I'm not saying this isn't a possibility, and from the looks of what Denver PD found – she's been planning revenge toward her ex for quite a while… and – heaven only knows why she'd be upset about the land deal when she's got more than she could spend – in a lifetime… but – you know how greed mixed with revenge can be…"

It wasn't much of a comfort seeing what's been done already – and I wasn't afraid for my safety… and that's what I told the guys… "I can take care of myself – it's my family I'm concerned about…" but Tony interrupted me:

"Jack – again – we're doing everything we can. The Chief even put in a call to get some advice from the Feds – a profiler to help us understand how deep she's going – and maybe what her next move is going to be…"

One of Sanchez' tech guys added "we've been trying to piece together everything we know from the computers we found in Julian Welch's place – even the ones we found in his aunt's place, and he's had some pretty impressive equipment we've been analyzing, but that aside – it's not unreasonable for us to think – that she could deduce - that the investigation you were working on with Wade is in part responsible for the land deal getting canceled."

I looked at Tony – I think he could tell what I was thinking…

"Can we have our tech guys do a 'once-over' on the hospital's system?

Sanchez scratched at his jaw – then cracked a half smile looking at our departments lead tech – "how fast can you guys get over to the hospital and start? I'll call the administration – and…" as he turned back toward me – "we'll have the 'dog-squad' start tracking with some of Marion's dirty laundry around the hospital."

The tech guys started to move – and I gave Stan and Nick the look – the look they knew well… and Athena was already on her feet – ready and eager.

Wade contacted the DEA so they could watch the sites Julian Welch could have used as product drops – while Chris Valenti was searching through video feeds – trying to pick up on anything we could use to identify what kind of vehicle Marion Welch would be driving. I could tell everyone was 'all hands on deck' again, but that still didn't make me feel any comfort.

The Chief said he'd post some patrol units at the hospital – maybe that would deter someone from trying something there. I still felt uneasy. I was pretty sure this crazy lady didn't want to go 'head-to-head' against me – and Athena, but if she wanted to get to me – would she try to hurt me by hurting someone in my family?

I knew Bell would have called Father Brian – she's always been more religious than me, but no comfort or counseling from him could comfort her - when a passionate revengeful fanatic was out there… somewhere.

As we started to leave – to begin our searches at the hospital – Tony turned to me "Jack – guys… try not to scare the 'straights' – try to blend in a little – maybe?"

I turned back from the doorway to the Detectives squad room – Athena at my side…

"She wasn't made to blend in… She was born to lead the way."

Chapter 62

No Safe Place

I called Bell as I was driving. I could see Nick and Stan in their K9 Trucks in my mirror close behind. My wife tried to hide her concern, but I could tell how she felt. She met us at the hospital main entrance.

"We thought you'd want some company while you're at work." I smiled nodding at Nick and Stan – holding Thor and Aries on their leashes. I reached down and clipped a standard leash onto Athena, and then we opened the bag Denver PD gave us… dirty laundry.

Each dog took in the scent, and I told the guys I'd walk with Bell so she could show me the most likely areas an experienced Nurse would infiltrate a hospital. I asked my wife if she was ready to work…

Bell took a long breath – showing her courage while caressing the Cross she wore around her neck *"With Jesus in my heart, and a German Shepherd at my side – I'm unstoppable."*

Nick began working Thor on the exterior of the hospital grounds. Stan took Aries and began working inside – the freight areas – maintenance coves and such… My wife - Nurse Isabel walked me up to the room where Julian Welch was murdered. Immediately – Athena indicated what we already suspected. She started getting 'hits' all around the room, hallway, and led us to the linen storage. Bell didn't have to show us anything Athena wasn't already leading us to. Nick and Stan radioed they too were getting 'hits' all over as well. Bell was surprised how much of the hospital Marion had been through. Undetected.

"See babe – you see why I wanted you to keep that little fanny-pack close to you?"

She stared silent, just nodded her head. But that silent moment was cut short when Nick called out that Thor was tracking out to the parking lot "We're getting some good hits out here." He said with some excitement.

I called Sanchez – told him what we were finding – " talk to your tech guys and see if they can trace back – maybe see what kind of vehicle was parked out there – I mean – as far back as you can – especially to the night her nephew was killed."

We kept searching – everywhere the dogs indicated – we looked, but each empty search brought disappointment. I called Tony back "we know she was here, but – she's not here now."

"I've got the tech guys working on it – but for now – get your team over to the high rise where her apartment is – she's most likely not going to be there, but it's all we've got to go on – for now." Tony's voice back to his normal 'down to business' demeanor.

Before I left – Bell walked me back out to the truck and asked "You doing ok?"

"Yeah – I'm ok, but a little hungry now… I didn't feel much like eating this morning." As she kissed me and gave Athena one last hug.

I didn't like having to leave Bell at work – unprotected. But I did like having Officers posted at all the entrances and patrolling the grounds. I drove off with Stan in the lead as we were trying our best – to pick up on any kind of trace – any kind of lead in search of a ghost. She slipped in to a hospital and killed – nearly right in front of a police officer. She killed Annette Kingman – with State investigators watching… my mind kept thinking…

We searched the high rise where Julian held my granddaughter Izzy captive, and we found hits, but no sign of Kingman's ex. We tried picking up her scent at many of the old Kingman properties, and once more… nothing. I called Tony.

"So Tony – you're a Chess player?" he said yes… and I went on… "If a King is dead and the Queen keeps playing – how do we guess her next move?"

Tony was silent for a moment, and then "we've been playing this game all wrong Jack – she's been making all the moves and we've been playing 'catch-up' but – I may have an idea, but it may mean luring her into a trap – come on in, and we'll start playing by our rules… not hers."

**

Athena trotted alongside me as we got back to the Detectives squad room. No leash, just pride – she knew she was the real queen – even if the one who thought she was a queen – was still lurking in the shadows…

"Jack" Tony said with purpose… "just in time for the run-down" as he shuffled some of the papers on the large table… "she's been playing the game – the game where she's known the board, and the pieces better than us, and so – look…" as he started drawing on the white board…

"She's known the Kingman residence – the neighborhood, and all the roads in and out of that area – so getting to the widow Kingman – that's no surprise…" as he started marking the hand-drawn map on the board…

"And – she's a nurse – obviously scoping out the hospital ahead of time, and pretty much disappeared without us even seeing her…" as we all watched him intently…

"We found some of the documents about the plan Annette Kingman was working on with her husband – Bane – and it looks like it was Marion's idea for the nephew to start killing the homeless men – so the city would devalue the property, and motivate them to sell it to the Kingman estate quickly…" as we started noticing a pattern growing…

"Julian Welch was already using his uncle to launder the drug money, and so it wasn't hard for Marion and Annette to convince Bane Kingman to step deeper into the underworld, and agree to the killings – even though Marion was secretly working behind her protégé – Annette…"

The room was silent – as we started seeing the picture come together, but Tony… Sanchez continued: "So gentlemen (and ladies)" as he looked at the many eyes glued to his demonstration… "how do we get this Marion to come out of the shadows, and into our trap?" he said with a half chuckle…

Wade didn't hold back and asked "I can tell you've got an idea – and we're listening… spill it!"

"All this time – I hadn't realized the answer is sitting right in front of us." As he looked at the small property bag still holding Julian Welch's fancy gold chains, watch… and cell phone.

Tony reaches for the bag – opens it, and asks the tech guys to scan the phone for the most probable numbers Julian would have used... to contact his dear Aunt Marion...

It was nearly a unison 'light bulb' came on over our heads as the team all saw what Sanchez was saying. And he continued...

"I've got one of the FBI profilers coming down – so we can use the same language nephew Julian would have used – if he was going to talk to her..." as he smiled watching the tech guys plug the phone into a computer... and start analyzing...

"I was wondering how we were going to keep her from leaving – getting away 'scot-free' with all that money" as I looked at Athena...

The door to the squad room opened, and the Chief walked in with an 'accountant mixed with psychologist' looking kind of woman – heavy rimmed glasses with hair pulled back tight – and a navy-blue suit with white shirt that screamed 'I'm a nerd.'

The Chief introduced her to the team – as she scanned Athena, Thor, and Aries... and with a hoarse voice a bit nervous asked "do they have to be here?"

Sanchez simply said "if it weren't for them – we wouldn't have gotten this far in the case – so yes... I think they're as much a part of this investigation as any of us..." and the FBI 'pencil-neck' relented... nervous, but she relented. The dogs just sat and smiled.

We all watched as she pointed out a few things here and there while talking with our tech experts, and then finally they stood a little straighter – looking pleased... and our guy said "I think we got it."

Tony shuffled past some of the Officers at the table and looked – and actually smiled before he said... "Send it."

It was a calculated guess – maybe more of an educated gamble, but the text message the tech guys, the FBI profiler, and Tony agreed on was:

*"**Sorry – didn't work – I know all the account numbers – better luck next time JW**."*

"I hope this works" Tony said with a bit of question in his voice.

The FBI agent – Dr. Catherine "Kate" Brennan simply said "it will." As she stood silent by the computers and tech equipment… then continued: "I'll guess – since she's been planning, and now playing the long game for quite some time – yet leaving evidence behind at her Denver home." As she paused again looking down at some of the papers on the table – then at the white board – continued:

"My estimation is that she'll respond in the next few minutes with some kind of threat thinking her nephew survived the murder attempt – and then try to locate where the phone was when this text was sent. So gentlemen – detectives…" then as she looked down at the K9's "Dogs – you better hope she thinks her nephew is at the police station turning States evidence against her – or that she's on to our plan to try and trap her, but in my educated opinion… she's thinking the former – and she'll be afraid her nephew is – how would you hicks say it – spilling the beans."

We didn't take offense, but didn't appreciate the 'hicks' comment… then she continued… "She's someone who is beyond obsession, needs to be in control, and her obsession for revenge far exceeds the 'woman scorned' scenario. If we haven't heard anything in the next – I'd say two minutes – here's what I'd send in the next message… then right as she paused… Julian's phone buzzed again.

The text message read: *"**keep silent or else**."*

Dr. Brennan watched with a little smirk – pleased if you will, and told Tony to respond with: *"**talking – no more silence – I told 'em where you're hiding**."*

Kate said "if this doesn't bring her out of hiding – nothing else will." And Tony responded "And now – what – we wait?"

Tony was on the phone with Valenti – asking if he'd gotten anything we could use – any kind of vehicle description surrounding the time Julian Welch really was killed by his aunt. Chris said they're working on it as fast as they could – since so many of the vehicles around that time, and the area Thor was indicating on in the parking lot looked quite similar…

"Then what are we looking for Chris?" Tony blurted out… Valenti said pretty much all of the vehicles in that part of the parking lot – looked like mini vans and small SUV's about the time the staff would have been leaving…

I called Bell and quietly asked her if she could get a roster of the staff working the evening Welch was killed – she said yes – and it shouldn't take long… "I'll tell Tony – Thanks – Love ya babe."

I told Sanchez – and that if we could get a team of Detectives to interview the employees known to have left around that time – that we could do some deductive reasoning – and see which one Marion could be driving. And unless she'd thought of this – maybe she'd still be driving the same vehicle.

Dr. Brennan – Kate – said in her opinion – "as careful as she's been – she's not thinking we would be apprised to her methods as of yet." As she looked to the ceiling in thought for a second: "This tactic we're using is going to draw her out – I am sure of this." She said in her near robotic manner – as if she's analyzing data – not real lives. But she added: "Just remember – she's more interested in being in control than survival… she's dangerous, and would rather die than lose the game she's playing."

Sanchez looked at the confident Dr. Brennan and simply said – "this lady has been mis-underestimated quite a few times before…"

But Kate interrupted "Yes Detective, but she was underestimated when she was playing the game… we, just turned the game into **our** favor."

Chapter 63

Tipping The Queen

Sanchez said his guys were working quickly to deduce which vehicle we could be looking for – anything could help. He said my wife was a huge help in getting him the information he needed for this.

I looked at Tony – "um – if she's had access to the hospital – you think we should pull down the crime scene tape from Julian's hospital room – hoping she hasn't seen it – yet?"

"Holy Sh… Jack" as he reached for the phone… dialing…turned back to me "great call Jack – it'd be these details – if we miss – I'm sure she'd pick up on – great call!" as he spoke to an officer stationed at the hospital… explaining to him…

Bell called – asking what she should say to her nurses at the hospital – since by now – everyone was asking questions – beyond what they already knew – I told her: "tell them everything – that if they don't know a Nurse – or anyone at the hospital – call the Officers – hit the emergency button – something – let them know the killer is 'on the loose' and posed as one of them – and has real nursing experience – maybe that'll get their attention…"

Valenti called back – told Tony that he's pretty sure from the deductive reasoning that the minivan is most likely our suspect vehicle. They can't get a solid color on it – but it's going to be darker – maybe mid range colored – like a beige, medium grey, or something like a charcoal color – since the other colors would show some kind of hint in the cameras – and that's the best he could come up with at the moment – but they'd keep trying – looking – searching – like the rest of us…

I could tell the dogs were getting impatient – they can sense the excitement, and it isn't in their nature to just sit around… and wait.

"Dr, Brennan – um – Kate?" I kind of raised my hand toward the English-Teacher figure the FBI sent… "Is there anything we can be doing? I mean…" pointing my nose toward the dogs… "they're pretty good at what they do – and… they want to be doing – something."

"Well" as if she was talking to Tony – but looking at us… "I'm sure she hasn't been holding-up in any of the Kingman properties, so I would find a list of the cheap hotels – no – Motels in town or close by since I'm sure she's convinced herself she needs to be ready for anything – at any moment. That's where I'd start looking."

Tony nodded – "Jack – get with Wade and start searching for a ghost that may be driving a medium neutral colored minivan staying at a cheap motel – not owned by the Kingman empire…" as he was trying not to mock the stoic – stiff Kate Brennan…

I knew it wasn't much – but Stan and Nick followed Wade and me out to the parking lot – where I lit a smoke, pat Athena on the head, and told them I knew of a few places we could start looking, and "Wade – if you could go back in and work with Tony – maybe we could be doing something other than sitting on our – well backsides…" as I tried to chuckle.

Stan looked puzzled "and Wade – go ask 'Mrs. Pencil-neck' in there if that Marion Welch would be stupid enough to try and get to her nephew if she thought he was being held – here at the station."

"I'll look into that Stan – I'll try to keep you guys up to speed… and so…" as he pats his leg and said in an enthusiastic voice for the dogs… "Go Get 'Em." The K9's acted excited as we chuckled.

I didn't even have to look at a list – call it another hunch? Call it spending time on the streets posing as a homeless man? But there's always those kinds of places that attract the lower end of society – and don't ask questions if you want to pay in cash. Truth be told – they probably prefer cash…

I called Bell as we were driving – I told her to call the kids so one of them could pick her up from work. I knew her shift would be ending soon… "And whatever you do hon. Don't get a ride from anyone you don't know!" She appreciated my concern, and she said the kids would most likely be happy to pick her up.

Stan called over the 'car-to-car' mode on the radio – asking why we were stopping at this particular motel. I told him my thoughts, and both Stan and Nick agreed that this would be a good place to start. I pulled up to the side of the road – Athena hopped out beside me, and we just stared for a second while Stan and Nick pulled up behind us…

We all stood and chuckled…

It was the kind of motel that smelled like yesterday's cigarettes and last week's coffee - where the ice machine hadn't worked since Reagan was president, and the carpet had more stains than a crime scene file. The kind of place where a villain wouldn't stand out - because the motel itself was already guilty. The 'Desert Star Motel' was a chamber of bad choices and obviously had neither desert nor stars, just a sun-bleached sign with half its bulbs missing and a promise of cable TV that probably meant rabbit ears and static. Still, it hid stubbornly by the road, surviving on hourly rates, drug deals, and the occasional fugitive who needed anonymity more than comfort.

Nick kind of coughed and with a bit of a smile said "so how ya wanna proceed? Think we should try to go in quiet and just do a walk around?"

I turned to Stan – then looked at Nick and said "Sure – let's go in real quiet – stealth like…" and then I hopped inside my Police K9 Truck – repositioned it so the front of the truck was aimed right at the main part of the motel… I got onto my 'heavy-duty' loud speaker and announced:

***"DO NOT BE ALARMED – WE ARE UNDERCOVER NARCOTICS AGENTS – WE ARE ONLY LOOKING FOR DRUGS*!!!"**

Like rats scattering from a sinking ship – all sorts of shadows fled – got into mis-matched painted vehicles – some ran on foot, but the calamity was – I'd say… more than humorous.

"Well – I'd say that's going in quiet Sarge" Nick said trying not to spit out his coffee.

Stan – kind of stunned: "Really? Jack – I mean… really?"

I just smiled – "years of doing this – and what I learned from the streets – I knew we'd be able to ID our 'person of interest' if she'd run like the rest, and if she's here – then we've got her."

Aries and Thor began to walk the rows of doors searching for a trail. I walked Athena into the office where the nice man behind the desk barely even noticed me – well us… walk in. "No rooms available now sonny" he choked with a slight burp…

"I'm not interested in renting a room – I'm interested in someone who might be staying in one of your rooms…" my voice in command mode, yet - still trying to hold back a chuckle.

"I don't care who rents the rooms as long as I get paid – so we don't have any information for ya sonny" his nose still buried in a day-old news paper.

I nudged Athena with my leg – she knew what I wanted, and she hopped up onto the counter and gave a low growl… that got his attention. I slid a picture taken from the Colorado driver license – and gave the 'nice man' a current description, and he said "room 14 – check room 14" as he was trying not to swallow his tongue.

I radioed the guys "The manager here thinks our suspect is in room 14" and they responded 'copy that' . . .

I thanked the man behind the counter and started walking toward room 14, and Athena could already pick up on something. I think Aries and Thor could too. We took the standard position with our dogs – you know, the way we stand to the side in case someone were to fire a weapon through the door or window – but no answer. I looked at Nick – the long-time weight lifter and body builder, nodded my head, and he gently used his foot to quietly knock on the door. It blew open with a slam.

Thor charged in first since he was already at Nick's side but it was a race between Aries and Athena – with them nearly colliding as they burst past the broken door frame. They were getting 'hits' all over the room. But no sign of Marion Welch Kingman.

I looked at the guys – "you know – I bet Mr. nice motel manager could give us some more information…" as Stan was calling in what we found to Sanchez. A patrol car pulled up to where we were parked – I motioned to him, and he walked over to me… "go post up on room 14 – make sure you don't turn your back on anything – not even the shadows. This lady we're tracking is a real ghost."

The man behind the counter was even more surprised – maybe washed in panic would be a better way to say it – as the three of us – with our little pups walked back into the office. He gladly told us what she was driving – that she wasn't a brunette – but had blonde hair, and that he thought she was definitely traveling alone. He thought the dark-tan minivan had Colorado plates, but didn't see what the numbers – or letters were... we thanked him for his help, but he asked who was going to pay for the door to the room?

"Well sir" I said politely... "consider it a cost of doing business – unless you want us to post a police officer here for the next few weeks while we put the repair job out for bids, and go through an approved contractor list... you know – city politics, or..."

"Got it – I got it... understood officer" he muttered under his breath. Obviously upset, but when all three dogs turned to look at him – nearly rehearsed – he nodded his head again and again "got it sir – understood!"

As Nick and Stan were heading toward their trucks – Sanchez pulled up into the parking lot. He got out of his car – while a few more officers arrived. He ordered them to hit their lights – make a great show of presence: "we want everyone to know we're here." And while the Desert Star was basking in the dancing red and blue lights from the patrol officer's cars – I gave Tony the update on Marion's description, and confirmed the color of the once neutral minivan.

"Now – Jack – thanks to you and the k9's – we've narrowed down our search a little – as long as she's on the move and looking for someplace to hide – it'll give us a bit of an advantage. Now that ours – and every other Trooper in all the surrounding states are looking for her too? It shouldn't be long.

I called Bell – told her to stay close to the family... that we may have just 'tipped the queen' a little... and she may be pissed.

Chapter 64

It's Not Always Black and White

Sanchez was processing the motel scene – collecting every possible piece of evidence he could. Meanwhile Valenti was now searching every camera he and his team could – looking for a dark-tan minivan with Colorado plates. It had been a long day for me. I went from apprehension – to elation. From the thought of being scrutinized – to bringing our case a little closer to the light. "What a difference" I thought – today went from black to white – in only a matter of moments.

Athena looked proud. She too looked like she'd accomplished something good. I was driving home and my phone buzzed – I looked down at the display – it was Bell.

I looked down for only a second to press the answer button, then the speaker function... "hey babe – I'm on my way home" I said with a smile – even though she couldn't see me... but Bell wasn't talking.

"Butt dial?" I thought... I kept listening... I could hear talking, but it wasn't loud – I heard a woman's voice, but it wasn't Bell's voice...

Athena tilted her head – as if to listen maybe? Or was she picking up on something that started to bother me. I kept listening, trying to make sense of it. A muffled shuffle. Was it Bell's softer tone in the background? Then I heard a different female voice - not hers... and my heart sank deeper into my chest.

I picked up speed – kept listening – and radioed Tony: "put a track on my wife's phone – quick – not sure why – but quick!" my voice rushed with near panic... I kept trying to listen as the growl of my engine raised in pitch with anticipation. I knew Tony trusted my instinct – and the previous intrusion we'd discovered... at my own home?

Traffic lights – damn traffic lights, and for a moment my thoughts betrayed me... I have 'red & blues' I can flash... I hit the switch, and busted through the intersection headed toward... toward where?

I pulled over for only a second when Tony called back on the radio: "Jack – it looks like her phone is headed from the hospital…" he paused… and before my anticipation nearly broke free he said "Toward your house."

Before I could reach for the mic to respond he continued: "I've got patrol units en-route to intercept."

I 'copied' and headed toward the hospital – lights flashing as well. Athena sitting straight – alert – sensing what I was fearing.

Tony calling out updates – tracking her phone getting closer to my home. I picked up speed. Nick and Stan told me they were headed toward my house as well – more units chimed in – they could hear the fear in my voice.

Tony said the signal was slowing as it was approaching my house – we all copied – I told 'em that I was nearly there.

Down my street. Toward my home. The reflection of my emergency lights flickering off of my neighbor's houses – people opening doors to see… I wasn't alone. In my mirrors I could see several more patrol vehicles behind me. Lights flashing…

I screeched to a stop in front of my house – in the driveway – a blue Subaru – Athena charging past me - then poised – ready – and in near attack mode.

The passenger door opens and Bell stands – and looks at me gun in hand – dog in position with more units arriving positioned for rescue…

Another Officer arrives pulling up from the opposite direction – not seeing Bell standing puzzled at the side of the Blue Subaru – orders the driver out of the car – ***hands-up face the vehicle***…

Bell staring at me – at first her eyes flickered with fear, and then relief. And me? Not knowing which way to even think. The nurse driving the car? – Not Marion, but who? Bell looked calm, but the woman standing by the driver-side door in hospital scrubs – she was petrified seeing several K9's now staring at her – and a number of uniformed officers in position ready to strike. More orders shouted: "***hands on the car – feet apart!***"

Bell stood stunned – and sort of smiled – raised her hands recognizing many of the faces behind the badges and flashing lights… simply said: "*Ok you got me – I give up?*" with a chuckle and a hint of question in her voice…

The nurse who gave her a ride home didn't think this was funny. The Patrol Officers put their cuffs away, and she could relax a little. All I could do – is hug my wife. Athena hugged too.

Aries and Thor – they looked disappointed they didn't get to see any action… Stan and Nick gave the release command – and now – it was all back to puppy play at uncle Jack's house.

One by one – the flashing lights shut down – and Bell explained that for a moment – she was a little nervous when the 'new' nurse at the hospital – working for my wife – head Nurse Isabel Duncan – told her that she'd done her training at a hospital in Denver… right where our suspect Marion Welch used to teach…

"You did the right thing babe – I mean – after having our granddaughter abducted – and the force came to our rescue? You did the right thing, but I thought I told you to call the kids for a ride – and not to take rides from strangers" I said with as much of a chuckle I could muster…

By now – all the kids – and my grandkids were coming out of the house to see what all the commotion was – and thankfully – Stan took the lead, and in a kind of 'announcer voice' said looking at all the friends that came to help – and the neighbors wondering what happened…

"It's all right folks – drill number A-492 a success – we can all go back to what we were doing…" as I shook my head – his eyes meeting mine with a smile… but he continued – his voice softer now so only I could hear…

"Seriously Sarge – if she's watching – at least she knows – we've tipped the playing field… in our favor."

Granddaughter Izzy – named after her grandma – never missed a chance to play with the dogs – and now with Nick's and Stan's dogs – and with Athena and Kip – well it was a five-way game of tag where we all had a good laugh watching Izzy play with the once ferocious, and the near feral monsters… kiss, lick, play, and love…

Thirty plus years I'd given to this department. For more than thirty years I've had a family – that my family has grown to accept as their own… where that bridge – that bond extended both ways, and the loyalty to this day… has never failed me. Some departments can boast of unity…

Ours lives it.

The Chief called as our red and blue party was coming to a close – he told me Sanchez filled him in, and he was getting all sorts of information from the motel room: "Good call Jack – good choice on where to start looking – your instincts nailed this one."

I told him that the nurse who gave Bell a ride home – was also a student of this 'nurse Marion Welch' – that one of Tony's guys might want to have a chat with her – she might be able to think of something they could use – anything we could use might help that FBI profiler pick up on something that might tighten the noose – and keep the game in our favor.

The Chief agreed, and said one of Tony's guys – overhearing all our radio traffic - was nearly at our house. He suggested we hold the nurse there a little longer so she could be interviewed.

She seemed a little apprehensive, but cooperated – gave her name "Jesse Wilkes." Said she was living in a studio apartment – not one of Kingman's… and drove an older Subaru, and was barely getting by on her nurses salary. But she was happy and at least living on her own – making her own way… and was able to help our detective glean a little more information – the FBI profiler might be able to use.

After she'd calmed down from the excitement – she excused herself politely, and was allowed to leave… so did most of our uniformed Officers, and the detective. Stan and Nick were about to leave – they'd called their dogs from their romping, and we were ready to settle in for the evening… it was a long day.

Stan and Aries pulled away first – giving our traditional wave – then Nick loaded Thor into his truck. He fired it up – waved, then started the drive to his house.

The neighborhood was once again silent – and the only lights now came from the streetlamps and the slightly overcast moon. I looked at Bell while she invited me into the back yard – so I could sit on the patio for a quiet moment, a cold beer, and a peaceful smoke while I watched Izzy brush Athena before they went to bed.

I eased down into my creaky lawn chair, still in uniform – making room for my holster, radio, cuffs, and mag pouches – adjusting carefully…

It was 'beer-o-clock' and I was ready to crack open that beer, and relax with nothing but the breeze as my white noise, and the gentle smoke from my cigarette rising into the evening. Over the radio Nick called out… Nick's voice crackled through the radio, tight and urgent.

"Jack… I've got eyes on a dark-tan minivan. Colorado plates. Half a block from your house."

And just like that - the night went black again.

Chapter 65

Silent, But Not... Golden

For me... It has been a lifetime of living between the calm and the chaos – only separated by a single beat of my heart. I went from settled in my chair – to rushing out the door. From Izzy brushing Athena – to her loyal charge running at my side.

My family knew – they always knew... when I didn't have time to explain – it was time to 'circle the wagons.'

I wasn't even across the lawn – I hadn't even reach my truck, and I could see Nick – his overhead lights flashing in the dark – only a half block from my house. I could hear him calling dispatch as I was opening the door – Athena jumping in and Nick: "Dispatch, I've got the suspect vehicle matching - looks like our minivan. Single occupant – Colorado plate..."

The night air was pleasant – summer-time cool, and would have been a perfect night for relaxing. I swung out of the driveway. Sharp and fast. My Ford 150 roared to life, lights snapping on as I floored it toward Nick. We were so close – I didn't have to tell Nick I was on my way. He knew it... He could see us...so did our suspect... Marion Welch.

I could hear Stan's voice over the radio – knowing he'd only left minutes before Nick did – that he wouldn't be far away either.

Seconds – it only takes seconds, but time often blurs and our senses peak – time doesn't stand still – it allows us to function at kind of a supernatural rate – un-human really... how it works... I don't know.

In those seconds – a mere 75 yards... I could see Nick's unit in a text-book vehicle stop position behind the dirty-tan minivan. Spotlight shining at the driver's rear-view mirror – Nick approaching – his gentle tap on the rear of the vehicle – leaving fingerprints in case things went bad, and his palm sweeping the side feeling for any furtive movements within the car.

He had one hand at a near ready – almost resting, and gently caressing his sidearm. The other hand gripped tight on a flashlight – the beam of light stabbing through the tinted windows.

Closer to the suspect now – I could see Nick's light shine against the blonde hair. Her eyes glued to the spotlights reflection in the rearview mirror – Nick's shadow casting its reflection onto her face. In that micro second I had to decide – and my choice was to nose-in toward the front of the minivan to prevent her from leaving. My overhead lights now cast an eerie flashing glow inside the van. With my senses glued to the picture, I could still hear all the calls from Dispatch – coordinating, directing, and communicating with the other units… but it was still a haze – a distraction from what my focus was on in that instant.

I started nosing my truck into – toward the minivan. Athena growling low. I could almost feel my pulse in the grip I had on the steering wheel. Not nervous, just excited – almost vengeful. But that thought hadn't even finished… the van's engine revved, a burst of exhaust – I heard it slam into gear – tires screeching as it lunged forward.

Nick charged back toward his truck – I was trying to flip mine around – turning sharp Athena swaying against the passenger door – then steadying herself against the dash. I cranked the wheel hard to the left – as hard as I could – flooring the gas pedal, tires now smoking… I could look Marion Welsh in the eye – her stare – that glare… was the essence of pure evil. I cranked my steering wheel a little harder.

My front bumper clipped the back of the van tearing away the plastic cover. The van shook – swerved… nearly tipped – its front tires catching traction – the van straightened, and was now on the move.

So were we.

Athena never broke eye contact with the van. She was sharp, focused, and on her game.

I straightened the wheels and mashed the pedal to the floor. The engine roared hotter, the cab vibrating with its strain. My mind went mechanical - responding without thought, every move instinct. We were closing on the van, the gap shrinking. I could hear Nick's voice over the radio, he wasn't far behind me, and he was calm in the chaos, calling out speed, direction, and damage.

I tried to position my truck so I could catch the rear bumper – you know – the "PIT" maneuver – so I could spin the van out of control and bring it to a stop, but she turned too quick. I slammed the brakes – Athena catching herself again on the dash...

I gunned it again with the smell of rubber and heated oil – the acrid smell of heated brakes stung my nose – sharp and metallic. The small engine of the minivan was no competition against our Cop's big "V-8's"

All she could do is make quick turns – and with each turn engines heated, rubber burned, and so did my focus...

My mind told me my ears could hear more units responding – boxing in side streets – blocking roads. Traffic was light for a weekday evening, but comfort had to wait. I could hear the State Police, County, and officers from neighboring agencies responding... right now it was all hands on deck... again. I could hear Wade's voice and somehow I knew he'd never be far from my 'six' either.

Lights flashing against store front windows. Blowing through intersections I had to stop for – and although I wasn't a religious man – I prayed she wouldn't kill someone. It took me off guard but now realized... we were downtown.

The traffic may have been light, but I knew by now employees would be leaving late night jobs soon, and this had to end. Now.

I could hear Stan's voice – but didn't make out where he was. Wade too. I knew he was closing in, but from where? We were headed right for a busy entertainment section of town. I held in the breath I'd already been holding for an eternity. Heartbeat pounding in my ears. One last chance to "PIT" this chase...

I could see flashing lights from the units blocking the side streets to the intersection we were now entering. It was my last chance. I punched the gas – engine revved. Athena pressed against the back of the seat.

With one bright flash of confusion – my headlights reflecting off of the Sheriff's logo in front of me as I closed the distance. I slammed on the brakes – now soft – spongy even – hard to stop – I tried to miss Wades Chevy Suburban from the County Sheriff's as it slammed broadside into the passenger side of the minivan. But I couldn't.

Glass – chrome – body parts from all our vehicles... dancing with delicate precision in near orchestration now crashing through the tangled spinning ballet of twisted metal. Then the sudden silence when it all stops where each heartbeat felt like hours. My truck coming to rest against Wade's Suburban – the hood of my truck buckled and bent. Athena on the passenger side floor – tangled in the web of mic chords and papers.

I beat the door of my truck several times before it would open forcing me back as I was trying to escape the seatbelt catching on all of my duty gear. Amid steam – the smoke – the haze of impact... I could see Marion Welch run from the minivan – blond wig falling to the ground from a dazed shaking head. Running – staggering maybe even limping like a wounded predator toward a mob of fleeing teenagers at the theater.

I couldn't fire my pistol – too many kids. I had to clear my head, but no time. My left leg felt numb, but that wasn't going to stop me. I could tell without seeing – and my ears still ringing that the presence of Officers all around me were like the wave of blue crashing down on the queen of violence that plagued our city.

I shook it off, but where's Athena? I called to her, but she was now a ghost in the shadows queen Marion tried to hide in.

Screams – shouts – panic from young voices – the nightmare any cop dreads. And there she stood – ragged, torn and disheveled – Marion Welch now holding a teenage girl around the neck with her left arm, and a syringe in her right hand. All I could see in that moment – was the face of my Izzy in the terror of this young stranger.

Welch was panting with a mix of adrenaline and exhaustion. So was I. All I could see in the eyes of this teenage girl was the same fear my granddaughter Izzy had.

"It's over Marion" as I tried to catch my breath.

"It's not over – 'til I say it's over" she spurted – her voice tinged with the hint of that nasal tone – reminding me of what our FBI profiler said about Welch – always wanting to be the one 'in control.'

She knew she was surrounded – she probably knew we wouldn't negotiate. Now was the time for quick thinking – and even sharper reflexes. And like a ghost from the mist – a shadow springing from the darkness… without any thought for her own safety. Athena.

As if I watched a scene – disembodied from myself… a single leap – a single roar without command… where eons of evolution met with pure determination connected in near silence – maybe even peaceful… as if time slowed to watch poetry fly through the air came split second salvation where once again…

Teeth met flesh.

Wade rushed in breaking the hold Welch had on the girl. Athena now in a fight for her life, and whether or not she realized it. She fought on. Before any of us could count how many beats of a heart it would take to stop the syringe – the stab - Marion's arm flailing with every attempt broke free long enough to make one final swing toward Athena, but she missed.

Something so small… something so invisible – yet so deadly. Athena made one final lunge to stop her, but Marion's swing meant for my little girl – my partner… missed, and landed sharp – deep… into her own flesh.

The syringe was aimed for the dog, but really meant for something else – someone else… and as I watched her – I thought to myself "why was Marion Welch waiting… watching… outside my house."

But after the chaos of snapping jaws and flailing limbs, the needle found an unintended target. She collapsed – fell back against the theater wall, the fight draining from her as quickly as the plunger had emptied. Her breathing became ragged almost immediately, each breath a visible struggle as her chest rose and fell in increasingly shallow gasps. The blue crept across her lips like spilled ink, and her jaw locked tight as her muscles seized. The gurgling sounds echoed off the brick walls, as her body became rigid and trembled against the concrete. Athena backed away, still focused, but sensing this was no longer a threat but something else entirely - something final and desperate playing out the final piece where the queen gave up her final move.

The silence in that moment watching what we could not stop should have been rewarding. But it wasn't. It was real. It was messy. But it was over.

The reality – the exhaustion – the pain… I nearly collapsed, but I sat on the ground amid the broken glass and shattered lives – with parents consoling kids and ambulances arriving – the silence in my mind ebbed back to the turmoil surrounding me. Wade limped over to me – stood tall, and extended his hand to help me walk to an awaiting ambulance. He whispered with a choke…

"I'm here…"

I don't know how long I sat there, and probably didn't care. While EMT's bandaged Athena's feet – her head resting on my lap – my mind drifted to my family and I felt for my phone, but couldn't find it. I looked around – at my pockets… patting myself. When I looked back up the Chief locked his eyes onto mine – gently smiled… "I already called Bell – Jack – she knows it's over too."

All I could do in that moment, was smile back, and asked…

"Does this mean I get a new truck?

Chapter 66

Big Boy Games

The only true silence – comes from peace. And no one loves peace more than Cops and Soldiers. Wade and I were both.

They say there is no rest for the wicked… I've learned – the righteous don't need it.

But rest we did – with family all around in the cool evenings of the mountains – at a cabin that once gave sanctuary – now giving us solitude.

Grandkids played with the dogs. The sounds of splashing in the creek sang the song of joy – and calm once more filled my soul.

My Nurse - Bell told us that Wades and my bruises from the crash were healing nicely, and when she turned back into my wife she teased me about driving too fast.

This wasn't just a week of respite – it was a reunion of family. A family that extended beyond tradition. A family that embraced a cause – bonded through duty… and united a community…

This is a family that survived playing **"Big Boy Games"** and knew how to throw a party.

Yes. We were all there… and I may have even heard – the newly promoted 'Lieutenant' Sanchez – Tony… really laugh. He laughed even harder when… he learned his uncle survived the ambush with us… in Iraq.

Stan and Nick told everyone about the loudspeaker at the motel – I teased Valenti about his Hollywood Homeless disguise… but Wade?

Yes I teased him about always 'crashing through' at the last second…

"I'm here!"

But with the joy and levity came the memories of fear – the horror, and the pain. The looks on my granddaughter's face – the look in her eyes. The courage it took for her to do – what most kids wouldn't.

It was all there – in the meadow by a cabin – far up a canyon that sheltered us from the summer heat. It was all there – the friendship. The family... the memories.

But peace will come when courage wins.

**

It was a good week in the mountains... but we still had work to do. So the calm turns back into the routine of life, and our everyday tasks return. We wake – drink coffee, a little breakfast? I give my wife a ride to work... in my personal truck.

Athena loved her hugs from Bell as we dropped her off at work. I looked around the hospital parking lot – in part because of always being vigilant, or maybe even kind of hoping I'd see that little blue Subaru the nurse – that Jesse Wilkes drove, so I could apologize for what happened... and when I couldn't see it – I asked...

Bell said she no longer work at the hospital – I asked "why?"

"She told us a distant aunt left her some money and that she could do some volunteer work – somewhere in some islands..."

We both paused – eyes locked onto each other... "J.W. and an aunt? You don't suppose...?"

I don't know if it would have been coincidence – or not, but then again... I've seen too much not to question it.

Experience has taught me that coincidences are often anything but, and that vigilance is the price of protecting what you love.

**

Like I've said – the routine of life goes on – even when things like an honors ceremony are involved. The Chief wanted all of us in our "monkey-suit" class-A uniforms so the Governor, County Sheriff, and Mayor could tell us what a good job we did – when we simply did what we were supposed to do. Cops, Soldiers, and every kind of first responder knows…

"We may walk among the Sheep – but make no mistake… We Are The Sheepdogs."

The ceremony was nice – lots of nice words… each one of us we awarded a little ribbon.

The Governor looked at my wife – Bell sitting with my whole family on the front row – and invited her to come up to the stand to pin the little ribbon onto my uniform with Athena standing stoic at my side… but really – what I remember most wasn't the speeches – the ribbons – or even the tears of gratitude in my wife's eyes…

It was when I looked back down to that front row – the eyes of my granddaughter Izzy locked onto mine smiling, and she simply…

Blinked Three Times.

Chapter 67

Open Sky

Peace is often an illusion… tranquility – a dream.

And yet, for a moment, I believed in both. But every man needs to chase them, if only to remember why he fights. And just when you start to believe in them, life reminds you that the story isn't over.

The warmth of the time we all spent at the cabin still lingered in my memory – the laughter, the clink of glasses, the quiet sigh of relief that comes when a job is done. But the edges of that warmth felt fragile, like smoke slipping through your fingers. Outside, the world was still turning, indifferent to victories won or battles survived. I felt it in the air: the subtle shift, the tension under the calm.

Somewhere beyond the hills, beyond the streets I know so well, something was waiting - patient, silent, and relentless. And as always, the question lingered: were we ready to meet it when it came?

The Chief had me working with our States wildlife Officers – we'd been teaching them how to use their new K9 division to track evidence – and maybe reduce the poaching… it had been working well, better than expected and…

Word got around… There were officers from Alaska, and even the Montana wildlife service's that arranged for us to teach some workshops on how to use K9's. They saw our success, and wanted to see if they too could benefit from how we'd been doing things. And that's how it ended up – two men, one dog, and a mission that was supposed to be routine.

And at first – it was…

Wade came over the night before we left for our adventure – he offered to drive us, but I told him the Chief already arranged for our State Wildlife pilot to take us. Wade hung out with us for a while - the house was full. It was the way Bell liked it.

The grandsons were camped out on the living room floor, shouting at the TV while some racing game buzzed with engine noise. Athena lay stretched out between them, ears twitching every time one of them yelled, "Go! Go! Go!"

They invited me to join in – playing the game with them, but they beat me every time… Bell was in her chair, pretending to read, but mostly watching us. She always did that the night before I left - said it was her way of "taking a picture without a camera."

I had to finish packing my bag – and left for a minute, and when I returned, I leaned against the doorway, mug in hand, just… taking it all in.

"Routine trip," I told her later, when all the kids were asleep and the house had gone still. "Teach a few classes, shake a few hands, I'll be back before you can miss me."

She smiled - but her eyes said more than her words did. "You always say that."

"I always mean it."

"I know" as her smile never quite made it to her eyes.

When I zipped up my bag later that night, I laid Athena's vest on top – her badge polished, the patch stitched clean. For a moment, my hand lingered on it. It wasn't superstition. Just… respect. You don't walk into the field without remembering what it asks of you.

The airstrip the next morning was quiet, the kind of quiet that comes before sunrise has the nerve to break the chill. I was expecting something bigger - maybe a twin-prop, something with room to stretch. But the plane parked on the tarmac looked like it had stories older than I did. A sun-faded Cessna 185, paint peeling at the tail, a couple of fresh dings along the wing edges that told me she'd been through weather and worse.

And then there was Skip.

He was leaning against the wing, coffee in one hand, clipboard in the other - mid-60s, weathered, lean as a fence post. His jacket bore the insignia: State Wildlife Division.

"You must be Jack," he said, offering a hand that felt like sandpaper and trust.

"And you must be the man brave enough to fly this thing."

He grinned. "She's not much to look at, but she'll get us there. Name's Skip. Forty years chasing elk surveys and duck counts. This old bird's done more miles than a Greyhound bus."

Athena trotted up, nose to the wind, tail wagging.

"Well, look at that," Skip chuckled, crouching to meet her. "You bringing the muscle, or the brains?"

"Both," I said. "Depends who you ask."

He laughed, a gravelly, easy sound. "Any dog that gives me the once-over before letting me touch her's got sense. She can ride up front if she promises not to bite the pilot."

By the time we were strapped in, I could already tell I liked the man.

There's something about old-timers - the ones who've lived their share of long winters and bad landings - that settles your nerves.

We lifted off just as the sun spilled over the Wasatch range. The mountains fell away beneath us, the light turning the peaks gold. Athena's head rested on my knee; her eyes followed the shifting shadows on the floorboard like she was tracking clouds.

Skip talked as he flew, showing me which instruments indicated what, and how each knob and lever made the plane do things. "This gauge shows altitude - altimeter. This here's the throttle - push in to climb, pull back to descend. And see these pedals? That's how you steer - most folks don't expect that." He was telling stories of his time serving in the Air Force – a C-130 Pilot… he also remembered narrow ridges, glacial lakes, and one time he had to land on a gravel bar with a bear watching. He grinned as he talked – it told me everything I needed to know about him. He was cool-headed, confident, and he loved flying.

I laughed. "You ever scared?"

He shrugged. "If you ain't scared once in a while, you ain't paying attention."

As we were getting ready to land in Idaho for a quick fuel stop, Skip wasn't hitting the usual place on the runway to slow the plane and taxi in... I had to ask... and he laughed:

"Small plane like this? – If I drop the flaps just right and catch the right breeze, well I could probably set her down in a grocery store parking lot – watch – I'll show ya..."

I watched as he cranked the flaps – cut the throttle, and then pulled the nose of the plane back, and... he just about – even did... set the plane down close to the refueling station. Almost like landing a helicopter. I was impressed because – I'd never seen that done before.

As the plane was being fueled I admitted, "Always wanted to learn to fly. Closest I ever came was getting dropped out the back of a C-130 - the old Hercules - a flying freight train that could take a beating and still bring you home, or in a chopper back when I was in the Army." Like I said: Skip told me – he'd flown the Hercules when he 'was in' the Air Force... and who knows – he could have been flying one I'd ridden in...?

"Tell you what," Skip said, glancing over the dash. "You teach me how to make my dogs listen like Athena there, and I'll show you what keeps a bird like this in the air."

I grinned. "Deal."

And we shook on it, 7,000 feet above the plains - a pact sealed by wind and trust.

The training in Anaconda – Montana, went smoother than I'd dared hope. The officers from Alaska, and the ones from Montana were skeptical at first, watching Athena like she was some kind of circus act. But once she started tracking, their tune changed fast. She picked up trails invisible to the eye, signaled on a shell casing half-buried in mud, and when a call came in about fresh prints on the ridge, she went from demonstration to deployment in seconds.

The mock drill turned real when a cornered poacher refused to drop his rifle. The standoff stretched thin. Then Athena flanked him - silent as breath - and when he turned, she was already there, disarming and holding him in place until the others moved in.

Skip was there too, watching from the truck, wide-eyed.

"Holy hell," he said later, shaking his head. "She's better than most of the men I've worked with."

"She's better than me," I told him. And I meant it.

That night, over coffee, we laughed about everything from bad camp food to busted radios. Two men on different ends of the same road - one who flew over the wild, one who walked through it - both just trying to leave it a little better than they found it.

The next leg of the trip was supposed to be a short one – a couple of days in Hardin – just a little east of Billings. A routine hop, a few more officers, one more demonstration before heading home. Skip said we'd be back before the coffee in Anaconda cooled off.

The forecast looked fine. A little turbulence expected over the ranges - nothing unusual. Skip said we'd be flying along the highway routes so we could bypass any trouble.

I remember thinking how calm the air felt that morning. Funny, how the world always feels so still right before it breaks.

Our ride to Hardin was a little bumpy. The look on Skip's face gave me confidence that we would be fine.

Our training session there was typical, and before we left, Skip wanted to take me to a place all 'Vets' should visit. And our visit to the Little Bighorn monument about 10 miles or so south of town was humbling. Our time there was a mix of duty, and reverence. The Custer National Cemetery – like all the other places we honor our Military fallen – brings back the memories of war, or loss, but also…

The memories of where I met my wife – my first K9 Gunner… and the bonds we make amid the losses. Moments like this make these kinds of trips worth the effort. Skip wasn't just flying me around – he was becoming my friend. I told Skip "I need to make a weekend trip up here with my wife – she'd love to see this too…"

Skip told me "Hell – Jack – just say the word, and I'll fly ya both – even all three of you up here… just say the word!" as he clapped me on the back. I could see his eyes smile – even through his 'aviator' sun glasses.

We finished up our last training workshop with the Montana Wildlife Officers, and prepared to leave for home in the morning. Everywhere we went – Athena was the star who shone, and the clown that could make us laugh.

Chapter 68

Wild

The flight home started easy.

The kind of morning that tricks you into thinking you've earned a quiet ending.

Skip was in rare form - humming off-key, reminded me of Wade. Skip was tapping the dash, bragging that if the brass ever put him behind a desk, he'd retire to Alaska and fly fish until his arms gave out.

He told me "I'm not the kind of 'catch and release kind of guy…" and before he could finish – I chuckled…

"You're the – kind of 'hook 'em and cook 'em kind of guy?" Skip laughed a little – shaking his head, and even ribbed me about how Athena had stolen the spotlight.

"Careful, Jack," he grinned. "Word gets out that she's the brains of the operation, they'll start sending her to conferences instead of you."

I smiled, scratching behind her ear. "Wouldn't be the first time my partner got more attention."

Skip laughed, shaking his head. "She's something special. Never seen a dog so steady. You're lucky, you know that?"

"I know."

The mountains rolled beneath us in layers of gray and green, sunlight breaking through the clouds like veins of gold. From up here, the world looked peaceful. Small. Like maybe we'd finally learned how to live with it.

Skip checked the gauges, and then leaned back. "We'll cut south once we hit the ridge line - that'll shave twenty minutes off. You'll be home by dinner."

"Bell will like that," I said. "She pretends she doesn't worry, but I know better."

"Good woman," he said, smiling. "Keep her close, Jack. They don't make many like that anymore."

Then his hand froze midair.

At first, I thought he'd dropped something - but then his eyes flickered, unfocused, and he made a low sound, like a groan caught in his throat.

"Skip?"

He winced, hand to his chest. "Ah - hell… Jack…"

The plane drifted slightly, nose dipping before he pulled it back just in time. His breathing turned ragged.

"Something's wrong," he said through clenched teeth. "Arm's numb. Damn it"

"Skip, stay with me. What do I do?"

He tried to speak again, but the words broke apart. His eyes darted between the gauges and me.

"You… got this," his voice rasped - the words barely audible. "Just… keep her steady…"

And then his head fell forward against the harness.

For a moment, I didn't move. The world narrowed to the sound of the engine and the rush of wind across the windshield.

"Skip?"

No response.

I grabbed the yoke with one hand, reaching over with the other to shake his shoulder. "Skip! Hey - look at me, man. Come on!"

Nothing.

Athena whimpered from the back seat, ears pressed flat, eyes locked on him. She knew.

"Don't do this," I said - louder now. "Come on, buddy, wake up! You hear me?!"

The silence that followed was worse than any storm I'd ever heard.

The plane drifted again, left wing dipping. I fought the controls, forcing it level, breathing through the panic clawing its way up my throat. My hand found the headset - my mind racing for what Skip had said before. The altimeter, the compass, the throttle… everything blurred together in a mess of noise and instinct.

"Okay… okay…" I muttered to myself. "Keep her steady, Jack. Keep her steady."

But the truth hit hard. I didn't know how. Not really. Not enough to bring her home.

I looked over one last time. Skip's face was still, peaceful in a way that tore something open inside me. The man who'd taught me to trust the sky was gone - and I was still flying it.

"Alright, partner," I whispered, glancing at Athena. "Looks like it's just us now."

Her eyes met mine -steady, unwavering -as if to say, 'Then fly.'

The horizon tilted again. The Uinta mountain range rose ahead, jagged and merciless. And for the first time in a long time, I felt small - a man clinging to a machine he didn't understand, talking to ghosts while the wind screamed outside the glass.

"Skip," I said quietly, almost to myself. "You said I've got this… I hope to God you're right."

He'd told me to keep her steady. So that's what I did - for as long as I could.

I looked at Athena – her head tilted slightly, and I reminded her something ol' Charlie once told me… "Any time you claim to know something – like an ability – or even try to explain something… it has to be the same to all kinds of situations that compare to each other – unless – there's a good explanation as to why something you can prove works against it."

So I slipped the headset on and keyed the mic "mayday – mayday… I'm in a small plane heading south, and the pilot is…" I couldn't bring myself to say the words…

"I'm alone up here – the pilot can't fly!"

All I could hear was static.

I adjusted the dial, tried again. "Mayday, mayday, small aircraft over the Uintas - pilot's down, repeat, pilot is down - requesting assistance."

Still nothing. Just that hollow hiss of empty air.

Athena's ears perked, nose to the glass. I could feel the vibration of her low whine against the back of my seat. The altimeter needle dipped another notch. My heartbeat pounded in my temples, louder than the engine.

"Okay… we can do this…" I said aloud, mostly for her, partly for me.

The yoke felt stiff - foreign - like wrestling the steering wheel of a runaway truck on ice. The plane responded too much, then not enough. I eased back, breathing slow.

The mountains were closer now - ridges folding in on each other, snow still clinging to the shaded crests. There was no highway, no flat ground, just pines and granite and nowhere to go.

I think I can see a small meadow – something… maybe a little flat – a place to aim for?

"Skip," I whispered, glancing sideways. His head leaned against the door, still. "You said I've got this… so help me prove it."

I trimmed the nose up slightly, felt the tail jitter. The wind picked up - a sudden downdraft shoved us sideways. The plane lurched hard; Athena braced herself, claws scraping the metal floor.

"Hold on, girl!"

The stall warning blared - that sharp, steady scream that means the sky's had enough of you. My instincts took over; I dropped the nose, praying for lift. The treetops flashed closer. The wind howled like a living thing.

Then - impact.

A metallic shriek. The right wing clipped first - tore loose. The cabin twisted sideways, weightless for a heartbeat. My shoulder slammed against the door.

Glass exploded. Athena barked once - sharp, trees and dirt scraped against the plane like whips against metal – or sandpaper against glass, and then a second hit crushed all the sound into thunder.

Then silence.

A ringing filled my ears, thin and high, like the world had been stripped of sound. Smoke drifted in lazy ribbons through what was left of the cockpit. The dashboard lights blinked weakly, fading one by one.

My hand still gripped the yoke, frozen in place. The smell of fuel and pine needles filled the air. For a moment, I wasn't sure if we were upside down or buried or both.

Then I heard her - Athena. A soft, broken whine.

"I'm here, girl," I rasped, voice shredded. I turned, pain lancing through my ribs. She was tangled behind the seat but alive - her eyes bright, tail trembling. I reached out, fingers brushing her fur. "We made it… we're okay."

I don't know how long we stayed like that. We were just breathing, trying to understand what happened, but we were still breathing.

The world outside was quiet again. The wind had calmed. Leaves and dust drifted lazily through the broken canopy like snowflakes - soft, almost merciful.

And somewhere beyond the wreckage, I could hear water. A stream, faint and steady.

I looked across the torn meadow - the bent grass, the twisted fuselage - and I spoke, though I didn't know if I was talking to Athena, to Skip, or to myself.

I could already tell, but call it habit maybe? I felt the side of Skip's neck – no pulse. Nothing. I sat back into my seat – Athena resting her head on my shoulder. I looked out through the shattered window at the forest. I tried to gather my thoughts.

The *wild* is *untamed, uncultivated, and unpredictable.* It describes the rawness of a storm over the mountains, the call of a wolf beneath the moon, or the wind that bends the grass without asking permission. The wild moves according to its own rhythm - not the order of man, but the pulse of creation itself.

I tried to shove open the door, but it wouldn't budge. I leaned against Skip and apologized "sorry bud" and then braced Athena with my right hand holding her back – then kicked as hard as I could. The door fell to the ground, and Athena followed me out of the plane.

I felt myself all over – I checked Athena. I could tell she was shaken, and I had some bruises, but the tough little plane got us to the ground… and we were alone.

Alone in the wild.

To live by the rules of the wild is to learn from the weather that shapes the land, and from the trials that shape the soul. It means understanding that survival isn't only about endurance, but about harmony: knowing when to fight, when to yield, and when to simply stand still and listen to the wind.

I looked down at Athena – still shaken from the crash. I stroked her fur – our eyes met and I told her "The wild isn't just *out there*. It's *in here.*" As I held my hand to my chest – then smiled at her "And its rules, once understood, can guide us through every kind of terrain. From these mountain paths to the tangled landscapes of our own lives."

The rules of the wild - Nature's laws - are unwritten and unique to each individual, shaped by the relationships we form and the circumstances we face.

I looked at the meadow – scarred and torn, and then the trees that stopped us. But all I could really see was Skip.

The moment we step beyond the safety of civilization and into nature's domain, we enter a game where the rules are absolute, and there are no second chances. In the wild, you cannot break. You cannot bleed. You must become one with the beauty you admire… knowing it is trying to kill you.

And in the end, those rules teach a simple truth: **Nature always wins.**

I fumbled through the wreckage to pull free what I could – what we would need to get us through the night. I found a space-blanket and covered Skip as best I could.

I don't know how long I stood there thinking – wondering if anyone heard our call for help, but I stand at the crossroads of survival, where the only refuge was the knowledge I carried - the lessons learned from standing face to face with nature's unmatched energy, armed only with the will to endure.

The mountains whispered to me long before I even knew their names. They were my teacher – I was the student, and now… comes the test.

Chapter 69

Big Boys in the Wild

"Be strong enough to stand alone. Be yourself enough to stand apart. And be wise enough to stand together when the time comes." Charlie's words echoed through my head one more time - but this time, as I looked into the eyes of my partner.

"Little girl," I said softly, "it's just you and me."

Her look - stoic, yet steady - said it all. Like she was answering me without words: *"Yes… we'll face this together."*

I scavenged what I could from the wreckage - a small tarp, a few flares, and Skip's and my sidearm's - and extra ammo. It wasn't much. The snacks we'd packed wouldn't last long. Then I found my bag - unzipped it - and the first thing my hand touched was a pack of cigarettes… and my lighter.

"How about we take an inventory of what we've got girl" Athena watching my every move… then she froze – ears up, and she turned and looked deep into the forest…

"Yeah – I know girl – we need to take an inventory of what's out there watching us too."

Athena looked back at me and all I could do is smile for her, and before I could even realize what I was saying – the words fell from me "we're not alone girl, and we're not at the top of the food chain any more…"

I pat the side of my leg – and felt the first of the many bruises that would haunt me. Athena knew what it meant and she leaned in closer to me.

I lit a cigarette – looked over the meadow, and then back to the forest. I wasn't new to any of this – not really, but all the times I'd been in the mountains before – I learned from hard experience, and I learned to expect the unexpected.

I don't how know how long I'd spent gathering things from the plane – maybe I was a bit dazed still from the impact of the crash. Maybe a bit dazed still from losing a friend. I had to shake it off – I had to get into the game. This was a big-boy game with no second chances, but then again – that's how it's always been with me.

The sun was still high in the sky, and by now I'm sure our arrival – or non arrival at the municipal airport would have been reported. Or would it? I know Skip filed a flight plan, but I kept second guessing myself. Thoughts coming and going with my mind reeling, and wondering if I should try to walk to safety – or to wait?

I looked at the wreckage again – my friend still sitting in the pilot seat. I knew I wouldn't leave a man behind – I'd wait.

"We'll get you home, Skip," I whispered, looking at the space blanket. "I promise you that." Athena looked at me like she understood.

I told Athena to stay – she didn't. She followed me into the meadow – out into the open. I scanned the sky to see if I could see anything. I couldn't. My ears were still ringing – I tried to listen for the sounds of engines – anything.

Nothing but silence.

"Think Jack – Think!"

Athena followed me back to the plane. I looked at the space blanket covering Skip – wishing I could see it move. I reached for the mic again – twisted some dials on the panel, tapped the mic into my palm a few times, but nothing. No matter how many times I wanted to hear something come over the radio – it was nothing but silent.

I looked at Athena "well that did a whole lot of good – didn't it?" She tilted her head – then turned to look toward the meadow. Maybe I heard it too – the sound of an engine.

We ran out into the open again and looked, but couldn't see anything. Athena kept looking. Nothing. But we heard something – it wasn't my imagination. I know it.

"Come on girl" as I ran back toward the plane – "I got an idea."

I fumbled around some more – felt under the seats – apologized to Skip for reaching past him – but I couldn't find what I hoped to locate. Athena looked more puzzled than ever.

"He's gotta have some – somewhere girl" hoping she could understand what I was saying… I tried to reach through the rear seats into the storage area – deeper this time, but the plane was too crushed.

I jumped back out – and grabbed a broken branch from one of the trees, and began to pry at the outer door to the storage compartment. I chopped away at it, and finally got the branch into the cracks enough to pry it open. Found it.

I looked at my little girl – still watching my every move – "I knew Skip would have a tool box – I think all pilots keep tools in their planes."

I grabbed the branch again – and the tool box. I tried to open the cowling that covered the engine – but had to use the branch again to break away the twisted metal. I felt around the bottom of the engine – and found the drain plug for the oil.

I found the socket that matched the drain plug, and then stopped. "So girl – what are we going to use to catch all this oil in?" I looked around – I had to find something. I stepped back toward the opening – stepped onto the door I had to kick open that broke off… standing there on the broken door – I looked down. Athena looked at me as if she could say… *"it was there underneath you the whole time."*

I shook my head – as if she had really said that – "Ok smarty pants – rub it in!"

I used my pocket knife and shredded strips of fabric from the seats, and tore out pieces of foam padding. "Ya think this'll make some black smoke girl?" I asked. Athena just looked at me like I was crazy. I pulled it all over to where the bent broken door could catch the oil I'd drain from the engine. I tried to work fast, but didn't want to work sloppy.

"Slow down Jack" I thought – slow is smooth, and smooth is fast…

I finally got the drain plug loosened and started draining some of the oil. I knew car and truck engines could hold a lot of oil, but didn't want to waste it all on one shot. I knew there were fire restrictions during the summer heat – that any black smoke would attract a lot of attention – so… "Here we go girl – let's see if this works."

I carefully dragged the broken door with my oily rags into the open. I paused – hoping to hear something hopeful. Nothing – nothing still, but – there was no wind – no breeze – so – I thought to myself – this smoke should rise straight up.

I waited for a minute – debating whether I should wait – or light my signal fire now. I turned to Athena hoping she would have the answer. She just looked at me.

"Ok then – I'll light it now girl."

I found a dry twig, and lit the end of it with my lighter. I gently held it with the palm of my hand so I wouldn't blow it out when I moved. I slowly lowered it to the slime I concocted, and… nothing - it just went out.

I tried some dry grass, still nothing. "Why won't this light girl?" she just looked back toward the plane – our 'camp' site… "Ok then – maybe you have the right idea – more heat!"

She followed me back to the plane, and I found one of the flares Skip had. We took it back to the meadow – lit the flare, and… Athena jumped slightly at the popping when the flare ignited – and when the shredded fabric, foam and oil caught – it bellowed black smoke like nothing else, and stung our eyes – smelled like burning tires.

"Well girl" as I coughed a little – "now all we can do is hope the smoke will speak for us."

We stood there in the meadow for a while watching the smoke rise – dark and greasy. I smiled at Athena "you know girl – if 'uncle Wade' were here – he'd be dancing around the fire like some Comanche."

The sun was finding its way toward the peaks surrounding us – the shadows now longer and the forest growing darker. "Come on girl – I think we need to make a place for us to get some rest."

We walked back to the plane – I grabbed the branch I'd used to pry open the parts of the plane, and started digging. I thought we could make a small fire pit, and keep warm – then use some rocks to surround it so – we could put them in the ground later, and cover them with dirt and sleep on them – because, as I turned to Athena again: "it gets really cold up here – even in the summer time." Athena seemed to know what I was saying. She always has.

I kept digging – working to make our visit here as pleasant as I could. I felt fur against my left shoulder… Athena was digging with me. Through all of what we had gone through – I still had to chuckle.

The night was the worst. Summer in the Uintas doesn't forgive mistakes, and still reaches freezing when the sun goes down.

After the crash, even a single breath felt sharp against the cold. I moved Athena close, feeling her warmth seep into me. She curled against my chest like a living blanket, her steady presence was the only thing keeping me grounded.

I'd heated some rocks by the fire I managed to get going. Placing the hot stones inside the small trench, and then covering them carefully with some dirt. I created a little pocket of warmth - a crude, improvised heater. Athena pressed closer, her fur brushing the sweat and soot from my face.

Sleep came in short bursts. Every breeze, every snap of a distant branch, kept me alert. I kept my pistol holstered – and Skip's in my hand while I kept my ears open for the hum of a helicopter or kind of engine, for any sound that meant rescue was near.

By the time dawn broke, painting the peaks in gold and shadow, I was stiff and raw, but alive. Athena nudged me, impatient for food and water. I moved slowly, gathering what I could from the stream and fed her the last of our snacks, still scanning the trees for any hint of movement.

Athena seemed to thank me for her breakfast – though it wasn't much. "Come on girl – how about we send some more smoke signals?" She stretched like she was camping – enjoying the nature, but I reminded her that – although this world is beautiful… it's dangerous.

Hours passed. The smoke rose – once again filling our world with the stench of hope – and the acid that burned our noses.

I listened, watched, and waited, telling myself: *Patience. Keep her safe – keep her steady. That's all you can do.*

Then we heard it - faint, almost imperceptible. The sound of an engine. Athena's ears perked – I think mine did too. It got louder.

I ran out to the meadow – Athena at my heel. We saw it – a small plane. It circled around the meadow – a couple thousand feet above, but tipped its wings and circled just enough to let us know we were seen.

Being alone is a power very few people can handle. But I wasn't alone – even though I felt an emptiness like a mission I didn't complete. A feeling I had to accept – that was a part of the life I chose to live.

Too many times I donned the armor – too many times I walked the line of duty prepared to face the inevitable knowing… what we hold precious is the illusion of security.

Gunner saw me through combat, and taught so many of my partners how to serve me. Tina knew me like she was a part of me. I could save Gunner, but I couldn't save Tina. It was the little girl sitting at my side that gave me the strength to get through – when I didn't know I could.

So I sat waiting by the remains of loyalty and friendship – the crash, and the man I'd only known a short time – only comforted by the companion that saw me through when I thought I'd seen enough.

So we sat. We waited…

And I hate waiting.

Chapter 70

I'm Here

My scars tell the story of how life tried to break me…but couldn't.

The sun was high in the sky – the mountain air warm enough for me to set my jacket aside. But doubt started creeping in when the help I hoped would come… didn't.

The black smoke from our signal fire smoldered – still rising, but fading as the last of the engine oil and fabric began to die. I clapped my hands – Athena jumped to attention – "come on girl – let's play old school."

I gathered up some of the pine branches and green leaves from the nearby aspen trees – and we got the smoke going again… but for how long?

I was hungry – I'd given Athena what little we had, and that was gone. I knew it wasn't enough to keep her going… it'd been 24 hours or more since we'd eaten, and I knew we'd have to eat soon.

I knew my wife would be worried sick because… I was starting to worry too. But I had to be strong – I had to keep strong… because this was the moment when strength is all I had.

Wade… where are you?

The fire had burned down to a whisper beneath gray ash. I watched the embers fade while Athena sat close beside me. Her eyes locked onto the tree line, as if she could will something – someone… anything to appear. I brushed my hand along her shoulder, feeling the steady rise and fall of her breath.

"Good girl," I whispered, though I wasn't sure who I was trying to reassure… her, or me.

The breeze shifted. A faint tremor rolled through the air - deep, distant sounds – familiar and rhythmic.

For a second I thought it was my heart, thudding too hard in my chest. Then I heard it again. The familiar throbbing of chopper blades.

I froze. Athena's ears shot up, and she turned toward the sound. She wasn't questioning – she wasn't doubting, she just knew.

I stood, scanning the horizon, the bright glare forcing tears into my eyes. At first it was only the sound, and then a speck appeared over the ridge, growing larger, shaping into a familiar outline.

"Come on," I said, my voice barely more than a breath. "Come on…"

Athena barked - sharp, urgent… or maybe it was excitement. The helicopter tilted into a slow circle above the valley.

I waved both arms with my jacket in hand. Then I stumbled forward, almost tripping over a rock. The motion must have caught someone's eye because the chopper dipped, swung back, and came lower.

The sunlight hit the windshield just right - and for a split second, I saw the shape of the man leaning out the side door. Ball cap turned backward. Aviator glasses.

Wade.

Of course it was Wade. He'd have volunteered before they even finished saying my name.

A flood of everything hit at once - relief, disbelief, and the kind of ache that only comes when you've held too much in for too long. I dropped to a knee beside Athena, wrapping an arm around her.

"You did good, girl… you did so damn good."

The wind from the rotors blew away the smoke and ash, scattered it, and lifted it away into wild spirals. The noise broke the silence we'd been used to, but it was the best sound I'd ever heard.

Wade hopped to the ground before the bird made final touchdown – he crouched as he ran to me then he straightened… and with his huge corn-fed hillbilly smile shouted above the sound of the helicopter – shook his head with a laugh…

"I'm here!"

Wade pulled me into a big bear-hug embrace. He didn't care who was watching – neither did I. Athena jumped between us as if to say *"where's my hug"* – we both hugged her like we never wanted to let her go. And then as I looked over Wade's shoulder I could see the flight Paramedic walk toward us.

Before he got up to us I told him: "Skip – the pilot – he's still in the plane."

The flight medic told me "Sir, I need to assess your injuries."

With all the strength I had left I told him "Take care of Skip first."

The look on my face told both of them more than any words could. Wade – still bracing me as I stood said "We'll get him."

"No – I made him a promise… one I intend to keep."

Wade took me by the arm – Athena at my side, and we walked toward the plane with the medic following.

The chopper pilot walked up to us – removed his helmet… he was slightly older – I could tell he'd seen his days in the service as well. He walked like a soldier – professional… kind eyes.

"Sgt. Duncan? We've got a weight problem. Altitude's killing our lift capacity. This little Bell 206 Jet Ranger… well - I can take the deceased and one passenger, or I can take you and your dog with medical personnel. Your call."

Wade started to object. I cut him off with only a look.

"Skip goes home first. We wait for the second bird."

The Pilot – I could tell, respected my decision immediately. "Understood – Jack, we'll be back within the hour or so. I've got some water and some sandwiches in the bird."

He stood with us for a moment, and both the pilot and the medic gave me one last moment with the friend I only knew for a short time… Wade stood back holding Athena – stroking her fur while I walked up to the wreckage.

I stepped over broken branches and twisted metal – glass and the remaining shreds of the seats I used to build a signal fire… I slipped the space blanket away from Skip, undid his safety harness – and brushed his grey hair as best I could with my hand.

Skip's eyes – now closed… looked pleasant – kind of like he was sleeping. A slight smile graced what was once his Veteran strength – a look as if he passed doing what he loved doing… the most.

I pat his shoulder – all I could muster was "you're going home Skip… I promised you – and you're going home."

I zipped up his Wildlife Resources Coat – and as I began to – maybe even try to lift him from his seat, I stumbled – fell back to the ground. Wade tried to catch me, but he simply helped guide me easily to the ground.

As the chopper Pilot and Medic began to lift my friend from the plane – with everything I had left – I forced myself to my feet – brought my hand to a proper salute… Wade snapped to attention – so did Athena. And while the crew carried a Veteran – a Pilot to his last flight – a public servant on his last adventure… we all gave him the respect – the love he deserved…

Skip was placed carefully aboard the chopper, and as the engines wound up again – Wade and I gave him one last salute as the pilot and crew of the bird lifted off. Then in unison as the chopper began to make its turn to leave… they all the saluted back.

We watched it disappear in silence… the three of us.

Wade opened the cooler the flight crew left for us – handed me a sandwich… I gave it to Athena. Wade just looked at me – shook his head and said "good thing they packed a bunch of 'em."

We all sat in the shade of the tree-line and ate. "Tuna-fish? Really Wade?"

He chuckled "that's just what they had…"

So we sat, we waited – drank soda… and I smoked a cigarette.

Wade broke our moment of silence "what you did for your pilot – Skip – that was something…"

"I wish I could have done more."

Athena turned and rested her head on my lap – looked at me as I stroked her forehead and I told her "pretty girl – such a pretty girl."

"Quite a set-up you made." Wade said low – steady…

"Something we'd do as kids – you know…" I whispered back

"Bell's been – well – she hasn't slept – hasn't eaten… ever since she heard your plane didn't arrive at the airport…" as Wade stared down at his feet – shaking his head… "Hell – man… I've been sick thinking what could've happened to ya."

"I kind a figured…"

Wade choked a little "I – I mean… I really don't know… what I'd ever do without ya bud."

"Same…" as I turned to look at him.

Wade's smile – his humor now faded – more somber as I could tell his mind was reflecting on our lifelong friendship – showing through his eyes… but then in that moment when I thought he would hug me again – I whispered back "I don't know what I'd ever do without you either, but…" as my voice lifted, and I chuckled: "don't ever ask me to brush your hair with my hand!"

Wade bust out laughing… "Well I love you too man!"

Before I finished my last cigarette – the echoes of the air beating against rotors broke the silence. Athena – still laying across my lap – raised her head – perked her ears… and smiled.

"Looks like our ride's coming" Wade grunted – standing – brushing the dirt from his legs… then reached his hand toward me – lifting me… Athena stretching.

My friend held me steady as I began my walk to the chopper. The pilot and crew jumped out to help – hollered above the sounds of the engines "Sergeant Duncan?"

I stopped – Wade held onto my arm guiding me to the waiting flight, but all I could do at that moment is remember walking with Wade after surviving the ambush in Iraq, and with all my strength – once again – I let out the long lost cry – loud enough for the dust to hear…

No – We Are The Wolf Pack

Wade – and the crew from the helicopter – had to nearly lift me into the chopper – I hadn't realized how bruised – maybe even beaten I'd been… I'd been running on adrenaline for so long – the thought of rest nearly collapsed me.

I sat back into the seat – Athena taking her position on my lap as she – and even how Gunner was trained to do when riding in choppers – and before we lifted off – the flight crew made sure we were strapped in… but – I asked…

"Ya think we could stop at this little place I know – and pick up some burgers – maybe some fries…"

Wade just shook his head – looked at the pilot, chuckled "How ya feeling today?"

The pilot shrugged his shoulders – with a puzzled look on his face tilted a little, and before he could say anything – wade blurted out… looking at me…

"This guy already lost one pilot – I'm sure he'd want to know if we're going to make it back Ok…"

The pilot wasn't the same one who'd been at the meadow before – but simply told me:

"Sir – you're headed to the hospital… some head nurse there said we had to make sure you were Ok before you go home!"

Wade? Broke out that corn-fed smile… shook his head again and chuckled: "head nurse?" All I could do was look down at Athena – and smile…

"Bell."

As the hum of the engines wound up, I sank into the seat, holding Athena close. As we lifted off I looked across the scarred meadow, the twisted fuselage, and felt the truth of the wild settle into my bones: it doesn't forgive mistakes. It doesn't wait. But it can teach, if you're willing to listen.

And today, we survived.

Chapter 71

The Patio

Coming home isn't always the hard part. It's realizing that part of you never does. Some pieces stay behind in the places you fought, in the people you lost, in the silences that follow. Maybe that's the price for a life that's been spared more than once.

Hemingway believed you had to know how to live before you could write about it. But my story wasn't written in living. It was forged in the space between the heartbeats - when death leaned in close and I told it:

"Not yet..."

Some have said they saw their life flash before their eyes during a time they thought they would die. I've stood at that threshold more times than most – between combat, being shot, buried a partner, and walked out of the wild when I shouldn't have. But I never saw what was behind me.

I only saw the solution… I saw - what I still had to do.

The sight of the city – familiar, and yet for a moment it felt foreign. The time I'd spent away, and was then lost - felt like a lifetime. A lifetime that lasted a mere twenty-four hours or so.

We were mostly quiet – we didn't need a lot of words to fill the time. My flight from the crash may have lasted an hour – maybe a little less. But – I wasn't counting the minutes.

Wade did lean in to speak with the pilot for a second… I couldn't hear what they were saying. I didn't care. The helicopter banked – I looked through the window. I could see the parking lot of the hospital was crowded with the familiar markings of our department's units.

When the skids touched down, the world felt suddenly too loud from rotor wash, and the distant echo of voices shouting our welcome.

And then, through it all, faces came into focus: my wife, Bell; the kids; the grandkids; my department – they were all waiting, all there. Athena whined softly beside me, tail beating against the seat. She seemed to recognize them before I did.

I tried to stand but the medic's hand caught my shoulder. "Easy. You're not done getting patched-up yet."

Wade slid open the door on our Bell Jet Ranger, and before it locked open – Bell's arms wrapped around me – tight… I couldn't help but wince in pain…

"Sorry" she chuckled through her tears. "I'm just… just so – so glad you're alive!"

Athena – part soldier – part cop, and always family, nosed herself into our embrace… and we were reunited. Wade and one of the medics slid me into a wheelchair, and the Chief handed me a bag – smiled, and simply said…

"Double Cheese Burger – from 'you know where' – hot fries, and large soda… Wade let the pilot know, and we wanted to make sure you got fed."

Athena looked at me with 'that look' and… before I could give her any – my friend Tony – Detective Tony Sanchez, well – he handed her a burger, and gave her a huge hug. I just looked at him…

"You old softy."

Tony chuckled "you told me that she'd grow on me – and you're right – she did."

He was about to give me a pat on the back, but Wade caught his arm in enough time to let him know – it might not be the right time for that – since they didn't know the extent of any injuries… then I heard Wade apologize for the 'bear-hug' back at the meadow…

Hours later, after X-rays and questions and too many pokes and prodding's, the verdict came in: two broken ribs, a cracked collarbone, a handful of bruises that would take on every color of the rainbow. The doctors called me lucky. I didn't feel lucky.

Outside the room, my family took care of Athena – Izzy held her tight – they all couldn't hug her enough.

Bell waited at my side. The nurse's badge on her scrubs caught the light, but her eyes said what her words couldn't. She just took my hand and let the silence say the rest.

Skip's family was there too. His wife, his kids – they were standing together, clutching each other in that dazed, hollow way that only fresh grief knows. There are no words for that kind of moment.

I held her hand – a widow, a wife in mourning. She was frail, shaking, and yet still holding onto that hope that faded into grief, but I told them what truth I could: that Skip never felt the crash. That he was gone before the impact. That I did everything I could to bring him home.

It doesn't matter if the bond of friendship – of family – was for an hour, a day, or a lifetime… because the words still echo in my mind… "Blood makes you related – loyalty makes you family." And to me – Skip, was family.

When I finally stepped outside, the cool air hit like a baptism. The department was waiting. Men and women I'd bled beside, worked beside, and laughed beside. They cheered, clapped, and hollered my name. I smiled because it was expected - but the weight in my chest didn't lift.

Then came the news crews, microphones and cameras flashing like lightning in the early evening.

"Sergeant Duncan! The FAA's initial report - do you have any comment? Was it pilot error?"

I looked past them for a moment, to where the horizon faded behind the hospital. "No," I said quietly. "Skip passed away before the crash. He didn't make a mistake. He just… didn't have time."

I swallowed hard and then paused. "There *was* no pilot flying when we went down."

They went silent for a moment. I turned, whistled softly for Athena. She rose, stiff but steady, then as another question coughed through the crowd… Athena turned, and smiled – smiled that way of showing just enough teeth to mean business, and that let them know we were done. And we walked away…

Two survivors carrying the weight of one man's final flight.

The wild doesn't care who you are, what you've done, or how many medals you've earned. It strips you down to what's real, and what can survive. Out there, there's no rank, no past, no second chances… only truth.

Here at home – it's not much different. I'm husband, dad, and grandpa… I'm friend, partner, and…

I look down at Athena - at those eyes, that heart. Words don't quite fit, so I just leave it there.

But Athena looks back up at me – her eyes tired, and her fur drying in the breeze, and we sit on the patio alone for the moment… the sounds of laughter – joy… the sounds I missed in the silence of a crash…

Wondering if I'd hear them again.

I won't try to tell you what your mind has already pictured – how our family came together, and how we celebrated… I'm sure you already know.

But as I sit here – the summer evening caressed only by the stars, and the comfort of home, and a lifetime of memories… and the partner who stayed by my side…

I simply look back through time… from the safety – the security of knowing I have survived – and that I will survive… so then and only then… I can sit quietly here on my patio, and only then… I can let the pictures of my life flash before me…

Chapter 72

Where Heroes Run

The real measure of a man, I think, is what he carries quietly. The memories that refuse to fade, and the ones he finally learns to love.

I used to think the hardest part was the fight. Whether it was the gunfire, the storm, or a crash. But it's not. The hardest part is what comes after. It's when we sit in the quiet, when we have to face the echo of everything we've survived, and we ask ourselves… why we're still here.

Charlie was right. About all of it. "Some scars you carry. Some carry you."

Every scar, every loss, and every breath I still take - it all asks the same thing: What will you do with what's left of you?

Survival isn't about being the strongest or the smartest. It's about being the one who keeps breathing when everything says to stop. And if you're truly blessed, you don't do it alone. You do it with a partner who won't let you quit, a friend who won't let you fall, and a woman who won't let you forget why you came home.

I've been asked: how many times a man can walk to the edge and come back? The answer is:

As many times as it takes.

But nobody asks me what I left behind each time I returned. Pieces of myself? Pieces of the people? Pieces of the partner I couldn't save? I guess maybe… I was held together - not by what remains, but by who remains.

There's a moment in every battle - whether it's bullets or mountains or even the weight of your own mind. When you realize you're not fighting to win anymore, and that you're fighting to get back to the people who are fighting for you. That's when survival stops being about you. And that's when you finally understand what you're made of.

I've lived a lifetime worth of loyalty packed into years too short. Gunner taught me duty. Tina taught me sacrifice. Athena taught me that even after loss, even after everything... I can still choose to stand. They didn't make me stronger. They simply taught me to try again.

In the end, it was never about the battles we fought, or the medals, or the titles that came and went. It was about the ones who stood beside us when the fight got ugly - and stayed when the smoke cleared.

Courage isn't born on the battlefield - it's born the first time you choose to stand your ground when no one else will.

Tears? They aren't a sign of weakness. They're proof that the heart still feels, and that we haven't hardened ourselves beyond redemption.

Duty has taught me that loyalty carries a price. If Charlie hadn't passed those values to his son, would Father John have survived? And would I have survived losing Tina? I often wonder how many unseen lives are shaped by the paths we choose, and how our loyalty to our standards, and to those we love, reaches farther than we will ever know.

Freedom isn't about running wild. It's about knowing where you belong and still choosing to stay.

Through it all, I've learned that loyalty doesn't end at the gravesite, and partnership doesn't die with the badge, the uniform, or the last command. It lives in every act of quiet honor, and every time we do what's right when no one's watching.

We are the sum of the lives we've touched, the oaths we've kept, and the things we've carried. And it's not because we had to, but because we couldn't set them down.

I've buried friends, partners, and a few pieces of myself along the way. But I've also found something deeper. I finally found a faith not in perfection, but in resilience. In the unspoken truth that sometimes... all that's left to do... is keep going.

The wild has its way of humbling a man. So does combat. So does love. But each time I walked away from the wreckage - whether it was steel, or fire, or grief... I carried something new with me: the proof that we were here. The proof that we mattered.

The measure of a man isn't written in his victories. It's carved into the quiet moments when no one else will ever know what it cost him to stand.

And if I've learned anything from all the scars, it's this - we don't survive by strength alone. We survive because somewhere out there, someone believes we still can.

That's the creed. That's the anthem.

To the ones who stayed. To the ones who tried. And to the ones who never stopped believing - even when the world went silent.

This story was never about how I lived.

It was about why I kept living.

So as I sit in the peace – the tranquility of the evening... the sky is kinder and the moon nearly full...

I hold onto a leash from the past remembering all of the paw-prints than have left their memories in my heart, and their legacy now sitting at my feet... and I know...

Somewhere between the chaos and the commotion of life is a bridge – a place of honor, and that is...

Where The Heroes Run

An Epilogue, A Note from the Author, and my Special Thanks...

On November 6th in the year 2000 President Bill Clinton signed congressional legislation into law... it was called "Robbie's Law."

Robbie's Law – or Public Law 106–378, 114 Stat. 1468 United States Code – transformed the lives of service members forever. It opened the door allowing for the partners of our Military Working Dogs to provide them a good home when leaving service.

It ensures the humane care for their service and proper medical care, treatment, and formalized adoption procedures after their service. It was applied across all branches of the U.S. military and is codified at **10 U.S.C. § 2583**. The law was named for Robbie, a military dog whose service highlighted the need for these protections.

It took years of letter writing campaigns – lobbying our legislators, and countless hours of compassionate work to bring this needed law... So our heroes can be honored in the manner they deserve.

This law was not about politics – it was about compassion. America came together with bi-partisan support - to save the lives of our trusted companions who bear the burden of service while offering the comfort and protection... of a friend.

Thanks to Robbie's Law, heroes like the character portrayed in this story - like Gunner, can come home, not as "just a dog," but as a trusted companion whose life of service is recognized, respected, and cherished. Yes - America came together to save them, and in doing so, reminded us all of the power of love, loyalty, and compassion.

Author's Note

These stories were never just about dogs - they were about partners. About the quiet understanding between those who serve and those who stand beside them without question.

When I began writing The Big Boys Series, I didn't know where the journey would lead. What started as a single story became a collection - a tapestry woven from memories, loss, courage, and the kind of loyalty that doesn't fade when the uniform comes off.

Through The Big Boys Series, we walked through action, adventure, and the aftermath - the weight of sacrifice, the silence that follows duty. We wrestled with what it means to keep faith when the rules change, and when life tests the limits of our endurance.

And now, in **Where Heroes Run: The American K9 Elegy**, all those roads meet. These stories - though fictionalized - carry truths I've seen, lived, and shared with those who wore the badge, the uniform, or the scars of service.

I wanted to honor them - the men, the women, and the four-legged heroes who asked for nothing and gave everything. Robbie's Law made it possible for many of them to come home - but it's love, loyalty, and compassion that keep their stories alive.

This Elegy is for them. For those who ran toward danger when the rest of the world ran away. For those who stayed loyal - to the end.

Thank you for walking this road with me.

Acknowledgments

I want to thank my real-life wife - my rock - for her patience, grace, and unwavering support. She has seen me through a career and a calling that took us through many highs and lows. She knows, more than anyone, that the life behind the badge comes with a cost. Her love and understanding have carried me farther than words can ever express.

I also want to thank my brother Lowell, my son Jason - and my wife once more - for their help as editors, for sharing ideas, for believing in this work, and for helping me shape it into something worthy of the stories it carries.

To all of my children: John, Angela, Matt, and Jason - thank you for forgiving me. For all the missed programs, parties, and family gatherings... the tryouts, the games, and the birthdays I wasn't there for. I was drawn to do what "Sheepdogs" do - to serve, to protect, to stand that post. Your understanding means more to me than I can ever repay.

To my grandchildren - especially my oldest granddaughter, Izzy - thank you for reminding me what joy really looks like. You and Athena have brought more light into my days than you'll ever know.

And finally, to those who stand by that line - those who do what they do not for recognition or reward, but because it's what must be done - this is for you. You know the cost. You know the weight. Yet you keep standing, quietly, faithfully, holding that line for the ones who can't.

Sometimes the world never sees it. Sometimes no one says thank you. But know this: what you do matters. The lives you touch matter. The stories you carry - the sacrifices you've made - they matter.

This book, this *Elegy*, is for all of you who keep walking forward, day after day, with the weight of the world on your shoulders and loyalty in your heart.

Thank you – for you guard that bridge between chaos an calm, and it's you... who walk "Where Heroes Run"

H. Jack Dunn

"The Sheepdog Is Tired"

There comes a time in every life of service when the shadows grow long and the armor grows heavy.

A time when the war-horse, once thunder in the earth, stands at the fence line and listens to battles meant for younger legs.

A time when the old K9, grizzled around the muzzle, still rises at the slightest sound… but slower now, because the years have carved their story into bone and spirit alike.

People see the strength, but they never count the scars. They see the uniform, but never the nights spent in cold rain, staring into the dark, waiting for the evil no one else could face.

They see the protector, but never the wounds of being unprotected.

They call when they're afraid, curse when they're safe, and forget who stood between danger and their sleep.

And still… the sheepdog rises. Every time.

Not for glory. Not for praise. Not for a pat on the back. But because something deep inside could never do anything else.

But now… the sheepdog is tired. Not broken. Although abused. Not defeated. Even though beaten… Just tired in the way only those who have carried too much, for too long, for too many, will ever understand. Maybe someday the world will turn, slow down long enough to notice the sentinels who stood the night watch when no one else would.

Maybe someday they will understand that strength like this comes with a quiet cost. And maybe… just maybe… someone will finally say:

"Rest now. You kept us safe. We see you."

H Jack Dunn